Praise for *New York Times* bestselling author Sarah Mayberry

"Mayberry's heartwarming story about the power of love to heal all features characters whose motivations and anguish are quite realistically depicted."
—*RT Book Reviews* on *The Other Side of Us*

"[Mayberry] really knows how to capture and express a modern woman that feels very authentic and relatable."
—*DearAuthor.com* on *All They Need*

"Thought provoking, uplifting, inspiring… this story has made it to my 'keepers' shelf and Sarah Mayberry is an author who I will absolutely be reading more of."
—*Goodreads* on *Within Reach*

"I've always enjoyed Mayberry's books, but reading this one was like finding a twenty-dollar bill in your coat pocket, then unfolding it and finding a fifty wrapped inside. It started out great and just kept getting better."
—*USATODAY.com* on *All They Need*

"A gripping book that's impossible to put down."
—*RT Book Reviews* on *Below the Belt*

"Sarah Mayberry truly is a gifted author and I can't wait for more of her work. Mayberry knows how to heat up the pages."
—*Fresh Fiction* on *She's Got It Bad*

SARAH MAYBERRY

New York Times bestselling author Sarah Mayberry was born in Melbourne, Australia. Ever since she learned to read and write she has wanted to be an author. She studied professional writing and literature before embarking on various writing-related jobs, working as a magazine editor and in story-related roles on Australia's longest-running TV serial drama, *Neighbours*. She inherited a love of romances from both her grandmothers and fulfilled her fondest wish when she was accepted for publication. Visit her online at her website, www.sarahmayberry.com.

New York Times Bestselling Author

SARAH MAYBERRY

Her Kind of Trouble

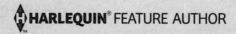

HARLEQUIN® FEATURE AUTHOR

Recycling programs for this product may not exist in your area.

ISBN-13: 978-0-373-60609-2

HER KIND OF TROUBLE
Copyright © 2014 by Harlequin Books S.A.

The publisher acknowledges the copyright holders of the individual works as follows:

HER KIND OF TROUBLE
Copyright © 2014 by Small Cow Productions Pty Ltd.

BACK TO YOU
Copyright © 2014 by Small Cow Productions Pty Ltd.

Printed in U.S.A.

CONTENTS

Her Kind of Trouble

Every book is a journey of discovery, frustration, elation, delusion and determination. I couldn't get through it without Chris, Max and Wanda.

A big thanks to my lovely writing buddies
Marie, Schwartzeputzer, Joan, Mel
and the fabulous Melbourne Mob.
It's so nice to know I'm not alone in the madness.

CHAPTER ONE

March 2004

"WELL. WHAT DO you think? Do I still look like an over-stuffed silk sausage?"

Vivian Walker winced as her sister spun to face her, the taffeta of her wedding dress rustling. She would never live down the scathing commentary she'd given the day she'd gone dress shopping with her sister. Next time someone asked for her opinion, she needed to engage her edit function first.

"It looks gorgeous," she said, because it was true and because the big day was tomorrow and there was no way she was critiquing the gown her sister had chosen.

Jodie smoothed a hand over her hip. She'd been dieting like crazy and the classic fit-and-flare dress clung to her curvy figure perfectly, with not a hint of over-stuffing. The lace overlay was delicate, the strapless sweetheart neckline flattering, the dove-grey silk belt the perfect accent for her slender waist. She really did look beautiful.

"You don't think I should have gone with something more modern?" Jodie asked, flicking her long, dark red hair over her shoulders.

"We can dash down to the mall now, see what the rental place has," Vivian suggested, poker-faced.

"Ha, ha, smarty-pants. That was your cue to tell me that this is the perfect dress, that there isn't a more perfect dress anywhere in the world, and that I look like a regal, sex-goddess-princess in it, et cetera, et cetera."

The guilt that had been hovering since her sister unzipped the dress's garment bag bit hard. Vivian scratched her nose to hide her reaction from her sister.

Was there anything worse in all the world than letting down someone you loved? She'd yet to find it, if there was.

"You look amazing, Jodie. Really, really stunning," she said, meeting her sister's eyes.

It wasn't a lie, not by a long shot, but they both knew that if things had gone according to plan, Jodie would be wearing a dress Vivian had designed. A one-of-a-kind creation that—in theory—would have been the culmination of all the hard work Vivian had put in over the past three years studying clothing design at the Melbourne Fashion Institute.

If only she hadn't made that stupid, impulsive offer when they'd gone shopping six months ago. If only she'd paused for a *second* to consider what she'd be taking on before she asked her sister to let her design something. But she'd been so disgusted by the safe, homogenized, boring dresses, and so full of herself after winning praise at a recent exhibition of student work at the institute, the offer—bold, brash, confident—had simply popped out of her mouth.

Jodie's eyes had lit up on the spot, and she'd done a happy dance around the changing room. "Viv, that would be *so* fantastic. And I know that whatever you come up with will be my dream dress, because you are so amazingly talented."

Panic had set in about thirty seconds later. This was

her sister's wedding day. Whatever Vivian came up with needed to be off-the-planet extraordinary. It needed to be the best, most creative, most sublime thing she'd ever designed.

Was it any wonder she'd choked every time she sat down with her sketch pad to try to rough out ideas in the following weeks and months? Was it any wonder she'd made no less than twenty starts on twenty wildly different designs before throwing each and every one of them out? And was it any wonder her sister had finally let her off the hook after three months of unreturned phone calls and excuses, assuring Vivian that she was more than happy to buy a dress off the rack if designing one was proving too difficult?

That Jodie had wound up selecting one of the dresses Vivian had so vehemently critiqued and rejected on their shopping expedition was the icing on the cake of her guilt and discomfort. "What do you think of the veil? I'm still on the fence about whether to wear it over my face, or to do something with it in my hair, or maybe not wear it at all." Jodie picked up a lace-edged confection of white froth. "I tried all three options when we did the practice run on my hair and makeup, but I still can't decide."

Vivian pushed her feelings aside and stood. "Let's have a bit of a play, see what we can come up with."

She fiddled with the veil, trying different ways of pinning and draping it before slipping out to her car to retrieve her workbox. Big, black and heavy, it was actually a portable tool chest that she'd modified for her own purposes, the compartments filled with all manner of trims, haberdashery and sewing supplies she'd collected over the years. She rummaged through the sections until she found what she was looking for—delicate grey feathers that had been dusted with silver and some paste diamond jewelry she'd picked up at a yard sale. She tried a few different options before hitting on the right combination of antique brooch and feathers, pinning the veil so that it fell in delicate, sensuous folds down her sister's back.

"Oh, wow." Jodie inspected herself in the mirror. "Viv, I love it. Thank you," she said, flinging her arms around Vivian.

Vivian hugged her sister, even though she knew she didn't deserve her gratitude. "If you like, I could come up with something similar for your belt, embellish it a little. I could do it tonight, have it ready for you tomorrow morning."

Jodie's smile faltered and Vivian knew she was thinking about the dress-that-never-was, along with all the other things Vivian had screwed up over the years.

"We've got the dinner tonight. I don't want you to feel pushed for time," her sister said diplomatically.

"I won't be. It'll take me an hour, two tops. I really want to do this, Jodie." She left the rest of her plea unspoken. They both knew that a few embellishments on a belt and veil didn't come even close to compensating for how badly Vivian had let Jodie down, but it was something.

"Okay. Sure. Why not?" Jodie said, and it killed Vivian that she could hear her sister talking herself into trusting her again.

"I'll draw up some sketches before dinner and run them past you."

"You don't need to do that. You have wonderful taste. Whatever you do, I'm sure I'll love it."

The bedroom door opened then and their mother and the other two bridesmaids barged in, laden with champagne and glasses, all of them talking at once.

"God, Jodie, you look gorgeous! Like a fairy-tale princess," one of them said.

Vivian smiled to herself as she cleared her things out of the way. The princess reference was sure to meet with her sister's approval.

She stayed for one toast, but the belt was playing on her mind—she refused to let her sister down again—so she made her excuses and retreated to her childhood bedroom to sketch some ideas.

Their mother had converted Jodie's room into a study the moment she moved out, but she'd kept Vivian's as it was when she'd struck out on her own a year later, "just in case" Vivian needed it. The message being that while sensible, down-to-earth Jodie couldn't possibly fail to succeed in the adult world of rent and utility bills, flighty, unreliable Vivian was a much shakier proposition.

The galling thing was her mother had been right. Vivian had had to move home twice—once when she'd lost her job working in retail fashion, the second when she'd had a falling-out with her housemates. Worse, things were looking shaky at the apartment she shared with two other students at the moment, too.

Vivian sighed. It would totally suck to crawl home a third time.

Sitting on her bed, she arranged the remaining feathers off to one side, placing a selection of antique brooches next to them. She had another rummage through her workbox and unearthed a packet of pewter-grey and white sequins, along with some seed pearls.

Perfect.

Taking up her pad and pencil, she started to sketch. She had roughed out a design and arranged the component pieces on the belt when someone rapped on her door. She looked up, only registering how long it had been since she moved when her neck objected.

Her mother entered, dressed in a bronze silk pants suit, her faded red hair sprayed into a stiff helmet, gold jewelry gleaming at her ears, throat and wrists.

"Vivian. I've been looking for you everywhere. We leave for the restaurant in twenty minutes." Her expression became exasperated when she saw that Vivian was still in her jeans. "You're not wearing that, are you? This is the first time we'll be meeting some of Jason's extended family."

Vivian resisted the urge to roll her eyes. Her idea of fashion and her mother's had diverged a long time ago, but even she knew jeans were not acceptable for the private dining room of a swanky restaurant.

"I'll be ready," she said. "And I brought a dress."

Her mother's gaze dropped to the bed. "That's not Jodie's belt, is it? Does she know you have it?" Her mother started forward, clearly determined to rescue it from Vivian's clutches.

Vivian rested a protective hand over the arrangement she'd spent hours perfecting.

"Jodie gave it to me. I'm finessing it."

Her mother pursed her mouth. "I hope this isn't going to be like the dress. The wedding is tomorrow."

"Thanks, Mum, I'm well aware of that."

"There's no need to take that tone. I'm thinking of your sister. This isn't the time for you to go off on one of your whims."

"I'll finish tonight." Vivian ground out the words.

It was one thing to admit to yourself you were a screwup, but it was another thing entirely to have it pointed out by your nearest and dearest. Repeatedly. Ad nauseam.

"I'll leave you to change, then." Her mother gave the belt one last mistrustful glance before leaving.

Viv growled, then carefully unfolded her legs so as not to disturb the sequins and pearls. She didn't have time for a shower, so she concentrated on fixing her makeup before shedding her clothes and pulling on her dress. One of her own designs, it was made from an inky-blue wool crepe and had a loose blouson top with a peekaboo central split and a fitted pencil skirt. She'd been growing her strawberry-blond hair out of a short crop for the wedding, and she pinned it up before spritzing on perfume and racing downstairs.

"Only five minutes late." Her father made a show of checking his watch. "Got to be a new record."

Vivian wrinkled her nose at him. "But worth every second," she said, twirling for him.

He whistled appreciatively.

Her mother made a clucking noise. "You're a born flirt, Vivian. Try not to give anyone a heart attack tonight, okay?" She tried to close the peekaboo slit that revealed a hint of Vivian's décolletage.

"Relax, Mum. I know CPR."

Jodie laughed. "Not much to say to that, is there?"

They trooped out to the car, her and Jodie piling into the backseat.

"So is what's-his-name going to be there tonight?" Vivian asked as the car pulled into the street.

"I may need a little more detail than that," Jodie said dryly.

"Jason's brother. What's-his-name." The mysterious best man who hadn't made it to either the engagement party or the wedding rehearsal because he'd been "touring with his band."

"Seth. You might want to make a note of his name, since he's going to be your brother-in-law. Sort of. Family by association anyway."

"Goodie. I always wanted a brother." Mostly when one of her boyfriends had turned out to be a jerk-wad.

"Yeah…Seth isn't really brother material."

Vivian gave Jodie a look. "What does that mean?"

"I think I'll let you work it out for yourself."

It was tempting to badger her, but Jodie was clearly bent on being mysterious so Vivian let the subject drop and asked about the itinerary for the honeymoon.

Their father was cursing under his breath by the time they entered the restaurant, ticked off after having to park on a side street because the restaurant's lot was full. Their mother murmured soothing words to him as they made their way to the private dining room.

Approximately half the guests had already arrived and her parents began to circulate, apologizing for being late, while Jodie made a beeline for a smiling Jason. Vivian lingered in the doorway to appreciate the lavish decor—over-the-top red velvet curtains with gold tassels, a long dining table surrounded by button-backed chairs in black velvet, lots of glittering candles and bevel-cut mirrors. Fancy.

Not really her cup of tea, but she could appreciate that a wedding called for a bit of pomp, and her parents would have the opportunity to do this only once, since it would be a cold day in hell when she agreed to marry someone. She might be barely twenty-three, but she knew that much about the life she wanted to carve out for herself. There would be no cozy domestic arrangements in the suburbs in her future. No matching rings and big white dress and public vows. There would definitely be no babies.

She was going to be a clothing designer. She was going to launch her own line and build it into a force to be reckoned with. One day, she would send a collection down the runway at Paris fashion week, and women would covet clothes bearing her brand.

One day.

The thought was still lingering in her mind when the huddle of people gathered at the far end of the table opened up and she caught sight of the tall, dark-haired man in their midst.

Hello, sailor.

His hair was raven-black, brushed back from his widow's peak in a careless, windswept style reminiscent of an old-school, bad-boy movie star. Unlike everyone else, he'd eschewed a suit and tie and instead wore an open-necked black shirt and leather jacket with a pair of tuxedo pants and scuffed biker boots. She wanted to smirk at how try-hard the ensemble was—he might as well have the words *wannabe rock star* tattooed across his forehead—but was forced to admit that he more than carried off the look.

He was, in a word, sexy. And boy, did he know it. The knowledge was reflected in the way he held himself, the way he studied the people around him and in the small, knowing curve to his lips. He thought he was too cool for school and the best thing since sliced bread all rolled into one, with a helping of God's gift to women thrown in for good measure.

So, this was Jason's mysterious, never-around brother, Seth Anderson.

Interesting.

A waiter glided by bearing a tray of champagne flutes and she plucked one for herself before he could disappear. Sipping at the bubbles, she went to greet her aunt and uncle, watching Seth out of the corner of her eye every step of the way.

He was easily the hottest guy in the room. She guessed he was about her age, maybe slightly older. She tried to remember what else Jodie had told her about him, but apart from the fact that he was lead singer in a band called Skunk Punk, Vivian came up blank. Since she'd never heard of his band—and who could forget that name?—she figured that his music career wasn't much to write home about, despite all the time he apparently spent touring.

But, hey, what did she know? Maybe he was about to break out and be heralded as the next Michael Hutchence.

He glanced up, scanning the room until he arrived at her. For a breathless moment their gazes locked, and a ripple of something forbidden and hot and reckless licked through her. His eyes were espresso-brown, and the glint in them was downright wicked.

He cocked an eyebrow, his mouth quirking into a speculative, assessing smile as his gaze traveled down her body and up again. Not to be outdone, she raised an eyebrow at him and gave him the same treatment, deliberately lingering on his crotch, just so he knew who he was dealing with.

He raised his glass in her direction, an unspoken acknowledgement that she'd trumped him. Or so she chose to think.

She turned her shoulder on him as she joined her aunt and uncle, exchanging kisses and greetings, doing her damnedest to appear as though she had better things to do than engage in eye-foreplay with him. Even though she was burningly aware of him.

Definitely interesting. Maybe this wedding wasn't going to be all pomp and circumstance, after all.

SETH TOOK A pull from his beer, not taking his eyes off the redhead who had just walked into the room. She was pretending that she wasn't aware of him, but he knew she was. He'd known it the moment their eyes locked. She was trouble, with a capital *T,* and he'd always had a thing for trouble.

He let his gaze slide down her body again. She had a great ass, something that was more than evident thanks to the fits-like-a-glove dress, and unless he missed his guess, she was rocking a C cup upstairs.

Very nice.

He bet she went off in bed—not because she was a redhead, but because of the suggestive curve to her lips. No fake orgasms and holding back for Red. She'd go all the way and then some.

Someone nudged him and he turned to find his brother scowling at him.

"No." Jason sliced a hand through the air.

"What?" Seth put on his best innocent face.

"That's Jodie's little sister, Vivian. She is absolutely out of bounds."

Vivian. The name suited her. A bit different and naughty.

"She doesn't look out of bounds." Seth gave her another once-over. Her high heels were serious business, the stilettos made from shiny silver metal.

Hot.

Jason moved to block his line of vision. "Think of her as a nun."

"Never gonna happen."

"Then think of my hand around your throat, squeezing slowly until your ever-loving eyes pop out of your head."

Seth laughed. "Wow, you are really serious about this, aren't you?"

"These people are about to become my family. Apologizing for my humpy-dog brother is not high on my list of things to do."

Seth sighed heavily and turned his back on the siren across the room. "Fine. She's off-limits."

Jason stared as though he was trying to work out if Seth was sincere. Seth rolled his eyes and drank the last of his beer. When had his brother turned into such a freakin' stiff?

"I so need another one of these." He dumped the empty on the table and, hands shoved into the pockets of his pants, headed for the waiter.

There were four years between him and Jason, but right now it felt like four decades. In the space of a couple of years, his brother had gone from being a fun guy who loved to party and hang out to a stay-at-home, cardigan-wearing family-man-in-training. He'd even bought a set of golf clubs last month, for Pete's sake.

Seth blamed Jodie. Not that she was inherently evil, but she had clearly done something to his brother's brain, changed its fundamental chemistry so that Jason was now a different man. And he was about to become a husband.

Seth shuddered. Was there a worse word in the English language? *Herpes,* perhaps. Maybe *fungus.* But *husband* had to be up there.

He snagged a beer and surveyed the room. His parents were schmoozing with Jodie's parents, all of them looking as pleased as punch that they would spend the next thirty-odd years doing exactly the same thing at extended family gatherings. His grandmother was seated, her cane dangling from the table by its crook. But his gaze kept sliding to Vivian.

To her ass, if he was being strictly accurate.

Her skirt was tight with no V.P.L. He bet she wasn't wearing underwear. She might be wearing a thong, of course, but he preferred his version.

He glanced to where his brother was talking with Jodie and some of her cousins. Jason was preoccupied, his head tilted toward Jodie as he listened to something she was saying.

So attentive. So domesticated.

Since he was otherwise occupied…

Seth headed across the room, only stopping when he was a few feet away from Vivian in her sexy blue dress. She made him wait a full ten seconds before pretending she'd just noticed him.

"Oh, sorry. I didn't see you," she said, her eyes sending him a very different message.

A shame he wasn't allowed to play with her properly. She'd give him a good run for his money.

"Seth," he said, offering her his hand. "And you're Vivian. We're about to become family, they tell me."

She considered his hand for a beat before sliding hers into it. Her skin was soft and warm, her nails surprisingly short and businesslike.

"Jodie warned me you aren't brother material."

She was more of a strawberry-blonde than a true redhead, he decided. Her eyes were an intriguing blue-green, her skin creamy smooth.

He bet she tasted *good.*

"Did she? I wonder why?"

"You think maybe it has something to do with the whole Marlon Brando *On the Waterfront* thing you've got going on?"

"Damn. And here I was, aiming for James Dean in *Giant.*"

"You'll need a cowboy hat to pull that one off."

"A cowboy hat, huh? I'll add it to my shopping list. So, Vivian, what do you do when you're not being the sexiest woman in the room?"

She huffed out a little laugh. "Wow, you don't mess around, do you?"

"Just calling it like I see it."

She took a sip from her champagne flute, considering him over the rim. "So, how do you see this working? We slip out between the main and dessert and I do you in the alley? Or were you thinking the bathroom?"

He choked on his beer, going from semihard to hard in no seconds flat. Then she arched her eyebrows and he knew she was yanking his chain.

"Funny."

"Just calling it like I see it." She lifted one shoulder in a casual shrug.

The movement caused the slit in her bodice to flare momentarily, offering him a heart-stopping view of cleavage. He was about to respond when he felt the heavy pressure of someone staring at him. He glanced around and met his brother's dark glare.

Okay. Time to wind up this little chin-wag before his brother burst an artery.

"Vivian, it was nice meeting you. I look forward to seeing you at the altar tomorrow," he said, offering her a mocking half bow.

"Tomorrow's a whole other day. And you know what they say about weddings." She winked then, the sexiest move he'd ever witnessed in the flesh.

Since he knew he couldn't top that, he offered one last smile and turned away. Jason was angling toward him, and Seth headed in the opposite direction and sat beside his grandmother. As he'd guessed, Jason stopped short, unwilling to give a lecture about keeping his pants zipped in front of an octogenarian.

Wimp.

"Seth, sweetheart. Good to see you. Tell me about all the trouble you've been causing," his grandmother said, patting his hand.

"I don't know who you've been talking to, but I've been busy working. No trouble here."

She laughed heartily, tickled, and he set himself to entertaining her. And all the while he puzzled over Vivian's parting words. What, exactly, did people say about weddings? And did it mean he was in with a chance tomorrow or not?

VIVIAN STAYED UP half the night hand-stitching the sequins, seed pearls and feathers onto the belt. She was bleary-eyed when she finished, but the belt was gorgeous and she was certain that Jodie would love it.

It wasn't a dress, but it was something.

She set her alarm before burrowing into the pillow and willing herself to sleep on the narrow bed. For some reason, her conversation with Seth slipped into her mind as she drifted off. Man, he was cocky. So confident he was almost offensive.

Almost. If he actually delivered on the promises he made with that body and those eyes... Well, it would be a whole lot of fun.

She fell asleep with a smile on her face, slept through her alarm and then had to shower in a panic before joining her sister downstairs to have her hair and makeup done with the other bridesmaids.

"Vivian," her mother said reproachfully as Vivian slipped into the lone empty seat at the kitchen table.

Vivian widened her eyes. It wasn't as though the makeup artist or hairdresser had eight arms and was able to work on more than one person at a time. She would have been sitting around twiddling her thumbs if she'd been on time.

The next hour flew by in a waft of hairspray and a dusting of powder. Then it was time to get dressed. She and the other bridesmaids shimmied into their pale green sheaths before helping Jodie dress. Then, holding her breath, Vivian handed over the belt.

"Oh, Viv." Jodie's eyes popped as she reached for it reverently. "It's so beautiful."

"Good. I'm glad you like it."

"I *love* it."

Vivian was pretty sure she'd remember the look on her sister's face for the rest of her life.

There were photographs to take next, then the drive to the church. In the vestibule Vivian and the other bridesmaids helped arrange the small train on Jodie's dress, then Vivian tweaked the veil one last time. The doors to the church proper opened, the organ chimed the opening chords to "Here Comes the Bride," and Vivian started down the aisle, her suddenly sweaty hands clutched around her bouquet.

She might not want this for herself, but it hit her that this was a big deal. Jodie was getting married. She was about to become someone else. Mrs. Anderson. She was about to lay the foundation stone for starting her own family.

Vivian blinked rapidly, worried she would ruin her makeup. Then her gaze found the tall figure of Seth standing at the head of the aisle, and she saw the smirk on his lips, as though he fully expected her to turn into a slobbering sentimental wreck any second. She sucked back her tears and lifted her chin. She loved her sister, but she had her dignity to consider.

The ceremony passed in a blur, the only stand-out moments in her memory being when Jason and Jodie exchanged rings, and the time when she got caught staring at Seth's profile and had to let her gaze drift as though she'd been examining the stained glass window over his shoulder and not wondering what kind of a kisser he was. She wasn't entirely sure he bought it, but she'd tried.

There were more photos—endless photos—after the ceremony, then they piled into the cars and drove to the Fairfield Boathouse for the reception. The food came quickly, which was just as well as Vivian was starving, having somehow forgotten to eat breakfast *and* lunch in all the rush. The champagne flowed freely, and before she knew it they were at the speeches part of the evening. Her father spoke well and made everyone cry, then Jason's mother took the floor and made them laugh. Seth told droll stories and earned his brother some raised-eyebrow looks from her sister. Then it was Vivian's turn to talk about the happy couple.

She'd never been crazy about public speaking, so she chugged down her glass of champagne before taking the mike. She'd written out her speech, and she pretty much stuck to the script as she shared how happy she was for Jason and Jodie, and how she thought they made a great couple and couldn't wait for little Johnny and Jan and Jill to come along. Everyone seemed to think that was funny—phew—so she finished on a high note.

With the official stuff out of the way, the music started. Vivian knocked back more champagne while watching her relatives make idiots of themselves on the dance floor, then went in search of the ladies'.

Afterward, she couldn't quite face returning to the rowdy din. Not just yet. She slipped out the front entrance onto the covered balcony that circled the Victorian building. The river was dark as night, but fairy lights circled the gum trees nearest the boathouse and the world seemed mysterious and full of promise.

The scent of smoke drifted to her and she glanced to her left. Someone stood in the shadows of the balcony, the tip of his cigarette glowing.

She smiled, because she knew exactly who it was. Full of champagne and mischief, she went to talk to Seth.

WHATEVER ELSE A person thought about Vivian—and Seth had had a few very detailed, very specific thoughts regarding her in the twenty-four hours since they'd met—it was impossible to ignore the fact that she knew how to move. There was a swing to her hips, a strut to her walk that issued a challenge.

Look at me. Take me on.

Watching her walk toward him, half her face in shadow, he could only admire the way she worked it.

"Ms. Walker. Taking a break from the festivities?"

"Avoiding the 'Chicken Dance.'"

He winced. "Really?"

"Yep. There will be some 'Greased Lightning' and the 'Bus Stop' before the night's over, too."

He swore under his breath and took another drag on his cigarette.

"You got another one of those?"

"Didn't realize you smoked."

"Only when I'm drunk."

He gave her an assessing look. She wasn't swaying on her feet or glassy-eyed, but her cheeks were a little flushed. She waved a hand dismissively.

"Relax. I'm not there yet," she said.

"Hey, whatever gets you through the night."

God knows, she'd get no judgment from him. He'd been guzzling champagne since they'd arrived at the boathouse, trying to anesthetize himself against the knowledge that his brother's life was officially over.

He offered her a cigarette and lit it, breathing in her perfume. Spice and musk. Nice.

"So I hear you're a fashion designer?" he said as she blew a stream of smoke into the darkness.

"Been asking about me, James?"

It took him a moment to remember their James Dean/Marlon Brando conversation from last night.

"My mother mentioned it. She seemed to think we might have a lot in common."

Her eyebrows shot skyward and she looked as horrified by the notion that his mother had matchmaking on her mind as he had been.

"Yeah, I know. I laughed so hard I think I broke my funny bone," he said.

"What is it with people always trying to pair everyone off in neat little couples? News flash—not everyone in the world wants to file two by two onto Noah's Ark and live like the Brady Bunch for the rest of their lives. There's a hell of a lot more to life than paying taxes and making babies."

"Man, don't get me started," he said, thinking of the grief his father gave him every few months about giving up the band to do something "realistic" with his life. No matter how many times he explained that music *was* his life, it never seemed to get through.

"No offense, but I nearly choked on my own tongue when Jodie told me Jason had asked her to marry him. I mean, she's only twenty-six. That is *young* to be getting married these days."

"You think I didn't freak when Jason told me he'd popped the question? Your sister is nice and everything, but come on."

She held her hands in the air. "Hey, preaching to the converted here."

He reached for the bottle of champagne he'd smuggled out with him and took a swig before passing it to her. He watched her pale throat as she tilted her head back and drank deeply.

"I've got to ask this, because it's been bugging me. What is it, exactly, that people say about weddings?" he asked.

She handed him the bottle. "I don't know. Why?"

He shook his head, confused. "You're the one who said it."

"Did I?"

"Yeah, last night. You said tomorrow is another day and you know what people say about weddings."

She laughed, the sound loud and delighted. "That's freakin' hilarious."

He watched her, unable to stop himself from smiling even though he had no idea what was so funny. "You want to let me in on the secret?"

"Sure. I have no idea what people say about weddings. I was trying to be mysterious. You were doing your whole brooding thing, and I wanted to make sure you knew I wasn't a pushover." She laughed again and this time he joined in.

"Well, mission accomplished. Congratulations."

"Why, thank you, James." She grabbed the bottle and took another swallow.

He took advantage of the opportunity to check her out again. The other bridesmaids looked okay in their dresses, but Vivian looked amazing. He especially liked the split in the side of the skirt that had tantalized him with glimpses of her thigh all day.

"I bet the other bridesmaids were pissed when they heard you'd be maid of honor," he said admiringly.

"You don't need to butter me up, James."

"Don't I?"

"Nope." Her gaze held his, and he was pretty damn sure that he wasn't imagining the invitation in hers.

Well, happy birthday, Mr. President.

"In that case, maybe it's time for me to bring out the big guns." He reached into the inside pocket of his jacket and pulled out the joint he'd rolled earlier.

"I see you've really committed to the whole rock-and-roll lifestyle."

"You got a problem with that?"

She gave him a slow, steady head-to-toe appraisal. "Not in the least."

He closed his eyes for a brief moment of thanks. Sometimes, out of nowhere, the universe delivered a perfect moment. He was going to grab this one with both hands and run with it.

VIVIAN WASN'T SURE if the limo was her idea or Seth's. It was all a bit hazy in her mind after that first kiss on the balcony. One minute they'd been talking, then she'd been pressed up against the building with Seth's body against hers and his tongue in her mouth.

And holy hell, could the man kiss.

He'd stormed her mouth and her body as though he owned her, and she'd been wet and desperate for him within seconds. The feel of him, hard and demanding against her belly, had her thinking of getting naked and horizontal pronto. Then he'd broken their kiss, taken her hand and led her to the stairs.

Now, he slipped the driver some money to take a walk. She shivered with anticipation as Seth opened the door and waved her inside.

"Madam."

One word, but so loaded with promise she had to squeeze her thighs together to contain her excitement. She crawled onto the backseat, kneeling as he got in and closed the door.

"You'll have to unzip me." She offered him her back. It didn't take three years of design school to know that precious little action would happen while she wore a figure-hugging, floor-length sheath.

"Totally on it," Seth said, his hands on her zipper.

She felt the fabric loosen, and she wriggled until she'd pulled it off and draped it over the driver's seat.

"Oh, man." His gaze was avid as he stared at her cream-colored balconette bra and matching panties.

She loved the slightly dazed look in his eyes.

"Brace yourself, I'm climbing on board," she said, slipping a leg over his body and straddling him.

"Permission to board granted. And anything else that strikes your fancy," he said. "And speaking of fancy…"

She bit back a moan as his hands slid onto her satin-covered ass, curving his hands to the shape of her body as he pulled her close. They kissed, his hands massaging as she ground against his erection. He smoothed one hand up to the clasp of her bra, and seconds later she felt it slacken around her rib cage.

"You've done *that* before," she murmured as she slipped the straps down her arms.

"I was a Cub Scout." He swore under his breath as her bra fell from her breasts. "Vivian, seriously. Could you be any freakin' hotter?"

She didn't get a chance to respond because he leaned forward and pulled one of her nipples into his mouth and she was lost.

Utterly gone.

Never had a man's mouth on her breasts felt so good. Hot and wet, his teeth and tongue teasing her. She gripped handfuls of his hair and held him in place, riding the waves of desire sweeping through her. Then he slid a hand onto her belly and beneath her panties and took her to a whole new level.

The feel of his clever fingers between her thighs was crazy-making, the pressure both too much and not enough. She started to pant, and when he slid a finger inside her she gave a low, guttural moan.

"These have to go," he said, and she heard a rip as he tore her panties off.

A part of her wanted to laugh at how mad and desperate it all was—the cramped quarters, him tearing her clothes off, their harsh breathing. But then he found her with his thumb at the exact moment that he bit her nipple and she was too busy coming, her head dropping forward as she clutched at his shoulders, needing an anchor to keep her earthbound.

Moments later she opened her eyes to find him watching her with a huge grin on his face.

"Like a handheld flare," he said.

"Sorry?"

He reached for the buckle on his trousers. "I'll explain later."

She stared as he slipped himself free from his pants. Wow. This was going to be *good*.

"Want to do the honors?" He held up a condom.

She smiled, relieved that they weren't going to have to have *that* battle. "Don't mind if I do."

She pulled the latex from the foil, slipped it over the head of his very hard erection and smoothed it on. The moment she rolled it home, she took him in hand and guided him to her entrance. Holding his eye, she slid onto him in one slippery, wet rush.

His breath sighed out on a wordless exclamation, and when she started to move, his hands tightened on her hips. He felt so good inside her, so thick. Desire tightened inside her again, stoked higher by every stroke of his body. He drew her closer, tonguing her nipples.

She tilted her hips and ground herself against him, one hand on his shoulder for balance.

For long moments there was only the sound of their breathing and their bodies coming together. He reached between them, finding her with his thumb again, and she keened desperately, so, so close to coming a second time.

Her movements became urgent, fervent, as she raced toward oblivion. This time he went with her, his hips surging off the seat, his hands dragging her down as he buried himself, his body shuddering. Her body tightened around his as she climaxed, her fingers digging into his shoulders as she kissed him deeply.

She lay limp as a rag doll on his shoulder for what felt like a long time afterward, trying to muster the energy to move. So many things to do—get rid of the condom, get dressed, check her makeup, go back to the reception—but she was so boneless with sated pleasure she could barely blink.

"How you doing there?" he said, his voice a rumble near her ear.

She pushed herself off his chest, letting out a gentle sigh. "I'm pretty good. How about you?"

"Fair to middling."

They began to laugh, then a car started nearby and they both ducked instinctively.

"Shit. What time is it? People must be leaving already," Vivian said.

She slid away from him, leaving him to do whatever it was men did with the condom, and reached for her bra. He made himself decent and buckled up, then helped her wriggle into her dress. It was impossible to pull the narrow skirt over her legs while kneeling, so she cracked the door slightly, did a quick scan, then got out. Standing in the V of the open door, she smoothed the skirt down.

"Decent?" she asked.

"Hardly."

"I meant the dress, funny guy." She rolled her eyes. Leaning past him, she scooped her panties from the limo floor. No way was she making the rookie's mistake of leaving those little puppies behind.

"You look fine."

He got out of the car and she gave him a once-over. It was hard to see much in the dim lighting, but apart from being a little rumpled, he looked fine, too. Which meant they were clear to head into the reception.

She glanced toward the boathouse, not sure how to say what needed to be said.

"Listen, Seth…I had a great time. But just so you know, I'm not really looking for anything. I've got a lot going on with my studies, I've got a graduate show to prepare for…" She trailed off awkwardly.

He was silent for a long moment, his expression unreadable. "So, what, this was just one night of the best limo-monkey-sex ever, no strings attached?"

She couldn't tell if he was pissed or not. He didn't sound pissed, but there was something about the way he was holding himself that made her a little nervous.

"That's another way of putting it."

He grinned hugely, his posture and expression relaxing. "I knew you were my kind of girl when I met you, Vivian Walker."

She punched him on the arm, aware that he'd played her. "Thanks for freaking me out, James."

"My pleasure." He tugged her ruined panties from

her hand. "I'm keeping these, too, by the way." He slid them into his pocket.

"Adding them to your collection, are you?"

"I'm going to frame them and hang them above my bed."

She couldn't help but laugh. "Man, you are so full of it."

But so charming and sexy, too. And, God, was he good in bed. Or, if they wanted to be strictly accurate, in car.

He pulled the cigarettes from his pocket and offered her one. She shook her head, and he lit up.

"We probably shouldn't go back in together," she pointed out.

"You want to go first or will I?"

"You go," she said.

He considered her for a moment, then reached out and tucked a strand of her hair behind her ear. "See you 'round, Vivian."

"Back at ya."

He started walking toward the boathouse, trailing smoke. She watched him, a frown forming as the repercussions of what they'd done finally made their way through her hazy, champagne-muddled brain.

Her sister was married to his brother. She and Seth would see each other at family functions for the next forever. Probably getting naked with him at the first opportunity hadn't been the best way to kick off their relationship.

Then she remembered his kiss, and the feel of his hands in her panties, and the hard, thick slide of him inside her, and she waved a hand in the air, shooing her concerns away like an annoying fly.

What had happened between her and Seth had been inevitable from the moment they'd laid eyes on each other. They'd simply gotten it out of the way sooner rather than later.

Which was a good thing.

Smoothing her hands over her hips, she took a deep breath and went to rejoin the party.

CHAPTER TWO

Ten years later

"WE READY TO go, people?"

The assistant's voice rang out over the chatter in the studio, causing a flurry of activity. Lights were tweaked, reflectors placed at the ready. Robin changed lenses on his camera, his dark head bent, his focus on the task absolute.

Vivian shook her head in admiration. He was so damn good at what he did; taking him up on his offer to become business partners was one of the best decisions she'd ever made.

The model she was dressing shifted her weight and Vivian turned to her own task, concentrating on knotting the scarf around the pretty blonde's neck in a jaunty and sexy bow.

When she was finished she stood back, eyes narrowed as she studied the effect. The model raised her eyebrows, waiting. Vivian nodded.

"You are good to go, sweetie," she said, patting her on the shoulder.

The girl beamed—and she *was* a girl, barely sixteen—and took her place on the purple velvet chaise that was the centerpiece of the photo. Vivian sighed.

Were the models getting younger or was she getting older?

Probably a bit of both.

This was the last shot before lunch, but she went to the clothes rack to check that the next couple of outfits were ready to go anyway.

"Viv."

She glanced over her shoulder, smiling when she caught sight of Jodie standing inside the doorway of the huge studio space.

"Hey. You found us!" she said, waving for her sister to come in.

Jodie glanced around anxiously, clearly worried about getting in the way. It probably looked chaotic to an outsider, but the organized mayhem was second nature to Vivian after five years working as a professional stylist. Taking pity on Jodie, she met her halfway, pulling her into a tight hug.

"Hey, gorgeous," she said. "Thanks for coming all the way into the city to see me."

Even though Vivian had been in Melbourne for over two months now, she hadn't caught up with her sister nearly enough to make up for the ten years Vivian had spent in the U.S.—something Vivian intended to change now that she was home for good. Hence today's lunch date.

"It was no big deal. This place is pretty amazing."

Vivian looked around, trying to see her new workplace through her sister's eyes. Once a factory, the building had been converted into studios and offices in the seventies. She and Robin had managed to snag the penthouse studio, a cavernous space with age-stained floorboards, rough brick walls that had been painted white and a vast wall of metal-framed windows that flooded the room with natural light, which was one of the many reasons she and Robin had gone gaga over it when they'd found it five weeks ago.

"It's working out really well."

Robin had been a friend and occasional work collaborator in L.A., but she'd still had her doubts when he proposed they join forces when he heard she, too, was planning to head home to Australia. All reservations had been blown away the first time they'd sat down to truly hammer out the details of their partnership, however, and from that day she'd been pinching herself that she'd gotten so lucky.

"So you're settled, then?" Jodie asked.

There was an odd intensity to her gaze as she waited for Vivian's answer.

"I'm well and truly, officially home," Vivian said. "No way could I face another transPacific move. Besides, I missed you guys too much."

Jodie's two boys, Sam and Max, were nearly four and five, her mum and dad were getting older... It had been time to return, and Vivian didn't regret it for a second, even if she *did* miss some aspects of her life in L.A. Her friends, the opportunities. Her very cool apartment in Los Feliz.

"Good. Because I like being able to do this instead of making do with Skype," Jodie said.

Vivian checked her watch. "You hungry yet? Robin doesn't need me until after lunch, so we can raid the buffet and go sit on the roof if you like?"

"That sounds suitably inner-city groovy and exciting for a mum of two from Balwyn." Jodie rubbed her hands together in comic anticipation.

"I might have a couple of scarves and handbags to throw your way, too," Vivian stage-whispered as they headed for a trestle table laden with food.

"Oh, goodie."

Vivian had been keeping her sister supplied with a steady stream of fashion and accessories for years. When she was in L.A., Vivian had packed up her finds every month and shipped them to Australia, causing Jodie to joke she was "dressed by Vivian."

"My God. How are you not the size of a house?" Jodie asked as she considered the array of food.

Sandwiches, subs, doughnuts, cake, lasagna warming in a bain-marie, three different types of salads. Vivian handed her sister a plate.

"I don't eat dinner most of the time. And usually this sucker has been gutted by the time I get here and I get a sandwich with someone else's fingerprints on it, and the slushy salad from the bottom of the bowl."

"Ew. Even I would lose weight in that case." Jodie patted her well-padded hips self-consciously.

"Jodie, if I ever have children, I will pray to the gods that I look half as good as you do," Vivian said. "Now, dig in before these vultures break for lunch."

They both loaded up their plates, then Vivian led her sister upstairs to the rooftop, an inhospitable concrete expanse she and Robin were attempting to humanize with a few deck chairs and potted plants.

They grabbed a chair each and chatted easily while eating—Jodie catching up Vivian on Max and Sam's latest exploits, Vivian filling in her sister on the challenges of launching a fashion styling and photography business.

"So who is the shoot for today, then?" Jodie asked as she finished the last of her carrot cake.

"Fairbank and Rose," Vivian said, naming one of Australia's most prominent and exclusive department store chains.

Jodie's eyes widened. "Is that an ongoing thing?"

"It's an audition. We've got a proposal in with them, and this catalogue shoot is the first stage. I guess you could say we're dating, but no one is ready to commit yet."

"They'll be down on one knee, begging you to marry them in a matter of days," Jodie predicted.

"I should record that and play it back while I sleep," Vivian joked. "On to more important matters. What would Sam love for his birthday?"

Her youngest nephew was turning four on the weekend, and Vivian wanted to get him something memorable and fun.

"Anything that references monkeys in any way will go over a treat," Jodie said. "Also, anything related to pirates. If you can find a pirate monkey, you'll have hit pay dirt."

"Pirates and monkeys. That should be enough to get me started."

Jodie set her plate on the ground and dusted off her skirt. She'd given up her work as an accountant when Max was born, and usually she spent the day in jeans and sweaters, but today she'd clearly gone to a bit of trouble, pairing a short-sleeved cashmere turtleneck with an Asian-print skirt Vivian had sent her.

"I wanted to ask you something important, Viv."

She looked so serious that sudden dread clutched

at Vivian's stomach. "Okay. Should I be sitting down for this?"

"You're already sitting down."

"Good point. Then do I need a box of tissues?"

Jodie smiled. "I really hope not."

Then Vivian twigged. "Oh, my God, you're pregnant again!"

Another niece or nephew. *Fantastic.* And this time she would be here to share the whole experience. She leaned forward to hug her sister but Jodie fended her off with a laugh.

"Will you calm down and let me get a word in sideways? I'm not pregnant. But you're kind of on the right track. Jason and I have been talking lately, and we realized that now that we have Max and Sam we need to stop living like kids and plan for the future."

Vivian blinked. She couldn't think of a single couple who were more grounded, sensible and grown-up than Jodie and Jason. They were both accountants, for Pete's sake, they managed their finances down to the cent, they had two children, a mortgage, a dog and a family wagon. How much more adult could a person get?

"Sweetie, if you and Jason consider yourselves kids, then I am officially an embryo. No, less than that, I'm the hopeful, horny glint in someone's eye."

"It might look like that from the outside, but we don't have life or disability insurance…. And we haven't thought about who we'd like to look after the boys if something happened to us."

Vivian stared at her sister, wondering if she was misinterpreting the hopeful expression on Jodie's face. Surely she wasn't asking if Vivian would be willing to step in if Max and Sam needed her to…?

"Jason and I had a big talk about it, and as much as we both love our parents, we think the boys would be better off with someone younger. Dad's slowing down a lot now, and Jason's mum adores the kids, but she has a bit of a short fuse when they're being rowdy. So we wondered how you would feel about being named as guardian to Max and Sam. In case anything, you know, happened."

Wow. Just…*wow*.

Vivian blinked away the hot rush of tears. She couldn't believe this. That her sister—and Jason—trusted her so much. Sure, she knew she'd done a lot to rehabilitate her reputation as the crazy, flighty sister over the years, but for Jodie to trust her with her beloved children…

"Are those happy tears or oh-my-God-get-me-out-of-here-I'm-so-freaked-out tears?" Jodie asked.

"These are happy tears. And the answer is yes. Times a bazillion. I would crawl over broken glass for those boys, and I would be honored to be their guardian," Vivian said earnestly.

"I was hoping you'd say that."

She was having trouble choking back a wellspring of emotion. "Jodie…I want you to know this means a lot to me. I will *not* let you down. I will do whatever it takes to make sure Sam and Max are happy and healthy, that they never want for anything."

"*Should* anything happen to me and Jason," Jodie amended with a twinkle in her eye.

"Right. Of course," Vivian added hastily. *"Of course."*

Jodie laughed outright. "Wait till I tell Jason you

were ready to drive over and pick the kids up straight away."

Vivian smiled sheepishly. "An enthusiastic guardian is a good guardian, right?"

"Absolutely. I hope Seth is as happy as you are. I'll feel so much better having this all settled."

Vivian frowned. "Seth?"

"Sorry, I should probably explain that, shouldn't I? We want the two of you to be there for the boys. A male and female influence."

"Right. Good plan," Vivian said, even though she was privately boggled at her sister's choice. Being based overseas, she'd seen Seth only a handful of times in the past ten years, but the family grapevine had kept her up-to-date on the headlines in his life. She knew, for example, that he'd given up on the band seven years ago and had been bumming around in various jobs in the nightclub and bar scene ever since. She knew that he was still a total pants man, showing up with a new girlfriend every six months, without fail. She also knew from the few times they'd been in the same room that he was still charming and cocky and sexy—but none of those characteristics were what she would have chosen for the man who would be guardian to her children.

But they weren't her children, they were Jodie and Jason's, and even though it almost killed her to bite her tongue, Vivian did. If they thought he would make a good role model and parental stand-in, then she would bow to their superior judgment. After all, they knew him much better than she did.

"How did he, um, react?" she asked.

"I don't know yet. Jason's seeing him tonight after work. He loves the kids, though, so I'm sure he'll be fine with it. Which is probably just as well, since he's going to be a father himself, soon."

Vivian nearly fell off her chair. "What?"

When did this happen? And how come she hadn't heard about it earlier? Surely if Seth had settled down with one woman long enough to get her pregnant, her sister would have considered it gossip-worthy?

A strange feeling gripped her. A little like vertigo, but not. In her secret heart of hearts, she'd kept a casual eye on Seth, ensuring she knew enough, but not too much about his life. Not because she was interested in him romantically, God forbid, but because he was the male approximation of her on Jason's side of the family—the younger sibling, a bit of a screwup, never one to color within the lines. In a strange way, he'd become the benchmark for her own success—or not—over the years. As long as he was still single, it was okay that things hadn't worked out with Franco and she was alone again. As long as Seth was still floating around, trying to find "his" thing, it was okay for her to be doing the same—although that hadn't been an issue for her for a while now.

But now he was in a relationship, having a kid…? Suddenly she felt left behind. She'd been so sure she'd be the first one to settle down and start a family.

"We found out about it just last week. Personally, I think it's because he worked out that if he's going to be hitting me up for babysitting duties, he should probably let me know there's a niece or nephew on the way."

Vivian chose her words carefully. "So, have you met his girlfriend?"

"Oh, she's not his girlfriend. This is Seth, remember? I think they were friends with benefits for a while and she got pregnant, yada, yada."

"How's he coping with that?" She honestly couldn't imagine Seth getting up to do a late-night feed or changing a diaper.

"You know, pretty well." Jodie nodded thoughtfully. "As Jason said, he's manning up. He's been to Lola's doctors' appointments and he's doing all he can to make sure she's got what she needs."

"Well. Good for him." Although, really, it was the bare minimum that should be expected of a man who had gone halves in a baby. Even accidentally. Mind, there were plenty of baby daddies who ran for the hills, so Vivian figured Seth deserved a couple of elephant stamps for effort.

"So, have you met Lola?" She was starting to feel like Mrs. Crab Apple, the gossipy neighbor, but she couldn't deny her curiosity.

"Yeah. She's a nice kid." Jodie kept her face absolutely straight, but Vivian didn't miss the implication.

"How old is she, exactly?" she asked, not sure whether to be amused or exasperated. Honestly, Seth was practically a caricature of himself.

"Twenty-four. Give or take."

Vivian blinked.

"It's going to be interesting, that's for sure," Jodie said, almost but not quite smothering a smile.

Vivian didn't bother trying. "Hoo yeah."

"You can tease him about it at Sam's birthday this weekend. He will *love* that."

"I bet he will." She grinned, thinking about how much fun it would be needling him. "So, do you have any paperwork I need to sign to get my hands on these kids of yours or what?"

"Not yet. We'll talk to our lawyer next week, though, so I'll let you know."

Vivian caught her sister's hand, the easy smile fading from her lips. She wanted—needed—her sister to know that this was a big deal for her.

"Thanks for trusting me, Jodie. I won't let you guys down."

"I know, sweetie. That's why I'm asking you."

They hugged, and the warmth of her sister's arms was the best thing Vivian had felt in a long time.

Yep, it was damned good to be home.

SETH PACED IN front of the clinic, checking his watch for the tenth time in as many minutes. Lola was late *again*.

Even though she hadn't responded to any of the other messages he'd left, he dialed her number, rubbing his temples. He stopped in his tracks when she actually picked up. Hallelujah.

"Hi, Seth. Sorry I didn't get back to you earlier but I was at the checkout and there was such a huge queue behind me, I didn't want to hold everyone up by talking," Lola said, her Yorkshire accent more evident over the phone.

Checkout? Queue? She was *shopping,* instead of turning up for her thirty-six-week checkup?

Unbelievable.

Although, considering it was Lola, only too believable. To his eternal frustration.

"Lola. I'm at Dr. Mancini's. Where are you?" He did his best to keep the impatience out of his voice, but wasn't certain he pulled it off. They'd learned a few weeks ago that their baby was in the breech position, and this scan had been scheduled to see if the baby had corrected his or her position.

In other words, it was bloody important.

"Oh, God, I'm so sorry. I totally forgot. I heard about this amazing warehouse sale for baby furniture, and… Well, I forgot. Can we reschedule?"

Seth gave a silent sigh. In any other woman, he'd blame Lola's lapse of memory on pregnancy hormones, but the truth was that she'd always been a bit flaky. Forgetful, more inclined to rub a crystal to get rid of a headache than take a painkiller, and absolutely hopeless with money. She also wasn't great at thinking through the repercussions of her actions, or planning ahead.

"I'll see if they can reschedule us and call you back with the time."

"Oh, you're waiting for me? I'm so sorry."

Of course he was waiting for her. He came to all her appointments. Where did she think he was?

He bit back his irritation. There was no point getting frustrated with Lola. Her feelings would be hurt, and then he'd get the silent treatment for days.

"I'll call you in five." He hung up and went to talk to the receptionist. She was very understanding, managing to find a spot for Lola the following day, then he called Lola and passed on the details.

"Why don't you set up a reminder on your phone for tomorrow morning?" he suggested.

"I'm not stupid, Seth. There's no need to talk to me as though I'm a child."

Dear God, not the don't-treat-me-like-a-child argument again.

"I was just making a suggestion. If you don't think

it has any merit, feel free to ignore it," he said, attempting to defuse the situation.

Too late, Lola was off and running. For the next ten minutes he listened as she enumerated her achievements—leaving her home in the United Kingdom to come here on her own two years ago, being promoted to shift leader at the call center where she used to work after only three months on the job, having to ask her parents for money only twice since she'd left home, while the girl she was living with practically had her rent paid by her father.

At times like these, he was reminded only too well of how young she was. At twenty-four, he'd been messier, less organized and a whole hell of a lot more irresponsible than her. Just as well one of his guys hadn't slipped through back then. Twenty-four-year-old him and twenty-four-year-old Lola would have been a disaster of epic proportions. As it was, it would be a line-call as to whether thirty-four-year-old him and Lola could pull this thing off between them.

Although it wasn't as though they had a choice.

Somehow he managed to assure her that he hadn't been taking a shot at her, agreeing that he'd meet her at the clinic again tomorrow before ending the call. He needed to get to the bar to make his six o'clock appointment with his brother, so he jumped into his Audi and wasted five minutes trying to get it to start before the engine finally caught and he could hit the road. He made a mental note to talk to the mechanic to get the ignition fixed. One of many things he needed to take care of in the run-up to Lola's due date. The last thing he wanted was to be stuck with a car that wouldn't start when she was in labor.

He was tired and hungry by the time he parked in the reserved spot behind the bar, not a great sign when his day wouldn't be over until at least midnight. Scrubbing his face, he let himself in the back door and hollered out a hello to the guys in the kitchen before heading upstairs to his shoe-box-size office.

He sat at his paper-strewn desk and stared bleakly at the scuffed wall. There was no getting around it—he was deeply, profoundly worried about how Lola would cope with being a mother. Not because she was a bad person, but because she simply didn't handle difficult situations well. Her default reaction to any stressful situation was to retreat to bed and stay there eating junk food for as long as she could get away with it. Yes, she could be fun—a lot of fun—when she was in the right frame of mind, but she could also be impatient, temperamental and self-centered.

Right, and you're a freaking saint. Perfect daddy material.

He wasn't. He was the first to admit that. He'd lived selfishly his entire life. About the only thing he'd ever fully committed to was the bar—and, perhaps, to being a decent uncle to his brother's kids. But he was fairly certain he understood many of the challenges that lay ahead. He knew there were going to be late nights and not a lot of sleep and periods of intense frustration and worry. He knew that no matter what else was happening for him or Lola, the baby needed them to put him or her first. Every time.

He wasn't one hundred percent certain Lola had the same take on parenting, however. He wasn't sure that she'd given much thought to the way things would work between them, in fact. She preferred to "take things as

they come" and not get "bogged down in all the details"—both phrases she'd used to fob him off last week
when he'd tried to discuss a care schedule for when the
baby was born. He'd wanted her to know that he would
be there to support her in any way she needed him to
be, but she'd shied away from the discussion. As though
by avoiding the conversation she could pretend for a little bit longer that she wasn't about to become a parent.

Which boded really bloody well for the future.

The phone on his desk buzzed, signaling a call from
downstairs.

"Hey, boss. Your brother's here," Syrie said when he
picked up. "You want us to send him up?"

"Thanks. And send up a couple of beers and a large
fries, too, okay?"

"I'll put it on your tab."

"Funny."

He took a second to check his emails—nothing urgent—before the sound of steps on the stairs announced
his brother's arrival.

"Good to see you," Seth said when Jason entered
the office. "Grab a seat. I've got some beers coming
our way in five."

"I knew I liked coming here for a reason," Jason
said as he loosened his tie and set down his briefcase.

Seth tried not to smile. He could count on the fingers of one hand the times Jason had dropped by Night
Howls for a drink. Usually he was either working late
or had some commitment with his family—which was
the way it should be when you had two kids under five.

"What did you have to do to get out of jail early?"
he asked.

Jason touched his briefcase with the side of his shoe.

"There's a reason why that bastard weighs a ton. Lots of stuff to go through when I get home."

"Man, I don't know how you do it," Seth said, shaking his head.

He'd long since given up the hard partying days of his youth, but the thought of showing up at an office in the city at eight every morning and sitting under fluorescent lights all day and not checking out again till it was dark outside made him want to launch himself from the top of the nearest building.

Jason shrugged easily. "Horses for courses, mate. No way could I stand working the hours you do, either. I'm comatose once it hits nine."

"That's because you're up at sparrow's fart. I don't start the day till ten, minimum."

"That is so going to change when the baby comes along." Jason's laugh held more than a hint of schadenfreude. "How many weeks is it now?"

"Four."

"It'll be so much fun watching you do this."

"This is an ugly side of you, just so you know."

"Consider it payback for all the years you gave me shit for not coming out to play because I had to be home with Jodie and the kids. I'm allowed to savor the irony a little."

Seth shifted uncomfortably. "Yeah, well, I was a dick. You're a good dad, and you have awesome cute kids. If they were mine, I'd want to be home with them, too, instead of out with a douche like me."

"Funny you should mention that." Jason yanked at his tie, loosening it further.

Seth braced himself. When his brother had called to ask if they could catch up tonight, he'd been a little surprised, given they mostly saw each other on Jason's turf. It had only taken him a few minutes' thought to work out what his brother wanted to see him about, however. Seth had dropped the big news about Lola and the baby on Jason and Jodie only last week, and he figured his brother was here to offer him some guidance, man-to-man. Which, frankly, he was more than happy to take. He figured he and Lola needed all the help they could get.

Syrie arrived and Jason held fire on whatever it was he was about to say while she distributed the drinks and fries. Once she was gone, Jason took a big mouthful of his beer before eyeing Seth.

"I know you've got a lot on your plate at the moment, so this is probably going to seem as though it's coming out of left field, but Jodie and I talked about it and we decided that we'd leave the decision up to you. If it's too much, we totally understand, given what you're taking on. But you're at the top of our list and we wanted to give you the option."

Seth was genuinely baffled about where this conversation was going. "You want to tell me what this list is for?"

Jason nodded, smoothing his hands down his thighs, and Seth realized he was nervous. Which made him nervous.

"Okay," Jason said. "You've always been really good with Max and Sam. The best uncle ever, is the way Max puts it. And Jodie and I have started putting things in place for the future in the past few weeks, just in case. Insurance, wills, that kind of thing."

"Cheery stuff. What brought this on?"

He shrugged. "Jodie saw some movie with her girlfriends a few weeks ago—I don't know the details, but she's been freaking out about making sure the boys are looked after if something happens to us. Which is where you come in."

"Me?"

"Long story short, Jodie and I would really like it if you'd be Max and Sam's co-guardian in the event that something happened to us."

For a moment Seth was literally speechless. He'd given his brother's wife a lot of crap over the years—a reciprocal arrangement that they both mostly enjoyed— although he'd never had anything but the utmost respect for her as a parent. Same for his brother. They loved their kids, were firm but loving, generous but measured, and Seth figured that Sam and Max would be a whole hell of a lot better adjusted than him by the time they were grown men. That Jason and Jodie wanted him to step into their shoes if necessary was both daunting and touching.

He realized Jason was waiting for his response, a small frown between his eyebrows.

"Sorry," Seth said. "You threw me for a second there. Yes, absolutely. I would happily be guardian to the boys. Whatever you guys need me to do." There wasn't a doubt in his mind.

Jason's expression smoothed out as he sat back in his chair a little. "Good stuff. Great."

"You didn't think I'd say no, did you?" Seth was more than a little astonished by the notion.

"No. I know you love the kids. But taking on some-one else's family is a big deal. I wouldn't blame you for hesitating, given your situation with Lola."

"Since the odds of anything actually ever happening

to you guys is ridiculously small, I'm not going to get too sweaty over it. But you should know that I would do whatever it took to make sure those kids get everything they want and need. As for Lola and the baby... I'd work it out."

"Good to hear. Thanks, mate. It's a load off, for sure. I know Jodie will be thrilled to have this all sorted. Assuming, of course, that Vivian is in, too."

Seth had just taken a mouthful of beer and he nearly choked as the meaning of his brother's words hit home. Because Jason had said "co-guardian," hadn't he? Which implied that there was at least one other guardian. And now his brother had mentioned Vivian.

"You're not seriously thinking of asking Vivian to be guardian, too, are you?" The words were out his mouth before he could think of a better way to phrase his objection.

"Why? You got a problem with Viv?"

"Not with Vivian herself, no. She's fine—awesome fun—as herself. But as a stand-in *mother?* Are you sure you've really thought this through?"

He didn't understand how his brother couldn't see what was so patently clear to him. Vivian was a good-time girl. She'd flitted from career to career for the past ten years, bouncing from the east coast of the U.S. to the west and then back again, rubbing shoulders with celebrities and professional party animals. Jason had regaled Seth with tales of her adventures. And now the guy thought she'd be a reliable substitute for Jodie should the worst happen?

Jason frowned. "She loves the kids. When she was in L.A. she spoke to them once a week on Skype, never fail. And since she's been back she's been making up for lost time with them."

"Right. Until the next shiny, bright thing comes along," Seth said.

"Viv's not like that anymore. She's grown up," Jason said.

"You need to know that whoever you choose is rock-solid. Utterly reliable. Take it from someone who is dealing with a flaky, unreliable woman every day, it's a nightmare and you don't want to be exposing your kids to that kind of uncertainty." Seth could hear the vehemence in his own tone, but he wasn't about to apologize for it. This was important.

"I take it you're having some issues with Lola?" Jason said carefully.

"Yes. Just a few." It was tempting to spill his guts, but this wasn't about him and Lola. This was about Sam and Max and doing what was best for them.

"You have my sympathy, but Viv isn't Lola. How many times have you even been in the same room as Viv over the years anyway? A dozen?"

"Enough to know what I'm talking about." Enough to know that he knew and understood Vivian far better than Jason ever would. He'd never told his brother about the night of the wedding and those mind-blowing minutes in the limo, and he wasn't about to now. But as far as he was concerned, that night was the perfect illustration of his worries. Vivian had been having a good time, and she hadn't stopped for a second to think about what the repercussions of her—their—actions might be. She'd just stripped off her dress and climbed on top because it felt good. From what he'd heard and seen over the years, doing what felt good was her life philosophy. Which was great if you were looking for a hot encounter in the back of a limo, but not so great when you were talking about ferrying kids to soccer practice and worrying about fevers at one o'clock in the morning.

In the back of his head, a voice piped up, pointing out that he'd done all those things in the back of the limo, too, and that he'd pretty much thumbed his nose at convention all his life, lived recklessly, done all the things he'd just accused Vivian of doing, and then some. He ignored it, driven by the anxiety tightening his chest. He couldn't do anything to alter the situation he was in with Lola, but his brother could definitely dodge this bullet.

He realized that almost every muscle in his body was tense and that he'd shifted to the edge of the chair. The need to reach across the desk and grab his brother by the lapels and shake him until he saw sense was almost impossible to resist.

"I appreciate your concern, but Jodie and I are pretty settled on this," Jason said evenly.

"Then maybe you need to talk some more. Really think about it."

"We have thought about it. A lot. That's why I'm here." There was a steely note beneath his brother's words. Despite his calmness, Seth had rattled him.

Good.

It was tempting to push harder, to drive home his point further, but there was a look in his brother's eyes that told him it was time to back off. He'd issued his warning in the strongest terms possible, done his best to alert his brother to the danger he was courting. The rest was up to him and Jodie.

"As long as you guys are going in with your eyes open. It's your decision," Seth said carefully.

"Yeah, it is. Our lawyer will draw up some papers. I'll get them to you as soon as possible so we can get this wrapped up."

"Let me know what you need me to do or whatever and I'll make it happen."

There was a weird vibe in the room. Jason was pissed with him. Well, so be it. If someone had tapped him on the shoulder nine months ago and told him how things were going to pan out with Lola, he would have set a new land-speed record bolting in the other direction. He'd simply given his brother good advice. He wasn't going to apologize for that fact.

"You want another beer?" he asked.

"Actually, I should probably head home so I can help get the kids into the bath," Jason said.

"Sure."

He walked his brother downstairs and through the bar, following him out to the street. They exchanged a little more small talk before Jason headed for the tram stop on the main street.

Seth stood watching him walk away. Then he went inside to prepare for a busy night.

CHAPTER THREE

"WHY DON'T YOU two walking, talking menaces take it outside for five seconds while your mum and I make the magic happen?" Vivian said.

Her two nephews skidded to a halt halfway through their fourth lap of the kitchen island. They'd been circling her and Jodie like electrons around the nucleus of an atom for nearly half an hour now, fueled by excitement and too many gummy snakes in the lead up to Sam's birthday party this afternoon.

"Are we getting in the way?" Max asked.

"What do you think?" Jodie asked.

"I think we are being superannoying," Max said, giving his brother a high five.

Vivian tried and failed to hide her amusement.

"Please don't encourage them. They already think they're a comedy duo." Jodie walked to the sliding door and pulled it open. "Outside. Now."

Sam and Max moaned and groaned but they did as instructed, trudging across the lawn to the play equipment in the corner of the yard as though they'd been sentenced to life imprisonment.

"Poor babies," Vivian said.

"Oh, yes, their lives are blighted. It's a wonder they can smile, let alone laugh." Jodie rolled her eyes.

They resumed work on the salads. Jodie mentioned

that she'd caught up with Nell, one of her bridesmaids, the other day, and Vivian heard the CliffsNotes version of the other woman's divorce. They talked about various school friends as they finished the prep work for the party, then Jason came inside from cleaning the barbecue, covered in black gunk and rust, and Jodie herded him into the laundry room to clean up. Listening to them bicker companionably and watching her nephews race up and down the climbing frame outside, a warm sense of belonging stole over Vivian.

She had loved every second of her time overseas, but there was no denying that it was good to be back. There was something about the clear, far-off blue of the Australian sky and the faint hint of eucalyptus that wafted through even the most suburban of streets on a sunny day and the flat, familiar drawl of the Australian accent that eased a pressure inside her that she hadn't even known needed comforting. Put simply, this was home, where she belonged, and it felt right and good to be here at this stage in her life.

Her small moment of introspection was broken by the arrival of her parents, loaded down with yet more food and presents for her nephew. The other guests poured in after that, and it wasn't long before the house and yard were alive with the sound of children playing and adults talking and laughing. Vivian did her best to be useful, circulating with platters of finger food and keeping one eye on the horde of children rampaging around the yard. She was, however, very aware of the fact that her gaze kept darting to the door every time a new guest arrived, and after catching herself doing it for the fifth time she admitted she was waiting for Seth.

It wasn't a comfortable admission, given their history, but there was no point denying the truth. From the first moment she'd laid eyes on him she'd been aware of him—drawn to him—and apparently time, experience and maturity hadn't changed that fact. Regardless of whatever else had been going on in her life, she'd always enjoyed matching wits with him at the family events they'd both attended.

That didn't mean that she wasn't fully aware of his many, many shortcomings, of course. She'd always known him for what he was—temporary fun—and had managed their relationship accordingly. But she'd be lying to herself if she pretended that she wasn't looking forward to seeing him today. Especially since she would have the opportunity to tease him about impending fatherhood.

Despite her vigilance, he must have somehow snuck into the party without her noticing, because the next time she scanned the yard to see if there was anything she could do to help her sister, her gaze got caught on a familiar dark-haired figure keeping Jason company by the barbecue.

Seth glanced over his shoulder at almost that exact moment and her heart gave a distinct excited kick as they locked gazes.

Just like old times.

He smiled, the same cocky, confident grin she remembered so well, and she grinned in return, offering him a nod of acknowledgement. It was tempting to weave her way through the crowd to talk to him, but that would be breaking her self-imposed rule where he was concerned. She was allowed to be amused by him, she was even allowed to indulge in a little flirting, but she was not allowed to make him *important*. Racing to his side the moment he arrived at the party definitely fell under that category.

Instead, she returned to the kitchen, eager to occupy herself handing around more food.

"Go away. You've done enough," Jodie said, shooing her away like a housefly.

"I want to help," Vivian protested.

"Great. Go and be charming and funny and make sure everyone is having a good time."

"It's much easier to hand around a platter of sushi," Vivian grumbled.

"Why do you think I'm here in the kitchen?" Jodie grabbed a clean wineglass and poured a generous amount of a sémillon sauvignon. "Here."

Vivian took the glass with good grace and was about to slip through the sliding doors when Jodie called to her.

"Wait. Jason probably needs a beer. Which means you should probably take one for Seth, too."

Vivian dutifully accepted the two bottles of beer, letting them hang between the fingers of her left hand. Taking a deep breath, she headed for the barbecue.

She could see Jason's and Seth's heads above everyone else's. They were both slightly taller than average, and they always seemed to stand out in a crowd. Seth's shoulders were broader than Jason's, though, his hair darker. He was dressed more stylishly, too, in a pair of low-slung jeans and a wrinkled black shirt with cowboy boots, as opposed to his brother's polo shirt and slightly too loose bright blue jeans—daddy denim, as she and Robin called it.

Her professional self had to give Seth points for figuring out early what suited him and sticking to it. He always looked effortlessly cool, as though he'd slung on the nearest thing when he rolled out of bed and it just happened to be a very hip shirt and the latest in edgy jeans.

"Apparently you two reprobates aren't capable of looking after your own hydration levels," she said as she drew closer, causing both Seth and Jason to swing to face her.

"Finally. I was beginning to think Jodie had forgotten me," Jason said, his eyes lighting up when he saw the beers she was carrying.

"You could have gotten a beer yourself, you know," she said as she handed one of the bottles over.

"And leave my sacred post at the barbecue? What sort of heresy have they been teaching you over in the U.S.?" Jason said.

Finally Vivian allowed herself to look at Seth. He was watching her with lazy approval, his gaze sliding over her face before dropping to her body.

"Looking good, Viv," he said. "As always."

She was suddenly very aware of the warm sun on her face and how cool and slippery the bottle was as she passed it to him.

"High praise from a connoisseur like yourself, Seth. Thank you."

His mouth kicked up at the corner at her dry tone. "And she comes out fighting."

"Self-defense. As always."

He glanced at the beer label. "I take it there were no Peronis?"

"I don't know. Would you like me to race back and check for you?"

He offered her the beer. "You're a champ."

She let the bottle hang between them, her smile becoming a grin. He knew she wasn't going to scamper off to fetch him his preferred brand of beer, and she knew that he loved suggesting that she might.

All part of the game.

"Better drink that while it's still cold." She took a mouthful of wine. "Might be the only one you get."

He laughed. "You haven't changed much."

"Neither have you." It had been two years since they'd last seen each other, and any changes in his appearance had all been in his favor as far as she could see. There were new lines around his eyes and mouth, but they only served to underscore the rugged handsomeness of his face. He'd been good-looking when he was younger, but now he was truly a man, and it showed in the hard, slightly cynical light in his eyes and the density of the two days' worth of scruff shadowing his jaw. He seemed more comfortable in his own body, too, as though he'd settled more deeply into his own skin.

"Jason tells me you're back for good this time?"

She couldn't help but register the skeptical note in his voice.

"A friend and I have started a business together. We've got a studio in West Melbourne."

He looked surprised. "Yeah? So you really have given up all that la-la-land stuff?"

"That's right. How about you? A little birdie tells me you're running a bar somewhere suitably grungy."

"Collingwood. And I own the place." His tone told her he was aware she'd been taking a retaliatory shot.

"The same little birdie tells me that congratulations are in order." She raised her glass. "Here's to becoming a daddy."

He snorted his amusement. "Go ahead, get your digs in while you can. Everyone else has."

"Have they?" She glanced at Jason, who shrugged apologetically.

"You've got to admit, it's pretty ironic. Considering."

She knew exactly what he meant. Seth had always been a walking, talking poster boy for an unencumbered, live-for-the-moment lifestyle.

"So have you swapped that little car you used to drive for an SUV yet?" she asked.

"Not yet."

"You should probably get onto that," Jason said. "Not much room in that Audi TT for anything."

"It's a baby, not a refrigerator," Seth said.

"Still. You're going to need to haul a lot of stuff around," Vivian said. "Diaper bag, pram, portable cot, baby seat... You might even need to get a wagon."

"Enjoying yourself?"

She pretended to consider. "You know, I am. Is that wrong?"

Jason laughed. Seth gave him a sardonic look.

"Your burgers are burning, by the way," he said.

"Shit." Jason turned to the barbecue and started urgently rotating hamburger patties.

Seth didn't even bother trying to stifle his smile.

"This'll be you soon," Vivian said, unable to resist teasing him some more. It wasn't every day a girl was handed such a golden opportunity. "Barbecues, kids running all over. The whole nine yards."

"I'm up for it," he said, surprising her.

She cocked an eyebrow and gave him a look, but his gaze remained unwavering.

"Well, look at that. James has grown up."

"It's not that much of a stretch, believe it or not. You'll see when it happens for you."

She laughed, acknowledging the hit. "That about makes us even, don't you think?"

"I don't know. That stuff about my car was a low blow. I might need to get a few more digs in."

She held her arms wide. "Free shot. Head or gut, your choice."

His gaze ran down her body, lingering on her thighs in her tight black jeans.

"Can I choose a different body part?"

She checked her watch. "And there it is. A new record, even for you. Less than five minutes before the first innuendo passed your lips. Impressive for a new father."

He tried not to laugh but couldn't pull it off. "Jesus, you're a smart-ass."

"Thank you. I've had ten years of practice."

"Has it been that long?" His gaze narrowed.

"Jason and Jodie's ten-year anniversary was two months ago."

He whistled. "Time flies when you're having fun."

"Doesn't it?"

Seth took a pull from his beer. "So, tell me about this business you're starting up."

They talked for half an hour, filling in the gaps in each other's lives. As always, she was hyperaware of everything she said and did while near him. He'd always had that affect on her, magnifying her self-awareness to almost painful levels.

Probably that was the rampant sexual awareness that always seemed to be unleashed when they were within a few feet of one another. As she'd acknowledged to herself all those years ago, it had been inevitable that they would sleep together, given that they enjoyed what could only be described as sizzling sexual chemistry. It was just as well that they'd gotten it out of the way early, when it meant about as little as was possible. She wasn't so sure that she would have escaped unscathed by Seth's charms if she'd held off any longer. He was simply too magnetic, too attractive and sexy.

Plus, she liked him. She was aware that if one of her girlfriends was dating him, she would advise her to expect nothing but great sex and lots of disappointment. But since neither she nor anyone she personally cared about was emotionally invested in him, she was free to enjoy and celebrate his good qualities.

He was funny. He was hot. He was self-deprecating in the best possible way, yet also charmingly unrepentant about his worst characteristics. He knew who he was, and he liked himself. The older she got, the more important— and rare—both those things seemed to be.

Their conversation ended naturally when Jason started transferring the cooked food to the table that was serving as a buffet. She went one way, Seth the other, and while she remained aware of him for the next few hours, she made a point of not looking in his direction or engaging with him again.

It would be too, too easy to allow their light flirtation to become something else in her own mind. She'd sidestepped that pitfall when she was twenty-three, and she wasn't diving headfirst into it now she was thirty-three. No matter how wicked and compelling his dark brown eyes were.

The party began to die down after the birthday cake had been dispensed. Children started to become over-tired and the high-pitched wail of an upset child became the norm not the exception. A steady stream of parents made their way out the door, and even though Vivian was starting to feel the call of an afternoon nap—one of life's greatest pleasures in her book—she wasn't about to abandon her sister to clean up alone. She was returning to the kitchen with yet another armful of dirty plates and cutlery when she found Seth saying goodbye to her sister.

"Great party, as always, hostess with the mostest," he said, dropping a kiss onto Jodie's cheek.

"Glad you enjoyed yourself," Jodie said.

To an outsider, the way her lips curved upward would have looked both welcoming and friendly, but Vivian could see that there was absolutely no sincerity behind either her sister's smile or her words. In fact, if she had to guess, she'd say Jodie was mightily pissed with Seth. Which was weird, since they had always got on surprisingly well.

"I did, thanks," Seth said after a small hesitation. "The cake was amazing. I got some good pictures of Sam blowing out the candles. I'll email them to you when I get home."

"Thanks, that'd be great."

Seth's eyes narrowed at Jodie's cool tone, but he didn't push the issue, shifting his focus to Vivian and giving her a quick nod. "Good to see you, Viv. Good luck with the business."

Behind her, Vivian heard a sound, but when she glanced at her sister, Jodie's expression was carefully neutral.

"You, too," Vivian said. "Maybe I'll drop into this

sleazy dive of yours sometime and have a drink on the house."

"You do that."

Seth glanced at Jodie one last time before heading for the door. Vivian waited until he was gone before turning to her sister.

"What was all that about?"

Jodie went to the sink and rinsed the sponge. "What do you mean?"

"All that stuff with Seth just now. Are you guys fighting or something?"

"No. Of course not."

Jodie had always been the world's worst liar. Her voice got all funny and high, and her gaze started wandering all over the room. Vivian decided to take the fact that her sister was currently addressing the light fixture rather than looking at her as a sign that she was onto something.

"If you don't want to talk about it, it's fine with me," she said.

Jodie pressed her lips together as though she was trying to contain herself. "He's such a bloody hypocrite, that's all. I saw the way he was looking at you when he was talking to you earlier. Like you were a woman-shaped lollypop and he wanted to lick you. If I could get away with it, I'd kick him in the shins." The words burst out of Jodie as though propelled, and she immediately started wiping the counter as though she would mop up her words in the same way.

"Okay. Is there any reason why Seth flirting with me is a problem? I mean, I know he's having a baby with someone else, but they're not together, right? And he and I have always had that little flirty routine going on.

It's our thing. It doesn't mean anything, if that's what you're worried about."

"I know it's your thing. And I've never had a problem with it. I thought you guys were friends. But—" Jodie took a deep breath. "You know what? This isn't even worth getting into. Forget I said anything."

Vivian weighed her sister's obvious desire to drop the subject against the rather disturbing snippet Jodie had let slip and decided that she simply wasn't able to let this one go through to the keeper.

"I was under the impression that Seth and I were friends, too. What makes you think we aren't?"

"Nothing. It was a slip of the tongue. Ignore me."

"Jodie."

Her sister closed her eyes for a beat. "Viv. You don't want to get into this. It's between me and Jason, really. Not even that. It's been Seth and himself. The idiot."

Vivian watched her sister clean the already pristine granite counter. She wasn't sure why, but for some reason she found herself thinking about the conversation they'd had earlier in the week when Jodie had asked Vivian to be co-guardian to Max and Sam. She felt a little crazy linking the two things, but her intuition was going nuts and she'd learned to trust it over the years.

"Is this to do with the guardianship?"

Jodie went very still, and Vivian knew she'd hit pay dirt.

"I don't think we should have this conversation," Jodie said miserably. "I shouldn't have said anything in the first place. Can we please forget it?"

Jodie looked so unhappy, Vivian swallowed her objection. "Okay. If that's what you want."

"I do. I want us both to erase the last five minutes."

"Okay." Uneasy, Vivian went to collect more plates.

She couldn't stop herself from mulling over what little Jodie had said while she worked. Did Seth have some sort of problem with sharing guardianship with her? Did he want it all to himself, perhaps? Was he worried she'd fight him for custody...?

She couldn't get her head around it. She definitely couldn't imagine Seth agitating for sole guardianship of Sam and Max should anything happen to his brother and her sister. But clearly *something* was going on. Something that involved her and Seth.

"Vivian..."

She turned to find an uncomfortable-looking Jodie watching her from the patio.

"Please tell me you're not out here imagining a million different horrible scenarios."

"I'm not. Just one or two. That way I can get the details nice and vivid."

Jodie groaned. "God, sometimes I have such a big mouth." She joined Vivian at the buffet table. "Are you going to be able to forget what I said?"

"Of course. Although I've got to admit that I'm tempted to ask Seth what the problem is. Straight to the horse and all that."

Jodie's eyes went round. "God. I almost want to encourage you to do that."

Vivian set down the dirty forks she'd collected. "Are you going to spill or what? Because you can't keep dangling the carrot forever."

Jodie glanced toward the house. "I promised Jason I wouldn't say anything to you."

"Right."

"But I've already kind of ruined that, haven't I?"

"A little."

"Promise me that you won't take this to heart, okay? This is about Seth, not you. About his stupid situation. Which is why he's such a freaking hypocrite."

"Jodie, come on. You are literally killing me here."

"Seth doesn't think you're a good fit to be guardian to the boys." Jodie said it in a rush, almost as though she was afraid that she'd lose her gumption if she went any slower.

"*A good fit.* What does that mean, exactly?" Vivian asked carefully.

"He's an idiot, Vivian. His head is messed up over this baby stuff with Lola. He's having problems with her. It's a classic case of projection."

"What did he say?"

"He thinks you're unreliable. A party girl. Flighty." Jodie curled her hand around Vivian's. "But he doesn't really think that, Viv. Or, if he does, it's only because he doesn't know you well enough to know the real you."

Her sister's words seemed to come from a distance, as though she was shouting them from another room. Suddenly all Vivian could remember was the way Seth's gaze had slid down her body and lingered on her thighs when he'd asked if he could pick another body part. Meanwhile, he'd been dripping poison in her sister's and brother-in-law's ears, trying to convince them not to trust her with their precious children.

How. Freaking. Dare. He.

She inhaled slowly through her nose, trying to order her chaotic thoughts. There were so many directions to go, after all. Outrage, hurt, shame, anger.

"What did you say?" she asked.

"I wasn't there. Jason spoke to him alone. But he told him that we'd made our decision."

"Was Jason worried? After what Seth said?"

"No. Not for a second."

Vivian was hugely grateful for the fact that her sister didn't hesitate to reassure her.

"In fact, he thought Seth was way out of line. It's not like Seth's got a fantastic track record himself. He's hardly been the poster boy for upstanding citizenship over the years. He's got a good heart, though, and we both think that is way more important than either of you having nine-to-five jobs. Who cares if it took you a while to find yourself? Who cares if you used to party like it's 1999? All of those things mean that you'll be able to offer Sam and Max awesome advice when they need it. If they need it."

Vivian blinked. "He brought up my career changes? And my lifestyle?"

Jodie slapped a hand to her forehead. "Why do I keep making this worse?"

Vivian gripped her sister's shoulders and looked her dead in the eye. "You need to tell me everything he said. Every word."

"I don't want to."

"You need to."

Because Jodie might think that Seth was being a jerk, that he was projecting, that this was some kind of manifestation of the stress he must be feeling as a parent-to-be, but she didn't know the full story. Jodie didn't know that ten years ago, Vivian and Seth had had wild limo-monkey-sex at her wedding.

And that changed everything. Big-time.

"Start at the beginning, and don't stop until you reach the end," she instructed. And then she braced herself, because she knew it wasn't going to be pretty.

CHAPTER FOUR

IT TOOK VIVIAN half an hour to drag a full account of Seth's assholery from her sister. Then it took another half hour of cajoling, begging and bullying to extract his address.

"It's okay, Jodie, I'm not going over there with a loaded gun," she'd assured her sister.

"You could still do plenty of damage without a gun," Jodie protested.

Vivian planned to. And then some. But she didn't want her sister worrying in the meantime.

"I'm simply going to let him know that he's got it wrong. Take the higher ground. Be mature," Vivian said. "I don't need to stoop to his level."

How she managed to stop her voice from trembling when she was sitting on a veritable volcano of fury was a mystery to her. But she did, and Jodie seemed somewhat mollified by her calm words and grounded demeanor.

"Okay. But just…take it easy, okay? I feel horrible telling you any of this. You weren't ever supposed to find out."

"I would have found out eventually, Jodie. You really think people can hide that kind contempt from one another?"

Because that was what this was about. Seth was contemptuous of her. He had judged her and found her wanting on almost every level.

The hypocritical jerk.

Never mind that he'd been in that limo, too. Never mind that he'd been the one to produce the joint, and that she was sure that weed wasn't the only substance he'd abused during his many years of wannabe rock-and-roll stardom. Never mind that the man practically needed a revolving door installed in his bedroom to keep up with all the women he bedded, and that he'd been colossally irresponsible enough to get one of them pregnant. Never mind that he was the one who'd made a second pass at her during one of her visits home five years ago when they'd happened to be staying under the same roof for a night.

Nope, none of those things counted because he was a *man,* and he could do anything he wanted with impunity.

She glared out the windshield as she drove to Seth's address in the eastern suburb of Ivanhoe, her hands clenched tightly around the steering wheel. Beneath her anger, she was aware that there was a wellspring of hurt, but she refused to acknowledge it. She already felt foolish enough. For years she'd been under the illusion that she and Seth were kindred spirits. She'd believed that they'd both experienced a moment of recognition at the rehearsal dinner, that they'd understood one another intrinsically. Instinctively. Those crazy, hot minutes in the limo and all the interactions they'd had since and everything she knew of his life had only reinforced that notion.

Like her, Seth had had to shelve his dream of living large and instead find another, more realistic niche for himself. Like her, it had taken him a while to discover what that niche would be. They'd both resisted the call of convention, living their lives in ways that worked for them. And they'd both made mistakes—sometimes big ones—but managed to power through them and come out the other side with a semblance of dignity intact.

That *had been* her take on their relationship and on him. Clearly, Seth saw things differently. Apparently, he saw her as a sluttish loser who couldn't get her act together. An unreliable, insubstantial party girl who shouldn't be trusted with the well-being of two people who were incredibly precious to her. All of which made him one of the most judgmental, uninformed, narrow-minded ass-hats she'd ever met.

She found his street easily, slowing to a cruise so she could find his house number. The houses were old and large, most of them built from the deep red clinker bricks that had been popular in the twenties and thirties. She made a rude noise in her throat when she found Seth's place. It had a high gabled front, bow windows and a neatly manicured formal garden.

Mr. Respectable. What a crock.

She slammed the car door shut with a satisfying thud. Chin high, she took a deep breath, eyeing the door of his house. Then she stalked up the driveway, suppressed rage grinding the spiked heels of her boots into the concrete with each step.

She hoped Seth had medical insurance, because he was going to need it after she'd finished with him.

SETH WAS IN the backyard scooping leaves from the swimming pool when he heard the doorbell ring. He leaned the skimmer pole against the pergola and made his way to the front door, his bare feet almost silent on the polished floor. He could see a slim silhouette through the frosted glass, and he frowned as he reached for the handle. He wasn't expecting anyone, definitely not a female anyone. Whoever it was, he really hoped she wasn't about to interfere with his plans for the rest of his one free evening of the week—pizza, the footy on TV and then maybe a movie. The perfect antidote to an afternoon of screaming, raucous children and his mother's endless questions regarding Lola and the baby.

"You are a flaming hypocrite of the highest order, Seth Anderson. In fact, I don't think I have met a more sanctimonious asshole in my entire life."

The words flew at him the moment he opened the door, and a heartbeat later something solid thunked him in the chest. He looked down to see Vivian's hand drawing back before the heel of her hand smacked into his sternum a second time, the power behind the blow enough to force him back a step.

"How dare you bad-mouth me to your brother? How dare you even imagine that you have a clue as to who I am or what I'm capable of, you judgmental, self-righteous prick?"

He blinked rapidly, scrambling to catch up. Vivian was clearly angry about something. Really angry, if the way she was snarling at him meant anything. Then his brain kicked in and he understood that his brother—or more likely Jodie—had shared his concerns regarding Vivian's suitability for guardianship with her.

Awesome.

"You have no idea how lucky you are that I'm a girl and no one ever taught me to punch properly, Anderson, because your nose would be a pancake right now if I had my way."

He caught her hand as she took a third shot at his chest, a little surprised at how hard he had to work to keep her at bay. Apparently rage bestowed unnatural powers on a woman. Who knew?

"Listen—"

"No, you listen. You don't know me. Just because you once had the privilege of being inside my body for a few minutes—something that would never have happened unless I was very drunk and very stoned, by the way—does not mean that you get to pass judgment on me. No freaking way. You have no idea who I am or how I live my life or what my values are. You know nothing about me. *Nothing*. And yet you dared to try to cut me out of my nephews' lives. Do you have any idea how freaking evil that is?"

Her blue-green eyes were bright with fury, her body rigid as she fought him for control of her arm. Her jaw-length hair swung around her face, the ruler-straight fringe ruffled by her exertions.

"Look, I have no idea what Jodie told you, but I think you might be overreacting," he said. *"Ow."*

Pain bit into his shin. She'd kicked him. Shock made him loosen his grip on her arm and she wrenched it free, taking a step backward so that she was out of his reach.

"Don't you *dare* tell me I'm overreacting, you snake in the grass. You told Jason I would make a shitty guardian to Sam and Max. You said I was unreliable and a bad role model."

"I asked Jason a few questions, that's all. Appointing guardians is a serious business. I wanted to make sure they understood what they were signing up for."

Truthfully, he didn't have great recall of the conversation he'd had with Jason. He'd been so worked up over Lola, so worried about what would happen once the baby came, hearing his brother was relying on Vivian to put Max and Sam first had pushed about a million different buttons for him.

Buttons that maybe had more to do with his situation with Lola than they did with Vivian and his brother's kids—something that was far clearer to him now than it had been then.

"And did you think to use that same scrupulous microscope to examine your own life, Seth? Did you take the time to consider if a man who knocks up his casual girlfriend and runs a bar is the kind of guy you'd want looking after your kids? A guy who has wasted half his life chasing a juvenile dream, a guy who wouldn't know commitment if it bit him on the ass? Would *that* guy be the kind of person you'd want guiding your kid through life if you weren't around anymore, Seth?"

He held up his hands. "Look, I'll be honest. I was having a very crappy day when Jason came to talk to me. It's possible I overreacted a little. Said some things I should have maybe kept to myself."

She swore, and the next thing he knew her bag smacked into his face, something metallic landing a glancing blow on his brow before it fell to the ground.

"Jesus. Could you stop attacking me, please?"

"You have no right to judge me, privately or publicly. You think I didn't have a moment of doubt when Jodie told me you were going to be the boys' other guardian? You think I wasn't worried, given everything I know about you?"

He frowned. She nodded, a grim smile twisting her lips.

"Doesn't feel so great, does it, Seth, being judged and found wanting? You know why I didn't say anything, though? Because I figured that Jason and Jodie know you a hell of a lot better than I do, and that even though I think I have a grasp on who you are and the way you live your life, I really only know what I've cobbled together based on a handful of conversations over the years, one encounter in the back of a limo a decade ago and whatever gets filtered through to me via the family grapevine. I figured it would be arrogant and ignorant *in the extreme* to think that was enough to judge you by."

There was a hot, accusing light in her eyes, but beneath the anger he could see there was hurt. It was evident in the quaver in her voice and the way she was holding herself.

He closed his eyes for a beat, unable to deny the truth of her words. Because she was right, he didn't know her. Not really. When he'd mouthed off the other night, Lola had been at the top of his mind, not Vivian. He'd funneled all his frustration and fear about his own situation onto the whole guardianship issue, and the result was that he'd made a big freaking mess of everything.

And hurt and insulted Vivian on a massive scale.

Damn.

"I'm sorry, Viv, okay? I just—" He lifted his hands helplessly, then let them drop. "My head is up my ass at the moment. I've got a lot of stuff going down, and I just… You know what? There's no excuse for it. You're right. I don't know you. Not really. And I should have shut my cakehole and trusted my brother and Jodie. But

I didn't, and I said a bunch of stuff I shouldn't have. And I'm really sorry about that."

She didn't say anything for a long moment, her eyes never leaving his face. "You're lucky you still have testicles, you know that?"

He rubbed his chest where she'd hit him. "I'm pretty sure I'm going to have a bruise if that makes you feel any better."

She shook her head, then bent to collect her handbag. She slid the strap onto her shoulder. "You know what the worst bit is? At the party today you acted as though you liked me. As though we were friends. Stupid me, I always thought we were, too." She pressed her lips together, almost as though to stop herself from saying more, then turned for the door.

Damn. He was such an asshole.

"We *are* friends, Viv. And I *have* always liked you. Right from the start, I liked you."

"No, you wanted to screw me. Big difference, apparently," she said over her shoulder.

He couldn't let her leave like this. He wasn't under the illusion that he could erase his words or make her hurt disappear, but he wouldn't sleep tonight if he let her walk away without trying to fix things.

Slipping around her, he blocked her access to the porch steps.

"Don't go yet. Stay and let me grovel some more."

"No, thank you. I'm not going to hang around so you can feel less guilty about being an ignorant jerk."

She'd always been good at nailing him to the wall with the unvarnished truth.

He was about to try again when the phone rang.

"Give me two seconds to get that," he said.

She raised her eyebrows and he knew that the moment he moved out of the way, she was out of here. He snagged the strap of her handbag, slipping it off her arm before she could react.

"Hey!"

"You can have it back in a minute," he said, heading for the phone.

He heard her follow him, the *tap-tap* of her heels ominous as she stalked him.

"Give me my bag, Seth," she demanded as he picked up the receiver.

"Anderson speaking," he said into the phone, ignoring her.

She tried to snatch the bag but he turned, offering her his back.

"Is this Seth Anderson?" an officious female voice asked.

He rolled his eyes. Another telemarketer. He had to remember to add his name to the do-not-call list. "Thanks, but I've already got one."

"Mr. Anderson, I'm calling from Monash Medical Centre. Can you confirm that you are the partner of Dolores Alice Brown, please?"

Seth went very still. "You mean Lola? Has something happened to her?"

"Dolores's housemate gave me your contact details. Can you confirm that you are her partner, please?"

"Yes. I am. I mean—" This woman didn't need to know about his complicated relationship with Lola. "Yes. Is she okay? Is the baby okay?"

"I'm afraid Dolores has been involved in a car accident, Mr. Anderson. She's in surgery at present, and I understand her condition is critical."

It was like a gut punch. The room was airless. He let Vivian's bag drop to the floor as he reached for the pad and pen he kept by the phone.

"Where is she? How do I get there?"

He scrawled the details she gave him, his heart pounding in his chest.

"Is the baby okay? What happened? Was she driving?" He'd heard terrible stories about women sustaining injuries from the steering wheel in the late stage of pregnancy.

"I don't have any of those details, I'm afraid."

"Okay. Thanks." He set the phone down, his mind racing. He needed to get to the hospital. Now. He turned, only to find Vivian standing there, a frown on her face.

God. He'd completely forgotten she was here.

"Is everything okay?"

"Lola's been in an accident. She's critical and they're operating on her." He scooped up her bag and handed it to her. "Sorry. I need to go."

"Of course."

He yanked open the drawer where he kept his car keys and swore when he saw the empty space they should have occupied. Of course, his car was in the workshop. He'd dropped it off after leaving Sam's party. Why on earth had he decided he had to get the issue with the ignition checked out *this* week?

"What's wrong?"

"I dropped the Audi off at my mechanic's this afternoon." He pinched the bridge of his nose. Taxi. He needed to grab a cab. He had no idea how much cash he had in his wallet, but if he had to, he'd get the driver to swing past an ATM on the way.

"I'll drive you. Where do you need to be?" she said without hesitation.

He glanced at her, relief warring with guilt. "You don't need to do that."

Not after the way he'd pissed her off.

"Do you need to grab anything?" she asked, reaching into her bag to palm her car keys.

He stared at her, but she simply stared back at him, signaling her willingness to do this for him.

"Thanks," he said, and he spun on his heel to grab his wallet and coat.

"WHAT'S THE BEST way to get to that side of town?" Vivian asked as she pulled away from the curb.

Seth shoved his seat belt into the clasp, a fierce frown on his face as he considered her question. She could feel the anxiety coming off him in waves.

"Take Burke Road to the Monash, then take the Stephensons Road exit," he said.

She nodded, picturing the route in her mind. Putting her foot down, she concentrated on cutting through the early-evening traffic.

For as long as she lived, she would not forget the way the color had drained from his face when he took the call from the hospital. One minute they'd been squabbling and wrestling over her bag, the next he'd been as still as a statue, his whole being focused on the words coming down the phone line. Then he'd started to ask questions, and she'd understood that something terrible had happened.

"Did they say anything else?" she asked. "How did it happen? How is the baby?"

"I only know what I told you."

She glanced at him. He scanned the road ahead restlessly, his body leaning forward as though he could will the car to go faster.

"Does she have family you need to contact?"

He shook his head. "Not here. She's English."

"Do they know about the baby?" She slipped in front of a hatchback before darting into the left lane.

"Yes. I think they were planning to visit sometime soon."

He pulled out his phone then, and she listened to his end of the conversation as he spoke to someone whom she guessed was Lola's housemate. It was clear that the other woman didn't know much more than Seth, and he spent five minutes reassuring her that he would let her know what was going on the moment he heard anything before ending the call.

"At least the traffic's not too bad," she said as she squeaked through an amber light.

"Yeah."

Neither of them spoke again until they'd exited the freeway, then Seth used the map function on his phone to direct her to the hospital. She dropped him at the entrance, barely catching his urgent "thanks" before he raced into the building.

She parked, then pulled out her phone and called her sister, passing on the information.

"Oh, God. How horrible. Keep us in the loop, okay, Viv? And if there's anything we can do, let us know."

"I will." Vivian locked her car and made her way to the entrance, glancing around as she entered the vast lobby. She had no idea where Seth might have gone or what department would be looking after Lola, but she approached the information desk and threw herself on the mercy of the attendant.

She was directed to the waiting area in the emergency department, and she followed the signs until she found a low-ceilinged space filled with bank after bank of seating full of people in various stages of dull-eyed boredom or muted distress.

Seth was talking to the woman at the counter, his expression tense as he listened. Vivian found a couple of seats near the corner and reserved one with her bag before sitting in the other. When Seth turned from the counter, she lifted her hand.

"Seth. Over here."

He seemed surprised to see her, confirming as much when he sat. "You didn't need to stay."

"I'm not going to let you wait on your own."

He glanced at her. "Thanks."

There was a world of meaning in the single word, and she knew he was thinking of the reason she'd been at his house. She didn't owe him anything, but she could hardly abandon him, either. He was family. Sort of.

"Did they tell you anything?"

"Yeah." He breathed out through his nose, clearly affected by whatever he'd heard. "She was on foot, heading to her car at the supermarket, when someone backed into her. She's got multiple internal injuries, head injuries...."

Vivian's clutched her knees. This was so awful.

"Did they say anything about the baby?"

"Just that they're operating." A muscle jumped in his jaw and he blinked rapidly. Despite all the stupid things he'd said about her, she couldn't stop herself from resting a hand on his shoulder.

They sat in silence until her phone beeped with a text message. She checked and saw it was from her sister.

"I called Jodie so they'd know what was going on, I hope you don't mind."

"Was that her now?"

"Yes."

"I'll call her. Fill them in on where we're at."

He moved off to make the call and she watched him pace as he spoke to her sister. He'd been barefoot when he answered the door, and he'd shoved on a pair of old Converse sneakers before racing out to her car. His hair stood on end from where he'd been raking it with his fingers, and his big body was tense, his movements edgy.

She wished there was something more she could say or do, but knew there wasn't. This was a waiting game, pure and simple. If Lola died, if the baby died... Vivian didn't even want to think about what that would do to Seth. It was too painful to contemplate. Too huge a loss.

The row of seats rocked as Seth dropped down beside her.

"She wanted to come wait with us but I told her there wasn't much point at the moment."

He braced his elbows on his widespread knees, and stared blindly at his phone, his head lowered. She set her bag on the floor and wondered how long it would be before they heard anything.

After an hour, she went to get them both coffees. She bought muffins, too, even though she knew Seth probably wouldn't eat. She certainly wasn't hungry, but lunch had been a long time ago, and he needed to keep his energy levels up.

"So, how did you and Lola meet?" she asked as she handed over the coffee and muffin.

"She was a regular at the bar."

"Must be handy owning your own pickup joint."

His mouth curled slightly at her dig. "Believe it or not, I try to keep my work and personal lives separate."

"So what happened with Lola? You slip on the floor and accidentally fall into her vagina or something?"

He almost smiled again before taking a swallow of coffee. "God, this is awful."

"I know. But we're both going to drink it anyway. It's part of the whole waiting-room ambience."

He tore off a chunk of the muffin and chewed on it. "She seduced me. And I didn't have the good sense to say no."

"That hot, huh?"

"Yeah. Blonde. Great legs. Great…you know. Your basic male fantasy."

"Hard to turn down."

"Apparently. I'm not sure I tried too hard, to be honest."

"That surprises me."

He shot her a dry look. Good. If she could distract him, feed him and help the time pass, she'd probably done all she could.

"When did you find out she was pregnant?"

"About six months ago. We'd stopped seeing each other, but she came into the bar one afternoon to talk to me. Just handed me the pregnancy test and told me that I was going to be a father."

"Wow. That must have been more than a little surreal." She'd never really thought about it before, but it occurred to her that men—some men anyway—must secretly dread getting a visit like that. At least as a woman the realization that you were pregnant came in stages—suspicion and maybe symptoms, followed by confirmation. Men just got cold-called with the news.

"It was."

They were silent as they sipped their awful coffees.

"It wasn't a disaster, though," Seth said, surprising her. "I mean, it was a surprise. And obviously it's not ideal that we're not together, and that she's so much younger. But after I got my head around it, I realized it wasn't the end of the world. That I could do this."

"Be a parent, you mean?"

He glanced at her. "Yeah. I figured I maybe wouldn't suck at it too badly."

She considered his profile for a beat. He had a strong nose. Forceful. She'd never consciously noticed that about him before.

"You're a smart guy. You can probably do almost anything if you want it enough."

"Yeah." He glanced toward the counter and she knew he was wondering if this conversation was already defunct. If his baby had survived or not. If Lola was still alive.

The next hour crawled. Vivian was checking her emails for the fifth time when a tall, thin man dressed in scrubs entered the waiting area.

"Seth Anderson?" he called out.

Seth looked up, then stood, and the doctor gestured for Seth to join him. He glanced at her.

"I'll be here," she said.

He nodded. She watched him disappear around the corner, feeling sick and worried for him.

Not so long ago, she'd wanted to tear him a new one. Now, she just wished she had the power to set his world to rights.

But she didn't. All she could do was sit here and wait.

SETH STEPPED INTO a small, stark room that was obviously set aside for the delivery of bad news to patients' loved ones.

Holy shit.

He sat on one side of the table and watched as the surgeon took the other seat. The muffin he'd eaten had congealed into a lump of concrete in his stomach and his mouth was cotton-dry.

"As you know, Ms. Brown was brought in with extensive head and internal injuries. In situations like this where there are potentially two lives at risk, we try to consider the outcome for both mother and child. Especially in such a late-term pregnancy where the fetus is highly viable."

Seth pressed his back teeth together so firmly they ached. When was this guy going to cut to the chase?

"It was evident to us early on that the baby was alive but in distress, and we decided to deliver her while at the same time working to stabilize Ms. Brown. The baby is small, but she is holding her own. Ms. Brown, however, remains in a critical condition. We have repaired a laceration to her liver and removed a length of ruptured bowel. Both injuries are stable, but the trauma to her head is profound. My colleague, Dr. Conrad, has operated to remove a section of her skull to relieve the pressure on her brain. Even so, there has been significant bleeding and swelling, and we've been forced to put her into an induced coma to give her body a chance to rally."

Seth swallowed, trying to keep track of all the information. "The baby. The baby is okay?" he asked, seizing onto the only piece of positive information the man had passed on.

"She's a little underweight, but she's responding well. You can visit her in the neonatal unit shortly."

"This coma…that's reversible, right?"

"Yes. But I need to stress to you that she's suffered profound brain trauma."

"So, are you saying that she's going to die?" Because if that was what the guy was getting at, Seth would prefer for him to put it out there rather than hedge his bets with medical mumbo jumbo.

"The next twenty-four hours are critical. But you should know that even if Ms. Brown does survive, she will more than likely have significant mental deficits. I'm not sure what plans you have in place, but it's highly unlikely that she will be in a position to be the primary caregiver for her child in the near future, if at all."

Seth sat back. He had that airless feeling again, as though someone had punched him in the solar plexus.

"She's only twenty-four," he said stupidly.

As if Lola's age made a difference to anything.

"I know this is a lot to process. Take as long as you need in here, and if you have any further questions for me, feel free to call." He handed over his business card before standing.

Seth stared unseeingly at the black words on the square of card.

"Is there anyone we can call for you, Mr. Anderson?"

"What? No. No, I've got it covered."

"Then I'll speak to you later. Don't hesitate to make contact if you have any questions."

Seth had barely finished nodding before the doctor was gone, pulling the door shut behind him. Seth set the card on the table and planted his hands on either side of it.

Lola was teetering on the edge of death.

He had a daughter.

It was unlikely that Lola would ever be a true mother to her child.

He swore, the single word hissing between his teeth. This was…not happening. It was too big. Too much. Too terrible.

He had no idea how long he stared at the table, but the sound of the door handle brought his head up as a nurse appeared in the doorway.

"Oh, sorry. I didn't realize anyone was in here," she said, quickly shutting the door again.

It was enough to jolt him from his stupor. He slid the doctor's card into his pocket and made his way to the waiting area. Vivian came to meet him the moment she spotted him.

"You're as white as a ghost," she said, resting her hand on his forearm.

"The baby is okay," he said. "It's a girl. But Lola's in an induced coma."

"God, Seth. You must be reeling."

"Yeah, I am a little."

"Come and sit down for a moment." She led him back to their chairs.

"Can you see the baby?"

"Yes. I need to find the neonatal unit…." His gaze went to the sign hanging from the ceiling, but there was no mention of a maternity ward, just X-ray and Admissions.

"What about Lola's parents? Do you have any way of contacting them?"

He stared at her, then the import of her words sunk in. His brain cleared and he could see all the steps that lay before him. All the things he needed to do, the calls he needed to make. He took a deep breath, pushing his hair off his forehead.

"I'll need to go to her place, see if she's got anything there with their contact details. She's got a laptop. Maybe Zara knows her password."

"Where does she live? We can go there when we leave here."

He frowned. "You must have stuff to do. I can't let you be my personal taxi service."

Maybe he should call Jason, see if he could borrow his car for a few hours. Although the logistics of how his brother would get the car to him and then get home again were beyond him right now.

"Seth, you've got more than enough on your plate without worrying about how you're going to get around. Let me do this for you."

He wanted to argue—she didn't owe him anything—but she was right. He was in the middle of the biggest crisis he'd ever faced and the last thing he needed was more stress.

"Okay. Thanks. I really appreciate this, Viv."

"I know. What do we need to do now?"

"Find the neonatal ward."

Her expression softened. "To see your daughter."

"Yeah."

He had a daughter. Not just a notional bump, or a blurry outline on a scan. A real, live, breathing baby girl. She'd survived the accident and the surgery, and she was waiting for him somewhere in this massive edifice of concrete and steel.

"Come on, let's go," he said, suddenly urgent.

He needed to make sure his little girl was okay.

CHAPTER FIVE

THE BABY WAS small, but that was to be expected considering she was only thirty-six weeks. Vivian stood at the viewing window and watched as Seth spoke to the nurse on the other side. He looked so grim and scared as he gazed into the crib. And no wonder. This was a nightmare of epic proportions. Every single plan he and Lola had made for the future had been scuttled in one fell swoop.

But his daughter was alive, and, by the look of her, well. That was a huge, huge positive to cling to.

The only positive, really, until they heard more regarding Lola's condition.

The nurse reached into the crib and lifted the baby out. Seth accepted the tiny, white wrapped bundle, automatically drawing her close to his chest, nestling her head into the crook of his arm. Vivian blinked, surprised by how natural he looked holding his child. Then she remembered that he'd had plenty of practice with Sam and Max. He might come across as a die-hard bachelor, but in some ways he'd been training for this for years.

He lowered his head and said something to his daughter, his expression almost unbearably tender. It was such an intimate, personal moment Vivian had to look away. A lump of emotion swelled her throat and she swallowed a couple of times, wishing there was something more she could do for him. For all of them.

When she was confident she wouldn't turn into a one-woman waterworks, she let herself look again. He was rocking the baby in his arms, his shoulders hunched as though he wanted to curl around her to protect her from the world. And the expression on his face—it was a mix of wonder, grief, fear and bafflement.

He glanced up, and their eyes met. A shy smile curved his mouth before he caught himself. She knew exactly what he was thinking—that it was wrong to feel anything but bad given the circumstances. But he was holding a new person in his arms. How could he not celebrate that? How could he not feel enormously relieved and grateful and honored?

She smiled to let him know it was okay to be happy that his daughter had arrived and survived. Then he returned his attention to his girl and she knew that everything and everyone else had been forgotten. As it should be.

Some of the color was back in his face when he left the nursery. He looked…determined. As though he knew exactly what needed to be done. And who needed to come first.

"I have to talk to someone about paperwork, apparently. Then we can get going. I'll call Zara, and make sure she's going to be around."

It took another hour for them to escape the hospital. Zara had assured Seth that she'd be at the town house she and Lola rented, and Vivian drove toward the city, finally parking in front of a small two-story town house situated opposite the train line in Malvern East.

Seth didn't immediately get out of the car and she

saw he was bracing himself. Preparing himself to deal with Zara.

"She was pretty upset, huh?"

"Yeah. They're both English, and they've become pretty good mates even though they didn't know each other before they came to Australia."

Vivian didn't point out that dealing with Zara would be ten times easier than breaking the bad news to Lola's parents. She was sure that Seth was already painfully aware of that fact.

"You don't need to come in if you don't want to," he said suddenly.

She considered the town house and what was likely to occur once he went inside.

"It might be helpful to have another woman around."

"Yeah, but this isn't your mess."

"You can be grateful later, okay? Let's just get through this."

His dark eyes were unfathomable as he looked at her. "Viv, all that stuff with Jason and Jodie and the kids… If I'd stopped to think for even a second, none of that crap would have ever come out my mouth."

"No kidding." She opened her door. "Let's do this."

He joined her on the pavement and squared his shoulders before reaching for the catch on the waist-high gate. The garden was overgrown and neglected, a handful of junk mail rotting into the garden bed beside the letter box. Remembering the share-houses of her youth, Vivian had a fair idea what she was about to walk into—Ikea furniture, cask wine and the kind of clutter that only two young women can generate.

The door opened as they approached, revealing a

wan-looking, fuller-figured brunette dressed in an over-size sweater and black leggings.

"I heard you pull up," she said. Her eyes were puffy and red-rimmed and she clutched a scrunched-up tissue in one hand.

"I'm really sorry, Zar," Seth said.

Her face crumpled and Seth stepped forward, wrapping her in a hug. "She's in a great hospital, and they're doing everything they can."

Vivian tried not to stare. Over the years, she'd seen Seth flirt and tease and be charming. She'd seen him argue with her sister and roll his eyes at his father. She'd seen him be both playful and stern with his nephews. But she'd never seen the side of him she'd witnessed tonight—empathetic, gentle, patient. Emotional.

Not so much the battle-hardened bachelor. Maybe more of a well-disguised marshmallow in wolf's clothing.

"She just went out to grab some stuff for dinner," Zara said, her voice thick with tears. "I invited her to come to the movies with me but she said she didn't feel like it."

"I invited her to come to my nephew's party, too," Seth said. "Don't give yourself a hard time about those sorts of choices. Best way to drive yourself nuts."

Zara blew her nose, then she seemed to register Vivian for the first time.

"This is Vivian, my sister-in-law," Seth explained.

"I'm so sorry about your friend," Vivian said simply.

Zara nodded, her chin wobbling. Seth put his arm around her.

"I need to work out how to contact Lola's parents. I

don't suppose you have any idea where she keeps that kind of stuff."

Zara's forehead wrinkled as she thought for a moment. "I know she emails them pretty regularly. And they sent her a parcel for her birthday in March. There was a card…."

Vivian followed them as they disappeared into the house. Zara led them past an overcrowded living room and upstairs to Lola's bedroom, where it looked as though a clothing bomb had exploded.

"Her computer password is legseleven." Zara's mouth formed a weak smile as she passed the laptop to Seth. "She loves bingo like nobody's business."

The battery was flat, and it took them a while to find the charger in all the mess. Eventually Seth was able to access her email account, and it didn't take long to discover her parents' email address. Vivian jotted it down in the notebook she always carried in her purse, but she could see that Seth wasn't satisfied.

"I don't want to send them an email telling them what's happened," he said.

"If we can find an address, we can look up their phone number online."

More searching unearthed a stash of Christmas cards in Lola's bedside drawer, most of which were still in their envelopes. It only took a few minutes to find one from her parents.

"I'll take this, if that's okay," Seth told Zara.

She shrugged, looking lost and very young. Vivian remembered how alone and isolated she'd felt when her grandfather had died while she was living in New York. Being overseas was a fantastic adventure—until something happened to remind you of how precious and far away home was.

"Is there someone who can come stay the night with you?" she asked.

"My boyfriend works night shift. He's coming over as soon as he finishes," Zara said.

Vivian made her a cup of tea before they left, and Seth showed her a photograph he'd taken of the baby, which sent Zara to the bathroom to procure a fresh fistful of tissues.

"Can I come see her? Does she look like Lola?"

"Of course you can see her. And she has blond hair, like Lola," Seth said.

It was nearly midnight by the time they got in the car to drive to Seth's place.

"You okay?" she asked as she started the engine.

"Yeah." He sounded infinitely weary.

"What's the time difference between here and the U.K.?"

"Nine hours, I think. Depending on whether they're on summer time."

She saw the familiar golden arches of a McDonald's ahead. "You want a burger? You must be starving."

He shrugged, but she pulled into the drive-through anyway and ordered two cheeseburger meals. She parked in the lot, and they were silent as they unwrapped their food.

"I haven't had a cheeseburger since I was a kid," he said.

"What do you normally have?"

"Big Mac, of course." He waved the cheeseburger between them. "This is a girl's burger."

"I guess these fries are probably girly, too, right? Not chunky and masculine enough for you?"

"These fries are just fine," he said, grabbing a handful and stuffing them into his mouth.

She laughed, the sound very loud in the confines of the car. Then she remembered why they were parked at McDonald's at twelve-thirty on a Saturday night and the smile slipped from her lips.

"I might check in with the hospital," Seth said, his mind clearly on the same track as hers.

He made the call, only to be told that there was no change in Lola's condition. They finished eating and headed for Seth's place.

"When do you get your car back?" she asked as she pulled into his driveway.

"Not till Monday afternoon at the earliest. But Jason texted me earlier—he's going to drop his car off in the morning, so I'm covered. Thanks, though."

"Oh, good. That's great." She thought about all the things he needed to sort out. Lola's parents, Lola's treatment, the baby... She felt overwhelmed just thinking about it. She could only imagine how he was feeling. If he was a friend—as opposed to a sort-of relative that she only had a very loose relationship with—she'd offer to come in and do whatever it took to ease his burden. But she was very aware of the fact that the only reason she'd played a part in this small tragedy tonight was because he'd needed to get from A to B. Under normal circumstances, she would have heard about this via her sister, a few days after the event, and it would be months before she'd be in a position to offer him her sympathies in person.

"I'm starting to feel like a broken record, but thanks

for everything." He faced her. "I would have been screwed if you hadn't stepped up. And no one would have blamed you if you told me to go hang."

"You can suck up to me for the next ten years to make it up to me, don't worry."

"Deal."

"Try to get some sleep, okay?" she said. "As well as doing all the other stuff you need to do."

"Yeah."

He surprised her then by leaning across the hand brake and kissing her cheek. They'd never really done the kiss-hello, kiss-goodbye thing. For obvious reasons.

"Night, Viv."

"Night, Seth."

She caught a waft of his aftershave as he turned away, and she could feel the spot where he'd kissed her, her skin tingling from the slight rasp of his stubble. He shut the car door quietly, then disappeared into the house. She waited until a light came on inside before reversing into the street.

She felt both relieved and guilty as she headed home—relieved because she was in a position to drive away from the heavy sadness that had taken over Seth's world, and guilty for the same reason.

He would be okay, though. She wasn't sure how she knew that, but she did. Despite his devil-may-care demeanor, there was a very grounded solidity to Seth, something she'd only really understood tonight.

Yep, he was going to be okay. But it might take him a while to get there.

CALLING LOLA'S PARENTS was the hardest thing Seth had ever had to do in his life. It had been tempting to put it off even after he'd done an online search and confirmed it was 10:00 a.m. there, but his gut told him that the news wasn't going to get any better.

Maybe that made him the world's biggest pessimist, but the doctors and nurses had been very conservative in their predictions for Lola's chances. He figured he'd be an idiot to ignore their expertise.

Lola's father, Dennis, answered, and Seth introduced himself before saying he had some bad news. By the time he'd finished, Seth felt ten years older and as close to weeping as he'd ever been.

Dennis and Melissa signaled their intention to be on the first plane possible, and they exchanged contact details before Seth assured them he would be in touch the second he heard anything new. One of his key roles in this drama, he was quickly learning, was keeping all of Lola's loved ones informed.

It was the least he could do, as well as the most. At the moment anyway.

Afterward, he floated around the house, gritty-eyed with tiredness but still buzzing with adrenaline, his mind crammed with thoughts. Chief amongst them was his daughter, the red-faced little miracle he'd held in his arms for too few minutes tonight.

She'd been so light. He hadn't expected that. It had been a few years now since Sam had been a baby; he'd forgotten how damned tiny they were. Little fingers, microscopic nails. Squashed-flat noses and curled-up bodies. His daughter's head had been beautifully round, however, unlike his nephews', since she'd been in the breech position and had been delivered via emergency C-section.

She'd been deeply asleep, her eyes screwed tightly

shut. He could still remember the incredible softness of her cheek and the silky texture of the shock of blond hair on her head.

They wanted to keep her in the hospital for a while to monitor her progress and ensure she gained weight, but after that she would be ready to come home. His home, now, not Lola's.

He pivoted as the thought hit him, heading up the hallway to the room he'd mentally allocated as the baby's when he'd learned Lola was pregnant and had finished freaking out about it.

It was a junk room at present, filled with all the flotsam and jetsam that hadn't found a home anywhere else. An old bed frame, the office chair he'd used before he bought a more comfortable one, boxes of old CDs and books, a lamp with a crooked shade. He'd thought he would have time to prepare it for the baby, figuring she would need to be near her mother for at least the first six months of her life and that sleepovers would be some way off as of yet.

But Lola would not be breastfeeding their child. She would be lucky if she even knew she had a daughter.

It hit him then, the visceral reality of it. Lola, all blond hair and long legs and loud, raucous laughter, was fighting for her life in a hospital bed, her baby cut from her body to save them both.

"Jesus." He pinched the bridge of his nose so hard it hurt, but it didn't stop the tears from coming.

He sank into the manky office chair, hung his head and let the tears roll down his face and drip from his chin. He might have felt like a complete moron for getting Lola pregnant, and he might have had some serious reservations about how they were going to negotiate their relationship once the baby was born. But he wouldn't wish this on his worst enemy, let alone a woman with whom he'd laughed and had sex and more than his fair share of vodka shots.

Come on, Lola. Show us all what you've got. Show those doctors they don't have a clue. Get through this. Wake up and meet our girl.

His hands were fisted with the force of his plea to the universe. Slowly he loosened them. He wiped the tears from his cheeks and pushed himself to his feet.

He turned off the light and went to his bedroom, stripping to his underwear before hitting the en suite. He eyed his reflection in the mirror while he brushed his teeth. He looked fifty, every line etched deep, his skin pulled too tightly over the bones of his face.

He expected to stare at the ceiling for hours once he hit the bed, but he dropped off almost immediately, his weary mind checking out. He woke to the sound of persistent knocking at the door, and it took him a moment to blink himself to wakefulness.

As soon as he opened his eyes, it was all there, bearing down on him. Lola, the accident, the baby. He threw back the covers and went to let in his brother, smiling wearily when Jason passed him a giant coffee as he stepped over the threshold.

"You're a legend. Bless you."

"I got bagels, too. How are you doing?"

Before he could answer, Jason enveloped him in a hug that threatened to crack a rib or two.

"I'm so sorry, man. So sorry," Jason said brokenly. He and Jodie had met Lola a couple of times before she'd gotten pregnant.

"Yeah. Me, too." Seth had to blink to clear his vision. He led his brother into the kitchen and set down his coffee. "Give me two minutes to shower."

"I'll save you a bagel."

He was back in five, reaching for the coffee before taking a seat opposite his brother.

"Did you contact Lola's parents?"

"They're flying out as soon as they can."

"Jodie wants to know if you need help with the baby. Did they say when she can come home?"

Even though he'd spent time in the spare room last night, thinking about what needed doing, he still felt a bone-deep shock at the notion that home would be with him for the foreseeable future. Maybe forever.

He explained that the doctors wanted to keep an eye on the baby until they were confident she was gaining weight and holding her own.

"As for her coming home, I need to sort out the spare room. I thought I had a few months before she'd be able to stay nights with me."

"Jodie and I will clear it out for you today," Jason said without hesitation. "Leave your house keys with me. Anything in there you want to keep or should we donate it all?"

"Just dump it. I've been meaning to get rid of it all for ages." Seth's throat got tight. He'd always known his brother was solid, but it was insanely reassuring to know he had his back. Jodie, too. And the way Vivian had stepped up last night…she'd been incredible.

"I owe Vivian the mother of all apologies," he said, rubbing his forehead.

"Yep, you do. But she'll forgive you. Probably already has."

Seth scowled into his coffee. He didn't want to be

forgiven because this shit storm had descended on his life. He wanted to earn it.

The phone rang, making him start. He practically leaped out of his seat to grab it. As he'd hoped—and feared—it was the hospital, and he listened intently and made notes as they told him that Lola had stabilized and that he would be allowed to visit her if he wanted to.

"Thank you. I appreciate the call," he said.

He filled in Jason, then texted Zara. He checked the time in the U.K., and decided to send an email instead of calling to update the Browns. Then, after a small hesitation, he asked his brother if he had Vivian's number.

"Sure. I'll shoot it to you."

A second later, his phone chimed with the shared contact and he texted Vivian a quick update.

Lola stable, am allowed to visit. Hope you got some shut-eye. Thanks again for last night.

"Eat this in the car." Jason passed over the bakery bag, clearly sensing Seth's eagerness to be on his way to the hospital. "Anything we're unsure about tossing I'll store in the garage, okay?"

"Cool. And thanks, Jase."

"Mate, I wish this wasn't happening, but you gotta know you're not in this alone. Whatever you need."

They hugged again, and Seth had to fight the prick of tears. Apparently almost losing your ex-girlfriend and your daughter turned a guy into a complete sooky la-la. Something he could have lived without knowing.

Minutes later he was on the road, eating a bagel one-handed while steering through dozy Sunday-morning traffic. His thoughts raced ahead of him to the hospital. He wanted to hold his daughter again. Maybe this time she would open her eyes for him.

And he wanted to see Lola, no matter how traumatic that might prove to be. She needed to have someone who cared for her with her. She needed to know she had reasons to live.

God, he hoped she was going to be okay. That the doctors had gotten it wrong this time. That he wouldn't have to deliver more bad news to her parents.

The hospital parking lot was depressingly full, and he had to park in one of its far-flung corners. He sat in the car for a few minutes, trying to get his thoughts straight before heading inside.

He needed to keep a clear head today. He needed to listen, to ask the right questions, and be the best advocate he could be for both his daughter and Lola. Because neither of them had anyone else.

Letting his breath out on a harsh sigh, he opened the door and went to face the future.

VIVIAN WOKE AT ten and immediately rolled over to check her phone. Sure enough, there was a text there. The only surprise was that it was from Seth instead of her sister.

Lola was stable. He was allowed to see her.

Thank. God.

She closed her eyes for a moment, images from last night flashing across her mind. The hospital. Seth's face as he held his daughter. The life-interrupted messiness of Lola's bedroom.

It was all so sad. Poor Lola. And poor Seth.

She flung back the covers. After Jodie's revelation yesterday, sympathy was the last emotion she'd expected to be feeling toward Seth today, which just went to show that life was a complete crapshoot.

She was tempted to call Seth for a more current update now that she had his number, but managed to stop herself from doing so. He had enough people hanging on his coattails, asking for reassurance right now. She would not add to his stress by making herself one. She would ask her sister to keep her up to speed. That would have to do.

She spent the day setting her place to rights, leaving all the doors and windows open to let the warm summer breeze sweep through her second-floor apartment. Part of a boutique development, the space had been carved out of an old shoe factory, and the walls were exposed brick, with bright red water pipes running from floor to ceiling in one corner. It was a rental, but she already felt at home here.

She'd brought only a few items she couldn't bear to part with from L.A., freight costs being so exorbitant. The huge chinoiserie chaise she'd bought at a yard sale in Beverly Hills, the Hollywood Regency dining chairs and table, a few boxes of kitchenware. And, of course, her clothes.

It was late afternoon by the time she'd finished washing the floors and finally gave in to the need to call her sister.

"Hey. Have you heard anything?" she asked the second Jodie picked up.

"Seth's been at the hospital all day, but he rang a couple of hours ago to say that he'd seen Lola." There was an ominous heaviness to her sister's words.

"That bad, huh?"

"I gather she's pretty messed up. Seth sounded like someone had hit him on the head with a shovel."

Viv sank onto the arm of the chaise. "What about the baby?"

"She's doing fine. He gave her his first feed, and the nurses were apparently impressed by his diaper-changing skills, something I'm more than happy to take the credit for."

"That's great."

"He's under orders to come up with a name. We can't keep calling her The Baby."

"They must have had some names picked out?"

"According to Seth, they had a short list of ten for each gender."

"Wow. That's a long short list."

"I know. I think Seth wants to talk to her parents before he makes the final decision. Since Lola can't cast her own vote."

Vivian sighed. Every time she thought she had a grip on how grim this situation was, something new popped up.

"How's Seth sound?"

"Tired, but he's hanging in there. You'll be pleased to know he told Jase he owed you some serious belly crawling."

"He does, but it can wait."

"Listen, I gotta go. We're clearing out Seth's spare room for the baby and Jason needs my help moving the bed frame."

"What? You should have called, I could have helped." Vivian frowned as she registered the strident urgency in her voice. She figured her sister must have noticed it, too, because there was a small silence.

"I didn't think you'd be that keen on helping Seth out again, all things considered," Jodie said carefully.

"It's kind of an all-bets-are-off situation, don't you think?"

"I guess. Listen, I'll call you if there's anything new, okay?"

Vivian dusted her hands down her vintage 501 jeans after she ended the call. She wasn't quite sure where the urgent I-must-help-Seth impulse had come from. She felt sorry for him, of course, but there was no need for her to be *insistent* with her sympathy. And she was still pissed with him. So, really, there wasn't a single reason under the sun for her to be feeling the urge to snatch up her car keys and go help her sister and Jason fix up Seth's spare room.

"I feel sorry for him. That's all it is. Pity," she said out loud.

It sounded perfectly reasonable, and she decided she was going to roll with it, even though her gut told her it wasn't the whole truth and nothing but the truth.

Jodie kept her informed on Seth's progress through-out Monday, but the reports dried up on Tuesday. Vivian fretted all day, unable to concentrate on the upcoming shoot she had for an online fashion retailer. It was only a week away, and generally by this time she liked to have all her clothes and accessories specified, with a few variations at the ready should the client not be happy with what she'd come up with. So far, she had about half the shoot complete and a mishmash of props and accessories chosen.

Every time she hit a snag or paused to consider a color or texture combination, her brain slid from work to Seth. He was in such a difficult situation, with so much weight bearing down on him. If she were in his shoes, she would be freaking out 24/7.

It didn't help that it was a stinking hot day and every time she glanced out the window, bright blue skies beckoned. She gave up the battle at four, tossing down her pen and heading off to search for Robin.

She found him in the stockroom, rummaging amongst his light stands, muttering to himself. As usual, he looked runway-ready good-looking—hair perfect, clothes crisp and effortlessly stylish despite the hot day.

"Hey, crazy man, I'm outta here."

"You haven't seen my spare umbrella stand, have you?" Robin sat back on his heels, an exasperated expression on his face.

"Didn't we use it for the ad shoot last week?"

He snapped his fingers. "You're right. It's still in the van." He sprang to his feet, ready to race off.

"Before you go. What should I buy for someone who has just had a baby and almost lost his ex under tragic circumstances and who may or may not be completely freaking out about all of the above?"

Robin paused, his grey eyes narrowing. "This is your brother-in-law, right?"

"My brother-in-law's brother, if we're being technical about it."

"Well, if we're being technical about it, I think he's still your brother-in-law."

"Okay, Rain Man. Yes, it's for my brother-in-law. I was thinking I might drop in on my way home to see how he's doing."

"I thought you said his place was in Ivanhoe?"

"I did."

"And you live in Brunswick, which is five minutes

from here, versus almost half an hour to Ivanhoe, in the wrong direction."

"What's your point?" she asked, feeling caught out for the second time in as many days.

"No point. As long as you're aware that you're making excuses to see the guy."

"I feel sorry for him."

"Okay. Sure." Robin tilted his head, considering. "Scotch. I'd buy him a bottle of expensive Scotch."

"He owns a bar."

"So he'll appreciate the good stuff. See you tomorrow." Robin strode off, pastel-pink Ralph Lauren shirt billowing behind him.

She tried to come up with a better option as she took the stairs to the parking garage beneath the building, but the more she thought about it, the more she realized Robin was probably right. Strong alcohol would be pretty welcome in Seth's life right now.

She stopped by the liquor store on her way to Ivanhoe and bought him a stonking great bottle of Johnnie Walker Black Label. The sun-warmed bitumen was so hot she could feel it through the soles of her shoes as she walked to the car, and she could literally see the haze of vaporized eucalyptus oil coming off the leaves of the gum tree next to her car.

Summer in Melbourne. She'd forgotten how damn uncomfortable, sweaty and scorching it could be.

The blithe belief that she was doing a good thing for someone in a tough spot carried her all the way to Seth's front door. Then doubt kicked in, and her courage—or whatever it was—failed.

She had no idea why she was here. They weren't buddies. In fact, he'd gone out of his way to prove just how not-buddies they were only a few days ago, doing his best to talk her sister and Jason out of appointing Vivian as co-guardian. He'd proven himself to be a jerk of the highest order, and the fact that tragedy had since come crashing into his life didn't change that.

So why was she on his doorstep, the harsh afternoon sun burning her back through her jacket, a bottle of Johnnie Walker in her damp hand, her heart pounding a little faster at the prospect of seeing him?

Put the bottle on the porch, text him to let him know it's there and go home.

Excellent idea. Much, much smarter.

She placed the bottle in the corner, where it couldn't be seen from the street. She was turning away when an image flashed across her mind—Seth offering comfort to Zara on Saturday night, his face creased with worry. There had been so much kindness and goodwill in that small act. So much decency.

Seth might have royally ticked her off recently, but he had a good heart, and right now he was hurting. She didn't have it in her to ignore that.

So...

Rolling her eyes at herself—had she been this indecisive and dithery even when she was a teen?—she collected the Scotch and knocked on the door.

Butterflies took flight in her belly as she heard the sound of someone approaching. She frowned. This was not a butterfly-worthy occasion. This was a mission of mercy. End of story. Then the door opened and Seth was standing there wearing a pair of jeans cut off at the knees, a sheen of sweat and nothing else.

"H-hey," she stuttered, trying not to stare at the bare expanse of his chest. "I was in the neighborhood and thought I'd drop in, see how you were doing. And if you needed this." She offered him the bottle of Scotch, the movement so jerky she could hear the violent slosh of liquid against glass.

He'd been scowling when he opened the door, but his expression cleared when he saw her. Or maybe it was the alcohol that did the trick.

"Don't they normally send in a Saint Bernard with a little whiskey barrel on his collar?" he asked.

"You're thinking of Alpine disasters. For the run-of-the-mill urban kind you get a bottle and a hot babe."

His mouth turned up into a grudging smile. "You want to come in? I'm probably due for a break anyway."

He stepped aside, and she walked into the house. She hadn't noticed much of anything when she'd steamed in the other day, but this time she looked around. The floors were polished wood, the small hall opening into a spacious, high-ceilinged living room. The decor was Early Bachelor—leather couch, chunky coffee table, no cushions—but he had some funky black-and-white photographs on the wall and a huge, colorful canvas over the open fireplace.

Seth noticed her looking. "There's a gallery near the bar, and the owner and I are mates. She recommended this guy to me. Told me it would be a good investment."

"I like it. It's got good energy."

Before she'd narrowed her focus to fashion styling, she'd dressed her fair share of interiors and the professional in her wanted to soften his couch with some throw cushions, and maybe a couple of blankets. A rug wouldn't go astray, either. And the curtains… She'd bet a month's salary they'd come with the house and he hadn't even thought to change the heavy dark green velvet for something more modern and light.

"You want something cold? Or maybe Scotch on the rocks?" he asked, indicating the bottle.

"Scotch sounds good, but I take mine neat."

He raised his eyebrows. "That'll put hair on your chest."

"And yet somehow it remains resolutely hair-free."

His gaze dropped to her breasts. "I remember."

"'Course you do. Luckiest night of your life."

The look he gave her was pure cocky male. "Funny, I was thinking the same thing about you."

She wrinkled her nose. "Nah. I've gotten luckier."

He laughed as he turned away. "Sure you have."

He led her into an airy kitchen that had clearly been recently updated.

"This is nice," she said, scanning the shiny dark grey cabinets and the crisp white stone counters.

"The owners had this all geared to go when they were forced to sell, so I decided to go ahead with it anyway." He sounded almost indifferent.

"I take it you're a big foodie," she said dryly.

"No one makes toast like me. As for what I can do with a can of soup…"

"Wow. Be still my heart. You're a regular Renaissance man."

"I'll show you my etchings later." He grabbed two tumblers and poured a couple of fingers of Scotch.

"Feel free to ruin yours with ice and something fizzy if you have to. I won't tell anyone," she said as she accepted the drink.

"I'll cope."

She took a mouthful, grateful that the warm burn

of alcohol sliding down her throat gave her something else to concentrate on apart from his bare chest and the overexcited thud of her own heart.

"Jodie said that Lola's parents arrive tomorrow."

His expression sobered. "Yeah. It took them a day or so to get themselves sorted. Her father had a heart bypass six months ago and they had to get the all-clear from his doctor before they could fly. I'm picking them up from the airport in the afternoon."

She grimaced. "This must be so horrible for them. Do they have any other kids?"

"A son. I get the feeling they're not close, though."

He scratched his chest absently and she couldn't stop herself from following the movement. She'd never really had a chance to get a good eyeful of his chest before, but it was very nice, verging on exceptional. His pecs were clearly defined, his chest hair neither too wild nor too sparse. Just right, as Goldilocks would say. As for his flat belly...

A woman would feel awfully good pressed up against all that hardness.

There was a gleam in his eye when she dragged her gaze to his face and she knew he'd caught her looking.

"Any reason you're stroking around looking like a reject from an all-male strip club?" she asked, offense being the best form of defense and all that.

"I'm setting up the nursery. Finished painting last night, so it's down to assembling the furniture now."

"Ah. That explains why you looked like an angry bear when you answered the door. I'm betting you're one of those men who doesn't bother reading the instructions before he wades in," she mused.

"It's a crib and a change table. How hard can it be?"

"How long have you been at it now?"

"I suppose you're an expert on self-assemble furniture, as well as all-male strip clubs?"

"You want my help or not?" As the words came out of her mouth she wondered at herself. She should be cutting this encounter short, not prolonging it.

"I'll take whatever is on offer, but in case you haven't noticed, I don't have air conditioning. I wouldn't want to ruin your look."

She glanced down at the slim-cut black linen trousers and jade silk jersey tank she'd paired with a light grey short-sleeved bolero jacket. "I'll survive."

"Just remember, you asked for it."

He walked ahead of her, and she allowed herself a single glance at his ass. She'd dressed men in Gucci, Armani, D&G, in silk, wool, linen and cashmere, but there was no getting away from the fact that a firm, round masculine butt outlined in soft denim was one of nature's miracles, and Seth's ass scored extra miracle points thanks to his slim hips and cocky, cowboy-moseying-to-the-rescue walk.

Maybe you need to stop by the convenience store on the way home, stock up on batteries. Because this man is family, in case you had forgotten, and strictly verboten.

Maybe she did need to get some batteries for her buzzy boyfriend. And maybe she needed to start thinking about getting out there again. Now that the business was up and running, she could afford to invest a bit of attention in her private life again.

Seth waved her into a butter-yellow room with a large

white-framed window that overlooked the yard. "Should I start the clock now?"

A half-assembled crib sat in the middle of the space, hand tools strewn around it, while a heavy-looking carton leaned against the wall. The change table, she presumed. The smell of fresh paint hung thickly in the warm air, despite the fact that the window was open.

"Have you got a fan?" she asked, shrugging out of her bolero jacket.

"In the bedroom."

"That seems like good logistics," she said, not bothering to hide the sarcasm in her tone.

"I bet you're a pain in the ass to work with," he said as he headed up the hallway.

To fetch the fan, she assumed.

"People love working with me. I'm intuitive and awesome at anticipating problems," she called after him.

"Is that what they tell you?"

She was toeing off her shoes when he returned with a floor fan.

"So. Where are the instructions?" she asked, taking a sip from her Scotch.

"I can already tell this is going to be so much fun."

"I know. So can I." Even though a part of her knew she shouldn't be here, and that she definitely shouldn't enjoy playing games with Seth as much as she did, she couldn't stop herself from grinning.

His eyes lit with amusement and speculation. "Don't think I don't know what you're up to with all of this."

She felt an absurd stab of self-consciousness. "Sorry?"

"Coming over here, helping me out in my time of

need, making me feel even worse than I already do about being such a douche bag about Sam and Max."

"You are so on to me. And by the way, if that was your big apology, you get an F for effort." She could feel heat stealing into her face, the sensation so unfamiliar it took her a moment to work out what it was. She never blushed. Ever. And not only because it clashed horribly with her hair. Blushing was for virgins and debutantes, and it was a long time since she'd been either.

"Oh, I know I have some serious groveling to do."

"Good." Because she found it disturbing to look at him for too long, she made a big show of surveying the half-assembled crib. "So, where do you think you went wrong?"

CHAPTER SIX

TWO HOURS LATER, she was sweaty, frustrated and ready to unleash a missile on the sadistic torturer who had invented self-assemble furniture.

"These instructions are wrong. You know that, don't you?" she told Seth. "They don't even mention these little dowel thingies you're supposed to use to stabilize the legs. And there is no way this would stay together without glue, which they also haven't mentioned."

They were both kneeling on the floor beside the pile of furniture parts that were supposed to slot together to form a change table. She looked up from the much-pored-over, highly inaccurate instruction booklet to find Seth wearing a big grin.

She narrowed her eyes at him. Her hair was stuck to her neck, her tank top to her chest, and she felt about as far from fresh and cool as was possible.

"I know me being wrong is worth its weight in gold, but we still have to finish putting this stupid thing together," she reminded him.

"Come on, you have to admit it's a little bit funny."

His hair had curled into little commas where it was damp at his temples, and every time she breathed she inhaled the sporty scent of his deodorant.

"I'm finishing this. If it kills me," she said, resolutely ignoring the pull of attraction for the millionth time that night. It was easier when she concentrated on the job at hand, she'd found. And when she didn't stare at his body.

"I believe you, Red."

"Pass me the screwdriver."

"How about we take a break for dinner? The pizza place in the village delivers."

She barely looked up. "No anchovies, heavy on the olives. And if you have a cold beer in the fridge I will seriously consider forgiving you some of your sins."

"I have beer. Give me five."

She grabbed the screwdriver while he was gone, undoing the two side pieces that were supposed to go together but simply didn't match up with anything else. She experimented a little, reversing their order, then flipped them around. Miraculously, they slotted together as though they were made to do so.

"No way. The instructions are back to front," she said under her breath.

The realization gave her a second wind, and by the time Seth had returned with her beer she had one side of the table completed.

"Bloody hell." He stopped on the threshold, a stunned expression on his face.

"The diagrams are back to front. Someone doesn't know how to use Photoshop," she said triumphantly, pushing her hair off her forehead as she grinned at him.

"Get out of here."

He handed her the beer and she closed her eyes in gratitude as her fingers curled around the icy bottle. "Oh, that feels so good."

She tipped her head back and drank half the bottle in one hit, tapping a fist to her diaphragm afterward to release the gas her guzzling had generated in a short, sharp burp.

Seth blinked slowly. "You're all class, Walker. Anyone ever tell you that?"

"Many times. That doesn't give you a free pass to fart in front of me, either, by the way."

"Don't worry. When I'm around you, everything is clenched."

She tried not to reward him with a laugh but it snorted out her nose anyway. "Come on. If we motor, we can get this finished before the pizza gets here."

True to her prediction, he was tightening the last nut when the doorbell rang.

"You mind getting that?" he asked. "My wallet's on the kitchen counter."

"Sure." She pushed to her feet, wincing at how cramped her muscles felt. She'd been crawling around on the floor for hours without a break.

She found his wallet where he'd said it would be and pulled out a fifty as she made her way to the door. The pizza guy handed over two boxes and a long, foil-wrapped parcel that could only be garlic bread. Yum.

She took her bounty to the kitchen, sliding the change into Seth's wallet. Her gaze was caught by the pronounced ring that time and wear had scuffed into the surface of the leather. Giving in to curiosity, she flipped his wallet open and checked the inside pocket. Sure enough, a condom nestled there.

Trust Seth to always be prepared. Like a really dirty, overgrown, oversexed Boy Scout. He'd had a condom that night in the limo, too, she remembered.

He entered the room, arms stretched over his head as he worked out the kinks. "Tell me they didn't forget the garlic bread."

She tore her gaze from his muscular belly. "They didn't forget the garlic bread." She gestured toward his wallet. "How did Lola get pregnant?"

He blinked. "Is that a trick question?"

"You're a condom guy. I remember. So what went wrong?" She wasn't sure why she was so curious. Maybe because she'd been a little surprised when Jodie told her he was about to become a father. Seth had always been a bit reckless and wild, but he'd never struck her as being careless.

He sighed and looked deeply chagrined. "I have no idea. There was one night when we'd both had a bit to drink and my memory's a bit fuzzy. But I'm always careful. I had a scare with a girlfriend in high school, and ever since I've always used condoms, every time." He shrugged, clearly unable to explain what had happened.

"It's pretty much my worst nightmare," she confessed. Especially in her current situation.

"An accidental pregnancy?"

She nodded. "I don't want to be forced into a corner, so I'd rather avoid the situation in the first place. If I ever have kids, I want them to be planned."

"We talked about termination, but Lola always planned on having kids and she figured she was getting a head start." He frowned suddenly, and shook his head. "Damn."

"What?"

"I just realized I'm talking about her in the past tense." He looked stricken and tired and guilty in equal measures.

"Have the doctors said anything more?"

"They did a scan and some other tests this morning. There's no brain activity to speak of."

"What does that mean?"

"We're going to have that conversation tomorrow, when her parents are here."

They were both silent for a beat, the only sound the hum of the refrigerator. Vivian had never been close to this sort of tragedy before. It was so hard to work out what to do or say.

"Come on, we can eat by the pool. With a bit of luck a cool front will have come through," Seth said.

"Unless its arrived in the five minutes since I opened the door to the pizza guy, I wouldn't hold my breath."

They headed outside anyway, Seth stopping to snag two more beers and some paper towel. As she'd predicted, the night air was close and warm, the outdoor furniture still holding the heat of the sun. Vivian was so hot and sticky, she figured a little more sweat wouldn't make any difference, so she simply flopped into a seat, flipped the lid on the pizza box and reached for a slice.

"So, what brought you back home?" Seth asked as he twisted the caps off the beers and passed her one.

"Robin was heading home, and he asked me if I'd be interested in becoming business partners. We'd worked with each other a lot, knew we got along. It seemed like a great opportunity."

"So it was a work thing?"

"No." She picked an olive off her slice and bit down on it. "I'd been thinking about it for a while. Feeling homesick, I guess. I missed Jodie and the boys. And looking at pictures of birthday parties and Christmas instead of being here was getting old."

"Vivian Walker, you big softy." His smile was lazy, teasing.

"Guilty as charged."

"So tell me about this business you've got going. You didn't say much the other day."

She gave him a look. "You don't need to make small talk with me."

"I'm interested. Humor me."

She couldn't tell if he was sincere or not, but she was a little worried by the warm glow that sprang to life in her belly at his interest.

Ah, the ever-present danger of a charismatic man.

"Robin takes the pictures and touches them up digitally, I style them. Which means I select which clothes go together, put them together in a story so that they have context and appeal."

She was aware of two forces at war within herself as she talked—the need to show off and impress him versus the desire to play it cool.

Because she *was* cool. Normally. Around men. Even gorgeous male models who wore a lot less than Seth was right now. So why did he inspire this heart-beating-too-fast, everything-heightened feeling in her?

Seth polished off a slice and reached for another. "So you're responsible for the props and the background, all of that?"

"Yep. I scout locations with Robin, and we work together on themes if the client doesn't have a direction of their own. We don't always work as a team, though. Sometimes clients want him and not me, and vice versa. If we land this contract with Fairbank and Rose, for example, I'll be heading up a group of in-store stylists for customers looking for a personalized shopping experience, as well as styling their catalogue and web shoots."

"Personalized shopping. Smart. Make them look good and feel like movie stars and prize open their purses."

"I prefer to concentrate on the looking-good part.

You'd be amazed how many years you can take off a woman by putting her in the right clothes. It drives me crazy when I see people wearing ugly things because they don't want to look like mutton dressed as lamb or because someone once told them they had chunky legs."

Seth assessed her. "You like it."

"I love it."

"I wondered if it was a make-do thing, since you didn't make it as a fashion designer."

She pulled a face, embarrassed at being reminded of her childish ambitions. "I sucked as a fashion designer," she said. "Took me a while to work it out, but I finally got the message. I've got a great eye for color and structure and texture, and I am awesome at putting other people's clothes and accessories together. But give me a blank page and a pencil and tell me to design something original and I will hand it back to you with a doodle of a dog in the corner."

He smiled around the mouth of the bottle as he took a pull. It had been easier to stop herself from ogling his chest every five seconds while they worked on assembling the furniture, but it was much harder to avoid looking at him—okay, at his chest—when he was stretched out in the chair opposite, his long, muscular legs crossed at the ankle.

"What about you? Do you regret giving up the band?"

It was his turn to wince. "No."

He didn't say anything else and she raised her eyebrows. "That's it? I tell you my life story, with appendixes, and I get a one-word answer in return?"

"You want more? Okay. I hated being on the road. I started to hate the other guys. And I really, really hated holding my breath, waiting for people to work out we were freaking sensational, and then watching as some wet-bottom-lip kids with perfect hair rocketed to the top of the charts."

"Wet-bottom-lip kids? Please explain."

"You know, those kids who always have a shiny lip." He demonstrated, adopting a vacant expression and licking his lower lip before jutting it out.

She got the gist of what he was aiming for, but he was so attractive it was impossible for him to ever look truly gormless.

"So, basically you hate every boy band that ever drew breath?" she said.

"Hell, yeah."

"I never got to see you play. Did you do the whole white-dude-dancing thing like Mick Jagger?"

"You will never know." He smiled mysteriously, and she threw her pizza crust at him.

"This is why you don't have hairs on your chest," he said, picking the fragment off his right pec. "You're supposed to eat your crusts."

"Doesn't eating your crusts give you curly hair?"

He thought about it for a beat. "You could be right. I'm a little rusty on my folklore."

He set his bottle on the table, then stood and reached for the stud on his jeans. The action was so unexpected, she jerked back in her chair.

"What are you doing?" she asked, her voice squeaky with sudden panic.

"Going for a swim. Why? What did you think I was doing?" His eyes were so knowing she was hard-pressed not to throw a full pizza slice at him.

She settled for rolling her eyes and trying to look elsewhere as he pushed his cutoffs down his legs.

And failed miserably.

He had spectacular thighs. Beautifully muscular without in any way being beefy, dusted with dark hair. And she wasn't going to even start on the impressive package that was showcased by his snug black boxer briefs.

"You coming in?" He started for the pool.

"I haven't got anything to swim in."

"Hey, swimsuits have always been optional in this pool, babe."

She could hear the laughter in his voice, knew he was winding her up. He didn't really expect her to skinny-dip. He didn't think she'd be so foolish.

So reckless.

Something irrepressible bubbled inside her as she contemplated his dare, an echo of the wildness that had sent her sashaying toward him across the balcony at her sister's wedding all those years ago.

She stood and reached for the hem of her tank top. Seth was waist-deep in the water at the shallow end but he went very still as she whipped her top over her head. Her gaze holding his, she undid the snap on her pants, then unzipped the fly and shimmied her hips to work the linen down her legs.

She'd been busy establishing the business since she'd landed back home, but her body still retained the muscle tone from the twice-weekly Pilates classes she'd attended religiously when she lived in the States. She knew she looked pretty damn good in her plain black Calvin Klein bra and knickers—not perfect, by any means, but she'd never been one of those women who made a sport of hating her own body. It had given her—and others—a lot of pleasure over the years, and that totally worked for her.

She took a step closer to the pool, arching her back a little to make her breasts pop. Seth's mouth dropped open a gratifying half inch. Reaching behind herself, she found the clasp on her bra. She held the pose for a long, suggestive moment.

"In your dreams, Anderson." She took a running jump off the side of the pool, one knee curled close to her chest in classic bombing posture.

Water flew everywhere as she hit the surface and she laughed gleefully as Seth copped a mouthful. He was still spluttering when she surfaced. She pushed her hair off her forehead and gave him a smug smile.

"I'm going to let you have that one because I owe you," he said sternly.

"You're a generous guy."

"So they say."

She didn't bother responding, striking out for the far end of the pool. She hadn't gotten halfway before Seth drew alongside her, arms moving powerfully. He beat her there, then paused to wait for her.

"Ian Thorpe, eat your heart out," she said.

He shrugged, his eyes dancing with mischief. "I tried to let you win, but if I went any slower I'd have sunk like a rock."

"Like a block of concrete, you mean."

He pushed his hand into the water, sending a plume straight up her nose. "Now we're even."

"What happened to you owing me?"

"I'll pay you back some other way."

She swam to the tiled ledge and pulled herself out,

glancing around at the attractively landscaped yard. She was no expert on Melbourne real-estate prices, but it was clear to her that this place must have cost some serious money.

"So, this bar of yours must be doing all right."

"I get by."

"I've got to admit, I'm a little surprised. I expected a babe lair with shag carpet, a vibrating bed and mirrored ceilings. This is all very civilized."

"You haven't seen my bedroom. Yet."

"Right. That's going to happen." She considered the house. "This is a lot of house for one man, you know."

"What are you getting at?"

"Just wondering if it's a sign of things to come. Seth Anderson, finally growing up. Business, house, baby. Anything could happen."

"And probably won't."

His answer didn't really surprise her, but she couldn't stop herself from prodding some more. "Are you telling me you've honestly never been tempted to settle down? That there hasn't been one woman who made you think about tomorrow?"

"Yep."

"Really? Not even a hint of it? You're that much of a hardened bachelor?"

"It's got nothing to do with being a hardened anything. I'd rather be alone than trapped in a relationship that's destined to fail."

"How do you know if something is destined to fail if you've never even given it a shot?"

"Because it's never felt right. Whatever that thing is that makes people sign up for joint bank accounts and shop for rings, it's never happened for me. I've never met a woman amazing enough to make me forget all the stuff that can go wrong." He shrugged, as though it was that simple. And maybe it was.

"Okay. I suppose that makes sense."

"Of course it does. You're still single. Obviously you haven't met someone who fits, either."

Vivian forced a smile, thinking of Franco. "Oh, I wouldn't say that."

His gaze sharpened and she realized she'd dangled an almost irresistible conversational gambit. But that was not a conversation she intended to have with him.

"Have you worked out how you're going to manage things once the baby comes home?" she asked, heading his question off at the pass.

"Not yet. The bar is closed Mondays, and Tuesdays and Wednesdays are quiet nights, so I've managed to fake it this week. But I'm going to have to sort something out once Daisy comes home."

She smiled. "Daisy. You've named her."

He looked rueful. "Not officially. Not until I speak to Lola's parents. But yeah, it's my choice."

"I like it. I've always thought daisies were happy."

"Yeah, me, too. I figure she needs all the good omens she can get."

She drew her legs up so that her heels were resting on the edge of the ledge and wrapped her arms around her knees. "How are you coping with all of this, Seth?"

He paused. "Yeah, I'm good."

As convincing replies went, it left a lot to be desired. But she wasn't prepared to push. If he didn't want to talk, that was okay.

After a second, his expression became rueful. "Okay, honestly? I have no idea what I'm doing most of the time. I know what needs to be done, I'm going through the motions, but none of it feels completely real. Even seeing Lola yesterday, lying there with so many tubes coming out of her... I feel like I've been sucked into the trailer for a bad movie of the week, you know? One of those ones that has lots of tampon and chocolate commercials."

She didn't say anything, simply waited for him to continue.

"And I'm really not looking forward to tomorrow. Meeting Lola's parents. Taking them to see her. That's going to be some serious hard yards. And as much as Daisy is amazing and miraculous and so freaking cute, I am terrified about bringing her home." He gestured with one powerful arm. "I mean, look at my life. I'm so not the guy you'd pick to be primary caregiver to a little girl. I know how to change a diaper and run a bath and read a bedtime story, but that's pretty much it. I've read one parenting book. I'm about as clueless as it gets."

She could see the uncertainty in him, the fear and doubt. "This is a big freaking deal," she said.

"Yeah."

"You don't get do-overs with a kid."

"Tell me about it."

"So I guess that means you just do your best, and hope it works out okay." She offered him a small smile, aware that her advice was not the silver bullet he was looking for.

"What if my best isn't good enough?" Seth's voice was gravelly with emotion, and she knew it had cost him a lot to ask the question.

"It will be. It'll have to be."

Seth mouthed a four-letter word, then surprised her

by dropping beneath the surface of the water. He drifted to the bottom before using it as a springboard and propelling himself toward the far end. The world was very quiet as she watched him glide underwater.

After what seemed like far too long, he broke the surface, standing and taking a moment to slick the water from his face and hair. He looked like something out of an erotic movie, his body glossy with water, his muscles working smoothly, and she felt the distinct tug of desire between her thighs.

Vulnerability and masculinity. Had to be one of the deadliest combinations in the world.

But as long as she remained aware of that—of his appeal, and her susceptibility to it—she was solid.

Seth swam toward her, his head above the water, his biceps bulging with each stroke. He stopped in front of her, treading water, and she raised an eyebrow in silent question.

"I probably owe you more than a little face splash after that move you pulled earlier," he said.

"The bomb, you mean?"

"And the other bit."

The bit where she'd let him think he was getting something that was never going to be on the menu.

"What are you going to do about it?" she said.

"I'm not sure yet."

He moved so fast he was a blur, but she still anticipated him, attempting a half-assed dive over his head. He caught her foot, causing her to fall short of her goal, jerking her toward him. They wrestled like kids under the water for a minute, then broke the surface, both gasping for breath.

"Too fast for you, Anderson," she panted.

God, she loved teasing this man. It was like poking a stick at an almost-domesticated panther.

"Says who?"

"Says me." She slipped her hand past his guard, grabbing a fistful of his boxer briefs at the small of his back and yanking firmly upward. His hand shot out to stop her, but it was too late, she'd given him a solid atomic wedgie.

Laughing gleefully at his disgruntled expression, she took off while she still could.

"That's right. You run for your life," he called.

She heard him come after her, the fierce slap of his arms as he churned the water. She was laughing so hard it was difficult to maintain her pace. She made it to the shallows and had her foot on the first step when his arm snaked around her waist, yanking her into the water. Dragging her against his body, he easily resisted her attempts to escape. She gave a gasp of protest as he fisted his hand in the waistband at the back of her panties.

"Don't you dare," she warned him.

"What? Do this?" He gave a small tug.

Wet fabric pulled tight between her thighs, rubbing against places that were already dangerously hot and sensitive. Excitement thrilled through her—along with a rush of blood-chilling, visceral fear.

"Don't." The plea came from her gut, from the part of her that comprehended exactly what was about to happen and understood how enormous a folly it would be. Suddenly this wasn't a game anymore. Suddenly it was very, very serious.

"How are you going to stop me?" He tugged again, his eyes dancing with intent and desire and mischief.

Then, before she could gather her thoughts, he lowered his head toward her, his hand sliding down to cup her ass cheek.

Her hands instinctively latched onto his shoulders, shock stiffening her body as panic shot through her. If Seth kissed her, she'd be lost. In more ways than one.

"What are you doing?" she asked.

He paused, his mouth inches from hers. "You want me to draw you a diagram?"

"No. I really don't." There was a whip-crack sharpness to her tone, and he blinked, the heated intensity of his gaze instantly cooling as he understood she was serious. A second later, his grip loosened and he took a step backward, letting her go.

"Right. My mistake. Sorry."

She was practically panting, she had so much adrenaline buzzing through her. She couldn't look at him, and turned her back on him as she rearranged her panties. She was painfully aware that her nipples were hard— and not because the water was cold.

Back ramrod-straight, she climbed out of the pool, making a beeline for her clothes. It was time to go. Past time.

She was pulling her tank top over her head when Seth exited the pool.

"I'll get you a towel."

"I'm fine," she said, reaching for her trousers.

She wasn't fine. She was uncomfortable, her clothes clinging to her damp skin, her wet underwear quickly soaking her top and pants. But she wanted out of there more than she wanted comfort. She wanted to be alone, in the safety of her car, with several miles between her and Seth and that moment in the pool.

He didn't say a word when she headed inside to grab

her stuff from the baby's room. When she returned to the kitchen he was behind the counter, a towel around his waist as he folded the pizza box into the recycle bin. He eyed her steadily, but still she found she couldn't quite look at him.

"Listen, Vivian—"

"I really need to get going," she said. "The baby's room looks great, though. Really great."

She was already walking toward the front door. Seth took the hint, as he followed her and reached past her to open it for her. She scooted outside the moment she could safely do so.

"Good luck with everything tomorrow." She practically ran down the porch steps to the driveway.

Embarrassment hit her the moment she was safely in her car and the full scale of her ignominious retreat hit her. She'd always prided herself on being able to hold her own against Seth, but she'd scuttled out of his house like one of the three little pigs running away from the big, bad wolf. Scared off because he'd tried to kiss her. She'd handled far cruder passes in her time with a million times more finesse—so why the urge to bolt tonight?

Perhaps inevitably, anger followed hard on embarrassment's heels. Because they'd been having such a good night until Seth had taken things too far. They'd been talking, laughing, enjoying each other's company. But that hadn't been enough for him. He'd had to push, to see how far he could go. God forbid that he have a member of the opposite sex in his pool and *not* make a pass at her. God forbid that he exercise a little self-restraint for once in his life.

Right, that little scene in the pool was all on him.

Where, exactly, did you think things were going when you jumped into the water in your underwear? And when you flirted with him and wrestled with him and grabbed a handful of his boxers?

The starch went out of her backbone and her outrage simultaneously, and she bowed forward, resting her forehead on the steering wheel.

The truth—difficult as it was to acknowledge—was that she'd been dancing with the devil tonight.

Toying with herself, with Seth, with the situation. Enjoying the heat of their chemistry and the spark of their banter and the sheer electric thrill of the potential that always seemed to arc between them.

Wondering what would happen if they got naked again, and if the payoff would be worth the risk.

And Seth had called her bluff. He'd read her signals, interpreted them to suit his own agenda—which was pretty basic and predictably male and not that different from her own—then gone for it.

And she'd reacted like a startled horse.

She could still feel the echoes of her panic, it had been that strong, that instinctive.

That revealing.

She lifted her head. It was time to be honest with herself. Finally. She took a deep breath, feeling more than a little shaky. As though she was about to open Pandora's box and unleash something that could never be contained again.

All these years, ever since she'd met Seth and they'd exchanged their first ripostes, a part of her had known that he was dangerous to her. That if she allowed herself to, she could fall for him. Hard.

Hence her constant efforts to keep him at arm's

length. To define, limit and control her responses to him. He was her Achilles' heel.

Every time she saw him she felt the same *zing* of attraction she'd experienced the first time she'd laid eyes on him, a testament to the enduring chemistry between them. And it wasn't just a sexual thrill—although there was plenty of that going on. Absolutely. She loved matching wits with him. Loved dishing it out and getting it back in equal measure. He was one of the few people with whom she could be completely honest. She wasn't sure why that was. Maybe because they both understood that neither of them was perfect, and therefore that screwing up was part of the rich tapestry of both their lives.

The thing was, Seth had never had a long-term relationship. Ever. The longest she'd heard of was six months. And while she'd had her fair share of just-for-the-hell-of-it flings, she'd also been in love with Franco and had wanted to stay that way. To her knowledge, there were no broken hearts in Seth's past. Not on his side anyway.

An affair with him would be mind-blowing, but it would also be a one-way ticket to Disasterville. She didn't doubt it for a second. And she was sane enough and sensible enough, she liked herself and valued her happiness and peace of mind enough to want to avoid that kind of pain if she could.

Hence her undignified retreat of ten minutes ago.

Well, I guess that clears a few things up.

It did. It definitely did.

There would be no more cozy drop-in visits for her and Seth. It didn't matter that he was in the toughest spot of his life. He had friends and family aplenty to support him. He'd survived a whole ten years while she'd been in the U.S., after all. He didn't need her. And she didn't need him.

Feeling calmer than she had in days, she headed for home.

SETH KICKED THE fridge shut so hard it rattled. He'd screwed up. Big-time. He and Vivian had been having fun, and he'd messed it all up because he'd misread a bit of playful flirting and horseplay for something more adult. She'd come over to make sure he was okay. She'd labored in the stuffy torture chamber of the spare room with him to help him assemble baby furniture—and he'd paid her back by trying to get it on the second an opportunity presented itself.

He was pretty good at reading signals, female and otherwise. But when Vivian was involved, he was usually too busy being turned on, amused and challenged to engage the executive part of his brain. Which was probably why he often wound up looking and feeling like the humpy dog his brother had once accused him of being when she was around.

Such a good look.

He went outside and turned off the pool filter, then stared at the glint of the patio lights reflected in the water, guilt and regret tugging at him. There were so many reasons for him to have kept his hands to himself tonight that it would take him hours to enumerate them all.

For starters, he was a father now. He had a daughter who relied on him for *everything*. In a few days' time, she would be home with him and it would be up to him and him alone to ensure her health and happiness. His days of letting his whims guide him were *over*.

Then there was the fact that Vivian was family. Not blood-family, obviously. But there was no getting around the fact that she was someone who would be a part of his life as long as his brother was married to her sister. Which looked like a very long time, the way Jason and Jodie still looked at each other when they thought no one was watching. Vivian was the last woman he should be hitting on. The very last.

None of which had stopped him from trying tonight, though.

Reminds me of something else.... Oh, that's right— this is like the last time you tried to get Vivian into bed, isn't it, humpy dog?

Seth tried to silence the cynic in his head, but it was too late, the memory was already rising out of the dusty corner of his mind he'd consigned it to five years ago. For good reason—it was far from his fondest or finest moment, and he'd been more than eager to pretend it had never happened.

Vivian had been living in New York at the time and had come home on a flying visit. He hadn't approved of her cropped, dyed blond hair, but he had liked the way her jeans fit her and the way she'd flirted with him over dinner. If he was asked to swear on a stack of Bibles, he'd be forced to admit that he'd drunk a little too much on purpose that night so he'd have an excuse to crash at his brother's place.

So they'd be under the same roof.

Jodie had insisted he take the trundle bed in Max's room, since Max was just a baby and could easily spend one night in with her and Jason. Seth had waited impatiently till the house was silent before sneaking to the living room, where Vivian had crashed on the sofa bed. In hindsight, simply lifting the duvet and attempting to climb in with her had perhaps not been his smoothest move. He could still remember the way she'd rolled over and stared at him incredulously.

"You have got to be kidding," she'd said.

"What?"

"No. Not while my sister and baby nephew are sleeping down the hall."

"*Now* you're shy?" he'd said.

Again, not his best line ever.

"There's some hand cream in the bathroom if you're that hard up," she'd said witheringly, then she'd rolled away and done a very convincing job of falling asleep.

He'd lain in the dark with a throbbing hard-on, hoping against hope that she'd change her mind and put him out of his misery. She hadn't, and he eventually returned to Max's room, where he spent half the night staring at the ceiling feeling disgruntled, horny and stupid.

Seth winced. There was a reason he'd worked hard to pretend that moment had never happened. He'd been drunk and cocky. He'd shown about as much finesse as a brown bear in mating season.

Kind of like tonight, minus the drunk part.

The apology he owed Vivian was growing longer and more elaborate by the day. The way she'd beaten a retreat tonight… She hadn't even waited long enough for him to get her a towel—that was how desperate she'd been to get away from him.

More than a little over himself, he entered the house and locked up before making his way to bed. The light was still on in Daisy's room, and he stopped in the doorway. In the time it took him to inhale and exhale, all the stuff with Vivian shrank to assume its rightful proportion.

Yes, he'd screwed up tonight, but he had bigger fish to fry. He would apologize to Vivian when he saw her next—which would probably be next year if she had any say in the matter—but the person he needed to focus on wasn't Vivian or himself. It was the little girl who would soon occupy the crib lying on its side in front of him.

She was it. The one thing he had to get right. Everything else was white noise.

He knelt and put his screwdrivers in his toolbox. Then he tidied the packaging and other debris. Once the floor was clear, he pushed the crib into the corner, then placed the change table opposite it. His parents had brought bags of clothes and other gear over the moment they learned about the accident, and he opened the closet and rifled through the carefully folded and stacked shelves until he found the bed linen and quilt. He made up the cot, then somehow found himself unpacking and assembling the musical mobile his mother had insisted Daisy would love. When it was suspended above the crib, he turned to the change table, stacking it with diapers and wipes, setting a diaper bucket beside it.

Both the crib and table looked way too sterile when he'd finished, and he frowned at them, trying to work out what was missing. Max's and Sam's rooms were colorful, chaotic messes, with decals on the walls and posters of their favorite cartoon characters and tote bins full of toys. They felt alive and warm; his daughter's room looked like an ad from a catalogue.

He shrugged. He had no idea how to make things homey. He was a guy. He killed spiders, changed flat tires and watched sports on TV. His gaze fell on the big bear Jodie and Jason had given him, and he plunked it in the cot, adding a couple of other colorful plush toys to the change table.

Better. Definitely better. There were probably things that creative people like Vivian could do to make it warmer and livelier, but that would have to wait for another day. On impulse he pulled out his phone and took a picture. Before he could think about it too much, he called up Vivian's contact and typed in a message so he could send it to her as a text. She'd sweated with him to get it finished, after all. Seemed only fair that she see the end result.

Getting there. Thanks again for your help. I'd still be ignoring the instructions if you hadn't shown up.

He started adding another apology, then deleted it. The least he could do was look her in the eye while he owned his screwup. Apology via text was not going to come even close to cutting it.

He hit Send on the abbreviated message and went to brush his teeth, keeping an ear out for the chime of a return message. His phone hadn't made a peep, however, by the time he'd climbed into bed.

Maybe she was asleep already, or elbow-deep in her own work. Or maybe she simply didn't want to encourage him.

Either way, it was late, and he had a big day ahead.

CHAPTER SEVEN

VIVIAN DIDN'T SEE Seth's text message until the next morning when she collected her phone from the charger.

She read the message, then stared at the image he'd sent—the carefully arranged plush turtle and rabbit on the change table, the big bear in the crib with the *Sesame Street* mobile hanging overhead. He'd clearly spent an hour or two setting up the room after she'd left. Making sure it was perfect for his daughter.

The thought made the back of her eyes prickle with emotion, amplifying the unease she'd been feeling. He was trying so hard. He was scared spitless by the enormous responsibility that had landed so unexpectedly in his lap—and she'd made his life that little bit more confusing and difficult with her reaction last night. The look in his eyes—equal parts chagrin and confusion, with a dash of humiliation thrown in for good measure—as he stepped back from her in the pool had haunted her dreams.

She stared at her phone, debating her next move. They'd always been straight with each other, and the need to apologize to him—or at least explain—was almost irresistible. But she hadn't forgotten that today was huge for Seth. He was picking up Lola's parents at the airport, and they were having difficult conversations with Lola's doctors.

Vivian doubted very much that she was at the top of his mind right now. As uncomfortable as it felt to wait, she would hold off on clearing the air with him. She could afford to wait—Lola and Daisy could not.

The sky was clear blue again, and the weather bureau predicted another scorcher. She dressed in tailored black shorts, strappy wedges and a black-and-white diagonally striped silk tank with acid yellow straps before heading into West Melbourne with the air conditioning blasting.

She managed to get yesterday's outline finished by early morning, and she had it finalized and off to their client by one. Robin had a shoot the next day for a housewares importer that was using its own stylist, and she worked with him to ready the studio space so everything would be ready for an early start.

She was helping Robin unpack the stock he'd be photographing when her phone buzzed at two-thirty.

"Won't be a sec," she told Robin when she saw it was her sister's number. Jodie was a great respecter of work hours and never called between nine and five unless it was something that couldn't wait.

She moved toward the window as she took the call. "Yo, what's up?"

"Thank God you answered. Please tell me you're not in the middle of a million-dollar shoot that can't wait, because I really need your help." Jodie sounded about three seconds away from outright panic.

"I'm not in the middle of anything that can't wait. What do you need?" she said calmly.

"Sam fell off the monkey bars at kindergarten and they think he might have broken his arm. I'm on my way to the hospital as we speak."

"Is he okay?" Vivian was alarmed by the tight sensation in her chest. Sam was so sweet, so bright and funny—the thought of him being in pain made her feel more than a little sick.

"I don't know. I haven't seen him yet. I got the call about five minutes ago. The thing is, I was on the way to the airport to pick up Lola's parents as a favor for Seth, but now I can't do it and Jason's in a meeting and Mum isn't answering her phone...."

Vivian shook her head, confused. "I thought Seth was picking them up."

They'd talked about it last night, about how much he wasn't looking forward to it.

"He was, but someone threw a brick through the window at the bar after lunch, and one of his staff was hurt. The police need him there and he doesn't think he's going to be able to get away."

"Bloody hell, he can't catch a break at the moment, can he?"

"Nope."

"Okay." Vivian walked toward her office, where her handbag was stowed in the bottom drawer of her desk. "I'm on it. What time do Lola's parents land?"

"*Thank you*. Bless you for coming home from L.A. I have been freaking out the last five minutes, ringing everyone I could think of."

"Next time call me first, save yourself some stress."

"You can take that to the bank."

Vivian grabbed the flight number before telling her sister to keep her up-to-date regarding Sam's broken arm, then took two minutes to check on the flight status on her computer. It was running on time, with an expected arrival time of 3:30 p.m.

"Robin, I'm bailing on you," she said as she strode

to where he was stuffing shredded paper into a box. "I need to pick up some people from the airport. I'll come back tonight and help you finish."

"We're almost done now. I don't think there will be anything to come back to. Which means you are free to go save the world and I'll see you tomorrow."

He blew her a kiss and she pretended to catch it and put it in her pocket. "For later," she told him, and his laughter followed her out the door.

She had a clear run to the airport, arriving in plenty of time to ensure she had a long period of kicking her heels before Lola's parents might be expected to appear in the international arrivals hall. The enforced breather gave her ample opportunity to consider why they were coming and what they were about to face. They'd be expecting Seth, of course, and she'd need to explain why he couldn't be there as well as her relationship to Seth.... Messy. But this was a messy situation, wasn't it?

Belatedly it occurred to her that she had no way of recognizing the Browns when they arrived, nor they her, and she made the trek to her car to grab some paper and a marker to make a sign. It was forty minutes before a soft-looking, weary couple exited the quarantine area, their gazes lifting to Vivian's face when they registered her sign. Mr. Brown had faded blond hair and bright blue eyes, Mrs. Brown long brassy blond hair that could only have come from a bottle. They looked to be in their forties, which made sense, given Lola's age. Vivian offered them a smile as she walked forward to greet them.

"I'm Vivian, Seth's sister-in-law. He had something he needed to deal with, so he asked me to collect you on his behalf," she said.

Mrs. Brown blanched. "Is it Lola? Is she okay? Please tell me she hasn't died." She clutched her husband's arm, her fingers showing white around the knuckles she was gripping him so tightly.

Vivian kicked herself for not choosing her words more carefully. "Lola is still stable, as far as I'm aware. Seth had some trouble at his bar. Someone threw a brick through the window and one of his staff was injured."

"Oh. Thank God." Mrs. Brown swallowed nervously.

Her husband slipped his arm around her shoulder and gave her a bracing squeeze before offering his free hand to Vivian. "Good to meet you, Vivian. I'm Dennis, and this is my wife, Melissa. We appreciate you helping us out."

"I just wish you were coming to Australia under better circumstances." Vivian glanced at their baggage. "My car is a few minutes' walk away. What can I carry for you?"

She wound up with two overnight bags while Dennis and Melissa guided their larger wheeled suitcases across the air bridge to the parking garage. Vivian tried to generate conversation, but after a few minutes it was clear that the Browns were in no place to make small talk.

"How about this," she proposed once they'd found her car and stowed their baggage in the trunk. "You two sleep or talk or do whatever you need to do on the way across town, and if you have any questions about anything, I'll try to answer them. But if you just want to be quiet, that's okay with me, too. All of which is my long way of saying that we don't need to be polite to each other right now."

Dennis gave her a tired smile. "That sounds pretty good to me, thanks, love."

He looked very small and sad all of a sudden, and Vivian had to quell the urge to offer him a hug. What a terrible flight it must have been for both of them.

"Here," she said, finding Seth's number and handing him her phone. "You can call Seth if you like, let him know that we're on the way."

She concentrated on navigating her way out of the mazelike multilevel garage. She could hear Dennis asking questions about Lola and the baby as she drove, and she could see them visibly relax when they learned Lola was still stable.

Melissa had a relieved weep once Dennis signed off and Vivian spent the drive trying not to eavesdrop on their conversation while she battled the traffic-congested roads. They threw the occasional question her way, but it was evident that their thoughts were all for their critically ill daughter.

Finally they arrived at the hospital, and she felt the tension in the car rise. She pulled beneath the portico at the main entrance and turned to look at them.

"Why don't you call Seth again, and he can come meet you, instead of you having to find your way around this enormous place?"

"That's a fine idea." Dennis nodded approvingly.

She handed him her phone, even though it would have been easier for her to make the call. She wasn't sure why, but she felt oddly shy about talking to Seth directly. It had been completely unintentional, but she'd once again inveigled her way into his affairs when she'd agreed to pick up Lola's parents, despite having decided last night that the best and smartest thing for her to do would be to keep her distance.

"He's meeting us in the foyer in five minutes," Dennis reported as he returned her phone. "Thanks for the taxi service, Vivian. It's much appreciated."

"Yes, you saved us a lot of bother," Melissa said with a watery smile.

"It was nothing, and I wish I could do more," Vivian said.

They both slipped from the car, and it wasn't until they'd disappeared into the hospital that she realized she still had their luggage in her car.

Good one, Vivian.

Maybe she wasn't that great a taxi driver, after all. She found a parking spot, then went in search of the Browns for the second time that day. She was anticipating having to ask for directions to Lola's ward before she tracked them down, but they were still in the foyer when she arrived, talking to Seth, their faces set and pale.

Seth was pale, too, his hair rumpled as though he'd been running his hands through it. He glanced her way the moment she entered, as though some sixth sense told him she was there.

"Viv. Thanks for picking up Dennis and Melissa. I owe you," he said as she joined them. He brushed a kiss against her cheek, the gesture entirely natural and unconscious, the awkwardness of last night forgotten.

"Not a big deal, at all. As I've already told these guys," she said. "How is Daisy doing?"

"Daisy? You called her Daisy?" Melissa asked, eyebrows raised.

Vivian gave herself a mental slap for her slip of the tongue. So much for being helpful.

"Unless you have an objection to the name," Seth said. "It was on our list, and it seems to suit her."

"It's gorgeous." Melissa's eyes welled with tears again.

Seth glanced at Dennis, who nodded, blinking. "Daisy was my mother's name."

"I didn't know that," Seth said.

"Can we see Lola now?" Melissa asked.

"She's on the fourth floor. The elevators are this way." Seth started across the foyer, and Vivian had no choice but to fall in behind the others, kicking herself every step of the way for letting the cat out of the bag in regard to the baby's name.

She tried to catch Seth's eye to convey her apology as they all stepped into the lift, but he was frowning at the floor, clearly preoccupied. Once they arrived, Seth led them through a warren of corridors before stopping outside the intensive care unit.

"You should know she's on a lot of machines," he said, his tone serious. "There are at least three lines going into her arms, a catheter, the respirator, the heart monitor. Also, they had to shave off a lot of her hair and her head is bandaged."

"We understand. The doctors have kept us up-to-date," Dennis said.

"I know. It's just…different when you see it in person," Seth said, his expression stony.

Melissa reached for Dennis's hand.

Seth led them into the department, leaving them in the waiting area for a minute while he talked to a nurse. Vivian searched in her handbag and found a travel pack of tissues that she passed to Melissa, who gave her an almost-smile of thanks in return.

"Okay. They're happy for us all to go in. Normally they limit it to two visitors at a time," Seth explained.

Vivian glanced toward the nearby chairs. "I'll wait here."

Seth gave her a grateful nod before ushering the Browns into the clinical area. Vivian sat and tried to stop herself from crying. She didn't know Lola or Dennis and Melissa, but she didn't need to to appreciate the utter misery of their situation.

Her phone chimed with a text after a few minutes and she saw it was from her sister, checking to make sure everything was okay and letting her know that Sam had simply sprained his arm. Vivian had just texted an update back when Seth dropped into the seat beside her.

She glanced at him, startled. "Did they change their mind about the two-person policy?"

"No. I figured they might want a bit of privacy." He said it heavily, and she could see how tired he was in the lines around his eyes and mouth.

"They seem nice," she said lamely.

"Yeah, they do, don't they? Lola was—is—nice, so that makes sense."

"How are things at the bar?"

"A bloody mess. Ever seen a plate glass window smash? There's glass everywhere. We won't be able to open tonight, and Syrie's got a couple of scratches on her arms from flying debris. Thank God all our customers were in the dining room having lunch when it happened."

"I'll say. It sounds like you're lucky it wasn't worse."

"Yeah. I keep telling myself that, but it's not helping much."

"Do you have any ideas who did it?"

"There's not much information. All Syrie knows is that there was a smash and then glass was flying. By the time she got over the shock and the guys from the kitchen had come out, the perp had done a runner."

He rubbed his forehead, then rested his elbows on his knees as he contemplated the floor.

"I'm really sorry about blabbing Daisy's name out earlier. I wasn't thinking and it just slipped out—"

"I should be thanking you. You saved me a difficult conversation. Now it's sorted and I didn't have to put my foot in it."

He was sincere, so she decided to abandon the concern. There was enough angst in this situation without her generating any of her own.

"In that case, happy to be of service."

"Becoming a bit of a habit, isn't it? You being of service?"

She could feel her face heating. Where had this sudden propensity for blushing come from?

"Didn't I tell you? I'm trying to get a merit badge at Girl Guides."

"So this is like community service?"

"Exactly."

"I've got some laundry that needs doing at home if you want to score your cooking and cleaning badge."

"Cute," she said. "But not quite cute enough."

She noticed a fleck of red on Seth's thumb, and reached out to catch his wrist, angling his hand toward her. Sure enough, it was speckled with bloody marks.

"Is this from the glass?"

"Yeah. There were a few shards still hanging from the frame so I took care of them."

"With your bare hands?" she asked incredulously.

"I used a couple of bar towels, but it turns out glass is sharp. Who knew?" His smile was unrepentant.

"Worthy of the Darwin Awards, Anderson." She realized she was still gripping his wrist and let go.

"I'd barely qualify. Shows what you know."

A doctor exited the clinical area and they both glanced at him. When she looked at Seth again, his mouth was once again straight and grim.

"When is Lola's doctor meeting with her parents?"

He pushed back the cuff on his shirt to check his watch. "In about an hour."

"Does that mean you've got time to introduce me to Daisy properly, then?"

His eyebrows rose, as if the idea hadn't even occurred to him. Or maybe he was simply surprised she was interested.

"Sure. Let me tell Dennis and Melissa where we'll be."

He slipped into the clinical area, returning a minute later. She walked alongside him as they left the ward.

"Do you know where the Browns are staying? I've got their luggage in my car and I could drop it off for them so they don't have to lug it around the hospital."

"Thanks, but you don't have to do that. We can transfer it into my car," he said.

"Your little sporty thing?" she asked.

"Believe it or not, it takes luggage."

"As well as being a chick magnet? Who knew car designers were so practical?"

"You'd be surprised what I've been able to fit into that car over the years."

"Bet I wouldn't."

Seth entered the nursery with the ease of familiarity, talking to one of the nurses before gesturing for Vivian to join him on the other side of the glass. They both washed and dried their hands, then Seth led her to the crib holding Daisy.

Curled on her side, Seth's daughter was a study in pink, cream and gold, her tiny mouth puckered, her hands fisted tightly. Someone had put a soft-looking pink-and-white striped hat onto her head, but a few curls of golden hair had slipped out.

"A blonde. That's going to be fun for you when she's sixteen."

"You mean when she's thirty."

Vivian smiled. "If she takes after you, she will give you one hell of a run for your money. Poetic justice, considering how many fathers you've probably given sleepless nights over the years."

"You want to hold her or not?" he asked.

"Am I allowed to do that?" She glanced around, waiting for a nurse to offer a ruling on the issue.

"Believe it or not, she likes it. Crazy, I know." Without further ado, Seth reached into the crib and gently slid his hand under Daisy's neck and head before lifting her. He performed the action so confidently, Vivian had to blink.

"What's wrong?" Seth asked.

"I just realized you're a dad now."

He smiled faintly, and she knew he understood what she meant.

"Yeah. I am."

He offered the baby to her, and she slipped her hand beneath Daisy's head, necessarily standing close to him as they made the transfer. An odd sort of warmth came over her as her forearm brushed his chest and his fingers grazed her rib cage as he ever-so-carefully passed his daughter into her care. Not sexual warmth, something else. Something more generous and unfathomable.

"Hello, little girl," she said.

The baby wriggled, curving into the shape of her torso. Daisy's mouth worked, then her lids flickered and she woke. Deep blue eyes stared at Vivian, their regard so uncompromising and compelling Vivian couldn't look away. She was powerfully aware of how frighteningly frail and slight Daisy was, how small and defenseless, how completely, utterly dependent on the goodwill of others she was. And yet she stared at Vivian with not a shred of fear.

She hadn't learned to be afraid yet, which struck Vivian as being a wonderful thing.

And long may it be so.

"Aren't you just perfect," she whispered.

"She has awesome genes," Seth said.

She glanced at him dazedly. She'd forgotten he was with her for a few seconds there. Tradition demanded that she make some quip or crack—maybe a dig about Lola's awesome genes compensating for his, or something like that—yet she couldn't bring herself to do anything but smile goofily.

"I'm going to have to agree with you."

Daisy still watched Vivian with the same intense, slightly unfocused regard, as though she was trying to place her face or recall something she'd heard earlier.

"What's going on in that little head of yours, sweetheart? What are you thinking?"

"She's splitting the atom," Seth said. "If only she could speak."

"She will soon enough, don't you worry," Vivian

said. "If she's anything like Sam and Max, you'll have trouble getting her to stop."

She handed Daisy over after a few minutes, then watched as Seth put her down to sleep. They were silent as they left.

"I know that none of this is even close to being planned, Seth, but she's amazing. There's no way you can regret helping her come into the world."

"I know. She's already the best thing I ever did and she's only five days old." It was his turn to smile like a goof. He looked so endearing, hopeful and uncertain that this time she couldn't stop herself from giving him a hug. He hugged her a little more tightly than she'd expected. It was only then that she understood how worried and alone he was feeling.

Was it any wonder? A veritable storm of trauma had been raining on him since Saturday night. He was doing a damned good job of doing all the right things and covering all bases, but he was only human.

All it took was that single moment of insight, and last night's resolution to keep her distance burned to ash faster than she could snap her fingers. He and Daisy needed all the friends they could get, and Vivian intended to be one of them.

It wasn't a choice. It was simply the way it would be, because she couldn't turn her back on this man and his daughter. Not if her life depended on it.

And if that meant she would have to keep a close guard on her emotions…well, so be it.

SETH HAD TO force himself to release Vivian. She felt so good, and there was something about the straightness of her spine and the strength in her arms that made him want to stop and stay a while. A day or two, perhaps, while this crazy, chaotic sadness whirled around them.

But that wasn't possible, and this chaos was his to deal with, not hers.

A timely reminder.

"Show me where your car is and we'll sort out the luggage," he said finally.

She looked a little surprised by the abrupt shift in conversation, but led him to the parking lot and pointed toward where her car was located.

"I'll come find you in a minute," he said.

She cast a questioning look his way before heading for her car. He watched her go. He'd always admired her walk, the sass and confidence of it. It was one of the first things he'd noticed about her. That, and her sexy body.

It had taken him a lot longer to notice her quieter qualities, like her kindness and generosity. Over the years, he'd listened to Jodie rave about the clothes Vivian had sent home for her, and he'd watch her engage and play with her nephews. But the true extent of Vivian's generosity and care for her loved ones had hit home for him only in the past week. She was a giver, one of those people who showered her friends and family with gifts she'd picked up because she'd "seen it and thought of them." She wasn't precious or afraid of pitching in and rolling up her shirtsleeves. He bet she hadn't hesitated when Jodie had asked her to pick up Dennis and Melissa today. Even though his dumb-ass behavior had ensured that they'd parted in less than stellar fashion last night, and even though he'd said all those ugly things about her to his brother when he'd been flailing around in his own excrement.

Frankly, he was lucky she'd given him the time of day, let alone gone out of her way to help him.

He went to his own car, then drove through the lot until he spotted Vivian standing next to her SUV.

She eyed his Audi with a speculative gaze as he climbed out. "You know, we could do a trade if you like. My SUV for your TT."

"Like that's going to happen."

"Think about it and get back to me," she said, opening the rear hatch of her car.

He told himself not to look as she leaned forward to tug a case closer to the edge, but he'd been unable to stop himself from noticing a nice ass since he was in high school and it seemed he wasn't about to learn the skill now.

"Want to give me a hand here, Man of the Year?"

"Right. Sorry."

He gave himself a mental slap. He'd just been chastising himself for misjudging and undervaluing her, and at the very first opportunity he'd reverted to knuckle-dragging, drooling-idiot mode. Way to go.

He grabbed the case, brushing past her as he hefted it. She glanced at him quickly then, just as quickly, looked away. He transferred the first bag to his car, then the second, wedging in the two overnight bags. He had to push one side of the tiny rear seat forward to accommodate the luggage, but there would still be room for Melissa or Dennis to origami themselves into the rear while the other sat up front with him.

"Call me when you want to do the car swap," Vivian said knowingly.

He eyed her, standing there in the afternoon sun, her hair glinting red and gold. Her eyes were slightly squinted against the brightness of the day, and her mouth was curved into a cocky, smart-ass smile.

"I was a dick last night," he said. "I'm sorry for putting the moves on you. It was dumb, and a really crappy way to repay you for all your help."

It wasn't quite the eloquent, articulate apology he'd had planned, but it was out there now and he would have to make the best of it.

Her smile faded. "You don't need to apologize. It was a misunderstanding. Crossed wires. No one needs to be doing the whole mea culpa thing."

"It was still a dumb-ass move. You've been really great, helping me out with everything. Trying to make it something else was…dumb."

"Honestly? I was a little curious myself." She glanced at her shoes briefly. "I wouldn't have been in your pool in my bra and panties if I wasn't. So I apologize if I sent some mixed signals. Apparently all your prettiness went to my head for a few seconds."

Seth studied her. He knew at least a dozen women who would have taken his apology and run with it, but that wasn't good enough for Vivian. No, she had to step up and own her part. Because that was who she was, honest and fair to a fault.

"I'm not sure you should be letting me off the hook," he said slowly.

"It was probably bound to happen, sooner or later, given our history." She made a helpless gesture with her hand. "But the bright side is, we both know where we stand now, right?"

"Yeah."

He didn't miss the not-so-hidden meaning beneath her words. She was drawing a line in the sand, letting him know she wouldn't be jumping into his pool in her underwear again in the near future. Which was probably just as well. His life was complicated enough.

She shut the hatch, the thunk echoing. "I should let you get back to Dennis and Melissa."

He was aware that the debt he owed her grew larger by the hour. About the only thing keeping pace with it was his growing awareness of how much he liked her. On every level.

"Thanks for saving my bacon. Again."

"I happen to have a great fondness for bacon." She patted his arm in what he could only describe as a friendly manner and slid into her car. The window slid down as she started the ignition. "I meant to say, I have a gorgeous cashmere throw blanket that would be perfect for Daisy's room. I'll leave it with Jodie or drop it by when I get the chance."

"Thanks. I'm sure she'll love it."

"Look after yourself, Seth."

He watched as she reversed and drove off. Despite the many other things he'd had to worry about, last night had been weighing on him, and it was good to know that they were okay.

He glanced toward the hospital, aware of a bone-deep reluctance to go inside. It said something that he'd rather broil beneath the harsh sun than have to deal with Lola's heartsick parents. But he couldn't avoid reality forever. Letting his breath out in a long sigh, he headed for the main entrance.

Dennis and Melissa were still with Lola when he returned to the ICU, sitting by her bedside, their red eyes and set faces revealing the depths of their grief. He wondered if, like him, they had recognized that Lola—the essence of her, the spirit of her—was no longer in residence in the body. Over the past few days, everything about her had diminished. Her skin had sunken into the bones of her face, her complexion had turned grey. Modern medicine was keeping her alive—breathing for her, feeding her, ensuring wastes were eliminated—but the spark of life that made Lola Lola was gone.

"We've got a few minutes until the doctor's due. Do you want to come see Daisy?" he said.

Melissa nodded mutely, and Seth took them to the nursery and introduced them to their grandchild.

"Oh," Melissa said, one hand pressed to her chest. "She looks exactly like Lola as a baby. Exactly."

Seth stood back and watched them brighten as they hovered over the crib, both refusing to touch her until they'd changed out of their travel clothes.

"She's not quite as small as I thought she'd be," Dennis said. "I was expecting one of those tiny babies, like you see on the news."

She seemed more than small and frail enough to Seth, but he knew what the other man meant.

"They tell me that she should catch up with the full-term babies weightwise over the next few months," he said.

"Lola is going to love you so much, little one. She's going to adore you." Melissa rested a hand on Daisy's blanket, her voice thick with emotion.

They headed to the ICU afterward, quiet settling over them like a shroud as they neared Lola's bed. Dr. Patel was waiting for them, a frown on his face as he studied a printout. Seth hoped like hell it wasn't more bad news.

"Dr. Patel," he said, causing the other man to look

up. "This is Dennis and Melissa, Lola's parents. They just flew in."

"Of course. We've spoken on the phone. I'm very sorry to be meeting you under these circumstances," Dr. Patel said in his deep, throaty voice.

They exchanged small talk for a few minutes, then Dr. Patel guided them to the nearest meeting room.

An hour later, Seth led a shattered Dennis and Melissa to his car.

"Someone's going to be a little uncomfortable in the backseat for a few minutes," he said apologetically. "But your motel is only a few kilometers up the road, so it shouldn't be too bad."

He'd offered to put them up as his place, but they'd wanted to be as close to the hospital and Lola as possible.

"I'll take the back," Dennis said.

"Nonsense. You're as stiff as a board. I'll sit in the back," Melissa said.

Seth couldn't help but squirm as he watched her fold herself into the small space. Vivian had been joking about swapping cars, he knew, but maybe he should have taken her up on the offer.

Melissa's cramped posture provided much-needed comic relief as he drove to the motel, with Dennis checking on her welfare every few seconds and Melissa responding with ever more effusive descriptions of how comfortable she was. Even as he laughed along with them, Seth recognized it as a necessary release after the discussion they'd just had.

Dr. Patel had been kind but very clear as he outlined Lola's condition. Successive scans had detected no activity in her brain, and Dr. Patel and a colleague had examined her in detail. They'd both reached the same conclusion—Lola was clinically brain-dead, unable to even breathe on her own without the ventilator. Dennis and Melissa had asked questions and held out for hope, but Dr. Patel had been unable to provide it. Yes, he knew there were miracle stories of accident victims who had woken from years-long comas, but Lola would not be one of them. She had suffered catastrophic trauma to her brain as a result of the closed head injury, and there was no possibility of her recovering. At all. He'd gone on to state that he understood he was asking them to accept a painful truth, and encouraged them to do whatever they deemed necessary for their peace of mind, including procuring another opinion. Once they had satisfied themselves, they could discuss the next step.

Turning off Lola's ventilator.

Seth spotted the sign for the motel ahead and signaled to turn. The moment the car was stationary and the hand brake on, he shot out of his seat and flipped it forward so he could extract Melissa from her cramped quarters.

"I'll see if I can borrow my brother's car tomorrow," he said as he watched her stretch.

"It's a beautiful car," Melissa said, her gaze sliding over the TT's curvy profile before turning to study him. "It suits you."

"Did you want to go back to the hospital tonight?" Seth asked as he and Dennis hauled out the luggage.

"I'm not sure. Neither of us slept much on the plane. We might be better served getting a good night's sleep," Dennis said.

"Well, I'm going back to give Daisy her evening

feed. Call me if you need anything, otherwise I'll pick you up tomorrow morning at nine-thirty."

"That sounds fine," Dennis said. He extended his hand, and Seth shook it.

"You're a decent man," Dennis said, his throat bobbing sharply. "We appreciate all you've done for Lola and little Daisy."

Seth didn't know how to respond, so he settled for manhandling their bags into the foyer before bidding them both a good night's sleep.

Then he was alone in his car, and he could let himself feel the full horror of the news that Dr. Patel had imparted.

Lola was going to die. His little girl would never know her mother. He didn't want to even begin to think what that might do to a kid.

His chest hollow, he put the car into gear and headed back to the hospital and the only bright thing amongst all this tragedy.

CHAPTER EIGHT

THE CLOCK ON Vivian's dash showed five past eleven when she stopped in front of Seth's on Saturday morning—and yet there was no sign of her sister's car anywhere.

Perhaps something had come up with the kids. No doubt she would be here any minute now.

Any minute.

Vivian glanced toward the house, aware of a cowardly urge to circle the block rather than go inside where it would be just her and Seth until her sister arrived. Whenever that might be.

You signed up for it. This is the sort of thing supportive friends do, after all.

It was. And she had already decided that she would do whatever she could to help Seth and Daisy. Yet it was hard to let go of the instinct to protect herself.

The too-loud ring of her phone made her jump. Her sister's number filled the screen, and she started talking the moment Vivian took the call.

"Sorry. I'm running late. I'll be there in about twenty, okay? Did you bring those platters we talked about?"

"Yep. And I've already been past the bakery," Vivian said, preempting what she knew would be her sister's next question.

"You're the best. Okay, have to go. Jason got called into work and I need to drop Max at swimming. Grrrr."

The dial tone sounded before Vivian could say anything else. The curtains were still drawn at Seth's so it was impossible to tell what was going on inside.

Twenty minutes. She could do twenty minutes alone with Seth without anything untoward happening. Anyway, they wouldn't really be alone, because Daisy had come home last night. Hence today's celebration.

She got out and retrieved the platters, then girded her loins and headed for the front door. She could hear a baby crying as she approached, which relieved her of the quandary of how loud to knock.

The door opened almost immediately after her knock, revealing Seth wearing a harried expression, Daisy cradled in one arm. He wore faded jeans and a white T-shirt and looked better than anyone had a right to with a couple of days' worth of scruff on his jaw, and hair that had clearly not seen a brush or product in the past twenty-four hours.

"Hi. Sorry about the noisy welcome," he said, gesturing for her to come in.

"Jodie's running a little late," she explained.

"No worries."

"How did your first night go?" she asked, leaning forward to get a better look at Daisy.

Her face was screwed up as she gave vent to whatever frustration or discomfort ailed her.

"Hey, little one. Is it nice to be home?" She had to raise her voice to be heard over the screaming.

"We got about three hours sleep. On and off."

Vivian pulled a face.

"Yeah. I'm hoping she'll have a nap before everyone gets here," Seth said.

"Murphy's Law says that she'll be out the moment everyone arrives."

"Probably, but I'll still call it a win if she gets some sleep in."

"True. I'll just dump these in the kitchen," she said, already heading in that direction. "There's more stuff in the car that needs to come in."

"I'll get it. Is the car unlocked?"

"Is that your cunning way of passing me a screaming baby, Anderson?"

"I thought whatever it is might be heavy."

She slid the platters onto the counter and turned to find him wearing a mildly amused expression as he rocked Daisy in his arms.

He was barefoot, rumpled and clearly tired, but the sight of him holding his daughter so tenderly made her chest warm.

"A bunch of miniquiches and savory tarts? Hardly. But I'll have a cuddle. I have a feeling she'll be in high demand, so I should get in while I can."

She approached him, slipping her hand beneath Daisy's head, her other hand sliding beneath her body as Seth offered his daughter to her. Once again she felt a warm rush of…something as he passed over his precious burden. Sensing that something had changed, Daisy ceased crying for a moment, her gaze searching Vivian's face in confusion.

"It's okay, sweetheart, Aunty Vivian's got you."

Daisy's face crinkled into worried lines as she began to cry again, and Vivian tucked her into the corner of her elbow and rocked her gently. "Poor bubby. You'll be all right."

A few soothing pats and rocks were enough to calm Daisy and she subsided into confused silence. Vivian smiled at her.

"See? It's not so bad. We're all good." She glanced up to find Seth watching her with a frown on his face.

"What?"

"How come you don't have one of these? You obviously like kids."

"For the same reason you didn't until recently."

"Because you've never accidentally knocked someone up?"

She rewarded him with a wry look for his smart mouth but chose not to respond, hoping he'd simply drop the subject.

"I find it hard to believe that there hasn't been a guy who wanted to make babies with you."

"You're not great at taking a hint, are you?"

"Apparently not." He crossed his arms over his chest, signaling his intention to wait her out.

She continued soothing Daisy, trying to decide if she wanted to tell Seth about Franco. On one hand, it wasn't something she liked to rehash, but Seth didn't look as though he intended to let it go anytime soon.

"I lived with someone in L.A. for a few years. We talked about babies. But we didn't agree on how things might work."

"Define *things*."

She gestured impatiently. "He wanted me to stay home and be a full-time mum while he did the provider thing. And I didn't want to give up my career. He didn't understand why I would choose work over a family, I couldn't understand why it had to be a choice. I'm sure you can see where this is going." She shrugged, wishing she'd stuck with her policy of ignoring him and hoping he'd go away.

"Had this guy never met you?" Seth's tone was incredulous.

"What is that supposed to mean?" She narrowed her eyes. If he made one reference to her supposed party-girl past, he was going to be walking funny for a week. At least.

"You love what you do. Who in their right mind would try to take that away from you?"

She was so surprised by his answer that for a moment she could do nothing but blink.

"I suppose he gave you a vacuum cleaner for your birthday, too," Seth said, shaking his head. "Don't quote me on this, but sometimes I can fully sympathize with the feminist movement."

Probably she shouldn't feel quite so shaken that Seth understood her so easily, so clearly. It wasn't exactly a news flash that women were as attached to their careers as men—this was the twenty-first century, not the ice age. Yet she'd lived with Franco for two years and he hadn't been able to comprehend that her sense of herself was as tied up in her work and her creativity as his was in his career.

Seth, however, got it without even trying. But then he'd always got her, hadn't he? Just as she'd always got him.

"I hope you at least broke the knuckle-dragger's heart when you walked out on him," Seth said.

She wished.

"It was kind of the other way 'round, actually."

There was a strange expression on Seth's face when she glanced at him.

"Don't tell me you're still in love with the caveman?" he asked.

"No. Of course not. It's heading toward two years. He married someone else last March."

Seth watched her closely. "Did you fantasize about storming the church and screwing it up for him?"

She smiled faintly. "No. Like I said, I'm over him."

"You don't look over him."

There was a gruff note to Seth's voice. In another man, she'd be tempted to diagnose it as jealousy. But this was Seth. He'd never had any claim on her—or any designs, for that matter.

Well, unless wanting to sleep with her again counted, and, under the circumstances, she was pretty sure it didn't.

"I'll always have a soft spot for him. He's my one that got away, you know? Even you must have one of those."

"I thought I was your one that got away."

She laughed. "You were my lucky escape. My disaster waiting to happen."

"Let a guy down gently, why don't you?" He played wounded for all he was worth, but for a split second there was a look in his eyes that gave her pause.

Surely he hadn't been serious…?

She tried to discern the truth, but his expression was again impenetrable. Then she reminded herself of whom she was talking to—Seth, the guy she'd had sex with in the back of a limo more than a decade ago. The same guy who'd gotten a twenty-four-year-old bar bunny pregnant and who had made a hobby out of avoiding commitment.

As if he considered their long-ago liaison anything more than what it was. The notion was laughable.

Or the worst case of wishful thinking she'd ever encountered in her lifetime.

"You going to hold up your end of the bargain or what?" She gestured with her chin toward the front of the house. "Those quiches aren't going to march themselves up the driveway, you know."

"First she crushes me, then she dismisses me."

He headed for the door. She paced with Daisy while he was gone, jiggling her some more and trying to understand why she'd volunteered all that stuff about Franco. No clear answer had come to her by the time she registered that Daisy was on the verge of sleep, her eyes heavy as she blinked up at Vivian.

"Don't fight it, sweetheart. You go to sleep."

She brushed the back of her finger over Daisy's cheek, then couldn't resist tracing the curve of her ear. Seth had obviously just bathed her, and she smelled like fresh powder, warm baby and sunshiny cotton. Daisy made an inarticulate sound, and Vivian held her that little bit tighter, pressing a kiss to her gently rounded head.

Seth might not realize it yet, but he was lucky to have this miracle in his life. She would bring him joy, she would terrify him, she would push him to the edge and over—and it would be the ride of his life.

Vivian was aware of an odd, wistful ache in her throat, and she cleared it briskly. Someone was getting sentimental in her old age.

Toughen up, Walker.

She wandered into the living room in search of distraction, noting the packet of pink balloons on the coffee table, along with a roll of ribbon and a Welcome Home banner. Both bemused and amused by the idea of Seth voluntarily decorating his home with pink balloons, she picked up the ribbon as she heard his footsteps on the stairs.

"Pink is so your color," she told him as he entered carrying both bakery boxes.

"Just for that you can help me blow up some balloons."

"Okay."

He looked surprised. "That was easy."

"Don't get used to it."

He made a rude noise before disappearing into the kitchen, and she heard the sound of the fridge opening and closing.

She checked her watch, wondering what was keeping her sister. The sooner she got here the better.

Seth checked on Daisy when he returned. "Hey, she's almost asleep. You'll have to tell me your secret."

"The patented Vivian Walker jiggle. Works every time."

"Figures." He glanced at the clock on the mantel. "I might try to put her down while I can."

"Good idea."

She extended her arms, trying to make it easy for him to make the transfer, but somehow she wound up confusing him and she felt the distinct brush of his fingers across her breast as Seth scooped his hand under Daisy's head.

He froze. "Shit. Sorry. I totally wasn't copping a feel, I promise."

"I should hope not. Bit pervy using your newborn baby as a pickup prop," she said, more to cover how flustered she was than anything else.

He was standing so close she could smell the mint from his toothpaste and see the tiny scar on his earlobe from when he'd had his ear pierced.

"No kidding." He stepped back with Daisy, his cheeks burnished a dull red.

If someone had told her Seth was capable of blushing, she would have laughed out loud. It was a little scary how endearing the sight was.

"Might want to avoid a repeat with my mum, though," she advised. "She has a rape whistle."

"Right. Note to self—avoid feeling up Mrs. Walker. Thanks for the hot tip."

He headed off to put down Daisy and Vivian waited until he'd left the room before glancing down at herself. Yep, sure enough, both her nipples were hard, creating two give-away, look-at-me points beneath her simple cotton tank.

"Thanks for the support, girls. Way to have my back." She rubbed her palms over them, willing them to subside. "Settle down, damn you."

"Is this a private party or can anyone join in?"

Vivian spun to find her sister on the threshold, a huge salad bowl in hand.

"I was just— Here, let me help you with that." Vivian darted forward to relieve her sister of the bowl, aware that there wasn't an explanation in the world that could cover why she was feeling herself up in the privacy of Seth's living room.

"You're supposed to do breast exams when you're naked," Jodie said, clearly not prepared to let the subject slide. "Just so you know."

"Thanks. I'll remember for next time."

Vivian carried the salad into the kitchen, aware of her sister following her.

"Where's Seth?" Jodie asked.

"Putting Daisy down. She's been up most the night."

"Babies. They do that."

Vivian risked a glance at her sister and found she was the object of intense study.

"What?"

"Just trying to work out if talking to your breasts is an L.A. thing or if I should be worried about your mental health."

"My mental health is fine. Can we change the subject?"

"I'm not sure I'm finished with it yet."

"I'll pay you fifty bucks. And throw in my Prada scarf." Because any second now Seth would be back and she so did not want the subject of nipples to still be on the table.

"Wow. Okay. But I'd rather have that cute red hobo bag."

"Done. I'm going to go blow up some balloons." She escaped to the living room, pushing her hair off her forehead. Between fighting her awareness of Seth and ignoring his awareness of her and pretending that her sister hadn't caught her tête-à-tit, she had a feeling it was going to be a long day.

SETH RETURNED FROM putting Daisy down to find Jodie had taken over his kitchen.

"Hey. Wasn't there a younger, hotter version of you here a few minutes ago?" he said, feigning confusion.

"Good to see you, too, Seth darling," Jodie said good-naturedly, rising on her toes to kiss his cheek and give him a quick hug. Even though he knew she was probably still pissed with him over the way he'd bad-mouthed Vivian—as she should be—she'd been a rock since Lola's accident and he'd never been more grateful for his brother's good taste in women.

He marveled that two women who shared so many genes could have such profoundly different effects on him. Jodie could kiss him, hug him, sit on his knee, punch his arm, and he felt nothing apart from warm affection and the odd desire to yank on her ponytail.

Vivian, on the other hand, had only to walk into the room and his imagination and body immediately went haywire. Every look was fraught with potential, every accidental touch a form of torture....

He opened and closed his hand, unable to shake the memory of the warm curve of her breast against his fingers. It was...disturbing that the sensation lingered despite the fact that it had been a full fifteen minutes since their accidental encounter. He was tired, he needed a shave, he hadn't eaten since four or five in the morning. Sex should be the last thing on his mind, given all the balls he had in the air. Yet the fact that Vivian was in his house acted like a magnet, drawing his thoughts and his focus. Her presence distracted him even when he should be listening to Jodie's convoluted explanation for why she'd been held up and why Jason would be arriving closer to one than to twelve.

"...I told him that if this keeps up, he needs to be having a talk with the partners," Jodie said.

"It could be worse. He could own a bar," Seth said.

"True." She wiped her hands on the tea towel. "Have you heard anything more from the police?"

"Nope. Not expecting to, either. We haven't had any run-ins with nasty drunks or disgruntled patrons lately, so it was obviously just some moron who was determined to wreck something for the hell of it and my window happened to be handy. The police won't be knocking themselves out trying to hunt whoever it is down."

"How's your bartender? Is she recovering okay?"

"Yeah. Syrie is as tough as old boots. But I'm having security cameras installed, along with a panic button." He'd always prided himself on Night Howls' relaxed and friendly ambience, but he needed to protect his staff. Especially since he would be relying on them more than ever.

"Well, let me know if you need me to sit with Daisy. I'm more than happy to help, you know that. I'm sure Viv would pitch in if you needed her, too."

Seth was already shaking his head. "I can't ask Vivian for more help. She's done more than enough."

"She's family. Why do you think she came home if it wasn't to be a part of all this mess?" Jodie's gesture took in the kitchen, but he knew she was referring to the craziness of family life in general.

"I'm pretty sure it wasn't to help me with Daisy."

"You know that saying about it taking a village to raise a child? It's so true it's scary, and Viv is part of your village. Don't let pride get in the way of asking for what you need. It's the quickest way to wind up in the corner with your thumb in your mouth while the dirty diapers pile up. Trust me, I've been there."

Seth knew she was trying to help, but he wasn't about to explain that, apart from issues of pride—and he was honest enough to admit that he had his fair share of that— he simply didn't trust himself where Vivian was concerned. He'd been more than ready to put what had almost happened in the pool down to an unfortunate confluence of circumstances—the warm night, the beer, the pressure of his situation, the ten years of history, curiosity and fantasy—but it was pointless to bullshit himself.

He was profoundly attracted to Vivian. Always had been, probably always would be. And not just in a wouldn't-mind-getting-into-her-pants kind of way.

It was an uncomfortable truth to face, given his track record with women and the fact that Vivian was no longer living thousands of miles and a big, wide ocean away. She'd always been the last woman he should hook up with, and now that his life was infinitely more complicated and stressful, that judgment call only became more important.

He couldn't afford to mess things up with her. He needed his family right now, and Daisy needed him to be solid. For once in his life, he needed to be smart about a woman.

"You're probably right," he said neutrally, aware that Jodie would keep hammering the issue if he didn't appear to give in. Then he beat a retreat for the living room, only to pull up short when he realized Vivian was in there, tying a knot in a fat pink balloon. Several more dotted the couch, lengths of string trailing after them like tails.

"Hey. You started without me," he said stupidly.

"It's called taking the initiative. All the cool kids are doing it." She glanced at him before returning her attention to the knot. "I wasn't sure where you wanted to put them."

"I was thinking along the top of the windows. And the mantelpiece."

They worked in silence for a few minutes, blowing up more balloons. When they had nearly a dozen, Vivian gathered them into bundles and attached them to the curtain rods, then the mantelpiece, pretending to consult him but doing it her way anyway and creating an end result that was a million times better than anything he could have done.

"Where do you want the banner?" she asked.

"Over the doorway to the kitchen."

"Ah. Definitely a job for a six-foot-two man, then."

She handed over the banner, and he taped it above the opening before stepping back to consider it. He caught Vivian stifling a smile and threw her a look.

"You're thinking that this is a big waste on a week-old baby who won't be able to read for another five years, aren't you?" he said.

"I'm thinking that it's very revealing seeing this side of you, Mr. Mum."

He glanced toward the front door, checking to make sure that none of the other guests had arrived early before he tried to explain himself. "It's for Dennis and Melissa more than anything. The specialist they've found is testing Lola on Monday. I want them to at least have one good memory to take home with them."

Vivian didn't say anything for a moment, her blue-green eyes steady on his face. "There you go, surprising me again, Anderson. Just when I thought I had you pegged."

She slipped into the kitchen before he could respond.

He tidied up the scraps of ribbon and collected the scissors and tape, all the while wondering what particular heading Vivian had had him filed under all these years. And then he remembered—he was her lucky escape, her "disaster waiting to happen."

He frowned, his thumb smoothing over the ragged stickiness of the leading edge of tape. Then he shrugged. Her writing him off as an option was a good thing. It certainly made it a hell of a lot easier to keep his focus where it should be. Daisy was what was important.

Only Daisy.

VIVIAN KNOCKED HERSELF out staying busy for the rest of the afternoon. She helped her sister heat and plate food in the kitchen, then she circulated amongst Seth's guests with platters, chatting to family, meeting his neighbors and friends. When Jodie had told her that Seth wanted to hold a welcome-home party for Daisy, her first response had been to wonder if all the stress had gone to his head—he had enough to juggle without inviting people over the second he brought his daughter home. Her mother *still* complained thirty-six years after the event because their father's mother had turned up unannounced with a phalanx of friends in tow the day Vivian's mother had brought Jodie home from the hospital.

But seeing Dennis's and Melissa's faces as they sat in the living room and took turns holding Daisy, Vivian knew that Seth had made a good call. The Browns had had a brutal time since they landed, and offering them this brief respite had been a generous and sensitive act. He was good at playing the ne'er-do-well Casanova, but there was more to him than a cheeky glint in his eye and a tendency toward self-indulgence and excess.

Seth was kind. And he was gentle. And he was thoughtful.

She wasn't sure if she was thrilled or terrified by the discovery, given how hard she fought to resist the undertow of their enduring mutual attraction.

Maybe both.

IT WAS MIDAFTERNOON before the call of nature saw Vivian handing an almost-empty platter to her sister. "Five minutes for a pit stop and I'll be your slave once more."

"Good luck with that. I saw Jason's dad disappearing with the sports section five minutes ago," Jodie said meaningfully.

Vivian wrinkled her nose. "Really? Blurg. I don't understand how men can read on the toilet. It's a one-function space for me."

"Jason's father's record is an hour. I'd head for Seth's en suite if I were you."

Vivian frowned, not liking the idea of invading Seth's personal space. On the other hand, she wouldn't be able to ignore the message her body was sending for long. Feeling ridiculously tentative, she made her way past Daisy's room, past the occupied main bathroom, to the door at the end that she assumed led to Seth's bedroom.

"Hello?" she called softly, knocking on the almost-closed door.

No one responded, which she figured meant the coast was clear. Still, she glanced over her shoulder, unable to shake the feeling that she was crossing the line. Seth didn't magically appear, demanding to know what she was doing, so she entered the room.

The bed had been made in a rumpled, haphazard manner, one of the pillows still showing the indentation from Seth's head, the dark grey-and-white pinstriped duvet lumpy-looking and skewed to one side. Books were piled six high on the table, with another stack on the floor. In the corner, scuffed boots sat near a chair, the latter bearing a pair of folded jeans. Despite the fact that he clearly hadn't gone to any trouble to personalize the room, the space resonated with a sense of Seth.

The scent of his aftershave hung in the air, and a watch lay curled on top of one of the books. She took a step toward it, feeling the unaccountable urge to touch something that had rested against his skin.

Um, hello? There's only one reason you're in here. This is not a fact-finding mission.

She corrected her path, walking into the white-tiled en suite bathroom. She shut the door, took care of business, then washed her hands.

An electric razor sat on one side of the vanity, along with a disposable one. She couldn't help smiling. Seth hadn't been near either of those in the past few days, from what she could tell. He'd been too busy looking after Daisy to worry about being smooth.

She saw her smile in the mirror and realized she was doing it again, hovering and taking stock of Seth's private domain.

Anyone would think she was a lovelorn teenager, the way she was carrying on. She exited the bathroom, determined to head straight for the door. Then she caught sight of the book on top of the pile beside Seth's bed and stopped in her tracks. *Simplicity Parenting: Using the Extraordinary Power of Less to Raise Calmer, Happier and More Secure Kids.* She glanced at the stack on the table. *Parenting with Love and Logic, The Happiest Baby on the Block, The Baby Owner's Manual: Operating Instructions, Troubleshooting Tips and Advice on First-Year Maintenance...*

There were no less than eleven books here, and all of them were parenting manuals. Many of them had sticky notes poking out, some with notes Seth had scribbled to himself.

No wonder he looked like crap. Not only was he up tending to Daisy at all hours, but he was also taking a crash course in parenting in his downtime. Not to mention running a business and supporting the Browns the best he could. It was a miracle his eyes weren't hanging out of his head.

She remembered the expression he'd had on his face when he'd inspected the banner this morning. He'd been so earnest, so intent. So determined to get this right for his little girl.

It occurred to her then that while Lola had been incredibly, horribly unlucky, she'd had one stroke of sublime good fortune—of all the men she could have made a baby with, she'd done so with Seth. While he drew breath, Daisy would never want for a protector and a champion.

Vivian told herself that it was ridiculous to get so choked up over a few books and the idea that Seth wanted to be a good father. Didn't all men want that? Wasn't he simply doing the right, decent thing?

Maybe. Probably. But there was something about the thought of Seth handling this on his own that added extra poignancy to it. Especially when he'd all but admitted that he was terrified of messing up.

She forced herself to move on, making her way to the kitchen. Her sister had a plate of sweet things ready to be circulated, and Vivian headed into the living room to tempt Seth's guests. The first thing she noticed was that the Browns were gone, and she wondered if they'd called it a day already.

No one would blame them. Although Seth hadn't said as much, she gathered that Lola's fate was to be decided on Monday when the specialist handed down his verdict. Reading between the lines and judging by Seth's low-key delivery, she suspected that he wasn't anticipating a miracle. Which meant that the decision to turn off Lola's ventilator wasn't far off.

"Vivian. Come settle an argument for me," her mother called from across the room.

She was talking to Seth's mum, Angela, and Vivian circled the couch to join them.

"How many times did you move home before you finally got it right? I can remember at least two." Her rings flashed in the sunlight as she rested a hand on Vivian's shoulder.

"Seth came home three times," Angela confided. She was wearing her salt-and-pepper hair in an asymmetrical cut these days, a look that really suited her long face. "Although it wouldn't surprise me if he slept in his car a few times over the years to avoid having to face his father again."

"So, let me get this straight. You guys are having a competition over who raised the biggest loser? Am I on the money?" Vivian said it lightly, but she was pleased to see her mother squirm a little.

"No. Of course not. We were just reminiscing," Angela said.

"You've got to admit, Viv, it took you a while to find your feet," her mother said a little defensively.

"Yep. I've never been one of those people who likes to buy out of the box," Vivian said. "I guess Seth is like that, too. It takes longer to find your way when you're traveling in uncharted territory."

She didn't wait for them to respond, sailing off to the other side of the room to offer some caramel brownies to Seth's father. The urge to find Seth and vent to him regarding their apparent status as the family disappointments was irresistible, however, and she walked into the kitchen in search of him.

"Have you seen Seth?" she asked her sister.

"He's out by the pool talking to Dennis and Melissa," Jodie said, busy setting up cups for coffee and tea, a sure sign the party was winding down.

Vivian moved to the patio door. Sure enough, Seth was outside talking to Lola's parents. She was about to join them, but something gave her pause. The way Seth was standing, perhaps, his back straight, his chin slightly raised.

As though he was staring down a challenge.

Dennis and Melissa looked tense, too, his expression serious as he banged his balled-up fist into the palm of his other hand.

Okay. Maybe she wouldn't go out and bitch to Seth right now.

Ten minutes passed before the Browns came inside. They seemed subdued, and immediately said their goodbyes. Vivian was passing the milk jug to Seth's elderly neighbor when Seth entered. It took only a single glance at his face for her to know that something was very wrong. Leaving Mrs. Cottrell to find the sugar herself, Vivian crossed to Seth's side.

"Are you okay? What happened?" She reached out to touch him and the moment she lay her hand on him she could *feel* how wound up he was.

"I need to check on Daisy," he said.

He was gone so quickly she was left blinking, her mouth open. When she turned around, she realized Jodie had seen the whole thing. Stupid, self-conscious heat rushed into her face.

"We should probably start packing away some of this food, huh?" She moved to the table and started to consolidate leftovers onto a single platter.

Feeling indescribably foolish, she waited for Jodie to say something. During the course of the day, Vivian had woven a false sense of intimacy around herself and Seth. She'd been thinking about him so much, analyzing her emotions, watching him. She'd been in his room, in his bathroom. She'd felt close to him, and she'd been worried for him when she saw his face just now.

But all that had been in her head, and Seth's reality was obviously far different from hers. There was no reason at all why he would choose to confide in her, of all people, when he had a houseful of friends and family. Why would he, when their relationship, such as it was, was based on sexual attraction and propinquity and not much else?

The moment stretched, but her sister remained blessedly silent. Slowly Vivian released her breath.

At least she didn't have to suffer the ignominy of trying to explain her upset to her sister.

Hell, she could hardly explain it to herself.

CHAPTER NINE

SETH SAT ON the end of his bed and stared at the pink, scrunched-up face of his daughter. All day long people had been calling her beautiful, but he was under no illusions. Right now, she resembled a baby monkey more than the chubby-cheeked cherubs on the covers of the books he'd been reading.

He didn't care. To him, she was the most fascinating, compelling creature ever to draw breath. He could spend hours mesmerized by her steady regard, and he couldn't get enough of her sweet, warm scent.

She was a part of him, the best part of him, and he loved her so much it made his chest ache.

He glanced at his watch, aware of the pull of duty. He needed to go play host to his guests. More importantly, he needed to find Vivian and apologize for blowing her off.

After talking to Dennis and Melissa, the urge to hold his daughter, to look into her face and breathe in her smell, had been overwhelming. He'd still been reeling from the conversation he'd had with Lola's parents, and Vivian's concern, the touch of her hand, the worry in her eyes had been too much to handle. He'd been holding himself together with rubber bands and superglue for the past week, and at that second he'd felt dangerously close to breaking.

But Vivian didn't know that. She knew only that he'd brushed her off like a stranger.

A tap sounded at the door.

"Seth?"

He recognized his mother's voice.

"It's not locked. Come in."

The door opened and his mother peered in as though afraid she was interrupting something. "I just wanted to let you know that we're going."

"Right. I'll come out."

"Is Daisy okay?"

"She's fine. I was making sure she was dry."

His mother nodded, and he settled Daisy into her crib before heading for the kitchen. It soon became obvious that his parents weren't the only ones leaving, and he listened patiently as people offered unsolicited advice on raising a daughter before saying their goodbyes. When the exodus ended, he discovered that Jason, Jodie and the boys were the only ones who hadn't abandoned him.

"Where's Vivian?" he asked, earning him a sharp look from Jodie.

"She left just before Mum and Dad," she said.

Damn. Why could he never seem to get things right where she was concerned?

"I've put the leftover salad in the fridge, and divided the quiches and party pies into smaller batches and put them in the freezer. Should keep you going for a while."

"We're taking the cupcakes and the brownies home with us," Sam reported importantly.

"Just as well, because Daisy hates cupcakes," Seth said.

"Ha! Daisy doesn't even have *teeth*," Max said, clearly delighted by his own knowledge.

"I'll pick up my coffee urn next time I see you," Jodie said, gathering her bag and coat.

It hadn't escaped his notice that both she and Vivian had worked their butts off for him and Daisy today. Another debt he'd never be able to repay.

"I owe you," he said simply. "I couldn't have done it without you. Or Viv."

"It was fun. Jase, can you help me with these platters, please?"

"Already on it," Jason said, his arms full.

Jodie's expression softened. "That's why I love you. Always one step ahead." She kissed his cheek.

"Get a room. Blah!" Max said, Sam quickly chiming in with his own gagging noises.

"Excuse me," Jodie said, eyes wide. "Where on earth did you get that saying from?"

"Relax, they don't even know what it means," Jason said. "They might as well be saying 'get a banana.'"

"I wish they were." The outraged expression eased from her face. "All right, double trouble, to the car."

There was a last-minute scramble to collect Hot Wheels cars, handheld games and sweaters, then they were gone and Seth stood in his empty house with nothing and nobody to distract him from his thoughts.

She'd be better off with us. If you're honest with yourself, you'll acknowledge that. We can give her everything she needs.

Melissa's heartfelt words echoed in his mind as he tidied the living room. Maybe he was naive. Maybe he should have anticipated this. Dennis and Melissa lived far away, and they were about to lose their daughter. It didn't take a psychology degree to work out that they must be desperate for something positive to cling to.

And yet he *was* surprised. Beyond surprised, actually. He was stunned.

Because Daisy was his. She belonged to him, and he belonged to her. The thought that someone might expect him to give her up, to hand her over, had never crossed his mind.

Still, he'd promised Dennis and Melissa he'd think about it, even though his knee-jerk reaction had been to tell them where they could stick their offer. He'd held back because he felt sorry for them, because he knew that they would be facing great sadness in the days to come. But as Dennis had made his arguments, and Melissa had chimed in with her own thoughts, Seth had started to understand what they were offering.

There were two of them. They had an established home. They'd already raised two children. They were still young and active enough to take on the challenge of a child. Financially, they were stable, and it would be no problem at all for Melissa to quit her job and care for Daisy full-time.

On paper, they were ideal. Far better suited to raising a little girl than a single, thirty-four-year-old guy who owned a bar and had spent most of his life avoiding being tied down. It was a black-and-white, cut-and-dried decision—on paper.

But no logical assemblage of facts and details could capture the way he felt about the tiny being sleeping so soundly close by. Daisy was *his* girl. He adored her. Even when she cried for hours on end, his only thought was to comfort her. She'd had the rockiest start in life, and he was determined to make it up to her.

But what if he wasn't the best person to do that for her? What if this love he felt, this overwhelming need

to keep her safe and protect her, was just a selfish manifestation of what *he* wanted? What if she needed more
than his devotion?

Whenever he asked himself the question—and he'd
been doing so ever since Dennis and Melissa had presented their offer—everything in him recoiled from
even contemplating it. But he had to. He had to look
it in the eye and force himself to consider what the
Browns were offering.

For Daisy. Because he would have only one chance
to get it right. What had Vivian said that night in the
pool? *You don't get do-overs with a kid.*

He was painfully aware of it, and had been ever since
Lola had told him he was going to be a father. Vivian
was the only person he'd voiced his doubts to, however.
She was the only one he'd felt he could be honest with,
without fear of judgment or being misunderstood. She'd
never bullshitted him, or held back, and he trusted her
with his frailties.

She was the only person who would understand the
dilemma he faced, too. Jodie and Jason would be angry
on his behalf, their instinct being to circle the wagons.
His parents would think he was looking for a way out.
But Vivian…she would be honest.

Suddenly urgent, he headed for Daisy's room and
started packing her diaper bag.

VIVIAN DID SOME yoga when she got home, repeating the
"salute to the sun" until her arms and legs were shaky.
Afterward, she lay on her mat and tried to clear her
mind of the jangling anxiety that had kept her on edge
since leaving Seth's place.

She was worried about what he and the Browns had

been discussing by the pool—even though it was absolutely none of her business, times ten. She was worried that her sister might suspect that her feelings for Seth were more than they should be. And she was worried that her sister was right. Most of all, she was worried that she had no idea what to do about all of the above.

She was doing some breathing exercises when a knock sounded at the door. Lifting her head, she debated answering for a beat. She hadn't met any of her neighbors yet, so there were only so many options for who might come calling unannounced—her sister, or Robin. Pushing to her feet, she dusted off the seat of her pants as she crossed to the door, then pressed her eye to the spy hole. She went very still when she saw Seth, a frown on his face as he stared away.

As though he already regretted his visit.

"Where's Daisy?" she asked as she opened the door. "Oh."

Daisy was nestled into the portable baby carrier at his feet, her blue eyes blinking at Vivian curiously.

"I know you've already given me most of your day, but I need another ten minutes," he said.

"Okay," she said, more than a little baffled. "Come in. Do you need me to look after Daisy? Has something come up at work?"

It was amazing—and scary—how easy it was to push aside her hurt simply because he'd come to her.

He entered the apartment, glancing around briefly before placing Daisy next to the couch. His dark eyes were stormy when they met hers.

"I need you to be honest with me. Can you do that?"

A dart of panic shot through her. What was he about to ask her? Then she gave herself a mental shake. He had not driven to Brunswick to interrogate her about her feelings for him.

"Yes. I think so."

"I mean real honesty. The kind that hurts."

"That's my specialty where you're concerned, remember?"

"That's why I came. You're the only person I could think of who wouldn't tell me what they thought I'd want to hear."

"Do you want to sit?"

Seth glanced at the couch behind him. "I guess."

He was so tense, and obviously preoccupied. He sank onto the couch, moving Daisy's carrier closer to his feet. Vivian sat on the ottoman at right angles to him, a small, distant part of her brain marveling that Seth Anderson was in her apartment, and that he'd come to her for counsel. She'd had her fair share of fantasies starring him over the years, but none had looked like this.

"So. What's going on?" she asked simply.

"Do you think I'd be a terrible parent?"

"Is this something to do with the conversation you had with Dennis and Melissa today?"

"Is that your way of avoiding answering?"

"No. I don't have a problem answering your question. If that's what you want me to do."

His gaze never left her face as he waited for her answer. Her brutally honest, frank answer.

She took a moment to gather her thoughts. "Okay, here are the things I know about you. You're way too confident for your own good. Despite that, people respond to you because you're charming. You're a dreamer, but you know how to buckle down when necessary. You're smart. You've made a success of yourself. You're impulsive. Playful. Creative. Surprisingly moral for a card-carrying hedonist. And you've got a big heart."

"How do you know that?"

She understood he was asking her to justify her last assertion. "Because I've seen you with Sam, with Max, with Daisy. And because no matter how this pregnancy came about, I've never once heard you bad-mouth Lola or try to weasel out of taking responsibility for your own actions."

"Doing what any decent human being would do is hardly grounds for a ticker-tape parade and marching band."

"In theory. In practice, there's a reason the phrase *deadbeat dad* exists."

"Okay. So?"

She studied his face, taking in the worry in his eyes, the stubble on his cheeks, the faint stain on his shoulder. She'd bet her favorite pair of Jimmy Choo shoes that he'd just finished feeding Daisy. She wished like hell that she knew what had precipitated his question, but that wouldn't change her answer.

"I think you'll be a good dad, Seth. Not perfect, because no such thing exists. The fact that we're even having this conversation tells me you're going in with your eyes open and that you care. A lot. You'll do whatever it takes to give Daisy a happy, safe life."

"What if the best way of giving her that is for her not to be with me?"

She sat back, shocked by the question. Then the penny dropped. "Is that what Dennis and Melissa were talking to you about?"

"They want to take Daisy. They think they're in a

better place to provide for her. There's two of them, they're comfortable financially, they've raised kids. They said I could visit whenever I wanted, that Daisy could come here on holidays when she's older. That they'd never stop me from being a part of her life."

Vivian was so gobsmacked she couldn't breathe, let alone think or speak. Daisy was Seth's daughter as well as Lola's. He was her *father.* The Browns had no place to even consider taking away that right.

"What did you say to them?"

"That I'd think about it." There was a bleakness in his eyes and a steely note beneath his words that sent a chill down her spine.

If Seth thought Daisy would be better off with the Browns, he'd let them take her. There wasn't a doubt in Vivian's mind he loved his daughter that much.

"Seth, listen to me." Urgency pushed every other consideration aside as she grabbed his hand, determined to get through to him. "Daisy needs you. You're her father. She needs exactly what you have to offer—boundless love and a good heart and all the goodwill in the world. That other stuff means jack."

Seth stared at her, his expression unreadable. She gripped his hand tighter and gave it a shake.

"You love this little girl. You will regret it for the rest of your life if you do this. It will be with you every day. *Every day,* Seth. So what if you're not perfect? Who needs perfect? You and Daisy are amazing together. Please don't let them guilt you into doing something that will kill you."

Seth looked at their joined hands. Vivian held her breath, aware of the burn of tears at the back of her eyes. She didn't know what she would do if he didn't listen to her. It would be a tragedy of the highest order if he gave up his child because he was convinced it was the best thing for her—another terrible chapter in what was already a wretched tale.

Then Seth lifted his head and she saw his mouth curl up a little at the corners and an amused light glinted in his eyes.

"You had better not be laughing at me, Seth." She tried to jerk her hand free, furious that she had been on the verge of tears because she was so passionate on his behalf and he was *laughing* at her. He tightened his grip, however, refusing to let her go.

"I'm not laughing at you. Well, not *at you* anyway. I came to you because I figured you'd be objective. Guess I kind of got that one wrong."

She was too busy feeling exposed to register the warm note of affection in his tone.

"Yeah, you did. As if I'm going to stand by while you ruin your life, you idiot. Can you let go of my hand now, please?"

"Not until you've calmed down."

"I'm perfectly calm, thank you."

"No, you're not. You're pissed with me. And I'm grateful that you care enough to get this worked up on my account."

His words took some, but not all, of the wind out of her sails. "Don't flatter yourself. I was thinking of Daisy. If they took her to England she'd have to put up with those crappy English summers and she'd never know how a proper game of football is played."

Seth's gaze was steady, and she knew he wasn't buying a word of it.

"Thanks for giving a shit," he said simply.

She was powerfully aware of the warmth of his palm and how big his hand felt around hers.

"It's not like I really had a choice," she said. Even though it wasn't the wisest thing to admit.

Something shifted behind his eyes, then his gaze dropped to her mouth. Excitement kicked in her belly, illicit, unwanted and inappropriate. If she leaned forward a few inches, and he did the same...

He looked away, a muscle working in his jaw. She tugged her hand and he took the hint, releasing her.

"Just because I care doesn't mean my opinion doesn't count," she said.

"Yeah. I know."

She looked at Daisy. Vivian had held her only twice but already she felt fiercely attached to her. She could imagine how much more strongly Seth felt. "Did you really think I'd tell you to let her go?"

"If you thought it was the right thing, yeah."

"You have a high opinion of my compassion and tact, obviously."

He shrugged, his mouth turning up in a rueful half smile. "Maybe I just wanted to talk to you."

Her belly did the excited-kick thing again, but she tried to ignore it. "That's a step-up from the usual."

"Oh, I wanted that, too. That's always a given."

He was incorrigible. And honest. And too damned attractive for her peace of mind.

He glanced at Daisy, then back at Vivian. "Can I ask you something?"

A lock of hair had fallen across his forehead. Combined with his scruffy jaw and dramatic dark eyes, it made him look like a brooding teen hero from a John Hughes movie.

Molly Ringwald, eat your heart out.

"You can try."

"If all of this wasn't going on with Daisy and Lola… would you go out for dinner with me?"

"Going out for dinner being man-speak for screw like bunnies?"

"Among other things."

The thought of dinner and sex and *other things* with Seth was enough to steal her breath and make her liquid with longing. But what was new about that?

"No."

"Can I ask why?"

"Does it matter, since it was a hypothetical question?"

"No. But that doesn't mean I'm not going to lie awake thinking about it anyway."

She had a flash of Seth in his rumpled bed, naked and horny, thinking of her. She swallowed, aware of her own hot arousal and her heart banging against her rib cage.

"I'm not interested in that sort of thing anymore."

"You're not interested in sex?" His tone was flatly disbelieving.

She loved sex, and they both knew it.

"I'm looking for more these days." She held his eye, wanting him to get the message loud and clear. Her days of sex for fun were over. She needed more these days. The promise of something greater. A shared future, or at least the possibility of one. And that would never be on offer with this man.

"Right." Seth's gaze dropped to the carpet.

"That doesn't mean we can't be friends, though."

He took a moment to respond. "I guess we've never really tried that, have we?"

"Kind of hard when I lived on the other side of the Pacific Ocean."

"Yeah." He rubbed a hand over his chin. "In the interest of full disclosure, I should confess it's very likely that I'm always going to want to get you naked." His expression managed to straddle the line between apologetic and unashamed.

"Always is a long time. Wait till I'm fifty with a wide ass and extra chins," she said, needing to keep things light.

He didn't blink.

Heat unfurled in her belly. Dangerous and dumb as it was, there was something uniquely compelling about a man wanting her so unabashedly. Especially this man.

"Okay." She smoothed her hands down her thighs, doing her damnedest not to smile. She should not be encouraging him. In any way. It was confusing for him, and for her.

"That doesn't mean I can't control myself," Seth said. "Despite what my brother thinks, I'm not a complete humpy dog."

"When did he call you that?"

"I believe the first time was the dinner before his wedding. After I laid eyes on you for the first time."

"Huh. I take it you never told him about…" She made a vague gesture with her hand.

"No. I did not." He looked mildly offended and she guessed that talking about his sexual conquests with his brother breached some mysterious guy code she wasn't privy to.

"I never told Jodie, either. For the record."

"I figured as much."

"Top points to both of us for discretion. And we

didn't even pinky-swear on it," she said, suddenly keen to move on from this subject.

Talking about that night brought back too many memories. Memories she'd revisited so many times they'd taken on almost mythical power in her mind.

She stood. "Do you want a coffee?"

He watched her for a long beat before answering. "I probably shouldn't. This is only the second time Daisy and I have been out and about. I don't want to push my luck."

"She's been very good so far."

He looked at his daughter. "That's because she's a smart cookie. She's biding her time for when I'm home so she can really exercise her lungs." It was said with so much affection, and there was so much raw love in his face.

"You're not going to let Dennis and Melissa take her, are you?" she asked quietly.

"No. Maybe I should. Maybe it would be the best thing for her. But she's my girl, and I can't let her go. Even though I told myself I would if I had to. If you told me it was the best thing to do."

"Well, that was a pretty safe bet, wasn't it?"

"In hindsight, yes." He bent to tuck Daisy's blanket more snugly around her, then stood and hefted the carrier. "We'll leave you to whatever you were doing."

His gaze ran over her yoga attire and she was almost certain he knew she wasn't wearing a bra underneath her stretchy tank.

"I was saluting the sun," she said.

"Rewarding it for trying to cook us in our own skins for the past week, were you?"

"Something like that." She walked him to the door,

then, on impulse, grabbed the key and stepped into the hallway with him.

"Escorting me from the premises?"

"It's a policy of mine."

They took the stairs to the ground floor in silence, walking through the tiled foyer to the automatic glass doors that led outside. The warm night air was heavy and moist after the air-conditioned building and Seth groaned.

"Man. I can't believe I'm going to say this, but bring on winter."

"Wash out your mouth. Never wish away summer. It's a crime against humanity."

"Says the woman with air conditioning."

She gave him her best smug look. He unlocked the Audi and she watched as he maneuvered the baby carrier into the back and locked it in.

"I know, I know. I need a bigger car," he said as he extracted himself from the tight quarters.

"I didn't say a word."

"You didn't need to." He glanced up the street, then at her. "Thanks for listening."

"When are you going to tell them?"

"I don't know. Monday's not going to be good. But it's not like things will get any better."

"No. Not from their point of view anyway." She hesitated, then decided what the hell. "Is it okay if I hug you?"

He looked surprised. "Of course."

She stepped forward and wrapped her arms around him, pressing her cheek briefly to his. His arms banded her body, his palms flattening on her back. It felt indescribably good to be so close to him, to have her breasts pressed against his hardness, to feel the strength of his thighs against her own.

"You're a good man, Seth. Don't ever doubt that."

She gave him an extra squeeze, then released him, stepping away quickly. Just in case the temptation to do it all over again was too much for her.

"You're not so bad yourself," he said gruffly.

There were so many emotions in his eyes she had trouble separating them from each other. Desire and affection and frustration and resignation.

"Drive safely, okay?" she said, then she headed back to her apartment before she did something they'd both regret.

CHAPTER TEN

SETH WIPED HIS hands down the sides of his jeans for the fifth time in as many minutes. He glanced at the seat behind him, but knew that the moment he sat he'd want to be on his feet again. It gave him the illusion that he was doing something. That he was prepared for this day. For this moment.

Dennis and Melissa had been in with Lola for a while now, saying their final goodbyes. They hadn't asked if he wanted to stay while Lola's ventilator was switched off, and he hadn't offered, a fact which probably made him a coward, but so be it.

He didn't want to watch Lola die. He wanted to remember her at her laughing and playful best. He wanted good stories to tell Daisy when she asked about her mother, not sad ones.

And, more selfishly, he didn't want to carry around the memory of Lola's last, desperate minutes with him for the rest of his life.

He rolled his head, flexing his shoulders to try to relieve some of the tension. He'd dreamed of Lola last night, a disturbing dream full of regret, violence and remorse. At one point he'd been convinced that he'd killed her, although the precise cause of her death had been blurry, and he'd woken in a sweat, the sheets snaked around his legs, his heart banging at a million miles an hour.

He'd walked through the dark house to Daisy's room and stood at the end of her crib watching her sleep until the ugliness had faded from his mind. Only then did he go back to bed and risk sleeping again.

Movement caught the corner of his eye. Sure enough, Dennis ushered Melissa into the waiting area, both of them moving with slow caution, as though they were afraid of what might happen if they brushed against the wrong person or thing. They were both grey-faced, and it was only when he met their eyes that Seth understood that, despite everything the doctors had said and all the second and third opinions, they hadn't given up hoping until the very end.

They stopped in front of him, and Dennis took an audible breath. "Well. She's gone."

"It seems pointless to say it, but you know how sorry I am. I wish I could have done something to change this," Seth said.

"We know, son. We're all in the same boat," Dennis said.

Melissa made a small, sharp noise. "I might go outside, get some fresh air." She headed for the exit with a stiff, jerky stride.

Dennis stared after her, his face settling into the now-familiar lines of worry. "It's been tough on her, all of this. She and Lola never got along as well as they could have. I know she blames herself for Lola wanting to come here. She thinks that if they'd been better friends Lola would have stayed close…." He took off his glasses and contemplated the lenses, obviously trying to get a grip on his feelings.

"Lola was an adventurer. She would have always wanted to explore the world," Seth said.

"That's what I told Mel. Maybe it will sink in some-time."

Seth glanced toward Lola's room. "I should pay my respects."

Dennis nodded faintly. "Of course. You'll be want-ing to say your goodbyes." He put on his glasses, then glanced around helplessly.

"Why don't you go find Melissa and I'll meet you in the coffee shop?" Seth suggested.

"Good idea." Dennis grasped Seth's elbow. "And maybe we can talk. Get a few things settled."

Seth tensed. Damn. They wanted to talk about Daisy.

"If that's what you want." He'd been hoping to hold off longer, but if they wanted an answer now, he wasn't going to string them along.

Dennis headed off and Seth went to Lola's room. The space seemed incredibly quiet without the constant rush of the ventilator, and his steps grew heavy as he approached the bed. They must have removed her vari-ous drips and lines when they took her off the ventila-tor, because her arms were blessedly free. Her hands were curled loosely by her sides, her eyes closed. She was profoundly still and pale—there was no mistaking the fact she was gone.

"Jesus."

He gripped the end of the bed, his knuckles aching as he fought against an unexpected rush of anger. She'd barely started to live and now it was all over, thanks to bad lighting in a supermarket parking lot and a dis-tracted driver. It wasn't fair, it wasn't right, and there was no one who could do anything to change it.

He breathed through his nose and as quickly as his rage had arrived it was gone. He moved to the side of the bed, reaching for her hand. Her flesh was cool but not yet cold, and he held it between both of his, trying to think of what to say.

"I promise I'll always put Daisy first, no matter what. And I promise she will know who you are. I'll take her to visit your parents and meet your cousins, and I'll make sure she knows that you loved *Dr. Who* and chocolate licorice. I'll do whatever it takes to ensure she gets to see *The Wizard of the Oz* on the big screen, because you once said it was the highlight of your childhood, and I promise—"

He cleared his throat.

"I promise that I will love her enough for both of us." He lowered his head and pressed a kiss to her hand, not even trying to stop the tears that were rolling down his cheeks. "Thanks for your generosity and your fun and your laughter. We had some great times, Lola."

He remained with his head bowed for a few minutes, deliberately fixing memories in his mind. The time Lola had cooked him dinner and burned everything, so served him fish and chips from the local shop.

The time she'd laughed so hard watching an old Austin Powers movie that she'd had tears streaming down her face and was unable to talk for ten minutes.

The time when they'd seen Daisy move for the first time on the ultrasound and Lola had gripped his arm with unalloyed excitement.

"Goodbye, Lola," he said, giving her hand one last squeeze before turning away.

He went straight to the bathroom to get his head together. He washed his face, then braced his hands on the side of the sink and stared himself in the eye in the mirror. He was about to go break Dennis's and Melissa's hearts all over again.

But it wasn't as though he had a choice.

He found them at a corner table, both of them staring at untouched coffees. Melissa had been crying again, her eyes puffy and red.

He sat and rested his hands on his knees and took a deep breath. "There's no point beating around the bush, so I'll come right out and say it. I can't give Daisy up. I love her, and even if she might be better off with you, I reckon I can make a pretty good go of being a decent dad. And that's what I'm going to do."

Dennis nodded briefly, while Melissa closed her eyes as though he'd dealt an indescribably hard blow.

"I'm sorry. I know it's not what you want to hear. But she's my girl," Seth said.

Melissa spoke without opening her eyes. "I knew you were going to say no. I knew the moment we proposed it. But we couldn't not ask." She opened her eyes and there was so much unhappiness and grief in her that Seth had to fight to hold her gaze.

"I know," he said. "I promise that the moment she's old enough, we'll be on a plane to come visit. And you'll always be welcome here. Always."

"That's good to hear. Good to hear," Dennis said. Then his chin wobbled, his face crumpled and he lost it, tucking his head into his chest as he sobbed, his shoulders shuddering.

Melissa half rose out of her chair, wrapping her arms awkwardly around her husband, her own face twisted with sadness. Never had Seth felt more helpless, more inarticulate, more useless.

Aware of how vastly inadequate the gesture was, he reached for the napkin dispenser on the next table and pulled a wad free, placing them in front of Dennis and Melissa.

An hour later, he dropped off the Browns at their hotel, sharing a wan smile with Melissa as she unfolded herself from the cramped backseat for what was most likely the last time.

"Let me know if there is anything more I can do," he said.

He knew they had already spoken to a funeral company, but they were strangers here and there were bound to be things they weren't clear on.

"We will. And thanks again, Seth," Melissa said.

She surprised him then by taking his hand. "I won't lie, when I first heard about you and the baby, I cursed your name. I really did. Being a single mum was the last thing we wanted for our girl, especially on the other side of the world. But you've been wonderful, standing by Lola. And now, all of this... I want you to know that Dennis and I will always remember the kindness you've shown us."

"You won't have to remember. Daisy and I are going to be bugging you for a while yet," Seth said. "You'll be sick of the sight of us one day, I promise."

"That sounds just fine to me," she said.

Seth waited until they'd disappeared into the foyer before climbing into the car. Jodie was looking after Daisy for him and he headed home, aware she had her own life to get to.

It had been a tough few weeks, and more often than not he'd felt as though he was staggering from one near mistake to the next. All the decisions with Daisy, trying to do the right thing by the Browns, the constant siren's song of his desire for Vivian...

He was exhausted. The thought of crawling into his bed and pulling the duvet over his head had never been more appealing. Or maybe crawling into the bottom of a bottle of something twenty-proof and wicked, something that would help him forget for a few precious hours.

Neither option was really viable, however, so he put on a brave face for Jodie and took what solace he could from holding Daisy and breathing in her special smell, absorbing her warmth.

Jodie left and he found himself picking up his phone and scrolling through his contact list until he found Vivian's number. The need to call her, to hear her voice, to talk to her, was so powerful it scared him a little. He didn't know why or how, but his gut told him that she could make things better. Or, more accurately, that she could make *him* better.

He'd known her for ten years, and he'd wanted her, more or less, for that entire time. He'd never really seen her, though. Not the real her. He'd been too busy being the cool guy, Mr. No Strings. Too busy chasing dreams and avoiding growing up.

He'd seen her now, though, and he understood that she was far, far more than a sassy mouth and a sexy body. She was warm, smart, loving. She was generous. She was sweet.

And she was impossible, because his life had imploded and because he liked her too much to inflict himself and his shitty romantic track record on her. Vivian deserved more than a guy struggling to keep his head above water while he attempted to join the adult world.

He stared at her number for a long time, his thumb hovering over the call button. He didn't trust himself to speak to her and not ask her to come over or if he could come to her. And if he did that, he didn't trust himself not to reach out for something that he knew he shouldn't even try to take.

He settled for sending a simple text:

She's gone.

What Vivian chose to do with it was up to her.

VIVIAN HAD JUST stepped out of the shower after her first Pilates class in months when her phone chimed receipt of a text. She blotted her face and hair dry, then picked up her phone to make sure that it wasn't one of her designers with an emergency.

Seth's message sat on the screen, stark and small:

She's gone.

For a moment Vivian couldn't breathe, and she sank onto the closed lid of the toilet and hugged her damp towel to herself, overwhelmed with grief for a young woman she'd never had the privilege of meeting. There were so many layers of sadness to this small, very human tragedy. Daisy losing her mother. Dennis and Melissa losing their daughter. Seth losing the helpmate who had made plans for their child.

Water trickled down her back, and she shook off her introspection and pushed to her feet. Moving with brisk efficiency, she finished drying before running a comb through her hair and walking into her bedroom. Five minutes later she was dressed and on her way out the door.

She stopped at the same liquor shop as the last time and bought the biggest bottle of tequila she could find, then did a run through the nearby supermarket to grab fresh limes and some groceries.

Barely forty minutes after Seth's text had arrived, she was on his doorstep, pressing the doorbell. The moment she saw his face she knew she'd been right to come. His eyes were flat, devoid of their usual spark, and twin lines bracketed his mouth.

"I have tequila," she said, brushing past him. "Hope you've got your drinking pants on."

She made it all the way to the kitchen and was unpacking groceries before he appeared.

"I'm not sure babies and hangovers are the best combination," he said.

"So we drink until we have to stop. I'm sure we can both live with that. I'm making you dinner, too, by the way. Fajitas, Vivian-style. Wait till you try my pineapple-and-lime salsa." She chatted as she unloaded the bags and searched for a cutting board and sharp knife.

"In the drawer," Seth said, joining her behind the counter and sliding open the drawer in question. He passed her a cutting board, but when she tried to take it, retained his grip.

"You didn't need to come over," he said, his voice low and gravelly.

Only then did she understand that he'd wanted her to, but had been afraid—or unwilling—to ask.

"Yes, I did." She pulled the board free and began slicing the chicken breast into thin strips. "You can dice the pineapple for me. I need it really small."

She glanced at him, and found him watching her, a pensive expression on his face. Unable to stop herself, she set down the knife and slipped her arm around his waist, resting her cheek against his shoulder as she gave him a quick squeeze.

"It's going to be all right, Seth."

She felt his belly muscles tense beneath her hand at the same time that she registered her own reaction to his closeness, and slipped her arm free again.

"You want me to cut up the whole pineapple?" he asked, grabbing another cutting board.

"Half should do. Then you can have a go at this onion." She passed him one of the purple Spanish variety.

"I don't know how, but I forgot how bossy you can be," he said conversationally, slicing the skin off the pineapple.

"I'll do my best to give you a refresher course."

The repartee continued as they worked, the conversation moving from Daisy's health to the security changes Seth was making at the bar. Neither of them mentioned Lola, but they didn't need to.

Soon the kitchen was full of the smell of spices as the chicken cooked. She added the finishing touches to her salsa before shredding lettuce and dicing the flesh of an avocado. The baby monitor came to life as she was ready to serve, and he gave her a rueful look.

"She has a food proximity detector. The moment it looks as though I might get a hot meal, she creates a distraction."

"Let's see if we can outsmart her. This can wait while you take care of her," Vivian said easily.

He disappeared and returned with a red-faced little girl, her gummy mouth stretched wide as she cried.

"Listen to those lungs," Vivian said with a grin.

Seth smiled for the first time since she'd arrived. "She can pump out the decibels, that's for sure."

He paced, jiggling Daisy, murmuring to her under his breath to try to soothe her. Slowly Daisy calmed, and Seth brought in her carrier and nestled her into it while Vivian set the food on the table.

"This is great," Seth said after swallowing the first bite of the tortilla he'd assembled.

"That salsa is totally the business, right?"

"The mint works really well with the pineapple."

"I know. I'm a genius."

Seth's eyes were laughing at her as he took another bite, and something inside her relaxed. He was okay. Sad, exhausted and momentarily depleted, but okay.

Daisy let it be known that she wanted to be fed as they finished eating, and Vivian cleaned up while Seth made a bottle with endearing caution, double-checking his measures and the temperature of the liquid before offering it to his daughter. Daisy was drowsy and content by the time he took her to her room to change her nappy, then put her in the crib.

"She should stay down for a few hours now," he said. "At least, that's the routine she's been lulling me into. No doubt she's still got a few tricks up her sleeve."

He had a mark on his jeans, and his shirt was half tucked in, half out, and his hair mussed, yet Vivian was almost certain he'd never been sexier or more approachable. The pull she felt toward him was so powerful she gripped the edge of the counter to remind herself of why she was here.

For Seth and Daisy, not for herself.

"How's your liver?" she asked as she reached for the tequila bottle.

"I own a bar, remember?" There was a good measure of his old cockiness in his response.

"Big talk, Anderson. Let's see you put your money where your mouth is."

"That doesn't even make sense. You bought the tequila, remember?"

"You know what I mean."

She used a cutting board as a tray, taking the limes, a small paring knife, the salt shaker and a couple of shot glasses she'd found to the table. She then grabbed the tequila and poured them healthy shots.

Licking the skin between her thumb and forefinger, she sprinkled salt on the damp spot and placed a lime wedge at the ready. She waited until Seth had done the same before she lifted her shot glass.

"To Lola," she said solemnly.

Grief raced across Seth's face like a cloud across the sun. Then he raised his own glass. "To Lola."

They both licked their hands before knocking back the tequila and sucking on their lime wedges. Vivian inhaled sharply as the alcohol seared its way down her throat to her belly.

"Oh, man, I hate tequila," Seth said.

"I know. You could so strip marine varnish with this stuff. Brutal." She poured them a second shot as she spoke, and Seth reached for the salt.

"Gives the worst hangovers, too," he said.

"No way. Nothing is worse than a champagne hangover."

"Talk to me tomorrow," he said knowingly.

They both threw back their second shots, Seth wincing as though he'd swallowed acid.

"Feeling alive yet?" she asked him.

He nodded, reaching for his lime wedge to suck more juice into his mouth. "Getting there."

She poured them a third shot but didn't immediately pass it to him. "Tell me about Lola."

He gave her a look. "You really want to do this?"

"That's why I'm here." She could already feel the warm alcohol glow snaking through her body, making her limbs that little bit heavier.

He shifted the salt shaker between his hands a few times. "What do you want to know?"

"Anything and everything you want to tell me. The floor is yours." She made a dramatic gesture.

"Someone's a cheap drunk."

"I'm a fast starter, but I'm good for the long haul," she assured him.

Seth drank the third shot without salt and lime. He hissed the moment he'd swallowed, shaking his head from side to side as though he was in pain. Then he took a deep breath.

"Okay. Lola."

He told her about the night they'd met, how she'd come into the bar with friends from work and spent the night flirting with him. He'd written her off as just another pretty girl out for a fun night, but then she'd turned up the following night, and the night after that.

"Finally she asked me when I was going to take the hint," he said. "And I asked her how old she was. She winked at me and said she was old enough to know better but young enough to learn, and then she laughed…."

"And you were gone," Vivian finished for him.

She'd seen pictures of Lola in the town house the night she and Seth had gone looking for the Browns' contact details. Lola had been blonde and fair-skinned, with big, laughing eyes and the kind of well-rounded body that filled men's magazines. A pretty difficult proposition for most red-blooded men to turn down.

"She was fun. That was the thing about Lola. She knew how to have a good time. Knew how to make the most of situations and always find the good no matter how difficult it might be. Funny how I forgot all of that as her due date got closer and closer." Seth's mouth flattened into a straight line.

"Having a baby is stressful stuff, even when you're married and theoretically on the same page," she said.

"We weren't even in the same book. She wanted to do a water birth at home, even though all the research was against first-time mothers not having access to medical intervention if needed. We argued about it for months, and then the baby was a breech birth so all of that went out the window. Even then she was convinced that the baby would sort itself out." He stared off into the distance. "A few days before the accident, she missed a doctor's appointment and we fought about that, too. She thought I didn't respect her, and in a way, she was right. I worried about what would happen when the baby came along, how two people with not much in common would come together enough to get it right."

He said it like a confession, laying his guilt at her feet. She poured another round.

"Being worried about the future didn't make the accident happen, Seth."

"I know that." His response was knee-jerk fast.

"Sure you do." She knocked back her shot, aware that the world was becoming pleasantly fuzzy at the edges. They'd have to stop drinking soon because of Daisy, but for the moment Vivian felt no pain.

"It was an accident. The last thing I'd ever wish on anyone," he said.

"I know."

"I'd rather have her here, fighting with me every day than for things to be the way they are."

"I believe you, Seth. Do you?"

He stared at her, his mouth half-open in automatic denial. Then his shoulders slumped and he lifted a hand to his eyes.

"There were times when I wished this whole thing would go away—Lola, the baby, all of it. I wanted my life the way it was before it got complicated." He let his hand fall and looked at her, clearly waiting for her condemnation.

"Congratulations, you're officially human. And tempting as it is to believe in magical thinking, as far I know, your secret thoughts do not rule the world. If so, there'd be a hell of a lot more women walking around in bikinis and miniskirts."

His mouth crept up on one side, reluctantly amused by her words. "Sorry, I forgot who I was talking to for a minute there."

"A dangerous mistake."

"Tell me about it."

She eased off her shoes and lifted one leg up, propping her heel on the edge of the chair and wrapping her arms around her knee. "Have you spoken to the Browns about Daisy yet?"

He nodded.

"How did they take it?"

"About as well as you'd expect. Although Melissa said she knew I'd never say yes. Wish she would have told me that—would have saved me a trip to your place the other night."

She gave his forearm a little shake. "Genuinely thinking about what they were asking is proof that you're a good person, Seth. An asshole wouldn't have even considered their offer, but you did because you want what's best for Daisy."

"There was a fair dose of what's best for Seth in that decision, too," he said, his tone self-deprecating. "Let's not make me a saint just yet."

"Not exactly a high risk, but thanks for the warning."

His gaze went to his arm and she realized she was still touching him. She snatched her hand away. "Sorry."

"Don't be. I like it when you touch me." He paused. "Sorry. Guess us and tequila isn't the safest mix in the world."

"No."

And yet she couldn't have stayed away tonight if her life depended on it. It would have hurt something inside her to think of him rattling around this house on his own, just Daisy and his grief for company.

"Maybe I should make some coffee," he said.

"Probably a good idea."

"Tell me about your day. Especially if it didn't involve hospitals and deathbeds."

"You're in luck. We did a lingerie shoot for a boutique brand that's launching a national campaign."

She'd downloaded a few shots onto her iPad and she showed him what she and Robin had come up with—a circus theme, complete with trapeze swings and a mistress of ceremonies with a bullwhip and wicked six-inch stiletto heels. They drank their coffee, then Daisy stirred and Seth went to see to her. He returned with a wide-awake baby in his arms.

"She's not going to just nod off again," he said.

"Does that mean I get to have a cuddle?"

He handed Daisy over and they went into the living room, each of them laying claim to a couch and stretching out along its length. Vivian tucked Daisy into the crook of her elbow and listened to Seth talk about his expansion plans for the bar while she soothed a hand over Daisy's head and marveled at how soft her skin was.

Vivian wasn't sure when she dozed off or how long she was asleep, but she woke with a start, jerking against the cushions when she realized Seth was leaning over her.

"I'm going to feed Daisy," he said quietly. "Don't get up."

He lifted Daisy and Vivian blinked dazedly. The lights were dim, and she couldn't remember them being that way earlier. Seth must have turned them down after she'd fallen asleep, which suggested she'd been out for a while.

Awesome company she was, flaking out at the first opportunity. She sat up, glancing at the other couch where Seth was coaxing Daisy to take the bottle.

"She's always slow with nighttime feeds," he said when he noticed her watching.

"Sorry I fell asleep. I guess I'm more of a lightweight than I thought I was."

"I conked out, too. Best hour's sleep of my life." He smiled slightly, and there was something so warm, so small and intimate about the moment, that her chest became oddly tight, as though someone held her too firmly.

"Well, I won't feel so guilty if it was a group activity."

"I'm happy to work off the assumption that this is a guilt-free zone tonight," he said.

She ran a hand over her hair, sure she must be rumpled and mussed, aware that she was gasping for a drink.

"I'm going to grab some water. Do you want one?" She stood so fast that the floor wobbled beneath her feet and she put a hand on the couch for balance.

"You all right there?" Seth asked, looking more than a little amused.

"I lost my balance. That's all." Still, she moved cautiously as she walked into the kitchen, and had to admit that she felt decidedly fuzzy.

So much for calling it a night and heading home, then. She'd either have to phone for a cab or crash on the couch for a while. It probably would have been wise to consider that fact before she had those last couple of shots.

She poured a glass of water from the tap and gulped it down, then got another for Seth and took it to the living room, even though he hadn't said if he wanted one or not.

"Thanks," he said, his fingers warm on hers as she passed him the glass.

She smoothed her hands over the seat of her pants, suddenly nervous. "Listen, I know it's late, but I'm not sure I'm okay to drive yet. So I might crash on the couch for a little while, if that's all right with you."

"I got some sheets out for you earlier," he said, and she followed his gaze to where a set of sheets and a pillow sat on the armchair, ready to be deployed.

"Well. You're a step ahead of me," she said.

"It's an expensive taxi trip to the city, and I'm betting you need your car tomorrow for work."

"I do. We've got lots on. A ton of stuff, actually."

"Then we're sorted."

Daisy made a sound and he glanced at her, reaching for the corner of the towel he was using as a makeshift bib to wipe at the formula trickling down her cheek. Vivian stared at his head, unable to stop herself from tracing the line of his neck where it disappeared beneath the collar of his shirt. He had lovely shoulders, square and well-muscled.

Strong.

He glanced up and caught her looking, and she quickly turned away, a warm flush of awareness rushing up her chest and into her face.

"I'll just make this bed up," she muttered, busying herself tucking the sheets into the couch cushions.

That didn't take nearly long enough, and she was forced to watch as Daisy drank the last dregs.

"She's feeding well," she said inanely.

"She is, once she gets started." He lifted Daisy and lay her gently against his shoulder, supporting her while he patted her back gently. After a few seconds Daisy produced a handful of audible burps, causing both Vivian and Seth to smile.

"To think, I'm going to have to reprimand her for doing that in public in a few years' time," he said.

"It does seem the height of hypocrisy."

Daisy had again been reduced to dozy complacence by a full belly, and Seth rose.

"I'll go get her settled."

She waved him off. "I'm all sorted here. You head off to bed. And don't worry if I'm not here in the morning—I'll probably sneak out as soon as I feel up to driving."

"You're welcome to stay if you want to."

"I know."

He eyed her for a moment, his expression unreadable in the dim light. "I'm not going to sleepwalk, if that's what you're worried about."

"I'm not worried." Not about him anyway. Herself— her own willpower—she wasn't so sure about.

"Okay. Good night, then."

"Good night."

He hesitated before exiting, and she knew he'd considered kissing her and then abandoned the idea.

Wise man. A dim room, several shots of tequila and the two of them were about as volatile a mixture as she could think of. Retreat was the only sensible option.

She heard him walk to Daisy's room, then the sound of him talking to her as he changed her diaper. After a few minutes, the tinkling music of a mobile filtered into the room.

She sighed, then unbuttoned her pants. Stepping out of them, she folded them neatly and set them on the coffee table before reaching beneath her top to unclasp her bra. It joined her pants, and she padded across the room to turn off the light before slipping between the sheets.

It wasn't until she settled against the pillow that she realized she could hear the sound of running water. At first she thought it was simply Seth brushing his teeth, but it went on too long and it hit her that he was having a shower.

In an instant, her head was filled with X-rated images. Seth naked beneath the jets, water glistening on his hard body. Seth rubbing soap over his chest, his belly, his thighs....

She groaned, rolling onto her belly and pushing her face into the pillow as she tried to clear the images from her mind.

She had a big day tomorrow. She and Robin were shooting a huge spread for Fashion Week in a couple of days and she wanted to review everything to ensure there would be no surprises. She needed to—

The water stopped. Good. No more pictures of naked, wet Seth in her head. He'd be drying himself now, running the towel down his muscular legs, brushing it across that perfect, hard ass....

"For Pete's sake," she said, her voice rough with desperation.

She flopped onto her back, conscious that her breathing was shallow and that her sex was hot and wet with need.

And Seth wasn't even in the same room.

"This is crazy."

It was, because she'd been so sure that this feeling, this connection between them, would fade or weaken with time and familiarity. Instead, it was getting worse because it wasn't just about sex anymore.

She was intensely aware of the thrum of arousal in her blood and of the insidious little voice in her head that was whispering for her to go to him and give them what they both wanted. What they both needed.

After all, she'd tried to rationalize herself out of her feelings so many times she'd lost count—and yet she'd still wound up here, horny and needy on Seth's couch, desperate for his touch.

This *thing* between them wasn't going away anytime soon. It had survived ten years, the tyranny of distance and multiple partners on both sides. It was as persistent and irresistible as an itch beneath her skin. She couldn't ignore it, try as she might, even though there were so many reasons for her to do so.

She should call a taxi. She should do it now, while her willpower was still strong and the sensible part of her brain was still in charge.

"For God's sake, Vivian, who are you kidding?"

She flung back the sheet. One hand extended for balance, she made her way through the darkened living room to the hallway. Seth's door was ajar at the far end, and she walked toward it, aware of the almost sickening lurch of excitement in her belly. Her heart was pounding so violently she was sure her chest was vibrating.

She reached the door, the paint cool against the fingertips of her extended hand. She eased it open, her gaze going to the bed. Pale light filtered through a gap in the curtains and she could see Seth was lying on his back, the sheet around his waist, his arms behind his head. She knew without asking that he'd been fighting the exact same battle she had and that if she slid her hand beneath the covers he would be as hard for her as she was wet for him. His head turned toward her as she walked toward the bed.

"Vivian."

She pulled her tank top over her head. Then she

pushed her panties down her legs, leaving both items abandoned on the carpet as she climbed into his bed.

At last.

CHAPTER ELEVEN

SETH WENT VERY still as the bed dipped and Vivian slipped beneath the sheet.

"Are we sure this is a good idea?" he asked, despite the fact that he was hard and getting harder by the second. There had been a significant quantity of tequila consumed tonight, and as much as he wanted this to happen, he was all too well aware that Vivian had been adamantly against it until this second.

"Shut up before I realize what a mistake this is."

Her hand found his chest, then a smooth leg slid over his hips, and the next thing he knew she was straddling him and kissing him, her mouth hot and sweet. Reason flew out the window along with restraint as he wrapped his arms around her, both hands cupping the round curves of her ass as he pulled her closer, his tongue warring with hers, his body arching off the bed as he tried to get closer.

He'd been dreaming about this for ten years. Vivian Walker, naked, in his bed.

She moaned as he flexed his hips, grinding his erection against her, his hands massaging her in time with his thrusts.

"Yes. Please," she said, one hand sliding down his belly and wrapping around his erection. She stroked him once, twice, and then tilted her hips, rubbing herself against his hardness. It wasn't until he felt himself notch into place that he realized what she intended and he caught her hips a split second before she took him inside.

"What's wrong? Oh, right. Condom. Hurry up."

He smiled in the darkness. Trust Vivian to be bossy in bed, as well.

"Yeah, condom. Also, slow down a little. No one's on the clock here, baby."

"Are you kidding me? It's been ten years, Seth."

"I know. You have no idea how many fantasies I've got to live up to."

He slid his hands up and around her rib cage as he spoke, glorying in the smooth silk of her skin. Her breasts filled his palms, and she gave a gratifying little shiver as he found her nipples with his thumbs.

"These breasts, for example. I have big plans for these breasts," he said, pinching her taut nipples between his thumb and forefinger, squeezing until she shivered again. "I'm going to suck on them till you beg me to stop."

"Never going to happen." She arched her back, pushing her breasts more firmly into his hands.

He loved the way she owned her desire, the way she unabashedly went after what she wanted.

"Then I'm going to make you come with my mouth, until you're wet and desperate for me to be inside you."

"I dare you," she said, circling her hips, rubbing the slick heart of herself against him.

"And only then am I going to come inside you and make you fly all over again," he promised her.

"All I'm hearing is a lot of talk, but I'm not seeing a lot of action."

She gave a squeak of surprise as he twisted, rolling her across the bed so that their positions were reversed and he was on top of her.

In charge.

He stared at her face, framed by her strawberry-blond hair, her pale skin flushed with desire. Her eyes glinted with excitement in the dim light.

"Brace yourself," he said.

Then he cupped her breasts, plumping them deliciously, and surveyed the bounty laid before him. Creamy flesh, rounded and full, topped by taut peaks.

Oh, yeah.

He lowered his head, pulling one nipple into his mouth. Her body bucked beneath him as he sucked hard, his other hand busy teasing and stroking her left breast. She made an inarticulate noise and he softened his mouth before biting her ever so gently. Her hands found his head, her fingers combing into his hair as she held him in place, guaranteeing her pleasure in the crudest possible way.

The need to be inside her built with every wriggle of her body against his, every moan, every clutch of her hands. But he'd promised and intended to deliver.

He kissed and sucked and licked her breasts until she was quivering with need, then he made his way down her trembling belly to her thighs.

"Oh, yes," she whispered as he pushed them apart, unable to resist stroking a finger along her slick heat.

"How many times have you thought about me doing this to you?" He breathed in her musky smell.

"Too many."

He grinned, ridiculously pleased by the confirmation of what he'd always instinctively known. Then he lowered his head and kissed her, sending his tongue deep into her folds. She tasted as good as she smelled and he grew harder still as he imagined how it would feel sliding inside her, feeling the tight grip of all this heat around him.

He settled into a rhythm, sucking and licking where she needed him most while he traced her lips and entrance with his finger. Only when she was panting, her fingers digging into his shoulders, did he slip a finger inside her. Instantly she clenched around him, her hips lifting off the bed as she came with a shudder, his name on her lips.

He waited until the tremors subsided before kissing his way up her body, then reaching into the drawer of the bedside table. He sat back on his heels as he opened the foil packet, and Vivian propped herself up on her elbows, her flushed face avid as she watched him stroke the latex onto his erection. He took his time, stroking it down the shaft, watching the way her eyes followed the movement, loving the greedy way she licked her lips.

He moved over her, not saying a word, holding her gaze as he gripped himself and found her entrance. She lifted her hips to take him, and he slid in.

Yes.

He remembered this. How good she felt. How right. How on earth had he survived ten years without doing this again?

He started to move, needing to thrust, needing to make her his. She wrapped a leg around his hips and rode with him, her eyes slitted, her breath coming in ragged pants. He felt the tension rising inside her, and he slipped his hands beneath her, lifting her into his thrusts, driving deeper and harder.

She came silently, her face turned away, her chest bowing off the bed. The feel of her muscles pulsing around him pushed him over and he was gone, lost in the most necessary, essential climax of his life.

When he came back down to earth, he was lying on top of her, his face pressed into her neck, one hand still possessively gripping her backside.

"Sorry," he murmured, worried he'd been too heavy for her.

"You should be," she said as he lifted himself on his arms. "I think you ruined me for all other men."

He couldn't help but laugh at her chagrined, slightly dazed expression.

"Then my work here is done," he said.

He rolled to the side of the bed and went into the en suite to take care of the condom. While he was in there, he heard the thin wail of Daisy crying, and he washed his hands and hurried into the bedroom.

"Don't go anywhere," he said, stopping to pull on a pair of boxer briefs.

Vivian didn't say a word. His smile was grim as he entered his daughter's room. He would trust Vivian to have his back in a million different ways, but he had no idea if she would still be in his bed after he'd settled Daisy. It hadn't escaped his attention that, until tonight, Vivian had been opposed to sleeping with him. He knew she had her reasons, that the odds were against this being anything other than a mistake…yet he'd do it again in a heartbeat. In fact, he hoped to do it as soon as he possibly could.

They had ten years to make up for, after all. He hadn't even come close to satisfying his need for her.

Daisy's crying became more strident as he leaned

over the crib to pick her up. A quick check confirmed her diaper needed changing.

He couldn't stop himself from glancing toward the door as he worked, half expecting to see Vivian making her way to the couch. There was no sign of her, however, and he allowed himself to hope. Maybe she'd still be in his bed when he returned.

He didn't allow himself to want anything more than that. Not tonight anyway.

VIVIAN LAY ON her side and breathed in the smell of Seth. She'd never met a man who smelled so good to her. It wasn't simply his choice of aftershave or shampoo or deodorant. It was the essence of him, and she was surrounded by it.

She told herself that was why she was finding it so hard to make herself get dressed so she could go home. Even in the privacy of her own mind it was an unconvincing, hollow argument.

She couldn't make herself leave Seth's bed because she didn't want it to be over yet. Because it had been so good, and she was so greedy, and he was so lovely.

So lovely.

Intense, generous, perceptive, wonderfully instinctive. And, God help her, she wanted more.

She could hear Daisy crying, and she imagined Seth pacing with her, soothing her, the same infinitely patient, compassionate look on his face that she'd witnessed every time he'd comforted his child.

She experienced the now-familiar tightness in her chest and acknowledged she was in big trouble.

And still she didn't leave his bed.

She'd drifted into a doze when she felt the mattress

shift beneath his weight. She smiled as his hand slid over her waist, hooking around her body and pulling her close. She opened her eyes and found his head on the pillow, mere inches away.

"She's off again?" she asked drowsily.

"She is."

He slid his hand along her hip and down her thigh, the warm glide of his skin on hers sending an electric thrill through her body. He stopped when he reached her knee, his fingers stroking the sensitive skin behind it before cupping her calf and encouraging her to bend her knee and hook her leg over his hips. She let him do as he pleased, confident that she would be happy to follow wherever he led, and that every step of the way would be filled with pleasure.

His gaze was heated and lazy as he scanned her face, his focus finally coming to rest on her mouth. She smiled, knowing he was going to kiss her, appreciating that he was making her wait for it. She loved the anticipation, the tease of it.

He surprised her then, his hand stroking up her leg and brushing over her backside before slipping between her thighs. She swallowed a rush of need as his fingers ever so delicately began to explore her folds, his touch as gentle and insistent as a whisper.

Still he held back from kissing her, and with every second that passed, with every tender, subtle stroke between her thighs, she wanted it more and more. Wanted to taste him, wanted him to invade her, wanted the connection and the uncompromising intimacy of the act of joining her mouth with his. She stirred, aware of the excitement rising within her, of how wet she was, of how much more she wanted, and yet savoring the ride. Trusting him to give her more pleasure than she could handle.

She couldn't stop herself from moaning when he slipped a finger inside her, then another, taunting her with the satisfaction of being full before withdrawing and returning to his delicate ministrations. She could feel her heart pounding, could feel the echo of that beat between her thighs where an insistent, almost painful ache of arousal was building.

Finally she couldn't stand it another second, and she closed the distance between them, pressing her mouth to his. He tasted like desire, and suddenly her need was an undeniable, take-no-prisoners thing and she pushed him onto his back and climbed on top, reaching for a condom. She sheathed him with shaking hands, then slid onto him with clumsy haste.

"Seth," she groaned, momentarily swept away by how good he felt inside her.

His hands smoothed over her hips and onto her belly before cupping her breasts. She flexed her hips and thighs and felt the thick, hard glide of him as she al-most—but not quite—slid off him. She tantalized them both with the potential, then plunged down onto him, biting her lip to stop herself from crying out.

It felt so good. So full. So hard and slick and right.

Seth arched off the bed, pulling a nipple into his mouth, the suction of his mouth so fierce, so forceful, it almost hurt.

Almost.

Something inside her slipped its leash, and she gave up any pretense of control as she moved over him, grinding herself against him with every stroke, bring-ing them to the brink of withdrawal before taking him deep yet again. She got lost behind her closed eyes, lost in a world of sensation and building tension. Her breath was a hot rasp in her lungs, sweat prickled beneath her armpits, her body shuddered with the strength of her own desire.

And then it hit her, tightening her body hard around his as pleasure rocketed through her. She felt Seth come seconds after her own release, heard the primitive grunt as he gripped her hips and held himself deep inside her. She was boneless, flopping down onto his chest. She lay there for what felt like minutes, the part of her that was still joined to him throbbing with tiny pleasurable aftershocks, her breathing gradually slowing. He smoothed his hands over her back, butt and thighs, his touch soothing now instead of arousing, and exactly what she needed.

Eventually she stirred, sliding off him and rolling onto her back beside him. She felt…depleted. And wholly satisfied. And utterly at peace with herself, with Seth, with the moment.

She wasn't silly enough to think the feeling would last, but she would enjoy it while it did. Life was short, after all.

After a while, Seth rolled onto his side to take care of the condom before sliding an arm around her and pressing a kiss to her shoulder.

"Stay the night," he said simply.

"So you can do that to me all over again?"

"Among other things."

"Okay."

He pressed another kiss to her shoulder, then pulled the sheet over them. She lay in the dark, listening to his steady breathing, wondering at herself. It was one thing to tumble into something unexpectedly, but to walk in with her eyes wide open—that took a special form of recklessness.

His hand tightened against her side, drawing her closer, and she was powerless against the crazy sense of warm belonging that washed over her.

Silly girl, Vivian.

She probably was. But it was too late now, she might as well enjoy it while she could.

SETH WOKE TO find a slim arm slung over his chest and a knee nudging his thigh. The understanding that Vivian was still there, in his bed, made him smile faintly. He'd had to get up twice more for Daisy during the night, and both times he'd half expected Vivian to announce she had to go. Yet both times she'd simply curled into his side when he'd returned, asking if Daisy was okay before drifting off.

Now, he turned to look at her, relishing the chance to observe her without being observed himself. Any makeup she'd been wearing had long since worn off and he could see the dusting of freckles across her small nose. Her eyebrows were delicately arched, with subtle peaks that hinted at her mischievous sense of humor. Her mouth was a soft blush pink, the bottom lip full, the top lip deeply bowed.

Her hair was tangled, the strawberry-blond color muted in the morning light.

God, she was beautiful. And it wasn't just about the way her features were arranged. She was beautiful because she was funny and caring, smart and sexy. A woman of substance. He wanted her closer, so he eased his arm beneath her shoulders, encouraging her head onto his chest. She made sleepy noises, then snuggled in and it occurred to him that if the feeling he was experiencing right now was anything like the way his brother felt when he woke with Jodie every morning, then he could totally understand why a man might choose to get married.

It was such an alien, out-of-left-field thought that he tensed, more than a little freaked out by his own thoughts. They'd had one night together, after all.

"What's wrong?" Vivian lifted her head, blinking herself to wakefulness. "Is Daisy okay?"

"She's fine. I remembered something, that's all."

She looked at him, her hair wonky on one side, a crease on her cheek from the pillow, and the this-is-right feeling hit him all over again. He really liked this woman. So much so that it scared him a little.

"What time is it?" she asked, leaning across him to check the bedside clock.

"Just after six." He closed his eyes briefly as her breast brushed his arm. Man, but she turned him on.

"So, Seth…" She smoothed a palm onto his chest, down his belly. "Would you call yourself a morning person? Because I definitely am," she purred.

Her hand closed around his rock-hard erection, and she smiled a lazy, cat-that-ate-the-cream smile. "I guess you are."

He wasn't about to tell her he was an anytime-of-day person when it came to her. Not yet anyway. He needed to get his head around the thoughts and feelings bombarding him right now. Like the fact that if she hadn't wanted sex, he would have been happy to simply hold her, and the anxiety that was nagging at him as it occurred to him that once she left his bed, he had no idea when he'd see her again.

He never worried about stuff like that. In fact, he was usually the king of take-it-as-it-comes. Hell, he'd practically invented the concept.

She stroked her hand along his shaft, slipping her leg over his as she nuzzled his neck and shoulder.

"You might have to be gentle with me," she said. "Last night was pretty full-on. But it seems like a crying shame to let this go to waste."

She stroked him again, and he was powerless to stop himself from rolling toward her and kissing her. Their tongues met and teased, mimicking what she was doing with her hand. He eased her thighs apart and went on an exploratory expedition of his own.

She was already swollen and wet for him, and her hips lifted into his touch, encouraging him wordlessly. The thought of being inside her was urgent, essential, and he turned to grab a condom. No less than four foil packets littered his bedroom floor—a new record, he was pretty sure. If Vivian was willing to give him another hour or two, he would be happy to make it five.

She was that hot, and he was that hot for her.

He pushed inside her, and she sighed her pleasure, wrapping her legs around his hips. He ducked his head to tongue her breasts, rasping his morning bristle across them before teasing her tight, pink nipples to even greater hardness. She moaned her encouragement, her hands clenched on his backside, her hips undulating.

She felt so good, he couldn't stop the climax speeding toward him and he didn't try. Instead, he reached between their bodies, finding her with his fingers and making sure that she came with him when the world dropped away.

For long seconds they hung together, wordless, breathless, then they crashed to earth to the sound of a phone ringing and an almost simultaneous burst of crying from the baby monitor.

"My phone," Vivian said, her eyes popping open.

"My baby," he said.

They rolled away from each other, and Seth had the very gratifying experience of watching Vivian half walk, half run out his bedroom in the buff as she went in search of her phone.

He pulled on the boxer briefs he'd abandoned last night and went to Daisy, finding her grasping at the air and turning her head from side to side as she complained, a sure sign that she was hungry.

"Poor baby. It's been at least three hours. You must be starving," he said wryly as he checked her diaper before taking her into the kitchen to make up a bottle. Vivian was in the living room, talking quietly but urgently as she stood with one arm braced across her middle, a frown on her face.

Something was wrong, obviously. He divided his attention between Vivian, the baby and the bottle, but Vivian still caught him unawares when she appeared in the kitchen with her clothes bunched to her chest.

"I need to go." She headed for the bedroom, and he tested the bottle to ensure it was the right temperature before following her, Daisy in his arms.

"What's wrong?"

Vivian already had her panties on and was doing up her bra, her movements brisk. "One of my designers had a flood overnight. Some guy on the floor above is a photographer, and he forgot to turn off a tap or something. I don't know the details, but the short story is that the rack of clothes she had picked out for me is toast. Which means half my shoot for tomorrow has disappeared."

"Can you find replacements? Another designer?"

She gave him a tight smile as she pulled on her trousers. "That's the plan. Except there's a lot of Fashion Week promotion going on right now and it'll be a stretch to find clothes that aren't already being covered. I booked this designer *months* ago."

She strode into the bathroom and turned on the water, quickly washing her face before running her damp hands through her hair.

"Is there anything I can do?"

He felt faintly ridiculous saying it, standing in his underwear while his newborn baby guzzled her bottle, but the urge to help was very real and very sincere.

Vivian flashed him a quick smile as she scooped up her tank top and pulled it over her head.

"Thanks, but it's going to be one of those days."

"Well, the offer's there if you need it. Even if it's just Daisy and me picking up stuff for you."

"You're sweet," she said, but he could see her mind was elsewhere. She glanced around, then strode out of the room. He trailed after her, watching as she shouldered her bag and checked she had her phone and wallet before heading for the door.

"Good luck," he said as she stepped out onto the porch.

"Thanks. I have a feeling I'm going to need it." She palmed her car keys. "You and Daisy have a good day."

"You, too."

She hesitated, then turned and started down the

stairs. It wasn't until he heard the sound of her car that he realized that he hadn't kissed her goodbye.

Better yet, he had no idea when he would see her again, or if last night had been the start of something, or a one-off, or something they were never to speak of again.

He knew what he wanted—more. More nights, more mornings, more Vivian. He was, of course, aware that his life was hardly conducive to romance right now, but that didn't change the way he felt.

He had no idea where Vivian stood on any of the above, however. She enjoyed sex with him, obviously. But she'd also referred to him as her "disaster waiting to happen."

It had smarted then, and it smarted now. Okay, sure, he didn't exactly have an unimpeachable record where other women were concerned. But other women were not Vivian.

Seth automatically reinserted the bottle into Daisy's mouth when she pushed it out as he mulled over his options. He could wait and see. Or he could take the initiative.

He'd pretty much been a wait-and-see guy all his life until he'd stumbled into the opportunity to buy the bar. Only then had he worked out that sometimes the world didn't come to you, you had to go to it. He'd learned to be unashamed in his pursuit of what his business needed. Maybe it was time to apply some of that hard-earned knowledge to his private life.

VIVIAN DROPPED BY her apartment on the way to the studio, ran through the shower, dressed in clean clothes and was in West Melbourne by 7:30 a.m. Typically she would be geared up to go if she had a shoot the following day—outfits bagged with accessories, look sheets pinned to each garment bag detailing every item that was in the bag, all of it waiting on a rack to be transferred to the van to transport to the location. She liked to be organized and well ahead of the game.

This time, though, she'd been forced to hold fire because the hero designer for this particular shoot had had supply issues with certain fabrics and the garments Vivian had specified had only come off the production line in the past few days. Hence the clothing still being on the designer's premises this morning instead of safely here, out of harm's way.

The first thing she did when she arrived was to fire up her computer, then she turned to her filing cabinet and started pulling look books—a fancy term for collection catalogues—from her favorite designers. Tomorrow's shoot was for a supplement that would be inserted in all the daily newspapers in Melbourne and Sydney to celebrate Fashion Week. Whoever she found to replace the damaged stock needed to be local, with a big enough profile and distribution to be relevant, and to have stock available in the size of her models. Last, but not least, the substitutions needed to be approved by the fashion editor at the newspaper who had subbed the job to her and Robin.

Easy peasy. Not.

It didn't help that a part of her brain was still very firmly in the dim quiet of Seth's bedroom, marveling at the night they'd shared and puzzling over their confusing parting. Not that she'd wanted to hash things out with him in Freudian detail or anything, but she'd expected to at least have some kind of discussion with him about where they stood with one another. They couldn't walk away from each other the way they had ten years ago, not this time. She was too involved in Jodie's and Jason's life, and so was he, and she didn't think she could simply turn off the concern and affection she felt for Daisy if Seth saw last night as a disposable, pleasurable one-off.

Then there were her feelings for Seth himself...

She gave herself a mental slap as she started leafing through the first look book. She needed to concentrate on the crisis at hand. The crisis in her personal life would have to wait.

She flicked through three books before finding a couple of designers with clothes that would slot nicely into the shoot she had planned. With some tweaking, she might even be able to utilize the same accessories. Writing down style numbers and names, she made a wish list and hit the phone. By eleven she had replaced the garments and had the client's approval on the substitutions. By twelve she was zipping from one side of Melbourne to the other collecting the clothes. It was three o'clock before she returned to the studio, sweaty and tired, last night's lack of sleep well and truly catching up with her.

She could remember when she could party all night and work all day, then do it again the next night. But that stage of her life had passed, along with the stage when sex was as meaningless to her as scratching an itch or satisfying a craving. Not that she had to be in love these days to want to get naked with a man, but she definitely needed to be emotionally involved. She needed to like him—the way she liked Seth.

She made a small impatient noise as she grabbed the

first load of garment bags from her car. Seth had been sneaking into her mind every time her thoughts veered from work, drifting like a phantom on the periphery of her consciousness all day, waiting for any opportunity to claim center stage.

She thought about the things he'd whispered while he was inside her, and the sensual promises he'd made *and* fulfilled. She thought about the way he'd kissed her shoulder and asked her to stay.

And she thought about the out-of-step, discordant confusion of this morning—her panic and distraction, his concern for Daisy, the sense that the bubble of last night had been well and truly popped.

Most of all she thought about calling him, largely because she wanted to hear his voice, but also because she wanted to give him a chance to say something—anything—to indicate where she stood. Or where he stood. Where they both stood.

She wasn't going to, though, she told herself for the hundredth time as she entered the freight elevator and hit the button for the top floor. The very fact that she felt as though she needed to speak to him meant what she really needed to do was to back off. She and Seth might have a relationship that was based in truth-telling and honesty, but that didn't mean she was prepared to lay herself bare to him. Not yet. She needed a lot more than one night before she would be prepared to be so vulnerable to a man who considered a couple of weeks to be long term.

It hadn't escaped her attention that he was dealing with the recent death of his ex-girlfriend and the arrival of his daughter. It stood to reason that while all of this—him, Daisy, last night—loomed large in her life, it probably had a smaller presence in his.

Last night had probably been a very pleasant interlude for him. He was probably mildly concerned about how to navigate the ensuing awkwardness next time they saw each other, but was otherwise unfussed. Probably—

For God's sake, give it a rest. Enough already. If you want to know how he's feeling and what he wants, ask the man. If you're not prepared to do that, don't manufacture positions for him. You'll just make yourself more crazy-pants than you already are.

She sighed, knowing good advice when her superego offered it to her. Whether she was going to be able to take it was a different matter.

It was stifling when she entered the studio—Robin was out meeting a potential client and they didn't leave the air conditioning running when no one was around. She had to make two trips to bring up all the clothes, and by the end she was ready for a long shower and a glass of wine, both of which were far away since she still had hours of work ahead of her. To add to her joy, her stomach started to complain as she brought her laptop to the trestle table where she'd dumped the clothes. So much for the muesli bar she'd consumed while on the road at lunchtime.

She pushed her hunger aside and concentrated on the detailed, finicky work required to specify and perfect the looks for the catalogue. Fashion Week was one of the industry's highest profile events, and scoring this contract had been a real feather in her and Robin's caps—a direct result, Vivian suspected, of them both being new in town with the gloss of L.A. still attached to them. They needed to knock this out of the park to cement their reputations, which meant she had to make sure these substitutions blended seamlessly into the vision she and Robin had created.

She wheeled a couple of her expensive, articulated mannequins out of the storeroom and went to work setting up the first few outfits. By six she was halfway through the new selection, with a growing list of items she needed to dash out and grab before the shops closed at nine. She was rubbing her forehead, trying to massage away the stress headache tightening like a clamp around her skull, when a masculine voice spoke from the studio entrance.

"We were hoping we'd find you here."

She glanced up, blinking in surprise when she saw Seth standing there, Daisy strapped across his chest in a sling.

"Hi," she said, utterly flummoxed. She hadn't expected to see him—them—today. She definitely hadn't expected Seth to seek her out.

"We brought you dinner, since I figured you probably haven't had a chance to eat." Seth lifted his hand to draw her attention to the plain brown paper bag he carried. "Grilled chicken and avocado burger with spicy fries, or a cheeseburger with extra pickle. Your choice."

"I'm not sure I have time to eat," she admitted, even as her stomach emitted a loud growl.

"I think you've been overruled. Fifteen minutes to refuel won't kill you."

She checked her watch. "It might if it means I miss the shops."

"Ten minutes, then. You can't work all day and night on adrenaline, Viv."

She had no idea how he knew that she'd barely eaten all day, but she didn't have the time or energy to fight what she suspected was a losing battle.

"Okay. But this isn't going to be pretty, so you might want to avert your eyes," she said.

"When I took Sam and Max to the zoo we saw feeding time at the lion enclosure. I'm pretty sure I'm unshockable in this area," he said, coming closer.

"You keep believing that." She met him halfway, leaning in so she could see Daisy's face. She was fast asleep, being strapped to her daddy's chest obviously agreeing with her. "How are you, sweet girl?"

She could feel Seth watching her, and suddenly she felt ridiculously shy as the full impact of what he'd done hit her. He'd been worried about her, and he'd packed up Daisy and come into the city to ensure she had dinner. Warmth spread through her chest as she processed the import behind his actions.

Seth cared about her. And, unless she was wildly misinterpreting his actions, last night had not been a one-time-only event. The relief that washed through her was so encompassing and profound she had to blink away tears.

"You okay?" Seth asked, his voice worried.

"Yeah. Of course." She still couldn't quite look at him, so she concentrated on Daisy, stroking a finger down her cheek.

"Let's get some food into you," Seth said.

They walked to the kitchenette, perching on the stools placed beneath the window and spreading their feast out on the long, slim counter.

"Cheeseburger or chicken?" Seth asked as she tried not to drool over the smell of hot food.

"I don't know. They both look amazing," she said.

"Halvies it is, then." He stood to fetch a knife.

She watched as he carefully cut each burger in half, the warm feeling in her chest expanding to fill her stomach and pelvis.

"Thanks for doing this, Seth. For thinking of me."

"In case you hadn't noticed, thinking of you is pretty easy for me, Viv." He said it lightly, but there was a gravity beneath his words that made her want to touch him.

And so she did, sliding her hand onto his shoulder, then to the warm skin at the nape of his neck.

"In case you hadn't noticed, the feeling is entirely mutual." She did what she'd been wanting to do since he walked in the door, pressing her mouth to his.

He responded instantly, his tongue stroking hers, his desire evident in the way his mouth moved and the way he reached for her shoulders. She wanted to be closer, but Daisy was between them, and after a few seconds they broke apart.

"Have I mentioned that I have another woman in my life?" Seth said.

"Let me guess—I bet she's a blonde," Vivian said, settling back onto her stool.

"How did you know?"

"Just a feeling I had."

They started to eat, Seth asking about her day and making sympathetic noises as she described her many phone calls and frantic zigzagging across the city. The horrible, wound-up feeling eased as the food hit her stomach and Seth made her laugh. By the time she'd finished, her shoulders were a whole inch lower and her head clear for the first time in hours.

"God, I needed that," she said as she polished off the last of the fries.

Seth was checking on Daisy, but he glanced at Vivian, his eyes warm. "Thought you might have."

He returned to adjusting Daisy's position in the sling, and Vivian quelled the urge to kiss him again. It was just a burger, after all, and a little bit of consideration and forethought on his behalf. It shouldn't mean quite so much to her. Not after just one night.

She gathered the remnants of their meal and tossed them in the bin, then washed her hands at the sink.

"I hate to eat and run, but I really should get back into it," she said reluctantly.

"Consider us gone," Seth said, standing carefully, one hand supporting the baby.

Would she ever be unaffected by the sight of his tender concern for his child? There was something very simple and good about watching someone with so much physical power exert himself to be gentle.

He caught her watching him. "Yeah, I know, this thing is ridiculous, the most emasculating invention in the history of the world. But she loves it."

"Well, you do have a nice chest. She has good taste."

"Must take after her old man."

He followed her into the studio and paused to examine the garment rack. "So this is a whole outfit for the shoot, is it?" He indicated the look sheet pinned to one of the garment bags.

"That's right. I call these look sheets, for want of a better term, but everyone else calls them Vivian's anal retentive checklist. What you see there is a thumbnail image of the components that make up the look, and I use it to confirm I have everything I need at this end, and at the other end. You'd be amazed how easy it is to forget accessories on location, especially with make-shift change rooms. Sometimes they just add that little extra lift." She gestured, her hand mimicking a bird taking off.

"So where's tomorrow's location?"

"Robin and I found this amazing Victorian mansion an hour out of town. It's in the middle of a field, and it's perfect—peeling wallpaper, crumbling plaster, fabulous decayed decadence."

Seth was smiling by the time she finished and she gave him a look. "What?"

"You should see your face light up when you talk about your work. If your job was a guy, I might have to take it out back and give it a black eye."

The thought of Seth being jealous of her—pos-sessive of her—triggered the chest-pinching feeling again, and she turned away in case he could see how much his words had affected her.

Stupid, when being charming was in his DNA.

"Let me know if there's anything else I can do, okay?" Seth said.

"Thanks." She shuffled some papers.

His hand landed on her hip, and when she glanced over her shoulder he pressed a kiss to her lips. The need for more was like a drug in her blood, making her turn into his embrace and open her mouth. The low, insis-tent throb of need started between her thighs and when he lifted his head her chest was rising and falling as though she'd run a race.

"When am I going to see you again?" he asked very quietly, his hand sliding up into her hair so that he cradled the back of her skull. It felt so good, so reassuring, that she closed her eyes for a moment.

"I won't finish till late tonight. And tomorrow might go long, too."

"What if I promised you dinner after the shoot?"

"What if the shoot runs late?"

"I can wait."

"Okay. I'll come over afterward."

He pressed one last, quick kiss to her mouth. "See you then."

She rested a hand on her chest as he walked away, just to confirm that her heart really was beating that fast, that frantically. Like a bird fighting to be released from a cage.

This man drove her wild, there was no two ways about it. He affected her on every level, so much so that it bordered on scary.

She turned to her work. Whether she was comfortable with it or not, she'd started something when she went to Seth's room last night. Or maybe she'd started it when she returned to Australia. Either way, this was happening, and it was happening without a safety net because this was *Seth*.

She let her breath out on a sigh, deliberately letting go of all the doubts rattling around her head.

She was going to go to Seth's tomorrow night, and she was going jump his bones again and whatever happened after that was what happened after that.

CHAPTER TWELVE

SETH SPENT FRIDAY at the bar, working through the pile of paperwork on his desk, answering emails, returning phone calls. There were bank records to get to his accountant for the quarterly business activity statement, there was superannuation to pay into his staff's various nominated accounts, there was stock to order and promotions to consider and deals to hunt down. He did it all with Daisy slung across his chest and was a little astonished at how much comfort he gained from having her so close, and how much more settled she was in between feeds and sleeps.

Clearly, kangaroos knew what they were doing, keeping their babies close for so long. Now, if only he could grow a pouch...

He dropped by his friend Sue's gallery on the way home, collecting the commission he'd left with her that morning, and spent longer than he'd intended trawling the aisles at the supermarket, trying to decide between marinating some fish and making a salad, or making his never-fail chicken curry. He wanted Vivian to feel pampered and cared for after what had probably been a stressful, demanding day, an urge that would have seen him giving himself sideways glances not so long ago.

But this was Vivian. She was...something else, and the thought of easing her burdens in any way, shape or form made him feel good. Better than good.

He paused in front of the spice display, remembering the way she'd looked at him last night when he'd arrived with dinner. As though she didn't know whether to laugh or cry, she was so tired and freaked out. Being able to make her smile, and to smooth out the wrinkle of worry between her eyebrows, had made him feel ten feet tall.

Someone brushed past him, and he realized he was smiling at the curry powder like a goof. Feeling suitably idiotic, he glanced around to see if anyone had noticed before tossing a jar of his favorite into the cart and heading for the registers.

Not that he was embarrassed about caring for Vivian. Far from it. But he couldn't help thinking that maybe he was getting a little ahead of himself. They'd spent one night together. She was coming over for dinner tonight. No one had said anything about the future, about what they were doing together. Not something he'd ever worried about before, but it was different this time. Because it was Vivian.

Daisy started to fuss as he fitted her into the car seat, and she cried all the way home, the sound amplified in the small cabin of his car. He banged the back of his head on the car frame when he picked her up once he got home, then spent the next hour trying to get her to settle. She didn't want a bottle, she didn't seem tired, she didn't respond to cuddling, tickling or jiggling. Finally he tried bathing her, and she calmed down, then drifted off to sleep. He did a frantic once-over clean of the house, changed the sheets on his bed and started dinner.

The curry was ready to be deployed, a bottle of white wine was cooling in the fridge, and he was getting twitchy by the time Vivian called at nine.

"We just finished. I'm on the other side of town, so I won't make it to Ivanhoe for another forty minutes. Still want me to come over?" He could hear the weariness in her voice and the urge to reach through the phone and comfort her was a visceral, physical thing. If he could somehow magic her across town on the spot, he'd do it.

"Well, I could eat all of this awesome chicken curry on my own. I'm definitely capable of it. But I'm not so sure about the bottle of pinot grigio I've got in the fridge."

"Oh, that sounds good. If you're sure you're still up for a visitor, I'll hit the road."

"I'm up for it," he said simply.

Her laugh was low and suggestive. "I bet," she said before ending the call.

He hadn't meant his comment to be sexual, but he wasn't about to object to her interpretation, because, of course, he wanted her again.

He woke Daisy to feed her, then they sat on the couch waiting for Vivian to arrive. He was dozing with Daisy's barely there weight on his chest when the doorbell rang, and it took him a moment to come to wakefulness and get to the door.

Vivian gave him a faint smile when he opened the door. "One zombie, for your amusement and delectation." Her usually sleek hair was rumpled, her clothes wrinkled and dusty. Her makeup was smudged beneath her eyes, and she had a bandage on her thumb. "Safety pin injury."

"Nasty. I prescribe a glass of wine and dinner."

"Sounds wonderful."

She stepped forward and dropped a kiss onto Daisy's

head before finding his mouth with her own, her hand curling around his forearm in a warm grip.

"I've been thinking about this all day," she said when they broke their kiss.

He tried not to be alarmed by how fiercely pleased he was at her words.

"Come in." He held out a hand and when she slipped hers into it, tugged her into the house, kicking the door shut. "How hungry are you? Because I made a lot of curry."

"I could eat a small horse. But I'd probably prefer chicken."

"Good decision."

He pushed her into a chair at the kitchen table, and when she held out her arms for Daisy, he handed her over. He opened the wine and poured a big glass, then asked about her day as he served their meal. She proceeded to give him a humorous, vivid account of the shoot, pausing only to rain praise on him when she took her first mouthful of curry.

"This is amazing. Did you...?"

"I did."

"Wow. Then it's even more amazing."

"Thanks," he said dryly.

She smiled and then quickly tried to hide it with her hand. "Sorry. That wasn't very diplomatic of me, was it? It's just you have been at great pains to establish your nonculinary credentials. All that talk about cans of soup."

"I know. But I can rustle up a decent feed if I concentrate all my puny powers."

"Well, I feel honored." There was a warmth in her

eyes that made him intensely glad that he'd gone to so much trouble.

She was worth it. More than worth it.

True to her assertion that she was hungry, she polished off her meal in no time, sighing with contentment as she reached for her wineglass.

"That was so good it should be illegal," she said.

"There's more if you want seconds."

"I'll wait a bit, see if my stomach catches up with my mouth. But thank you."

"There's dessert, too, although I thought you might like a soak in the spa bath between courses."

"You have a spa bath?"

"In the main bathroom, complete with shag carpet and a mirrored ceiling," he said, quoting her own description back to her.

"You have a good memory."

Only for the things she said to him.

"Want me to fill the tub for you?"

She bit her lip, and he could see that she was torn—wanting the bath, but worried about how antisocial it would be to abandon him for a soak.

"I'm going to run the bath," he said, taking the decision out of her hands.

"Okay," she said meekly.

Ten minutes later, she handed over Daisy and disappeared into the bathroom. Seth changed Daisy's diaper before putting his sleepy girl to bed. He could hear Vivian splashing around in the tub next door and his head filled with vivid, steam-framed images of her as he made his way to the kitchen. He refilled her wineglass, then headed for the bathroom.

"Okay for me to come in?" he asked after tapping lightly on the door.

"Hang on. I'll just wash out this shampoo mohawk… Okay, it's safe to come in."

She was chin-deep in bubbles when he entered.

"A shampoo mohawk would suit you," he said.

"Sadly, my days of crazy haircuts are long gone." She lifted a foot to nudge the bottle of bath foam sitting on the ledge. "Did you buy that for me?"

"As if, Walker. I have bubble baths all the time. Right before I give myself a pedicure."

She huffed out a laugh and indicated the wine. "Is that for me, too?"

"What do you think?" He handed it over.

"I think I could get used to this. Better be careful."

He shrugged, pretending he'd barely noticed her words. He wasn't about to say it out loud, but he could get used to caring for her like this, too.

He took a step toward the door. "Give me a shout when you're ready for dessert."

"Where are you going?"

"I was going to leave you in peace."

"Maybe I don't want to be in peace. Stay and talk to me." She offered him a hopeful smile.

As if he was going to say no to anything this woman asked of him.

"I'll go find something to sit on."

He made himself stop and take a deep breath once he was in the hallway. Not so long ago, he'd been a pretty cool customer when it came to the women in his life. Since Vivian had returned, he'd forgotten what that felt like. Maybe it was time to remember, for his pride's sake, if nothing else.

Accordingly, he forced himself to walk slowly into the kitchen to grab a chair. Just to prove to himself that he could.

VIVIAN SET HER wineglass on the side of the tub and sank into the water until the spice-scented bubbles tickled her chin. Her belly was warm from food and wine, her body cradled by water, and any second now, Seth would return and she would have the company of the sexiest, most intriguing man she'd ever met while she soaked away the cares and stresses of the day.

Pretty much her idea of heaven, really—all thanks to Seth. He'd gone to a lot of trouble on her behalf. He'd knocked himself out to be thoughtful, and the knowledge he'd put so much time and effort into ensuring her comfort and happiness was more heady than any wine.

Although maybe she shouldn't be quite so surprised. She'd seen the way he'd pulled out all the stops for Daisy in recent weeks. When he cared, Seth didn't hold anything back.

The thought made her close her eyes against a dizzying rush of hope and fear. She'd been working very hard not to second-guess herself and Seth, and she'd come here tonight determined not to get caught up in all the what-ifs that surrounded them. Right now was what was important, and it was good. That was all she needed to concentrate on.

A breeze brushed her cheek as the door opened, and Seth appeared with a chair in one hand and his own wineglass in the other. Placing the chair in front of the vanity, he sat and took a sip.

"So. What do you want to talk about?" he asked.

"I don't know. Tell me about your day. I feel as though I've been yammering at you since I arrived."

"I'll save you a blow-by-blow account of the many diapers Daisy burned through and give you the condensed version. I sorted out a truckload of admin stuff at the bar today, and the Browns called to confirm Lola's funeral will be on Tuesday."

"Does that mean they'll be going home soon?"

"I assume so, although we didn't discuss it. I know they had to leave at short notice so they aren't really set up to stay longer, even if they wanted to."

"No. And I guess the comforts of home must look pretty appealing right now."

"Yeah."

Seth propped his bare feet on the rim of the tub as he talked about his day. She stretched out her aching feet and closed her eyes, listening to the low gravel of his voice, enjoying the undemanding pleasure of having him close. If someone had suggested a week ago that she could be naked and in the same room as Seth without being beside herself with longing, she would have laughed in their face. The hum of need was there, of course—it was always when he was near—but right at this moment it was enough that they were sharing the same space. That they would make love tonight was a given, and there was something decadently delicious about simply accepting that fact and allowing herself to savor the slow build of anticipation as they enjoyed each other in a different way.

"Here. Give me your foot and I'll rub it for you."

She opened her eyes to find him shifting the chair closer to the bath.

"You don't have to do that."

"So they're not sore, then?" His raised eyebrow told her he would be deeply skeptical if she tried to deny it.

"After twelve hours on them, it'd be a miracle if they weren't. But you've done more than enough."

"Pass me your foot, idiot."

"Well. Since you asked so nicely, you silver tongue, you."

She lifted her right leg from the water, aware of how heavy and warm the limb felt. God, it was good to let go of the day's tension. Seth placed her heel on his knee, immediately going to work on the arch of her foot with his long, strong fingers.

"Ooooh," she moaned, almost slipping beneath the water, the pleasure-pain of his touch was so good.

"You like that, do you?"

"Keep that up and I'm going to need a cigarette in a few minutes," she said, closing her eyes so she could concentrate on what he was doing.

"Interesting."

Her eyes popped open and she found he was regarding her with a smoky, patient intensity that made her sex contract instinctively.

"One thing at a time," he said, as if he could read her mind.

"You started it," she said as she closed her eyes again, unable to stop herself from smiling.

He didn't respond, but continued his good work, his thumbs digging into her heel, her arch, the ball of her foot. She relaxed, her body softening. After a while he tapped her other knee and she offered up her left foot to his ministrations.

"You still awake there?" he asked.

"Mmm."

"You sink any lower and you'll need a snorkel."

"Or maybe you'd have to climb in and rescue me."

His thumbs stilled on her foot for a second. "True."

She caught him looking at her with what she could only describe as carnal intent. One glance at the water revealed that much of the foam had dissipated and he had an almost clear view of her body.

"See anything you like?" she asked lazily.

"A couple of things."

"Only a couple?"

She glided her hand onto her breasts, using her thumb and forefinger to tease her nipple to hardness, not taking her gaze from his the whole time.

"I don't want to come across as greedy," he said.

"Greed is a very underrated sin, in certain situations," she said.

She smoothed her hand down her belly, slipping her fingers past the neat patch of hair at the juncture of her thighs and into the warm folds of her sex. She was already swollen with need for him, and she circled a finger leisurely, enjoying the gentle pressure and the way Seth's expression sharpened to a wolflike intensity.

"So, only a couple of things, you were saying?" she murmured.

"A couple of dozen, yeah."

"Is this one of them?" she said, stroking herself.

"Could be."

"Or maybe it's these?" She slipped her other hand onto her breasts and made her already tight nipples even harder.

"They're definitely on the list."

"So. What are going to do about it?" she said, knowing she was driving him crazy.

"This."

He moved so fast he was leaning over the bath, his arms slipping beneath her before she'd even registered he was out of his chair. Then he was lifting her, ignoring her halfhearted protests as he slung her over his shoulder.

As a show of strength, it was a feat indeed.

"You're going to be all wet now," she said.

"So that'll make two of us."

She'd barely got her head around the double entendre before she was bouncing on her back on his bed, Seth standing above her peeling off his clothes as though the fate of the world depended on him completing the task in under three seconds. The moment he was finished, he covered her body with his, his mouth taking hers in an urgent, hot kiss.

She let herself get swept away in the sheer, undiluted pleasure of it, moaning when his hands found her breasts before slipping between her thighs. She was gratified to feel that he was shaking with need as he stroked her before plunging one, then two fingers inside her.

She lifted her hips, encouraging his penetration, needing more, and he obliged, finding her with his thumb and starting up a counterpoint rhythm that quickly had her panting and clawing at his back.

"You, I want you," she begged, trying to pull away from his touch even as he pushed her closer and closer toward her climax.

He paused, his body warm and heavy over hers. "Where do you want me? Here?"

She felt the thick, firm pressure as he guided himself between her thighs, rubbing himself along the seam of her sex.

"Yes. Exactly there."

She tilted her hips, and she was so slick with desire that he slipped easily into place. Just one flex of his hips and he would be inside her, filling her....

He nudged inside a bare inch, then immediately withdrew, his face twisted with regret. "Condom."

She caught his hand before he could reach for the bedside drawer. "I'm on the pill. And I had a full health check before I left the States."

She felt the jolt of realization rocket through him as he registered what she was suggesting. That it aroused him even further was patently evident, his erection surging against her.

"I got the all clear a couple of months ago, too."

He frowned, though, torn between temptation and caution. She tucked a strand of hair behind his ear, oddly touched by his concern. He was so different in so many ways from the unrepentant pants man she'd been happy to categorize him as all these years.

"While you think about it, I'm just going to do this," she said, lifting her hips encouragingly.

He groaned, the sound absolutely primal. He gripped her hips and eased himself inside her in a slow, controlled stroke, his expression tortured.

"That good, huh?" she asked.

"Like you needed to ask."

He started to move, his fingers digging into her hips, his whole body concentrated on the task. She smoothed her hands down his back to his backside, then up again, reveling in the smoothness of his skin and the flex and release of his muscles. He was so big and strong, and she loved the way he felt inside her, how he made her feel both powerful and powerless at the same time, the way he looked at her as though he could never get enough of it, of her....

She forgot to breathe as her climax took her, her knees clenching around his hips as she shuddered out her pleasure. Seth followed seconds later, his body buried deep, his breath leaving him on a single, almost painful sigh as he gave himself up to it.

They lay profoundly still for a few seconds, arms wrapped tightly around each other. He was still inside her, stretching her, and she could feel the frantic thump of his heart against her chest. Then he pressed a kiss to her forehead and rolled to the side and she was alone again.

For a moment she let herself float in the afterglow, enjoying the warm languidness of her body. Her thoughts drifted toward tomorrow, and the day after that, and the day after that, but she diverted them ruthlessly. She was staying in the moment. Enjoying this for what it was right now, letting it become whatever it might become in its own sweet time, without her breathing down its neck.

In keeping with her philosophy, she turned to look at Seth. His eyes were closed, his big body sprawled on the bed.

"Tell me, who came up with the name for your band?"

He turned to her. "Skunk Punk?"

"Yeah. Skunk Punk." It was hard to say without smirking.

Seth gave her a dry look. "Are you trying to take the piss out of me, Walker?"

"No. I'm genuinely curious. What thought process was behind the creation of such a...unique name?"

"A lot of the guys were really into The Sex Pistols, and I pretty much worshipped Johnny Rotten until I realized what an ass he is."

"Right, so that covers the punk part. What about the skunk?"

"You know that old Warner Brothers cartoon with the lady cat and the Casanova skunk, where he thinks she's a lady skunk and chases her all over the place?"

"You mean Pepé Le Pew?"

"That's the one. Our drummer had a thing about that skunk. The rest is history."

Vivian tried very hard not to laugh. "That's it? That's the earth-shattering genesis of Skunk Punk? A cartoon skunk and a fondness for Sid Vicious?"

"In our defense, we were eighteen when we got together. And there may or may not have been illegal substances involved the night we picked the name."

"It never occurred to any of you that maybe it wasn't the kind of name that would look great in lights one day?"

"That's where you're wrong. Rock and roll has a long lineage of ridiculous band names. Regurgitator, The Butthole Surfers, Hootie and the Blowfish... Want me to keep going?"

"This is a bit of a sore spot for you, isn't it?" she asked, poker-faced.

"You keep that up and I won't give you the present I got for you today."

She sat up. "You bought me a present?"

"Sort of. Money changed hands for part of the present anyway." He rolled off the bed and stood. "I've got you all intrigued now, haven't I?"

"A little."

"A lot. Admit it."

"Okay, I am medium-level intrigued."

He walked to the closet, his body a superb study in light and shade as he opened the door and pulled out a thin, square shape covered with a bath towel.

Seth had bought her some artwork? How...odd. Not that she didn't like art, but he'd never struck her as the arty-farty type.

"I've been thinking for a while about how I can make it up to you for being such a dick when Jason approached me about being guardian to the boys."

"Good. So you should, you misguided idiot."

"Absolutely. Mea culpa, my bad, et cetera, et cetera."

"So sincere. It's beautiful. I'm touched."

He pressed his fingers to his chest, playing wounded for all he was worth. "I'm very sincere, as you'll see in a moment, because I'm offering one of my most treasured possessions to you. My way of letting you know that I'm fully aware of how far out of line I was."

She eyed the shrouded frame curiously. "Okay, fine, Anderson. I believe you. You're sorry."

"I am, but before I hand it over, I feel honor-bound to point out that while I'm giving this to you wholeheartedly, if you should ever find yourself in a generous mood, I'd be happy to share ownership with you. A sort of time-share arrangement, if you will."

She was starting to get a little worried. His eyes were laughing at her, but there was something about the way he was holding himself and his gift that made her think he wasn't entirely joking.

What on earth was he about to give her?

"Okay," she said slowly.

He slid the frame onto the bed in front of her, then stepped back, gesturing for her to do the unveiling. She rose to her knees and reached for the towel.

"This had better not be a velvet painting of Elvis. Because no way would I share that with you," she said, feeling ridiculously nervous.

"This is better than a velvet painting of Elvis."

She glanced at him, taking in his arms-crossed-over-his-chest posture and his utter comfort with his own nakedness. She refocused on the frame, pulling sharply on the towel…only to reveal a pair of cream lacy panties delicately arranged on a dove-grey parchment background, surrounded by a gold and darker grey double mount within a thick, burnished walnut frame. It took her a full second to recognize the panties she'd worn to her sister's wedding.

"You did not." She stared at Seth, flabbergasted.

"I did."

"You kept these for *ten years?*"

"I did."

"No way."

"Way."

She shook her head. It couldn't be true. But it had to be, because she recognized the expensive French brand and could see the torn lace at the side where he'd ripped them off her in those cramped, desperate minutes in the limo.

"I don't know what to say," she said.

"I was thinking you could hang them above your bed. And if you ever get sick of them, I've got a spot right here." He patted a spot on the wall.

She studied him, trying to get a read on him. That he was enjoying himself enormously was more than obvious, and it struck her that there was no way he'd offer these up to her if he'd genuinely held on to her underwear as a treasured keepsake all these years. It simply wasn't his nature to be so sentimental, or to reveal himself so thoroughly.

He must have faked it. He must have remembered the brand and worked out her size and bought a pair of panties that looked roughly the same. It had been ten years, after all, and she couldn't swear to the fact that these were hers.

"You are so full of it," she scoffed, amused despite herself by his cheekiness. He'd gone to a lot of trouble to wind her up, and she was smart-ass enough to appreciate it.

"You think I'm bullshitting you?"

"Yeah, I do. No way did you hang on to my panties for ten years."

"They were in a manila envelope, stuffed in a box of old bank statements and tax documents," he said. "Your sister and my brother found them when they cleared out the spare room for me."

"Dear God. Please tell me my name wasn't on the envelope."

"What am I, stupid? Besides, I could barely remember your name the next morning."

It was such an outrageous lie, and so calculated to get her goat, she couldn't help but rise to the occasion. She grabbed a pillow and slung it as hard as she could, hitting her target square in the belly.

He grinned at her, utterly unrepentant. "I'm happy to come over to your place on the weekend and help you hang it, if you like."

She grabbed another pillow and aimed it at his head. "You are a ten-year-old. You know that, right?"

He dodged the pillow and advanced on the bed. "This is a nice show of gratitude."

"Tell me you really thought you'd get anything else," she said.

She was tickled by his teasing and the knowledge that he'd played her beautifully, and that both had required a lot of effort.

He'd been thinking about her, plotting and planning ways to amuse, entertain and comfort her. The thought made her want to laugh. It made her want to grab him and kiss him until it hurt. It made her want to preserve this moment for eternity, it contained so much joy and potential.

"Should have known you'd take it the wrong way. You never were easy to predict."

She made a lunge for the last pillow at the same time he did, and they wound up in a tangle of limbs on the bed. It didn't take long for Seth to overpower her, as he pinned her arms and used his superior weight to hold her down.

"That's more like it," he said, a dirty glint in his eye.

She struggled to free herself, arching off the bed with the effort, but he was too strong for her. By the time she ceased, they were both panting, and she could feel how hard he was against her belly.

"You going to do something with that or is it just for show?" she taunted him.

He flexed his hips by way of answer, nudging the head of his erection inside her. She bit back a sob at how good it felt, determined to play out her end of this game.

"That all you got?" she asked.

He ducked his head and pulled one of her nipples into his mouth, the warm, wet suction exactly what she needed. Then he thrust the rest of the way in and the game was over for her as the feel of him stretching and filling her gained momentum.

"Yes," she panted, her hands finding his backside as she urged him to go harder, faster. "More."

He took her at her word, plunging deeply before grinding his hips against hers and withdrawing to start again. She lifted her hips to meet his, deepening his penetration, her eyes drifting closed as she tuned into the building tension. Seth slipped his hands beneath her and angled her even further, holding her steady as he worked inside her. Her climax hit her in rolling waves, wringing his name from her lips as she tightened around him.

As always, her pleasure seemed to trigger his, and he took her mouth in an urgent kiss as he thrust one last time. His lip curled back, his body becoming as hard as steel as he rode out his release.

He rolled to the side afterward, his breathing harsh. She stared at the ceiling and tried to remember her own name.

"I knew you'd like it," he said after a minute, and it was such an absolutely Seth thing to say that she couldn't hold back the bubble of laughter.

She was wiping the tears from the corners of her eyes when the baby monitor came to life.

"Better than an alarm clock," he said, moving to the end of the bed and scouting around for his underwear.

He slipped out once he was decent, and she listened to the sounds of him talking to Daisy. There was a special tone that came into his voice when he spoke to his daughter. Soft and gentle and patient.

Sitting up, she swiveled onto her knees and snagged the frame from where it was in danger of sliding off the bed. She couldn't look at her framed panties without grinning. Acting on impulse, she went to the wall next to the door, where a black-and-white shot of the New York City skyline hung in a black frame. Unhooking it, she rested it on the floor and replaced it with her panties.

"Now, that's art," she murmured as she stepped back to admire the effect.

Seth would have to take it down tomorrow, in case anyone else saw it and thought he really was the kind of desperate pervert who preserved sexual trophies, but for tonight, she figured her panties had found the perfect home.

Rescuing the pillows, she returned them to the bed, then pulled up the sheet and slid beneath it. Seth would be a while, she knew from experience, so she turned off the lamp.

It wasn't until she was drifting off that it occurred to her that Seth hadn't asked if she was staying the night, and she hadn't offered.

They'd both assumed she would be.

CHAPTER THIRTEEN

SETH WOKE TO sunshine streaming across the sheets and an empty bed. It wasn't until he glanced at the clock that he saw it was nearly ten.

"Whoa." He bolted upright, flinging back the sheet and racing out of his room to Daisy's.

He pulled up hard on the threshold, blinking stupidly at the empty crib. Then his brain caught up with the rest of him. Returning to the bedroom to pull on a pair of boxers, he walked to the kitchen. Sure enough, Vivian was sitting at the table feeding Daisy.

"Did I sleep through the monitor?" he asked.

"Nope. I woke up and couldn't get back to sleep so I brought it in here with me. I figured you wouldn't turn up your nose at more than three consecutive hours of sleep."

She was wearing last night's shirt and her panties, her hair all sticky-outy on one side. Her face was devoid of makeup, the freckles in clear evidence on her nose. She'd never looked better to him.

"You look like you just won the lottery," she said with a grin.

"Kind of feels that way. I forgot what it feels like to have enough sleep."

He came closer, peering over her shoulder to check on Daisy. His daughter stared at him, her mouth busy sucking on the bottle Vivian held for her, clenching and unclenching her hands rhythmically.

"Thanks," he said quietly, and when Vivian glanced at him he dropped a kiss onto her lips.

Her smile was almost shy, and he had to bite back the impulse to kiss her again.

"You hungry? I've got eggs, bacon, English muffins if you're up for it."

She didn't respond straight away, glancing at Daisy before looking at him. "That sounds great, thanks."

He realized he'd been holding his breath, waiting for Vivian's reply, and he told himself to relax as he turned toward the fridge.

He'd never been this edgy, this uncertain with a woman before—but he'd never been as invested before, either, and it was past time he admitted that to himself. This thing with Vivian had moved a long way beyond sex, very quickly. A long way.

He'd recognized that she was special—important—the moment he set eyes on her all those years ago, and he'd spent most of the past decade trying to pretend otherwise. She'd always been in the back of his mind, though, a tantalizing possibility that he'd been a little afraid to explore.

Despite that—despite all his posturing and all their mutual game-playing—they'd somehow still wound up here, both of them half-naked in his kitchen on a Saturday morning. And it felt pretty good. In fact, it felt better than good.

It felt right. Like the most right thing that had ever happened to him.

He stared at the contents of his refrigerator, aware that he was in danger of getting wildly ahead of himself. As vibrant and fun and sexy as Vivian was, she could also be incredibly hard to read. There were times when he was completely clueless as to what was going on behind her blue-green eyes.

He knew she'd had a good time last night and that she enjoyed his company, but beyond that, he had no idea how she viewed what was happening between them. She'd referred to them as a "disaster waiting to happen," and the night she'd climbed into his bed she'd told him not to say too much in case she realized what a big mistake she was making.

Not exactly encouraging words.

But then there had been other times that she'd looked at him and he'd seen the world in her eyes. And she was still here, wasn't she? She hadn't rolled out of bed, dressed and gone on her merry way. She was having breakfast with him and Daisy. He figured that was an encouraging sign.

The fridge started to beep and he realized he'd been staring into it far too long. He grabbed the egg carton and the bacon, then shut the door.

"Scrambled, poached or fried?" he asked.

Vivian thought about it for a moment, her brow furrowed, then shrugged. "Surprise me. I used up all my decisions yesterday."

The sound of the doorbell echoed, cutting off the tail end of Vivian's answer.

"Hold that thought," he said.

He didn't think to check who it might be before he swung open the door, assuming it would simply be someone selling raffle tickets or one of his neighbors asking if he'd seen their lost cat.

Instead, he faced his brother and sister-in-law.

"Hey. We need to grab the coffee urn. Got a dozen coffee-guzzling parents coming to our place tonight," Jason said, brushing past Seth into the house.

Seth was so thrown that for a full second his mind was a complete blank. Then it hit him what was about to happen and he spun on his heel.

"I'll get it," he said, abandoning Jodie at the door to follow his brother.

But it was too late. Jason was already halfway to the kitchen. Short of taking his brother down in a running tackle, there was no way to stop him from—

"Viv. What are you doing here?"

Damn.

VIVIAN TOOK AN involuntary step backward as Jason stopped in the doorway, a stunned expression on his face. The moment she'd heard his voice she'd shot to her feet and headed for the hallway. Not quickly enough, obviously.

His gaze raked her bare legs, taking in her rumpled shirt and bed hair, along with the baby in her arms.

Seth appeared at his brother's shoulder, his eyes apologetic when they met hers.

Jodie's voice filtered in. "Is Viv here? I thought I recognized her car in the street, but then I thought 'what would she be doing here at ten in the morning?'" Jodie joined the two men in the doorway, her expression morphing from interested to comically surprised as she took in Vivian's dishabille.

"Oh."

"Fancy meeting you here," Vivian said lamely.

"We needed to pick up the coffee urn," Jodie said after a too-long silence.

"Sure. For your parents committee meeting. You mentioned it was your turn to host when we spoke this week." Vivian's face was hot. Not just warm, blistering, painfully hot.

"You should have called. I would have brought it to your place this afternoon," Seth said.

Vivian had to steel herself to meet her sister's gaze. She was expecting judgment, maybe even disappointment, but Jodie's face was creased with concern, her eyes full of questions. As though she was worried for Vivian, deeply so.

Vivian looked away. She almost would have preferred judgment. Her sister's concern made her feel decidedly...exposed.

"I might go get dressed," she said.

A coward's move, leaving Seth to take the heat, but where was it written that a woman had to take on every dragon that crossed her path?

"I'll come help you," Jodie said almost instantly.

Vivian wanted to object, but she knew that nothing short of a major extinction event would divert her sister from her course.

Still cradling Daisy, Vivian slipped from the room. She was very aware of her sister's steady tread as Jodie followed. Jodie stopped in the doorway when they arrived at Daisy's room, watching from a distance as Vivian leaned over the crib and nestled the baby amongst the covers. Her sister didn't say a word, but Vivian could feel Jodie noting her every move as she smoothed a hand over Daisy's soft hair.

Jodie moved out of the way to let Vivian pass, then followed her to Seth's bedroom. The heat in Vivian's cheeks burned hotter when she saw the very rumpled bed. Not much doubt about what had been going on in *that* last night.

Vivian cleared her throat. "I might just—"

"What are you *doing,* Viv?" Jodie's voice vibrated with concern as she finally broke her silence.

"Because I know Seth, you mean?" His history. His appalling track record.

"Yes, Viv, because you know him. The man is charming but unreliable. He's had more girlfriends than you've had hot dinners. He's the human equivalent of white bread—delicious, tasty and completely lacking in nutritional value. You know this, yet you still slept with him? Why?"

"Seth isn't white bread," Vivian said, unable to stop herself from defending him. "He's closer to that new stuff they make these days, the bread that looks like white bread but has hidden fiber you can't see."

"Seth has no hidden fiber, Viv. You of all people should know that."

"That's not true. He's a successful businessman. He's been wonderful with Dennis and Melissa. He's a great dad. If that's not fiber, I don't know what is."

Jodie waved off her words with the bat of a hand. "Fine. Awesome. I'm talking about Seth's capacity to be a good partner to one woman for a period of more than a few weeks, though. And in that department, the man is white bread, pure and simple."

"You're wrong," Vivian said stubbornly.

"Viv, you're not thinking straight. He's worked his magic on you. But believe me, Seth is white bread."

"No, he's a doughnut. And I'll tell you why. He doesn't for a second pretend that he's good for you." Vivian counted her points off on her fingers. "He knows he's irresistible. He's all about gratification in the now, and the moment you're done, remorse kicks in with a vengeance. All of which doesn't stop you from wanting another one almost immediately. That is indisputably doughnut territory."

"Really? You regretted it the moment it was over?" Jodie asked, her gaze shooting to the rumpled bed.

Vivian realized how bound up they'd both become in a stupid metaphor. Or analogy. Whatever.

"I will never regret Seth," she said, because it was the truth and she couldn't not say it.

"Oh, Viv," Jodie said heavily.

"Don't get all mopey on me. I'm fine," Vivian said. "Seth and I both know what this is."

"Do you? So how does the fact that you've fallen in love with that little girl fit into all of this?"

Vivian stepped to the bed and started straightening the sheets, suddenly needing to be busy. "Does it need to? Are you telling me that you *don't* love Daisy?"

"Are you in love with him, too?"

Vivian concentrated on folding down the top sheet, making sure the crease was straight before pulling up the duvet. "I'm not sure. Maybe."

"Oh, Viv."

She shot her sister a look. "It's not a terminal diagnosis. No need to break out the black armbands."

"Does he know how you feel?"

Vivian plumped the pillows with more vigor than was strictly necessary. "What do you think? And if you're about to 'Oh, Viv' me again, I'm going to throw one of these in your face."

Jodie took a wary step backward. "Okay. Has he said anything about how he feels?"

"This is Seth we're talking about."

"I'll take that as a no, then."

"It's three days old. Did you and Jason send each other valentines after three days?"

"No. But we hadn't spent the previous ten years circling each other, either. And there wasn't a baby in the mix to turn up the temperature on everything. And I wasn't maybe in love with him."

Vivian stared at her sister, stripped bare by her simple, clean summary of the situation.

"I can't believe I'm going to say this, given the whole white-bread conversation, but you need to talk to him, Viv."

"No."

Jodie frowned. "Why not?"

Vivian threw her hands in the air. "He's just lost the mother of his child. He's been thrown into single-parenthood literally overnight. I don't want to become one more thing he doesn't know what to do with."

Her words echoed in the room. Jodie didn't say a word, and Vivian sank onto the bed. Talk about hoist on her own petard. It took a moment to gather her scattered thoughts.

"Honestly? I thought I could control it. I thought that we could keep it to just great sex," she confessed. "When it became clear that wasn't happening, I told myself not to overthink everything, to go with the flow. Talk about self-delusional, huh?"

"I think you should talk to him," Jodie said with quiet certainty. "Tell him how you feel. Find out how he feels. What do you have to lose at this point? And you never know, he might surprise all of us."

Jodie made it sound so easy, but she had no idea how

many years Vivian had invested in Seth. How many fantasies. It felt as though she'd been resisting the pull of her attraction to him since she first drew breath. Seth, on the other hand…

Seth was all about having a good time. She could still remember with painful clarity the relief that had radiated off him when she'd made it clear she didn't expect anything from him after their limo session. He'd since grown up—given up the band, bought a house and a business—but he'd said it himself, hadn't he? He'd never met a woman it felt right with, and he was quite happy to remain single if the alternative was settling for something less than amazing.

A pretty high standard for any woman to live up to. Especially a woman he'd had ample opportunities to categorize as amazing over the years and never had.

The thought brought the sting of tears and she blinked rapidly. Now was *not* the time to cry.

"I know it's scary, Viv, but how else are you going to know?"

"I already know." She'd always known. It was why she'd been so quick to be the one to reject Seth first years ago, and it was why she'd always been so careful to let him only so close. Until the night Lola died, when she'd been unable to stop herself from going to him.

Because she was a pain-seeking, self-sabotaging idiot, apparently.

"I still think you should give him a chance to surprise you."

"And when he doesn't, I get to spend the next forty years or so avoiding him at Sam's and Max's birthdays, just in case he gets the wrong idea? No, thanks."

The reality was, Seth had had plenty of opportunities

to tell her how he felt. And not once had he so much as hinted that he saw her as anything more than a smokin' good time in bed.

She caught Jodie glancing at the clock while wincing apologetically.

"Sorry. We need to go. Sam and Max are with our neighbors, but we said we'd only be an hour or so...."

"It's okay. I'm not going to spontaneously combust or anything."

Jodie stepped forward and wrapped her arms around her. "If you need to talk, I'm here, okay? If you need to watch bad movies and eat chocolate and drink wine, I am so your girl. Whatever you need."

Vivian kissed her sister's cheek. "Thanks. I appreciate it. As well as the tough love."

"Oh, this wasn't tough love. You ain't seen my tough love yet. I'm saving that for when you keep seeing Seth because you can't help yourself and it slowly destroys you from the inside out."

Vivian laughed, but there was enough dangerous truth in her sister's words to send a dart of nervous adrenaline through her belly.

"Never going to happen," she said bravely.

"I hope not, sweetie, because I like both of you far too much for things to get that sad."

Jodie gave Vivian's arm one last squeeze before heading for the door. Vivian's head was full of so many thoughts it was hard to sift one from the other.

But maybe it didn't matter. The important thing was that Jason and Jodie arriving so unexpectedly had been the circuit-breaker she'd needed. She'd been skating on thin ice for a while with Seth, and her sister had cut a hole in the surface and pushed her into the freezing depths. Suddenly Vivian could see everything clearly. And it wasn't particularly pretty.

She'd been lulled by empathy and sympathy into letting her guard down. Seth's charm, charisma and sex appeal plus Daisy's stunning vulnerability had done the rest.

Stupid. Really stupid, especially when Vivian had told herself she was smart enough to handle Seth and keep herself safe. She made a rude noise. Yeah, right.

She was so far from safe it wasn't funny. She was knee-deep in dangerous territory, vulnerable, exposed and teetering on the brink of enormous pain.

She heard the faint sound of the front door closing, signaling Jason and Jodie's departure. She collected her clothes and dressed, then stole a few minutes to wash her face and pull her hair into a ponytail. She took a deep breath and went to talk to Seth.

He was standing at the sliding door, staring out at the patio, arms crossed. He must have grabbed clothes from the laundry, because he wore a pair of rumpled jeans, the denim riding low on his hips.

"Well, that was fun," she said brightly.

He glanced over his shoulder and she could see he was angry.

"Jodie told you how to live your life, too, did she?"

"Not as such. I take it Jason did?"

"Oh, yeah. Apparently I'm a sleazy moron who can't keep his dick in his pants and you're my latest victim."

"Wow. Jason really takes the big-brother thing seriously, doesn't he?" Vivian had always known that Jason walked on the conservative side, but she wasn't sure how she felt about being cast as the hapless dupe who'd fallen for Seth's practiced charms.

"He's lucky he's still got all his own teeth." Seth's expression was dark. "I should have checked before opening the door. Sorry."

"It's not your fault." She paused. "And maybe, in a way, we should thank them."

"For what?"

Her heart was going crazy in her chest. She could hear her sister's voice, urging her to lay her cards on the table so Seth would have to reveal his. Standing in the same room as him, the notion didn't seem quite so suicidal. When he was this close—close enough to touch—it was impossible not to remember the way he'd brought her dinner the other night, and cooked for her last night. He'd run her a bath and bought her a present to make her laugh—a present that had meaning and significance for both of them.

All of that had to mean something. At the bare minimum, it suggested that Seth liked her a lot. It seemed to her that that was a pretty good start. Love started with liking, right? It certainly had for her.

She pressed a hand to her stomach, feeling more than a little queasy. "We both knew what this was going in. Right?" She watched him, waiting for some sign that her gut was wrong. "Probably better to have a wake-up call now, before things get messy."

She held her breath as she waited for him to respond. *Please say something, do something. Give me a little bit of hope, something I can hang on to so I don't have to do what I think I'm going to have to do.*

For a fraction of a moment he was still. Then he arched an eyebrow, his mouth quirking up at the corner.

"Calling time on me already, Viv?" There was something supremely knowing and assured about the way he said it. As though he'd been here before. As though he'd had this conversation dozens of times.

And for all she knew, maybe he had.

"Seems smart to leave on a high, don't you think?" she said as lightly as she could. She shoved her hands into the back pockets of her jeans, clutching the denim tightly in an attempt to retain her composure. "You've got Daisy, I've got my business. It's not like this was ever going to be a thing, right?" She manufactured a smile that was every bit as world-weary and wry as his.

He glanced at the ground, his smile twisting, one shoulder shrugging negligently. "Yeah. You're probably right. We've both been around the block too many times to believe in those kinds of fairy tales."

She had to bite the inside of her lip to distract herself from the insistent burn of tears. She would not cry in front of Seth. Not when she'd pulled out all the stops to preserve her dignity.

She had her answer. It was over. In reality, it had never really begun. In a way, that was the saddest thing of all.

"It was fun while it lasted, though," she said.

"Yeah. It was, wasn't it? You still up for breakfast?" Seth asked, walking to the counter.

As if she could eat.

"Thanks, but I might motor," she said. "I'll grab the rest of my stuff and say goodbye to Daisy."

"Sure." He shrugged again before turning to set the frying pan on the stove. Ready to start cooking his morning-after breakfast.

Life went on, after all. Eggs needed to be fried, bacon crisped. She was just another woman walking out the door. No big deal.

She waited until she was safely in Daisy's room be-fore she stopped and took a trembling breath.

She felt ambushed, and so stupid for feeling that way. Seth had never pretended to be anything other than what he was. She was the one who had ignored what she knew and allowed herself to play a very sophisti-cated game of chicken with him.

Well, game over.

Daisy made a small sound, drawing Vivian's atten-tion. She moved closer to the crib. Daisy's tiny form was snuggled beneath a colorful quilt, her eyes closed, her mouth pursed. Both her hands were up near her face, the fingers loosely curled. Her blond hair was sitting up in wispy tufts, and there was a faint powdery mark on her cheek where she'd dribbled some formula.

"How'd that happen, sweetheart?" Vivian asked softly, brushing away the powder with her thumb.

Daisy turned toward her touch, eyes still closed, and sadness gripped Vivian so tightly it was hard to breathe. She'd never allowed herself to see Daisy as anything other than Seth's daughter—she wasn't that crazy—but there was no denying that she had fallen under this tiny baby's spell. Daisy had come into the world in the most traumatic way possible, and she'd lost her mother after barely a week. A person would have to have a heart of stone to not feel for a girl who would never know her own mother.

Vivian didn't try to stop the tears that misted her eyes this time. Instead, she leaned forward and whis-pered a promise to Daisy, a secret deal just between the two of them.

"If you need me, I'll be here. Even if it's hard. I'll be the best aunt-in-law under the sun," she promised.

Daisy's eyes flicked open and she regarded Vivian unblinkingly for a long beat.

"It's a deal, then," Vivian whispered, watching as the baby blinked slowly a few times before slipping back into sleep. Then and only then did Vivian collect her bag and jacket from Seth's bedroom. She paused outside the kitchen to ensure she had her game face on, then breezed in, her car keys already in hand.

"Bacon always smells so amazing. Like coffee. Two of the best smells in the world," she said.

Seth was watching the frying pan, his expression closed off and unreadable. There was a moment when his gaze flicked to her that she thought she saw something troubled and deeply unhappy in his eyes...then he blinked and his mouth curled at the corners and he was Seth again, easy come, easy go.

"It's not too late, you're allowed to change your mind," he said.

For a second the world seemed to stop. Then she understood that he was offering her a second chance at breakfast, not his heart.

"Tempting. But I've got a ton of stuff to do."

He pulled the pan off the heat, but she waved a hand at him.

"No, don't do that. I can see myself out. God forbid you end up with rubbery eggs."

She forced herself to round the counter and press a quick, chaste kiss to his lips.

"Like I said, it was fun while it lasted," she said.

"I'm hardly going to argue with that."

Standing this close, she could smell the warm scent of his skin, and a sense memory hit her—Seth's arm slipping around her torso during the night as he spooned her, his lips a soft pressure at the nape of her neck.

"Call me if you need anything, okay?" she said, because she couldn't say what was in her heart.

I've fallen in love with you. Is it possible you could love me, too? Is it possible I could be amazing enough for you?

"Will do. Look after yourself, Viv."

"You, too."

Her footsteps sounded too loud as she headed for the front door. She fumbled the handle, then she was outside, momentarily blinded by the bright morning light. She forced herself to walk to her car, even though she really wanted to run. She managed to get her car started before it all caught up with her.

She point-blank refused to let herself cry, however. It didn't matter that her chest was aching. She'd walked into this. She had no one to blame but herself.

Although maybe she could spare a little blame for Seth. Because they could have been so good together. They could have really had something....

You always wondered what it would be like if you let yourself go there with Seth. Well, now you know.

She sure did. Moving with deliberate care, she drove toward the sanctuary of home.

SETH WAITED UNTIL the sound of the door shutting echoed through the house before flicking off the gas on the stove. He shoved the pan away, barely resisting the urge to chuck the thing across the room.

She was gone, just like that.

Probably better to have a wake-up call now, before things get messy.... It was fun while it lasted.

Man. He couldn't believe it had all come crashing down so quickly. One minute he'd been hoping Vivian might spend the day with him and Daisy, which might lead to more days and nights, and the next minute his brother was looking at him as though he was a dirty old man in a smelly raincoat with a pocketful of sweets, and Vivian was drawing a line under the best three days of his life before heading for the door.

Ten minutes, start to finish, and it was all over.

Unable to stand still, he walked out onto the patio only to stop and look around, not sure why he'd come outside. He turned to go inside and caught his reflection in the glass. He was frowning, his stance aggressive, a faint curl to his lip.

He looked as though he wanted to punch someone.

He let his breath rush out in an exasperated snort. If he was going to punch anyone, it should be himself. He'd known from the moment Vivian slipped into his bed that they were living on borrowed time. It had been the unspoken rider to everything they'd said and done with each other. As she'd so eloquently said, they'd both known what this was going in.

They knew each other, and they knew his circumstances. His life was a mess, after all. And Vivian had far better things to fill her time than to take on an instant family with a man who didn't exactly have a great pedigree when it came to long-term relationships. When viewed through that prism, the idea that anything that they started now had the chance to turn into something real and substantial was laughable.

And yet he'd let himself go there. There was no point pretending otherwise. In the past week, he'd imagined what it would be like having Vivian in his life. Nights with her in his bed, mornings when she was the first thing he woke to. A lifetime of laughter and smart-assery, sass and truth-telling.

Vivian, by his side. His friend. His lover. His partner.

"You stupid bastard."

He dropped onto an outdoor chair like a felled tree, the realization hitting him like a freight train. He'd had *years* to get it right with Vivian. He'd had opportunity after opportunity—and he'd wasted them all. Every last one of them. He hadn't understood, until right this second, what was at stake.

He loved her. He'd probably always loved her.

Of course he had.

Of course.

"Oh, God."

Their shared history unspooled in his mind, each scene, each conversation, each moment making him squirm as he understood himself. Finally.

He really was a stupid bastard. The dumbest man in the world. Why hadn't this epiphany hit him earlier when she was still under his roof, for example, or, better yet, still in his bed?

Right. Because it would have made such a huge difference. She's the one who walked, remember? She's the one who didn't want things to get messy.

She was the one who had insisted he not even walk her to the door. Who had thanked him for a good time as though she were thanking the host of a particularly fun party she'd attended. Who had considered Jason and Jodie's arrival "timely."

She was the one who had walked away without a backward glance.

He'd been pondering how hard she was to read as he

contemplated making a breakfast to knock her socks off, but in reality there wasn't any ambivalence in her actions.

He was in love with her, but Vivian saw him as a good time for a short time.

Okay, maybe it wasn't as cut and dried as that, but it might as well be. It wasn't that great a surprise, after all. He was the one who had worked the playboy thing so hard. Who could blame Vivian for taking him at face value? That was all he'd ever offered her, so why wouldn't she reach out and take it?

That, and a handful of real moments. Shared moments of desire and connection and comfort.

Not enough, though. Not nearly enough.

It was conceivable that one day he might be able to appreciate the irony of the situation—the dedicated playboy falling at last, only to find the woman of his dreams was interested in the playboy and nothing more—but right now it felt bitter indeed. All the years he'd wasted. All the opportunities.

The high wail of a distressed baby brought his head up. Daisy was awake. She needed him. His crisis—the mess he'd made for himself—would have to wait.

Feeling gritty and tired and empty, he went inside to see to his daughter.

CHAPTER FOURTEEN

VIVIAN DIDN'T KNOW where to put herself when she got home. During the drive, she'd imagined herself crawling into bed, drawing the covers over her head and simply lying in the dark, curled around her pain like an injured animal.

As appealing as that notion was—and it said a lot about how low she was feeling that it was genuinely attractive—once she was home she felt as though someone had put itching powder beneath her skin. She couldn't settle in bed, the couch held no appeal, food disgusted her and the thought of going out made her want to bang her head against the wall.

She settled for a shower—a long, steamy one, standing with her head bowed, the water streaming down her back. Images from the past few weeks flashed across her mind. Seth laughing. Seth giving her his cockiest, dirtiest smile. Seth's face blank with exhaustion the night Lola died. Seth whispering sweet, smutty somethings as they made love.

Jesus. Was it any wonder Vivian had fallen for him? She'd been playing with fire while juggling dynamite, and the only miracle was that she hadn't done something really crazy like blurt out her feelings for him in the heat of the moment.

The thought was enough to make her shudder as she

toweled dry. She could imagine his utter bewilderment so vividly it almost felt like a true memory. She could almost see his eyes going blank, him retreating as he grasped that she'd joined the ranks of women who had gone before her in craving something from him that he didn't have to give.

Or didn't want to give. Or wasn't ready to give.

Same difference, at the end of the day.

She pulled on panties and a tank top, then wrapped herself in the flowing silk robe a friend had brought from Vietnam. She always felt comforted by its billowing softness, and she needed that right now.

She lay on her side on her bed, imagining how the next fifty years were going to play out. All the family events where Seth and Daisy would be close enough to touch and yet absolutely out of bounds. The sound of his laughter in another room. His impersonal kiss on her cheek each time they said hello or goodbye. The inevitable time when he'd arrive with another woman on his arm.

This was why people didn't get involved with co-workers—when things went pear-shaped, it was hell having to look them in the eye every day. She'd bought in to a similar hell falling for Seth, and there was nothing she could do about it, short of packing up her things and running back to L.A.

The thought had no sooner crossed her mind than she dismissed it. Her days of running away were over. She had a growing business here, but more importantly, this was home. This was where her heart felt most at peace. In the short term, that meant she would live through some grief and pain as she taught herself to let go of wanting Seth. But that was simply the way it would have to be. She would have to come up with strategies for hiding her feelings when he was around, and keep herself busy the rest of the time. Maybe she would give herself permission to avoid him for a while. Just until the sharpness of her hurt and disappointment dulled. She could easily go several months without seeing him if she was creative with excuses. Surely by then she'd have a grip on her feelings.

Surely.

Then she remembered that Lola's funeral was Tuesday. As much as she wanted to protect herself, there was no way she could give herself a free pass on that one. She cared about Seth and Daisy too much to abandon them on such a significant day.

No, she would go. She would say the right things to Seth, to Dennis and Melissa. If she was lucky, she might get a chance to spend some time with Daisy.

She pressed a hand to her chest, bearing down on the ache there. And after the funeral she would come home and be kind to herself until she stopped wanting something she couldn't have.

In the meantime, she would simply have to live with the hollowed-out feeling behind her rib cage and the hot, pressured feeling behind her eyes.

Resolved, she sought the comfort and oblivion of sleep.

SETH HAD A crappy few days before the funeral. Daisy was fractious, and he wound up taking her to the clinic on Sunday afternoon because he wanted reassurance that he wasn't overlooking anything. He wasn't, they assured him, so he took his daughter home and invested in more pacing, jiggling and cajoling in an attempt to soothe her. Vivian kept slipping into his thoughts, and finally he gave up trying to distract himself from thinking about her.

She'd touched his life profoundly—touched *him* profoundly—and he was resigned to the idea that she would be with him, in his head, his gut, his blood and his dreams, for a while. There was no pretending otherwise. There was even a twisted kind of comfort in the notion.

Yeah. That was how messed up he was.

By the time Tuesday morning rolled around he was raw-eyed from lack of sleep and feeling more than a little frayed around the edges.

The perfect mindset for a funeral.

He dressed with care, thinking of Dennis and Melissa and what this day meant to them. Wanting to do the right thing by Lola.

Predictably, Daisy threw up on his suit jacket as he was about to start the long process of loading all her paraphernalia in the car. He tried sponging the mark, then wound up stripping off his grey suit and putting on his navy one. They were running ten minutes late by the time they hit the road, and he hit speed dial to call Jason, knowing his perennially punctual brother would be there and could pass on a message to Dennis and Melissa in case they were worried.

It wasn't until his brother picked up that Seth remembered that he was still royally pissed with him after the big-brother lecture he'd received Saturday morning. The only thing that stopped him from hanging up was the fact that his brother had caller ID and would know it was him.

"It's me," he said coolly. "Just wanted to let you know I'm running late, in case anyone is worried."

"I'm coming from work but I'm almost there. I'll pass it along." His brother sounded unnaturally stiff.

"Good. Thanks. I appreciate it." Seth, too, sounded

as though he was talking to a stranger, but he figured that was his brother's fault, not his. Jason hadn't bothered to pick up the phone to apologize since reading him the riot act, and no way was Seth going to be the one who extended the olive branch.

No way.

"How's Daisy?" Jason asked.

"She's fine."

"Good to hear. Which way are you coming?"

"Down through Camberwell to the freeway, then onto Springvale Road."

"Might be worth jumping on the EastLink if you want to make up time," Jason suggested neutrally.

Seth's patience was already thin and his brother's careful conversation shredded what was left of it.

"For God's sake. Is that the best you can do?" he snapped.

"What?"

"If offering me route suggestions is your way of apologizing for Saturday morning, you're going to have to try harder. A lot harder." He changed lanes and jockeyed for position at the lights.

"I wanted to talk to you in person. After the funeral," Jason said.

"Fine, do that, if that's the way you want to handle it," Seth said shortly, reaching for the button to end the call.

"You're still pissed with me."

It wasn't a question.

"What do you think?"

"I was out of line. I realize that. As you said, what you and Vivian do is between the two of you. You're both old enough and ugly enough to work it out for yourselves."

His brother was saying all the right things, yet Seth could hear the "but" lurking beneath his words.

"But you still think I'm a sleazy, opportunistic asshole, right? That I'm taking advantage of her?" He was so tired, and a part of him had been spoiling for a fight with someone—anyone—since Vivian had left.

Jason's heavy sigh came down the line. "I told you, I overreacted, and I said stuff I shouldn't have. I apologize for that. But I'm not going to apologize for looking out for Vivian and being worried about her. You don't know her the way we do. She's not as tough as she likes to pretend."

"You think I don't know that? Vivian has a heart the size of the moon," Seth said hotly. "She likes to come across as cynical and on top of things, but she chooses to see the good in everyone. She would lay down her life for the people she loves."

There was a short pause.

"Okay. Maybe you know her a little better than I thought you did." Jason sounded confused.

"Vivian and I understand each other. We always have. I like her more than almost anyone else I know, and if you think I'd voluntarily hurt her or take advantage of her, you really do need your head read."

Another pause.

"I thought you guys weren't seeing each other anymore," Jason said.

"That's right."

"Even though you like her more than almost anyone else you know?"

It was amazing how revealing his words sounded when they were being parroted back to him.

"I should probably concentrate on the road. I'll see you in thirty minutes, okay?"

Seth ended the call before his brother could ask more probing questions. The last thing he needed was his brother running to Jodie with some story about how besotted Seth was with Vivian. Neither he nor Vivian needed that kind of speculation buzzing around them. They'd made their clean break, kept things neat and tidy. He wasn't about to be the one to make them messy. It felt like the least he owed her.

Plus it makes it easier for your ego. Let's not forget that bit, stud.

Fine. And it made it easier on his ego. Since it was all he had left, he figured he was allowed to preserve it.

He was fifteen minutes late by the time he un-strapped Daisy from her car seat, put her into her stroller and made his way to the Wilson Chapel at the Springvale Botanical Cemetery. People were milling in the foyer still, and he relaxed a notch when he realized that he and Daisy hadn't held things up. He spotted his brother first, then Jodie, and was about to make his way to them when Dennis and Melissa waved from across the room. He corrected his course, glancing around the crowd. It wasn't until he spotted Vivian that he realized he was looking for her.

She was wearing a deep blue dress that made him think of a black-and-white movie from the thirties. She stood in profile to him, her eyes covered with large sun-glasses as she talked to her parents.

She looked so good his step faltered. The urge to go to her, simply so he could be close to her, so he could hear her voice and look into her eyes, was almost overwhelming.

He tore his gaze away and focused on the Browns.

"There you are. And there's our sweet girl. Can I hold her?" Melissa asked eagerly, already reaching for the baby.

"Of course," Seth said easily. Daisy was a living, breathing balm, and he figured Melissa and Dennis would need their fair share of cuddles today.

He watched as Melissa arranged Daisy's blanket to ensure she was warm in the chapel's air conditioning. Lola's mother had seemingly aged since arriving in Australia, and Seth had to look away from the grief in her eyes as she stroked her granddaughter's cheek. He glanced across the room in time to catch sight of Vivian following Jodie and Jason into the chapel.

One day it was possible he would be able to watch the provocative sway of her walk and not be affected, but today was not that day. God help him.

"We should go in. I think they want to start," Dennis said.

Seth piloted the stroller, walking behind the Browns as they made their way to the front pew. He recognized a few of Lola's friends in the crowd, as well as his own parents. Again, he couldn't stop himself from searching for Vivian's face. He found her sharing a pew with his brother's family. She'd taken off her sunglasses, and for the briefest of moments, their gazes clashed. He was the one who broke the contact, busying himself setting the stroller to one side as the Browns sat.

She looked beautiful. He wasn't sure if he'd seen her in that particular shade of blue before, but it suited her supremely.

Stop it. Today of all days, let it go. Let her go.

Easier said than done. He inhaled sharply through his nose, then fixed his gaze on the celebrant who was waiting at the lectern for everyone to be seated. After a few minutes, music came up—the Dixie Chicks' "Lullaby," one of Lola's all-time favorites—and people slowly fell silent. Seth listened to the lyrics about love and forever and knew this was going to be a tough hour.

Lola had not been his love, but she had been his lover. They had had some good times together. He'd enjoyed her, and he hoped she'd enjoyed him. He hoped that he'd never made her unhappy, that he'd never given her cause to regret the night she walked into Night Howls and took a seat at the bar.

"Good morning, everyone. I'd like to welcome you to the memorial service for Dolores Alice Brown," the celebrant said as the last notes of the song faded. "As we all know, Dolores preferred to be known as Lola, which her mother tells me suited her much more, and that is how we will remember her today.

"Lola was born two days early during a cold winter in Yorkshire twenty-four years ago. She was the much longed-for younger sister to Tom, and the daughter Melissa and Dennis had been hoping for to complete their young family. From the start Melissa says she knew Lola had a mind of her own...."

Seth bowed his head as he listened to the celebrant outline Lola's too-short life. Zara was invited to speak next, and Seth found himself laughing along with everyone else as Zara recounted some of her friend's more outrageous antics—the time Lola had tried to talk her way into an exclusive restaurant by pretending she was famous, the time she'd sent herself flowers to pique the interest of someone she worked with, her obsessive love for all things Dr. Who, especially if they involved David Tennant.

Another of Lola's friends spoke next, then Melissa passed Daisy to him while she and Dennis walked to the lectern.

"You'll have to forgive us if we get a bit messy," Dennis said, his already watery gaze scanning the audience. "Lola was our girl, our little firecracker, and we're still trying to get our heads around the fact that she won't be ringing up from the other side of the world with some outrageous tale, or clomping through the door in her sky-high heels."

Daisy was restless, so Seth put her in the stroller and rocked it back and forth, hoping the motion would settle her.

"As you've probably gathered, our Lola was a bit of a character. Never let *no* get in the way of a good time was her philosophy, and she prosecuted that belief to the hilt. As you can imagine, she led us on a merry dance through her teen years, and I don't mind admitting that there were times when we both despaired of her ever being fit for decent company."

A ripple of laughter ran through the room, and Dennis took advantage of the pause to dab at his eyes with a folded handkerchief.

"She turned out pretty bloody amazing in the end, though, I'm sure you'd agree…."

Dennis talked about what a good friend and daughter Lola had been, and how excited she'd been about coming to Australia. They'd worried for her being so far away from home, but they'd looked forward to her frequent emails and phone calls. When he talked about the accident, his voice became thick with emotion and it was clear he was struggling to continue. He paused, his face quivering as he attempted to regain his composure. After a beat of concerted effort, he shook his head, signaling he couldn't continue. The celebrant stepped forward, only to hesitate when Melissa reached out to tilt the microphone her way.

"I wasn't going to speak. Didn't think I'd be up to it. But there's something I want to say. Something I want you all to hear." Her voice was thready with emotion, her face creased with grief. "My relationship with Lola wasn't perfect, and there are things I would change if I could go back. But I can't. I can't tell Lola how proud I am of her. I'm not sure I ever did that enough. I can't tell her how in awe of her I was. And I can't tell her how much I love her. I'll never be able to do that again. All I can do is stand here in front of you and tell you that Dolores Alice Brown was an amazing woman, and I will be proud that she was mine until my dying day. It's not enough, but it will have to do. Thank you."

Melissa's regret was a palpable thing, a ghost at the feast. Seth swallowed a lump of emotion and focused on his hands where they gripped his knees. How terrible to realize too late what was important, to never be able to right the wrongs of the past.

The celebrant took control of the mike, wrapping up the ceremony by inviting everyone for refreshments in the foyer. Music came on, this time Coldplay's "Paradise."

Seth took a moment to wipe the tears from his cheeks, feeling hugely exposed even though he knew if there was anywhere a man was allowed to cry, it was at a funeral. He stood as Melissa and Dennis returned to their pew looking shrunken and weary, as though the simple act of getting through the ceremony had diminished them. He watched them sink onto the pew and wished he had something to say that would offer them even a scrap of comfort.

Typically, nothing came to him, and he glanced to where the rest of the mourners were making their way through the double doors into the foyer for the promised tea, coffee and cakes.

"Why don't you stay in here for a while?" he suggested quietly. "Take a moment to catch your breath, and I'll bring you both a cup of tea."

Melissa nodded, her gaze on the stroller, and Seth knew what she was asking with her saying a word.

"Daisy can stay here with you," he said.

"Thank you," she whispered.

Seth rested a hand on her shoulder, then turned away, woefully conscious of his own inadequacy. He was too scared of saying the wrong thing, of inadvertently increasing their pain. It was far safer to retreat to the foyer and do something concrete like stand in line for tea than wade into such deep emotional waters.

His mother came over to talk to him as he waited for the tea, and he agreed with her that it had been a lovely ceremony and that, yes, it was incredibly difficult for the Browns. He could see Vivian's bright head out of the corner of his eye, but he didn't let himself so much as glance her way. He felt…flayed after the Browns' heartbreaking eulogy. He wasn't sure he would be able to mask his own want if he let himself look at her.

He made two cups of tea, realizing belatedly that he had no idea how the Browns took it. He settled for grabbing a few sugar sachets and giving them both a dash of milk before returning to the chapel, where he found Dennis holding Daisy. He and Melissa appeared marginally better.

"I wasn't sure how you liked it, so I hope it's okay," Seth said as he handed a cup to Melissa and set the other on the pew beside Dennis.

"This will be fine," Melissa said with a small smile. "I hope everyone doesn't think we're rude, staying in here for a moment." She glanced over her shoulder uncertainly.

"They get it. My mother asked me to pass on that she thought it was a lovely ceremony. *Beautiful* was the word she used."

"Oh, good. We wanted to do Lola justice," Melissa said.

They were silent for a beat, and the conversational hum in the foyer filtered into the room.

"I should probably circulate a little," Seth said. There were people he needed to thank for coming, people who had come to support him.

"We'll be out in a minute," Dennis said.

Seth slipped into the foyer and scanned the room for people he should speak to. Zara, and Syrie and Jack from the bar, had come. Jodie and Vivian's parents had put in an appearance, too.

Somehow, he found himself making his way to where Vivian stood with his brother and sister-in-law. He was unable to keep his distance a moment longer.

"Thanks for coming, guys," he said.

Vivian's mascara was smudged, presumably because she'd been crying. She looked sad and beautiful, warm and real. It took every ounce of self-control he possessed to stop himself from pulling her into his arms.

She wasn't his to comfort. She never had been.

"How are the Browns holding up?" she asked.

"They're okay. Exhausted, I think," Seth said.

"That was a pretty special speech they gave. Straight from the heart," Jason said.

"Yeah, it was."

He could smell Vivian's perfume. The sunlight streaming through the windows made her hair glow. The ache of his need for her, his want, was a physical pain in his chest and belly.

It's over. You had your chance, and she called time. Suck it up and move on.

"I should keep doing the rounds, but I wanted to say thanks for your support. Not just today, but since this whole thing blew up." He sounded stiff, too formal, but there wasn't much he could do about that.

"You're family, Seth. We've got your back," Jodie said simply.

He ducked his head in acknowledgement. She leaned forward to kiss his cheek, then his brother slung an arm around him and gave him a half hug, his fist thunking Seth's back with a dull thud. Seth told himself it would be weird if he didn't kiss Vivian, too, so he turned to her. He looked into her eyes for the briefest second before focusing on the spot near the angle of her jaw-bone that he planned to kiss. Her skin felt warm and soft beneath his lips, and he breathed in deeply before stepping back.

He tried to think of something else to say, something innocuous, but he was too busy fighting the inexplicable push of tears. It hit him then that Vivian would be the single great regret of his life. The one he never got right. The one who might have made everything work.

He forced himself to turn away, to take one step, then another, then another. Soon he was across the room, someone handed him a piece of cake and he was agreeing that the music had been very interesting and surprisingly moving. He forced himself to count to twenty before he looked at her, for dignity's sake. For appearances, because he didn't want to embarrass Vivian or expose himself more than he already had.

God forbid his pride might take a pummeling, after all. Not when it was all he had left.

What he saw made everything in him go very still.

Jodie had flagged down a server with a tray of tea and coffee. She passed a cup to Vivian, who reached out to accept it, but her hands were trembling so much that she sent tea sloshing over the brim. For the briefest of moments, her composure cracked, her brow furrowing, her chin wobbling. Jodie acted quickly, relieving her of the cup, leaning close to say something. Vivian nodded, then Jodie glanced across the room.

Straight at him.

She looked away again almost immediately, but there had been so much emotion in that single look that Seth felt seared.

Fierce protectiveness. Frustration. Accusation. Sadness.

And it had been directed at him, by Jodie, on behalf of Vivian.

"Seth, help me out here—what's the name of Lola's friend from the call center? The little dark-haired one?" Dennis said at his elbow.

Seth blinked, wrenching his gaze from the tableau across the room. He had to force himself to focus on the other man, then he had to prod himself to remember what Dennis had asked, because the bulk of his brain was busy trying to understand what he'd witnessed.

"Bianca. Her name is Bianca," he said absently.

"Of course. And the other girl she's with is Zara. It was good of them to come."

"Yes. Yes, it was."

"If you haven't got plans this afternoon, I was thinking I might take Mel somewhere nice for lunch. You'd be welcome to join us. And Daisy, of course."

Seth frowned. This afternoon. He genuinely couldn't think that far ahead. Not when his mind was so full of Vivian.

The wobble of her chin.

The tremble in her hands.

The way Jodie had looked at him. As though she wanted to kick him. As though she wanted to hurt him.

There were probably lots of reasons for Jodie to look at him like that. And Vivian might well have been upset by something said during the service. Everyone had commented on how emotional it was.

She might also be upset because she'd spoken to him. Because he'd kissed her cheek and walked away.

Because—maybe—she'd spent the past few days being bloody miserable as she stared down the barrel of a life that didn't include him.

Was it possible? Or was he simply clutching at straws, a desperate, drowning man?

"I'm sorry, Dennis, but there's something I need to do," Seth said, already turning away.

He was halfway there before he realized the object of his intent was missing. Jodie and Jason stood alone, their heads together in private conversation. Seth scanned the crowd, standing on his toes in order to see every corner. There was no flash of deep blue dress, no flare of strawberry-blond hair. Urgent, he made his way to his brother's side.

"Where's Vivian?"

Jodie started, one hand clutching at Jason's arm. "You scared me."

"Where is she?" he asked again.

"She had a headache. She went home," Jason said.

Seth's gaze shot to the door. She must have slipped out while he was talking to Dennis. She could have been gone only a minute or two.

He took off, not bothering with explanations. He had to catch Vivian.

He erupted into the warm air, casting about for any sign of her. There was no one on the path to the main parking lot, and he spun to look in the opposite direction. Again, nothing, which meant he needed to guess and hope he got it right.

He broke into a run, his suit jacket billowing behind him, his tie flying over his shoulder, fully aware that he could have this whole thing totally ass-about and that he might be about to expose himself in the worst possible way.

He had no idea what Vivian's true feelings were. She'd never given any indication that she wanted anything from him beyond great sex and a few laughs. She'd talked about things getting messy, but she'd never said she wanted more. Not from him anyway. Like him, she'd always been very careful to guard herself when they were together. She'd kept things light, and she'd met every riposte he sent her way with a witty sally of her own. She'd never once let him see the chinks in her armor, just as he'd never let her see the chinks in his.

That was the way it had always been between them, right from the start. A battle of wills. A game. A dance. Parry, thrust, advance, retreat. Neither of them giving any ground. Neither of them showing any weakness.

It had always been part of the fun. Part of the danger and challenge.

It had also stopped them from talking about what they were to each other, what place they held in each other's lives. God forbid they let their guards down. God forbid they show weakness or risk hurt. Not after ten years. Not when there was so much at stake.

Potentially.

He rounded the corner to the parking lot and caught sight of Vivian as she walked the final few feet to her car. She pulled her keys from her bag—

"Vivian!"

He put on a burst of speed as she glanced over her shoulder. She froze when she saw him, then slowly turned to face him. When he stopped in front of her, she reached out and wrapped her hand around the door handle.

As though she needed the support.

"Seth. Is something wrong?"

She was utterly composed, a faint, slightly quizzical smile on her lips. Friendly, familiar, but not too familiar. Not too anything. If he hadn't seen that moment with the tea, if her hand weren't white-knuckle tight on the handle, he wouldn't have suspected that something far less orderly and controlled might be going on beneath the surface.

"There's something I forgot to tell you. Something important," he said. "That night, when we were talking about why I never settled down. I said it had never felt right, that I'd never met someone amazing enough, but that was a lie."

He studied her face, trying to get a read on her, aware of his heart threatening to beat its way out of his chest. He wasn't sure if he was hopeful or terrified, maybe a bit of both, but he was beyond the point of no return.

He'd sat in a room and said goodbye to a woman who should have lived a good, long life. He'd listened to her parents sob, and he'd paid witness to her mother's painful regret. He was *over* being safe. He was over letting this particular woman walk away from him because to ask her to stop and stay might mean he was exposing himself utterly. Something Seth Anderson never did, because he was just too damn cool for that kind of vulnerability.

So freaking cool it hurt.

If he was about to crash and burn, so be it. He'd rather risk humiliation and rejection than go to his grave not having tried to seize this thing that had always lived between him and Vivian and turn it into everything it could be. Everything he wanted it to be.

"It was a lie because it has felt right once in my life, but I was too young and too scared to acknowledge it. I met this girl at a wedding, you see—"

Vivian closed her eyes, her shoulders slumping. "Seth."

She sounded broken. Defeated. But he wasn't about to stop talking, not when he was knee-deep in his declaration.

"She was the sexiest, hottest, wildest, smartest woman I'd ever laid eyes on, and when I kissed her it was like finding the other part of myself. But I was only twenty-four, and I was frankly terrified that I could feel that way so quickly about someone I'd just met. I figured I had my whole life ahead of me, that there would be other amazing women. Truckloads of them, since I was going to be a rock star."

She now watched him with a quiet intensity, waiting him out.

"There never was, though, Vivian. No one else ever measured up. Never even came close, because none of them were you."

"I can't believe you're saying this."

"I should have said it years ago. I should have said it that night I tried to crawl into the sofa bed with you at Jason's place. I should have said it every time I saw you for the past ten years. But I've always been stupid around you. I've always been scared of the way you make me feel. Of the way you make me want. Vivian, I freaking love you. And I honestly have no idea how you feel, but I really bloody hope you're willing to give me a chance to prove to you that, despite appearances and a truly shitty track record and a life that's pretty much a one-man disaster zone right now, I adore you."

He'd run out of words. All he could do was stand there and wait. The toughest, most raw seconds of his life.

Vivian let go of the handle. Her eyes were as clear as the blue-green of ocean water as she took a step toward him. "I lied, too, Seth. I told you once that Franco was my one-that-got-away. But it's always been you. Always."

"Jesus." Relief was a blow to his solar plexus. He dragged her into his arms, foregoing any pretense at finesse as he kissed her so hard their teeth clashed. Her words were still ringing in his ears, but he couldn't get close enough, needed the reassurance of her body against his. He pulled her closer, his fingers digging into her shoulders as the full import of what she'd said sunk in.

She cared. She wanted this. She wanted *them*.

"Seth." She pulled back from their kiss, her face creasing into a frown as she looked at him. Then her expression softened, and she touched his cheek, which was when he realized he was crying.

Like a big baby.

"I love you." She cupped his cheek and kissed his tears. "You don't need these. I'm not going anywhere."

"I know." And he did, deep in his gut. He simply couldn't believe how close he'd come—they'd come—to letting this slip away. "I guess I'm a little freaked by the close call."

Her eyes were bright with understanding. "Yeah, we like to run things down to the wire, don't we? Such drama queens." She hooked both her arms around his neck, her body warm again his from breast to knee. "It's going to be a bumpy ride. You know that, right? There's a lot of ego to wrangle between us. And a ton of attitude."

He couldn't stop himself from kissing her. Because he could. Because she'd declared herself his, and it would take a decade or two before that ceased to be a wonder to him.

"I wouldn't want it any other way," he said. Then it hit him that while it was one thing to acknowledge how they both felt, they weren't exactly starting with a clean slate. "Daisy—"

Vivian pressed a finger to his lips. "You don't need to ask. She's a part of you, which means I will always love her. I don't pretend to be an expert on babies and children, but I can promise you that I already love her more than is wise. Holding your hand while we both make mistakes would be an honor, Seth. If you're willing to trust me with your girl."

He swore under his breath and had to tip his head back to get a grip on his emotions. "Sweetheart, I'd trust you with my life. Ten times over."

They kissed, a long, slow, intense meeting of mouths and tongues, arms tight around one another. He could feel her heart beating, could feel the intensity of her emotions vibrating through her body, and knew she could feel his in turn.

"No more lies," he said when they came up for air. "No more bullshit to save face. No more trying to out-cool each other."

"Deal, my love. My Seth." She smiled, a sweet, slightly wistful curve of her mouth. "Do you have any idea how many years I've wanted to say that to you?"

"No. But you can tell me later, when I take you home."

And he kissed her again, because the sun was shining, and they'd finally found each other, and they were alive, with a lifetime of adventures and challenges ahead of them.

Which pretty much made him the luckiest man in the world.

It had taken them ten years to get here, to this place and this time and this moment. One thing was certain—he wasn't wasting another second.

* * * * *

Back to You

A big thanks to Marsha for thinking of me for this anthology, and to Margaret for helping make the manuscript as good as it could be. None of my writing would get anywhere without the advice, support and inspiration provided by Chris, who really is my hero.

CHAPTER ONE

He's not supposed to be here.

Becky Taylor froze on the threshold of the restaurant. Across the room, Cal MacKenzie leaned against the far wall, tall and dark and gorgeous. After ten years, the unexpected sight of him stole her breath away and sent her heart hammering into overdrive.

He was supposed to be in London. He'd moved there five years ago with his new wife, and Becky hadn't had any word through the grapevine that he was back.

He had every right to attend the staff reunion—they were both ex-employees of Hannigan's Discount Emporium, a family-owned store that had paid many a student's way through college. The thing was, she wouldn't have come if she'd known he was going to be there.

Becky quickly corrected herself. Of course she would have come; staying away would have meant she still cared.

"Hey, look—Cal's here," her old friend Carolyn said behind her.

Becky forced a smile.

"How about that."

"Now it really is the old Hannigan's gang," Carolyn said.

"Yeah." Becky hoped she didn't sound as off balance as she felt.

She shot another glance across the room. This time Cal was staring back at her. He raised the beer in his hand in silent greeting, his blue eyes smiling at her.

It was a warm Sydney night in the middle of a hot Australian summer, but all the little hairs on Becky's arms stood on end. It had been a full decade since she'd last seen Cal, but he still had the same effect on her. Damn him.

Carolyn was already exchanging hugs and exclamations with the group of people nearest the door. Becky wiped her sweaty hands down the thighs of her jeans. She spotted a discreet sign for the ladies' room on the door to her left. Three steps, and she was closing the bathroom door behind her and sighing with relief.

A moment. That was all she needed. A short moment to get over the surprise.

She stared at her reflection in the mirror, unhappy with the dazed expression on her face.

He's here, get over it. It doesn't matter, it doesn't mean anything. It definitely doesn't mean anything to you.

She and Cal had gone their separate ways a long time ago. The memory of how shattered she'd felt when he called an end to their brief relationship might still make her squirm with self-consciousness, but the days of her mooning over him were long gone. She was thirty-one now, not twenty-one. She owned her own home, she drove a sleek and sexy sports car, and until recently she'd been in a live-in relationship with a successful, attractive man. She was worlds away from the girl she'd been when Cal MacKenzie had ruled her world. The only reason she'd felt that illicit surge of excitement when she'd seen his tall body standing there was because she'd been taken by surprise. He'd once meant something to her, now he didn't. End of story.

She squared her shoulders and dug out her lipstick, smoothing on a fresh coat then topping it with lip gloss. Her lips looked shiny and full when she'd finished. She fluffed her long, dark, curly hair and adjusted the hem on her red T-shirt. Determined to prove something to herself, she exited the bathroom and made a beeline for the far wall where Cal still lounged, laughing with a handful of men.

He straightened as he saw her approach. She found herself looking up into his tanned, handsome face, a hundred old memories washing through her as she noted the way his black hair still flopped over his left eye, and how his mouth still quirked up more on one side than the other when he smiled.

"Becky Taylor," he said. "Good to see you."

Before she could respond, he ducked his head and leaned close to plant a kiss on her cheek. For a few seconds she was swamped with his heat and scent. She had to blink to clear her head as he straightened again.

"Cal MacKenzie. Aren't you in the wrong hemisphere?" she asked, amazed at how casual and light and assured her voice sounded.

"Moved home last year," he said. He placed his empty beer bottle on a nearby table and angled his body so that he cut her off from the rest of the group he'd been standing with. Almost as though he wanted her all to himself.

She pushed the stupid thought away. She didn't care if he wanted her all to himself—she didn't want him. That was the important thing.

Sliding a hand into the back pocket of her jeans, Becky cocked her head to one side.

"Still in IT?"

"Yep. Started my own consultancy with a mate, actually."

"Brave of you. It's a pretty competitive field."

"We're doing okay," he said.

She'd already noted his Hugo Boss jeans, Gucci boots and the expensive Longines watch on his wrist. She guessed he must be doing very well—but then, Cal had always been modest. Even as a young man, he'd possessed a quiet confidence and charm that had drawn people to him. Herself included.

"I hear you're with David Jones now," he said, naming Australia's most prestigious department store. "Ladies' fashion buyer, is that right?"

Had he asked after her, or had someone told him what she did for a living?

"That's right."

"I suppose that means you've been jetting around, checking out the latest fashion shows?" he asked.

"As much as I can," she said. She could brag about Paris, New York and London, but she had no need to impress Cal. He was just an old work colleague. No big deal.

"I was admiring your boots when you came in," he said, and they both glanced down at her dark red, hand-tooled Western boots. "They look like the real deal."

"They are. Straight out of Texas."

She was very aware of the way his gaze travelled back up her jeans-clad legs and over her breasts before it returned to her face. She felt a flare of excitement when she saw the desire in his eyes.

Unbidden, a handful of sense memories raced across her mind: the feel of his long, strong fingers stroking her body, the way he used to whisper in her ear as he drove her to her climax, the aching, needful fullness of his body moving inside hers.

She licked her lips and tucked her other hand into her back pocket to stop herself from reaching for him.

Then she realized what she was doing and she snapped to attention.

Pathetic. Ten years, and he cocks his little finger and you're ready to go on the spot. Too sad for words, Taylor.

"So, is your wife here?" she asked pointedly. Time to nip this flirtation—if that was what this was—in the bud.

Cal held up his left hand, displaying his ringless fingers.

"Divorced," he said. "Papers just came through. How about you?"

Divorced. He was divorced. Which meant he was free. Available.

"I'm not married," she said evasively.

"But you're living with someone, aren't you?" Cal asked.

Becky blinked. He *had* done his homework.

"Not anymore."

He looked pleased. She glanced away to break the spell he was weaving around her. She'd always found him fatally attractive. Right from the very first day when she'd looked up from reading a book in the staff room at Hannigan's and Cal had been standing in the doorway, a dark-haired god with blue eyes and a roguish smile. She'd been nineteen years old, and his innate charm had hit her like a freight train.

Even though she knew it smacked of retreat, she cast a look over her shoulder, scanning the party for an escape route.

"Look, there's Cheryl. I haven't seen her in ages," she said with relief. "I'd better go say hi or she'll kill me."

She had a smile fixed firmly in place when she turned back to him.

"Great to see you, Cal," she said.

Before he could say anything else, she turned and walked away.

CAL WATCHED her walk all the way across the room. More specifically, he watched her ass. Becky had always had a great ass—full, high, firm—and time had not altered it one iota.

God, she looked good. And she was single. He couldn't believe his luck. If he was completely honest with himself, she'd been the main reason behind his appearance at the reunion tonight. Sure, he'd wanted to catch up with a few old buddies, but it was Becky who had really drawn him. For ten years, the memory of their time together had burned bright as the hottest, most sexually satisfying time of his life. They hadn't been able to get enough of each other. He could still remember how desperate he used to be to get his hands on her smooth, creamy skin after a full shift working alongside her. More than once they'd wound up in the backseat of his car in the parking lot or in the dark corner behind the box crusher in the stock room, tearing at each other's clothes until he was inside her, giving her what they both wanted.

Was it any wonder that his thoughts had gravitated toward her now that he was a free man again?

He kept his gaze on her as she joined the group of ex-Hannigan's employees near the bar. Her hair was longer than when he'd known her. Back then, she'd kept her curls short and well-tamed, but he liked the way they cascaded around her shoulders tonight, the overhead lighting picking out rich highlights in the tumbled, dark mass. She'd put on a little weight, just enough to make her hips rounder and her breasts fuller, but her face was exactly the way he remembered it—the small, upturned nose, the full lips, the big brown eyes. She had the smoothest, clearest skin of any woman he'd ever known, and he could still recall the way he used to chase the blushes across her body when he had her naked in his bed.

Cal registered the tightness in his jeans. If he didn't stop staring, he was going to embarrass himself in a very public way. He hadn't expected to be so struck by her. When he'd hoped that she'd be here, when he'd speculated as to whether the old fire would still be there between them, he hadn't imagined anything like the heat that had ripped through him the moment he saw her. It had honestly been as though the years had fallen away and they were two kids again—two kids who desperately wanted to jump each other's bones.

Across the room, Becky laughed and brushed a stray curl away from her cheek, tucking it behind her ear. Even though he'd been staring at her shamelessly for the past few minutes, she hadn't glanced his way once.

He was forced to a reluctant conclusion—that the heat he was feeling was one-sided and only one of them was interested in bone-jumping.

It had been a long time between drinks; it had been crazy to think that there might be something left between them. Just because his thoughts had constantly drifted to her over the years, wondering what she was doing, who she was with, who was to say that hers had done the same?

Which left him standing alone at a reunion with no beer in his hand and a hard-on in his jeans. Not exactly a recipe for social success.

Forcing himself to look away, Cal shoved a hand into his pocket and rejoined the group of men he'd been hanging with before Becky entered and rocked his world off its axis.

He had the answer to the question that his body had

asked when he received the invitation to the reunion—
yes, Becky was still the hottest woman he'd ever known.
And no, he would not be getting a chance to relive history.

A damn shame, but he would survive.

BECKY WAS so tense and wired after she got home from
the reunion that her T-shirt was damp with perspiration.
Nervous energy, caused by pretending that she didn't
care a hoot about Cal all night. What a joke.

The truth was, she'd been painfully aware of his every
move. His laugh, who he was talking to, what he ate or
drank. Seeing him so unexpectedly had really thrown
her for a loop.

If there was one saving grace to the whole evening,
it was that she was a better actress than she'd ever given
herself credit for. Despite how she'd been feeling privately, she was pretty damned sure that no one had
guessed how she really felt—least of all Cal himself.
She'd been cool with him every step of the way, even
when he'd approached her again after dinner and spent
half an hour lounging in a chair talking to her and Carolyn about old times. She'd been supremely conscious of
every pass his blue-eyed gaze made over her body and
her face—but not once had she allowed him to see how
much his slow, lazy appraisals affected her.

Being with the Hannigan's crowd had been the perfect incentive to keep her guard up. Carolyn had been
well aware of her crush on Cal all those years ago, and
she'd been thrilled when Becky and Cal had finally gotten together. When it had all fallen in a heap after just a
month, Carolyn had been a sympathetic and supportive
friend, but Becky's pride had demanded that she keep

the extent of her hurt to herself. To Carolyn and the rest of her Hannigan's colleagues, she and Cal had had a fling for a few weeks that hadn't worked out. They'd both moved on, and only Becky knew how big the hole was that Cal had left in her heart—and that was the way she wanted it to stay.

As Becky shed her sweaty clothes and stepped beneath the shower, she forced thoughts of Cal to one side. He was the past, history. She wanted to wash him off the way she was washing away the stress and tension of her evening. Down the plughole with him, and may he never blight her life again. He'd wreaked enough damage already, thank you very much.

After towelling herself dry, she slid into bed and switched the light off. Closing her eyes, she acknowledged to herself that she was pleased to have survived the evening with her dignity in tact. Willing sleep to come, she slowly relaxed her body into the mattress.

She should have known better. In the months following their breakup, dreams of Cal had tortured her endlessly. Tonight, she was revisited by them with a vengeance.

There was no narrative to her dreams, just flashes of memory twisted into new shapes by her subconscious. Images of Cal's tall, strong body naked and ready for her, the too-familiar need to be close to him pulling at her, the tearing hurt of knowing that having had her, he didn't want her anymore.

She woke panting, the sheets twisted around her legs. She growled low in her throat as she rolled from her bed and grabbed the low-dose sleeping tablets she kept in her travel kit to help conquer jet lag. Downing one with a mouthful of water, she returned to bed, smoothed out the sheets and pummelled her pillow into a new shape.

"Get out of my head," she told Cal, even though she felt a little crazy doing it.

Rolling onto her side, she stared at the darkened square of her bedroom window until the tablets kicked in and she drifted into dreamless sleep.

Tomorrow was another day—a beautiful, fresh, Cal-free day. Bring it on.

You're thirty-one, Cal. Too old for this kind of crap.

It was three in the morning, and he was standing naked in the living room of his penthouse apartment, staring out at the darkened waters of Sydney Harbour. To his left, the bridge hung like a fairy-lit coat hanger in the sky, and all around the harbor, lights twinkled in the predawn blackness.

Everyone was asleep—except for him. He was too horny to sleep. Too restless and unsettled. He should have asked Becky out tonight. He'd been waiting to get her alone before he tried his luck in case she shot him down in flames, but it had never happened. Possibly because she hadn't wanted it to happen. The jury was still out on that one. Now he wished he'd thrown caution to the winds and just asked her, witnesses or no witnesses.

He walked into the kitchen, fumbling in the dark for a brandy balloon before pouring himself an inch of the golden liquid. Back in the living room, he hit the play button on his stereo and sank into the comforting soft leather of his couch. The mellow sounds of Coldplay filled the room as he sipped at the brandy and let his mind wander.

In the twelve months that he'd been back in Australia, a lot had changed in his life. Generally he had a sense that they'd changed for the better. His marriage hadn't survived the changes, but he was becoming more and more philosophical about that. In the end, he and Natalie had wanted different things. When she'd pushed him too hard, he'd pushed back.

He liked being back in Sydney. It was such a dynamic city, full of brash confidence and energy. And the weather—it was unfair even to think of comparing the gray heaviness of a London winter with the clear blue skies of home. Then there was his company. He and his partner, Daniel Strong, had attracted an exclusive set of clients, all of them high-end, and business was booming. Hence his penthouse apartment and very nice lifestyle.

He was quietly satisfied with all that he'd achieved in his thirty-one years, give or take one divorce and a few foolish decisions here and there along the way. So why was he sitting buck-naked on his sofa, swilling brandy in the vain hope that it would send him to sleep?

Becky Taylor. She of the perfect ass and the creamy breasts and the fiery passion of yesteryear. Closing his eyes, he relived the moment when she'd walked in the door tonight and stood there in all her red-cowboy-booted glory.

To hell with it. He was going to ask her out. As soon as it was remotely close to business hours, he'd look up her number at David Jones and call her. That was the only way he was going to get any closure on this; he felt it in his bones.

As though he'd finally given his tired body what it needed to sleep, he suddenly felt gritty-eyed with weariness.

"About time," he muttered to himself as he downed the last mouthful of brandy.

First thing tomorrow, he was making his play.

"BECKY, HOW ARE you?" the deep voice asked.

Becky's fingers clenched the phone receiver and she shifted to the edge of her seat.

"Cal? How did you get my number?" she queried stupidly.

"I looked it up. I wanted to ask you something, something I should have asked you last night at the reunion."

Becky swiveled in her chair and stared out at the spectacular view she had of Sydney's Hyde Park, a swathe of oak-and-plane-tree-dotted open space that created an oasis in the middle of the city.

"Yes?" she asked cautiously.

A surge of excitement raced up her spine. She squeezed her thighs together, sending a silent signal to her body— *Not on your life, pal. Not in a million years is* that *going to happen.*

"Will you have dinner with me?"

She was holding her breath, and she let it ease out slowly. Cal was asking her out. She hadn't imagined the spark of interest in his eyes last night. He still found her attractive. He wanted to explore that attraction.

All very good reasons to say no. But she hesitated, the word on the tip of her tongue. The silence stretched between them as her mind raced. If she said no, what would he think? That she wasn't up to the temptation? Worse, that she still had feelings for him? Pride demanded that she protect herself, as it had demanded all those years ago that she walk away from their brief relationship with her head high when he told her he wasn't ready for a big commitment, that things were moving too fast for him.

"Sure. When were you thinking?" she said.

It was her turn to be on the receiving end of surprised silence. He hadn't expected her to say yes. Interesting.

"How about tomorrow night?" he suggested. "Café Sydney?"

"I love it there. Sure. Shall we say eight?"

"I'll be there."

"You'd better be, since you called me," she said.

He laughed, the sound low and deep and compelling.

"See you, Beck," he said. Then she was listening to the dial tone.

Regret kicked in immediately. Was she *insane?* She had no business going to a cosy dinner with the man who had snapped her heart in two so efficiently all those years ago. Talk about being a glutton for punishment. Why on earth would she put herself in such a precarious position, especially when it was clear that Cal wanted to sleep with her again?

She was reaching for the phone before she realized she had no way of contacting him. She didn't know the name of his business, and she was almost certain he wouldn't have a publicly listed home number. A quick check on the Internet confirmed it. She slumped back in her seat and slapped her forehead with the palm of her hand.

"Stupid," she said, just as a familiar face appeared in her office doorway.

"Oooh, self abuse. Please don't stop on my account," Gareth said, swaying his way toward her guest chair.

Gareth was her opposite number in male fashion, and so gay that one of the secretaries had jokingly dubbed him "super gay" at the office Christmas party one year. It was a badge Gareth wore with pride—literally. In the annual Gay Pride parade last March, he'd worn a cape and a skin-tight Lycra bodysuit with a specially designed SG insignia on his chest. Now, he folded his long, slender legs and rested his beautifully manicured hands on them as he waited for her to continue.

"It's not the same with someone watching," Becky told him.

"Tell me about it," he said, rolling his eyes dramatically. "This is why I always advocate video cameras—if you must share, technology makes it so much less intrusive."

Becky laughed. "Sometimes I think you have a Ph.D. in innuendo."

Gareth looked pleased. "I do try, darling. Now, tell Uncle Gareth what's wrong. You know I always offer the best advice."

It was true—for an outwardly frivolous person, he was very perceptive. Or, as he liked to put it, his "emotional IQ topped out at freakin' genius."

"Just wrestling with a ghost from the past," she said, shrugging. "An old flame asked me out to dinner, and I stupidly said yes."

Gareth's eyebrows wiggled.

"How old is the flame? And is there a spark still?"

"Ten years. And it's dead and gone. Just my pride left to rake over the coals, really."

"But he wants to reignite it?" Gareth asked, really getting into the whole fire metaphor thing.

"I guess so. I need to track down his phone number and cancel."

Gareth looked down his nose at her, and somehow she found herself telling him everything: how she'd fallen for Cal the moment she met him, how she'd found out almost straightaway that he had a girlfriend, how she'd worked alongside him for two years, the tension between them building every day. And how she and Cal had gotten together the moment he broke up with his girlfriend and fireworks had exploded between them.

"We saw each other almost every single day for a

month. I utterly adored him. And then he told me that he wasn't ready for another serious relationship after coming out of three years with another woman."

"Ouch. How old were you both?"

"Twenty-one when we broke up. Intellectually, I understood where he was coming from. He was a good-looking guy, he was studying, he'd been tied down for three years. He wanted to party. But I felt like I'd been given the keys to the kingdom then had them snatched back again. I'd been in love with him for a year, and I only got to have him for a month. Not nearly long enough."

"Poor Becky," Gareth said.

"Yeah, well." She sat up a little straighter. "Anyway, it's all ancient history."

"Uh-uh. No way. You have unfinished business with this man. He cut you off before you were ready. You need to readdress the balance. You definitely can't cancel. What you have to do, Becky, my girl, is knock that man off his feet, dazzle him utterly, then walk away and leave him with his tongue hanging out and his zipper bulging. Revenge," Gareth said, eyes wide for dramatic effect.

It was a compelling argument. She loved the idea of letting Cal think he was charming her all night, only to pull the rug out from beneath him at the last minute. It would give him a small taste of his own medicine.

"You're tempted, I can tell," Gareth said. "I should warn you I have a Ph.D. in temptation, too."

"It seems a little petty," Becky said.

It was a token objection, and they both knew it. She was already imagining the look on Cal's face when she sashayed away from him. Not that she'd be able to see his reaction, not having eyes in the back of her head. But she could imagine it. Oh, yeah, she could imagine it.

"Petty, schmetty. Life hands us very few moments to be true divas, Becky. We have to grab them with both hands and hang on tight." Gareth clutched at two fistfuls of air, hauling them flamboyantly toward his thin chest.

"Okay. I'll do it," Becky said impulsively.

Gareth smiled and clapped his hands. "Girlfriend, you will *so* not regret this," he crowed.

Becky grinned back at him, feeling empowered all of a sudden. If she were a man, she'd beat her chest and give a Tarzan yell. Instead, she sat back and crossed her legs, feeling very feline and satisfied.

Yes, indulging in a little revenge fantasy was petty. But it wasn't as though anyone was going to get hurt, was it? Just Cal's ego a little, perhaps. She was certain he had plenty to spare.

"I'll need a new dress," she said.

"Oh, yes. And killer shoes. And underwear—something really slutty."

Becky raised an eyebrow.

"It's a psychological thing," Gareth said. "Trust me. He will never know it's there, but you will. You'll feel like a warrior queen."

A warrior queen. After years of feeling not good enough and discarded.

It sounded like a damned good exchange to her.

CHAPTER TWO

HER CONFIDENCE LASTED until she was standing in front
of her bathroom mirror the next evening, mascara wand
in hand. Her whole body was shaking so much she was
in serious danger of taking out an eye. She had to steady
her wrist with her other hand before she could get a decent coat on.

Not a great sign.

She glanced down at her Slutty Avenger underwear.
Her breasts were pushed up by a black satin-and-lace
balconette bra. She wore matching panties and black garters and sheer black stockings. She was dressed to tempt
and seduce. She should be feeling in control.

She *so* wasn't.

Becky reached for the deep red silk dress she and Gareth had chosen for tonight's dinner. It was part of the
latest shipment of couture they'd received from Paris—a
sleek, fitted, cocktail-length dress with a startlingly low
back and neckline and a slit up one side. If she sat right,
Cal would get an eyeful of stocking and garter. She'd
practiced for ten minutes earlier in front of the mirror
and was confident she had the move nailed.

She slid her feet into a pair of suede stilettos in the
same deep red. They made her feet ache after about five
minutes, but like the underwear, they made her feel sexier, stronger, braver than she really was.

She sprayed on perfume, hitting all her pulse points. Then she picked up her elegant clutch purse. She was ready.

She was also trembling with anticipation and nerves.

So much for being the Slutty Avenger.

She took a cab to Café Sydney. Traffic was light and she arrived early. Taking the elevator to the top floor of the heritage-listed Customs House, she veered away from the restaurant's reception desk and made her way to the ladies' room. Sitting on the closed lid of a toilet, she waited a full fifteen minutes before reemerging.

Childish, but her knees were knocking together and she needed every bid of edge she could get.

Cal rose to his feet as the waitress led her to him. He'd scored a coveted balcony table that offered them privacy and a spectacular view of the Opera House and the Harbour Bridge.

"I was beginning to think you'd stood me up."

He had no idea how close she'd come to doing just that.

She went to flick her hair over her shoulder, then re-membered she'd worn her curls in a sophisticated updo. She dropped her hand lamely to her side.

Smooth, Becky. Real smooth.

"Traffic was bad," she fibbed.

He smiled, the left side of his mouth quirking up just a little bit more than the right.

"I ordered champagne. I hope you still like it."

He looked deep into her eyes as he said it, and a fierce, hot memory rose up inside her—Cal pouring champagne over her breasts, Cal dipping his tongue into her belly button to suck out precious drops, the cold fizz of champagne bubbles tingling between her thighs.

She opened her mouth to say something sassy and clever and tantalizing.

"Yes."

His smile widened. He was wearing a charcoal shirt with French cuffs and a pair of black wool trousers. Discreet cufflinks glinted at his wrists. His hair gleamed darkly in the candlelight. His skin was tanned, and his eyes looked incredibly blue by contrast.

He was so damn sexy. She wasn't sure what it was about him that had always got to her so badly. Sure, he was good-looking, but she'd slept with other good-looking men. And yes, he was charming, but so were a lot of other guys. There was just something about the knowing, slightly naughty look in his eyes, and the ready curve of his lips, and the way he seemed so comfortable in his own skin....

He signaled the waiter and a glass of pale-yellow champagne appeared in front of her. Cal raised his.

"To old friends," he said.

She slid her fingers around the cool glass of the champagne flute.

"Friends? Hmmm."

That was what the Slutty Avenger would say, right?

He tilted his head to one side. "Okay. To old lovers."

She couldn't exactly argue with that.

She hoped like hell that her hand wouldn't shake when she lifted her glass.

"Much more accurate," she said. "I think we were too busy having sex to ever really be friends."

He laughed. "True. Maybe I should have said to great sex, in the interests of being really accurate."

She raised her glass to her mouth. Her hand was

blessedly steady. The champagne tickled her tongue
and tasted pleasingly dry in her throat.

"Nice."

He sat back in his chair. "So, tell me about the last
ten years," he said.

She crossed her legs, but the table blocked his view
of her stockings. She frowned. She hadn't thought about
that minor detail when she'd practiced earlier that evening. She *so* wasn't cut out for this femme fatale business. Definitely an amateur.

"What do you want to know?"

"How did you get into fashion buying?" he asked.
"You were studying economics when we were working together."

She explained that she'd dropped out of her degree
in the third year and worked her way up from the shop
floor, and he told her about his start-up IT company. By
the time they'd given their orders and worked their way
through their starters, some of the tension banding her
chest had eased.

Probably the champagne had a bit to do with that. By
her count, she was on her third glass by the time their
mains were slid in front of them. She felt as buoyant
and full of potential as the bubbles beading her glass.

"I like your hair long," he said as the waiter moved
away from their table. "It suits you."

It was the first personal comment he'd made since
their toast.

"I keep toying with cutting it short again, but it takes
so long to grow. And the in-between stage was a bitch.
I felt like a human fuzz ball for months."

"Don't cut it," he said. His gaze slid over her face before delving into the deep shadow between her breasts.

That quickly, the tension was back between them. She squeezed her thighs together under the table, aware of the heat building between them.

She eyed his body and wondered if he still had the strong tan lines he'd had as a younger man. He'd surfed and spent a lot of time in the outdoors, and she could still recall the way the rich nut-brown of his flat, muscled belly had given way to paler skin low on his hips. She could also remember how quickly she could get him hard, and the way he always stared intently into her eyes as he slid inside her, hard and hot and ready...

"I've thought about you a lot over the years," Cal said, his words an uncanny echo of her own thoughts.

He cut a slice off his porterhouse steak. "Wondered what you were doing. Who you were doing it with."

Her heart kicked against her ribs and she swallowed a huge lump of lust. All she could think about was what it would be like to be with him again. To feel his skin against hers, his breath in her ear, his body moving against hers.

Their eyes locked across the table, and she knew he was thinking the same thing.

If she was really the Slutty Avenger, she would be doing a victory dance right about now. She had him exactly where she wanted him—hot for her, putting himself on the line. All she had to do was string him along for another hour or so, then sashay away, leaving him with a hard-on and the bill.

But she wasn't the Slutty Avenger. Not by a long shot. She was practically panting, and a throbbing ache echoed her heartbeat between her thighs. She wanted him. Bad. Just as bad as when they'd both been twenty-one years old and full of raging hormones.

She stared at him, her mind working like a hamster in a wheel, trying to get a grip on the situation. He was too sexy, too tempting. She wasn't going to be able to walk away from the invitation in his eyes.

As soon as she admitted as much to herself, a strange relief flooded through her. She was going to sleep with him. She was going to run her hands over his body and let him run his hands over hers. She was going to taste his skin and welcome him inside her. They were going to revisit the past in the most physical, real way possible.

But it will just be sex. That's all. I'll take what I want from him, and I'll walk away, she promised herself. A variation on her original plan, and nothing more.

It would be even more effective this way. She'd get to have a good time, and finally put the ghosts of the past to bed. And she'd get to walk away leaving *him* wanting more.

She closed her eyes for a second, savoring the knowledge of what was to come. Then she opened them and locked eyes with him again. His blue gaze was dark and smoky with intent. They stared at each other, neither of them eating.

She smiled a slow, anticipatory smile. She felt light, as though the champagne she'd been drinking had carbonated her blood. He smiled back at her. Her breathing was shallow, her belly muscles tight. Her breasts tingled, and she didn't need to look down to know they were already hardening with desire.

"Are you hungry?" he asked, his voice a low rumble.

"Not for food," she said.

He stood in one smooth, powerful move. "Then let's get out of here."

She stood. He stepped close and took her hand, looking deeply into her eyes.

"I thought I'd exaggerated how sexy you were in my mind," he said. "I thought there was no way you could live up to my memories."

His gaze swept over her, and she felt a surge of feminine power. He wanted her as badly as she wanted him.

He turned, tugging on her hand as he pulled her toward the reception desk so he could take care of the bill. She eyed his broad shoulders as they walked, his words echoing in her mind.

He'd thought about her. And he thought she was sexy. Sexier even than his memories of her.

Triumph and relief and need coursed through her. He shot a glance across to her as he handed over his credit card. The animal need in his eyes made her forget everything sane and sensible.

No man had ever affected her quite like Cal. No man had ever gotten her as hot or made her feel as decadent and wanton and wild.

Trepidation twisted in her stomach as she remembered how she'd felt in the weeks and months after they'd parted ways all those years ago. Empty and dissatisfied and terrified that she'd never find another man who would make her feel as good.

Was she about to make a very stupid mistake? Was she willfully deluding herself that she could handle this situation, that she could handle him?

"Come on," Cal murmured near her ear as he found her hand with his again and pulled her toward the elevator.

She followed him because she wanted to and because she had to. But she wasn't completely gone. No matter what, she would not stay the night with him. She made the commitment to herself as the elevator doors closed and Cal put his arms around her from behind and pulled her back against him.

Her breath got caught somewhere between her lungs and her throat as he splayed one big hand over her belly and the other just under her breasts.

"This is a great dress," he said, the warmth of his chest pressing against her bare back. "I've been wanting to get you out of it all night."

"That was pretty much the idea," she said.

She felt the warm, gentle press of his lips on the side of her neck, followed by the wet lick of his tongue. Desire shot through her like lightning as she arched her neck to allow him greater access.

"Becky, if you had any idea what you do to me…" he murmured against her skin.

Her whole body was trembling with need and anticipation. His hands clenched the fabric of her dress as he pulled her closer. She could feel the hardness of his erection against the curve of her bottom.

This felt so good. *He* felt so good.

She twisted in his arms so that she was facing him. She rose up on the balls of her feet and kissed him, her lips opening over his, her tongue sliding inside the hot, slick darkness of his mouth to caress his tongue, to suck on it, to bite it gently, suggestively.

Cal groaned low in his chest and grabbed her butt, dragging her closer to him and grinding his hips into hers.

"I don't think I can wait," she confessed as they broke from their kiss.

His cheekbones were dark with desire, his lips glistened from their kiss. He slapped a hand toward the buttons on the elevator wall, and the elevator stopped at the next floor.

Without a word they both stepped into the muted darkness of a four-sided balconied walkway that ran around the open space at the centre of the building. While Café Sydney occupied the top floor of Customs House, several prestigious businesses had their head-quarters there. Becky figured they must have exited onto one of the commercial floors.

They walked the length of one side of the walkway until Cal found a waiting area tucked into the corner of the building. Two floor-to-ceiling walls of glass came together to offer yet another amazing view of the harbor.

Neither of them gave it so much as a glance.

Cal moved in on her with intent, his fingers sliding up her neck and into her hair as his mouth angled down on hers. His tongue was hard and demanding in her mouth as his body pressed against hers. The pins and combs holding her hair in place fell to the ground and her hair was suddenly loose about her shoulders.

"I've been wanting to do that all night, too," Cal murmured as he kissed his way across to her ear.

She gasped as his tongue traced the inner curve before plunging inside. She was so ready for him it physically hurt. She reached for the buttons of his shirt, sliding them open by feel alone as Cal continued to plunder her ear.

Then she had her hands on his chest. His skin felt hot and smooth and she pressed her palms flat against him and curled her fingers possessively into the resilient strength of his pectoral muscles. He was bigger, broader than when they'd been younger. She mapped his width with her hands, then found his nipples and began to tease them.

His hands found the zipper at the back of her dress. The hiss of it descending was a seductive whisper. Cal lifted his head from her ear to gaze at her as he pushed her dress off her shoulders. Red silk pooled at her waist and he mouthed a four-letter word as he took in the creaminess of her breasts pouring over the black satin cups of her bra.

His hands slid up her rib cage and onto her breasts, cupping them, molding them. Then he pushed the satin down beneath her breasts and his fingers found her nipples.

He pressed kisses into her neck as he teased her with his hands, squeezing gently, flicking his thumbs back and forth, shaping her with his palms.

"Everything is better than I remembered," he said against her skin, his voice rough with desire.

She was so overwhelmed by sensation and lust that she could barely think. She knew she should probably be more worried about the fact that Cal was pressing her against a thick glass window, and that anyone glancing across from one of the neighboring buildings could see them. She simply didn't care. There was only one thing on her mind—satisfaction. She wanted Cal inside her, pounding into her, giving her what she'd fantasized about in the unacknowledged, dark corners of her mind for ten years.

Her hands shook as she reached for his belt buckle. His erection strained against the zipper of his trousers, thick and powerful, a promise she was about to collect on. He sprang into her hands as she released him. So hard. So silky and yet so strong at the same time. She wrapped her fingers around him as he lowered his head to her breasts and sucked a nipple into his mouth.

She clenched her hand around him as need pierced her, arrowing through her body to where she throbbed for him. He bit her nipple, then sucked it, hard.

She was panting, and so was he. He smoothed his hands down her hips, found the hem of her dress. She moaned as he slid his hands up her stockings. Then he was caressing naked skin, and his fingers were gliding between her legs to where she needed him the most.

The firm press of his fingers against the damp satin of her panties made her moan again. He gave an appreciative sound in the back of his throat as he stroked her once, twice. Then he slid his hand inside her panties and into her slick readiness.

A shudder racked his body as he felt how wet and hot she was. She pushed his trousers and boxers down his hips, then stroked her hand up and down his shaft. Her thumb found a single bead of moisture on the plump head of his penis and she knew he was just as turned on as she was.

"Becky," he groaned against her breast.

"Yes," she said.

His thumbs hooked into the waistband of her panties and pushed down. She took over when they reached her knees, stepping out of them. Cal immediately pushed her back against the window and hooked one of her legs up over his hip. She felt the delicious pressure of his hard-on sliding between her folds. Then he slid inside her, big and hard and thick.

"Oh, boy," she panted as she stretched around him. Her memory had been holding out on her, big-time. He felt so right, so perfect inside her.

He huffed out a laugh.

"Oh, boy? Is that the best you can do?" he asked. His hands gripped her bare backside as they both savored the moment.

She stared into his eyes. "I can do a lot better than that."

She tilted her hips and started to tell him what he was doing to her, her words a whisper against his skin as she kissed his neck and his mouth and his ear and his chest. Cal's grip intensified on her butt as he began to thrust into her—long, slow, powerful strokes that pushed her closer to the edge with each penetration.

She lifted her other leg so that he had her entire weight. She hooked her ankles together behind his back, gripped his shoulders and held on for dear life as he pressed her against the glass and pounded into her with increasing urgency.

"Yes," she sobbed as her climax began to sweep her away.

Cal's mouth found hers. Her desire peaked. She opened her eyes and gazed into Cal's blue eyes as she came and came and came, her body tightening around his, her breath harsh and desperate. His lips pulled back into an animal snarl as he found his own climax, but his eyes never left hers. He stared at her the whole time that his body lost itself in hers, his fingers clutched into her backside, his thighs trembling.

For a few precious seconds afterward, he rested his forehead against hers and they simply breathed together. Then he released his grip on her butt and she slid down his body and stood on her own two feet.

Her body vibrated with satisfaction and the echo of

passion. Her breasts were still wet from his kisses. Her dress was rucked up around her hips, the silk crushed.

She pushed her hair back off her forehead. Cal was busy tucking himself back into his clothes. She tugged her bra up over her breasts and slid her arms through the sleeves of her dress.

"Could you zip me?" she asked, turning her back to him.

His fingers were warm against the skin of her back as he eased the zipper along its tracks.

She wasn't about to climb into her underwear in front of him. Instead, she bent to collect her panties and stuffed them into her evening bag. Very elegant. She was sure there was a paragraph covering just this situation in an etiquette manual somewhere, but she'd never read it.

Cal was buttoning his shirt, and she watched him slide the last button home.

Time to walk away. Time to regain the dignity she'd lost ten years ago when he'd broken her heart.

"Well, Cal, dinner was lovely," she said with what she hoped was a casual smile.

"What we ate of it, you mean," he said drily.

She shrugged a shoulder.

"Dessert was worth it." She took a step forward and pressed a kiss to the angle of his jaw. "Thanks. It was great to catch up."

He frowned as she turned away.

"Where are you going?" he asked. He sounded surprised.

"Home. Where else?"

"I thought we could go back to my place," he said.

Despite what they'd just done together, a hot rush of

desire washed through her as she thought about what that would mean. More Cal. Much more.

What could it hurt? You still won't stay the night. And you'll get him out of your system once and for all.

Becky frowned. She'd been chipping away at her own resolve ever since she'd said yes to Cal's dinner invitation. She had to draw the line somewhere, or there'd be precious little of Operation Dignity left to salvage. And then she'd be back where she'd been all those years ago—left gasping and needy when Cal had had his fill of her.

"I've got an early start tomorrow," she said. "But thanks for the offer."

"Right."

She forced a smile. She had to get out of there before the word *yes* escaped her lips.

"See you round, Cal," she said.

Then she turned on her heel and walked away.

CAL STARED as Becky walked away from him once again, her high heels clicking on the tiled floor.

They'd just had stupendous, gut-wrenching sex, and she'd calmly put herself back together and said goodbye as though it was nothing special.

Not what he'd expected. Not by a long shot. But then, none of it had been. He'd known he was still attracted to her. The reunion had illustrated that in no uncertain terms. But he hadn't expected to be so hot for her that he'd abandon dinner and find the nearest dark corner to bury himself in her. He was a seasoned, experienced businessman, for Pete's sake. Not a randy kid anymore.

And he hadn't expected it to feel so good to be with her again, to touch her, taste her. She'd felt familiar, but also excitingly different, and she'd been so turned-on that he'd almost embarrassed himself before he could give her what they both wanted.

He frowned. He still couldn't believe she'd just asked him to zip her up and then left him standing there. In the old days, Becky had been affectionate, warm. She'd never been able to get enough of him. And he'd never been able to get enough of her. All that intensity had scared the shit out of him hard on the heels of his breakup with Virginia, his long-term girlfriend. As blown away as he'd been by the sex, as much as he'd always enjoyed Becky's wit and sense of humor and sharp take on the world, he'd felt as though he was jumping feetfirst into another serious commitment. He'd been twenty years old. It had freaked him out. All his mates had been partying, seeing the world, having one-night stands. And he'd been in danger of turning into Mr. Monogamy.

He'd told Becky how he was feeling, that he wanted to pull things back, lighten up. She'd been upset. She'd cried. But then she'd pulled herself together. She'd said she understood where he was coming from. They'd worked alongside each other for a whole year after their short, tumultuous relationship had ended, work buddies who knew each other's bodies really, really well.

He'd still been hot for her. He wasn't a saint. They'd been so good together, he'd been unable to look at her without remembering. He'd even tried to score with her again on a casual basis when he'd had too much to drink at one of the Hannigan's Christmas parties. She'd turned him down. Then the next thing he knew, she'd quit, and the only contact he'd had with her was through the staff grapevine.

Cal ran a hand through his hair, then checked to make sure his fly was closed and his shirt buttoned properly. Crossing to the elevator, he punched the button and checked his watch. It was only ten. If she'd come home with him, they could have had all night.

Get over it, Cal. She didn't want anything more than what she got. Suck it up and move on.

He told himself the same thing when the urge to call her gripped him the next day. Badgering Becky with phone calls was not going to change anything.

Still, his hand hovered over the phone. He laughed at himself. He felt as though he'd regressed ten years. Time to take his own advice and get over it. They'd had a great night, a one-off. End of story.

A MONTH LATER, Cal found himself sitting in a church in the richy-rich Melbourne suburb of Toorak on a sizzling summer day, watching another former Hannigan's friend, Carolyn, walk down the aisle to marry her high-school sweetheart, Phil.

Even as he marveled at the fact that their relationship had survived the transition into adulthood and beyond, he found his gaze constantly drawn to the pew near the front of the church where Becky sat. She looked gorgeous in a dark green dress with tiny black flowers on it. Her hair was loose around her shoulders, and he spent almost as much time watching her as he did the bride and groom.

Afterward, at the reception, he arrived early in the ballroom and saw they were sitting at neighboring tables. He hesitated only a second before switching placecards with the man sitting next to her. If someone had put him on the rack and shone a light on him and demanded he tell them why he wanted to sit next to her, he would have said it was because he liked Becky. He always had. But it was also because he felt as though there was unfinished business between them. And yeah, he wanted to have her again. So sue him—sex that great didn't come along too often, in his experience.

She raised an eyebrow when she entered the ballroom a few minutes later and found him seated at her table.

"I could have sworn Carolyn said she was putting me next to Roger Lee," she said.

He gave her his best faux-innocent look, and she shook her head and laughed.

"You always were used to getting your own way," she said.

"To the victor the spoils."

He stood and held her chair out for her.

"Wow. Next thing I know, you'll be throwing your tux jacket over the nearest puddle for me," she said.

He inhaled her spicy-fresh perfume as she sank into the chair. She smelled as good as she looked. And he already knew she tasted twice as good.

"What can I say? I've picked up a little polish over the years."

She eyed his suit knowingly. "More than a little."

She reached out and rubbed the fabric of his lapel between thumb and forefinger.

"Armani, yes?"

He shrugged, quelling an adolescent surge of pride that she'd noticed his expensive threads.

"If you say so."

Her eyes brightened with amusement. "Don't tell me—you have so many designer tuxes in your wardrobe, you can't remember which one you brought down to Melbourne with you?"

He smiled back at her. "Something like that."

"Oooh. Big guy. I bet you own your own company and everything."

She laughed then, and the low huskiness of it hit him in the gut. He shifted in his chair, aware that he was rock-hard for her all over again. His gaze dipped to the swell of her breasts, outlined by the silky fabric of her dress.

"You look great," he said.

The smile was gone from her face when he looked up and their eyes locked. Something dark and hot flickered in the depths of her big brown eyes, and she swallowed visibly.

A slow smile curved his lips. He might be hard, but she was just as aware of him. He knew it the way he knew the earth wasn't flat, the way he knew cats hated dogs and dogs hated postmen.

"Where are you staying?" he asked.

"The Hyatt. You?"

"The Adelphi," he said, naming one of Melbourne's smaller, boutique hotels.

She licked her lips. He flicked his eyes toward the bridal table where Carolyn and Phil were talking and laughing with family and friends. It was going to be a long few hours while they waited out the meal and the speeches and the dancing. Until he could get Becky alone again.

He made it to the end of the main course before sitting next to her and not touching her the way he wanted to became too much for him. He felt like a kid again, out of control. He wanted what he wanted—and he wanted it *now*.

She was talking to the person sitting on her other side, and he waited impatiently for her to turn to him.

"Want to go for a walk?" he asked.

"A walk?" She arched an eyebrow at him, a smile quirking the corner of her mouth.

"Yeah. A walk."

He found her knee under the table.

She sucked in a surprised breath.

He slowly pleated the soft fabric of her skirt beneath his fingers as he gathered it up, inch by inch. She stiffened in her chair as his hand found her silky stockinged leg.

"Tell me you're wearing garters again," he said, fascinated by the way her pupils had dilated with desire.

"Stay-ups. Garters ruin the line of this dress," she said.

He glided his hand up her thigh until he hit bare flesh. She shivered. He slid his hand higher and encountered the smoothness of her satin underwear.

"What color?" he asked quietly.

Her eyelids masked her eyes for a beat before she answered.

"Red."

"One of my favorites."

He stroked her through the satin, and she bit her lip.

"Cal," she said.

He wasn't sure if it was a plea or a warning. He knew what he wanted it to be. Leaning back in his chair, he glanced toward the entrance to the ballroom, then back toward the bridal party.

"I figure we've got about fifteen minutes before they even think about cutting the cake," he said.

She took a deep breath.

"Yes."

What am I doing? One look, one touch and I'm trailing after Cal again, looking for someplace to get hot with him. This is insane. I'm insane.

Becky knew she should pull her hand free and go back to the table and ignore Cal for the rest of the evening. She also knew she wasn't going to. She'd been dreaming about him for four weeks, ever since their dinner. She might have walked away from him, but he'd gotten under her skin.

Not like when they were kids. Definitely not like that. She'd assured herself of that fact over and over. This was purely a sex thing. But it had still driven her crazy for the past month.

As Gareth had said when she'd given him a shame-faced, bare-bones report of her evening at Café Sydney, she sucked at being the Slutty Avenger.

Right now, however, revenge was the last thing on her mind. As always with Cal, lust had short-circuited her higher brain functions. She wanted to get off. Nothing else. She was even prepared to miss dessert for the privilege.

"In here," Cal said, and he opened a door in the hallway they were traversing and pulled her into a linen cupboard.

She laughed. "You've got to be kidding," she said, looking around at the cramped space lined with shelves piled with tablecloths and napkins.

"I'd never joke about something this serious," he said.

Then he kissed her, pressing her back against the door, one hand finding her breast through her dress, his thumb teasing her nipple into hard, demanding arousal.

"You get me so hot," he said.

She couldn't speak. She was too busy gasping as his other hand slid up under her dress and inside her panties.

"Ohhh."

He grinned at her, a wicked, knowing grin.

"Spread your legs for me, baby," he said.

She did so mindlessly, watching as Cal shrugged out of his suit jacket and threw it onto a shelf behind them. Then he was on his knees, lifting her dress, tugging at her underwear.

Her knees went weak as she understood what he wanted to do. He'd always been so good with his mouth and hands. He was one of the few men she'd been with who genuinely got off on the act of pleasing a woman.

She flattened her hands against the cool wood of the door as she felt the warmth of his breath between her thighs. And then he was tasting her, his tongue by turns delicate and rough, his hands cupping her backside as he held her close.

She shuddered and bit her lip and closed her eyes. Within minutes, her orgasm washed over her with the force of a tsunami. Then Cal was unzipping his trousers, and she was gripping his big, hard erection and guiding him once more between her thighs.

"One day, we should really consider doing this in a bedroom," he said as he took her full weight and pressed her back against the doorway.

"Shut up and kiss me," she panted.

Afterward, they put themselves back together in silence. Becky slipped out of the cupboard first and made a beeline for the ladies' room. She closed her eyes briefly when she caught sight of her reflection. She looked like a woman who'd just had two orgasms in a linen cupboard—cheeks flushed, hair mussed, lipstick smeared halfway up her cheek.

"You are such an idiot."

The woman staring back at her knew it, down to her bones. She was playing with fire. And there was only one inevitable result—she was going to get burnt.

No more. No matter what it took, this had to stop now. Before she did something even more stupid than sleep with Cal.

She took a deep breath. Then she started to erase the telltale signs of their encounter.

CHAPTER THREE

THREE WEEKS LATER, Becky stepped out of the shower and reached for the towel folded neatly on the corner of the vanity. She blotted her face dry, then briskly toweled off her body. Naked, she crossed into the bedroom to find her clothes.

"Stay the night," Cal said the moment she entered the room.

He was sprawled across his bed the way she'd left him after they'd made love for the second time that evening, deliciously naked against chocolate-brown sheets.

His blue gaze followed her every move as she reached for her underwear and began to dress.

"I can't. I've got—"

"An early start at work tomorrow," Cal said drily.

It was the same excuse she'd used every time she'd seen him over the past few weeks.

"Tomorrow's Saturday, Becky," he said, propping himself up on his elbows. "That one's not going to cut it."

"I was going to say it's my nephew's birthday, and I promised my sister that I'd go over early and help her set things up."

"What, at six in the morning?"

She pulled her linen trousers over her hips.

"No, but I've got some running around to do before I get there," she said.

Cal dropped flat onto his back and crossed his arms

behind his head. For a few minutes there was nothing but the sound of her clothes rustling as she finished dressing.

"Is there some kind of unspoken rule against you staying the night that I don't know about?" he asked quietly.

Yes. It's the only way I can retain control of the situation. This way, we get what we need from each other, but I can't fool myself that it's anything more than what it is.

"It's easier this way," she said.

"How? It's two in the morning. Wouldn't it be easier just to go to sleep? I promise I won't snore or steal the sheets."

He kept his tone light, but she could hear the edge beneath it. She grabbed a scrunchie from her handbag and pulled her hair into a haphazard ponytail. This conversation had been coming for a while. Perhaps they should have had it up front when he'd called her after Carolyn and Phil's wedding. That way they would have clarified the ground rules going in. She'd thought they'd been pretty obvious, but apparently they were about to get even more so.

"Are you saying you want to turn this into a relationship, Cal?" she asked bluntly.

He blinked. The surprise in his face was like a slap. Clearly, having a relationship with her had not even crossed his mind.

"I've only been divorced three months, Becky. I'm still finding my feet again, remembering what it's like to be single."

She reached for her handbag, keeping her head down as she blinked rapidly. What had she expected him to say? Yes? That he saw her as more than just a warm body? That he'd asked her to stay because he wanted to wake up and find her lying beside him, not because he wanted to have more sex with her?

Maybe. Even though she'd convinced herself that she'd gone into this with her eyes wide open.

History repeating itself.

The thought lent steel to her spine. She eyed Cal coolly.

"You're not interested in anything else," she stated for him. "And neither am I. This arrangement suits me fine, and I would have thought you'd be happy with it, too."

Cal's gaze narrowed. There was a long silence as he studied her, apparently trying to work something out.

"So this is just about sex?" he said.

"Hasn't it always been?"

She busied herself with digging her car keys from her handbag, aware she was walking a dangerous emotional line. The truth was, she was close to sitting on the edge of the bed and crying like a baby. Or like the rejected young woman she'd been all those years ago when he'd first cut her loose. Because this was what had always been at the heart of the problem of her and Cal—she loved him, while he only loved having sex with her.

Cal sat up and reached for his boxers.

"I like you, Becky," he said.

She forced a smile. "I know that. I like you, too. But let's not pretend it's anything other than what it is. We're not kids anymore, we don't need to dress it up."

"Is that why you said no to dinner tonight? Because you didn't want to dress it up?"

"Yes."

He stared at her. He was pissed, she could see it in the firm line of his mouth.

"So you're happy to screw me in fifty different ways, but you don't want to break bread with me?"

If she thought his reaction was anything more than piqued pride, she'd be jumping with joy.

"If I wanted dinner and movies and whatever else, I'd be in a relationship. And that's the last place I want to be," she lied. "I've got a lot going on at work right now. This suits me. If it doesn't suit you, then I understand. It's been fun."

Where was this calm, cool voice coming from? She felt as though someone else had taken over her body while the real Becky quivered in the corner feeling nauseous and shaky and weak.

Cal rubbed the stubble on his chin.

"So we're what? Bed buddies?"

"Yeah," she said.

"And anytime I want some action, I just call you?"

"Yep. And ditto for me. No need to ask each other to the movies or out for dinner or whatever."

"For your information, I really wanted to see that new George Clooney movie last week."

She simply raised an eyebrow at him. They'd wound up skipping the movie and going straight to bed.

"Yeah, all right, point taken," he said grudgingly.

"I'll call you in a few days," she said.

"Hang on."

Cal stood and moved close. He slid a hand behind her neck. He kissed her, his tongue slow and silky in her mouth. His face was full of promise when he raised his head.

"You could stay a little longer, couldn't you?"

She searched his eyes, trying to find something more in them than sexual hunger. She already knew he was hard again, his erection straining against the soft fabric of his underwear. It would be so easy to let things start up again, to fall back into bed with him. She gripped the cold, hard metal of her car keys, hanging on to her self-control.

"I really have to go," she said.

"Okay."

He leaned in again for one last kiss, but she turned away, pretending she hadn't noticed. She suddenly knew she couldn't handle having him touch her right now. Her skin felt as fragile as gossamer. If he touched her, she was afraid it would rupture and all her feelings would tumble onto the floor between them and he'd see the truth.

She made it to her car before hot tears spilled down her cheeks.

She loved him so much. Seeing him again, sleeping with him, had resurrected all her old feelings and then magnified them tenfold. She'd thought she could handle the situation, that she could sleep with him and prove something to herself and to him.

She'd thought she could show him that she didn't care. That he hadn't hurt her. That she hadn't felt rejected and humiliated and somehow lacking all those years ago.

But Cal had grown into a dynamic, sexy, fascinating man, so much more compelling than the young man she'd fallen in love with on the shop floor all those years ago. In bed, he was instinctive, passionate, daring. Just looking into his eyes was enough to turn her on. And he had a great sense of humor and a knowing wit that never failed to make her laugh.

He was the man of her dreams. Again.

And once again he didn't want her.

She forced herself to remember what he'd said: *I've only been divorced three months. I'm still finding my feet again, remembering what it's like to be single.*

Just like last time, only then he'd been young and full of juice and feeling trapped after three years with one girlfriend.

They were both excuses. He didn't feel the same way about her. Never had, never would. She had to face that fact now and stop kidding herself.

She hunched in on herself as her shoulders shook. Her chest ached, and she rubbed her sternum with the heel of her hand, over and over. It hurt. She loved him so much, and it physically hurt that he didn't love her back.

Even though she was an experienced, grown woman now, for a few weak moments she allowed herself to ask the old, old questions.

What's wrong with me that he doesn't love me? What don't I have that he's looking for? Aren't I beautiful enough? Clever enough? Funny enough? Am I too needy? What's wrong with me?

"God!" she moaned, disgusted with her own wallowing.

Talk about a pity party. If she was listening to a friend vomit up all this tragedy, she'd give her a swift kick in the butt and tell her that the problem wasn't with her but with Cal, or fate, or pheromones or some crazy mix of all those things that decreed that people did or didn't fall in love with each other.

She was smart, attractive, a good person. She didn't need Cal's approval or love anymore to prove that to herself. It might hurt that she'd been foolish enough to fall for him again, but just as he'd become a more compelling, nuanced, multifaceted version of the young man he'd once been, so had she become a more sophisticated, confident woman. She didn't need Cal or his love. She *wanted* it, but it was not essential to life as she knew it.

She scrubbed at her wet cheeks with her hands. No

doubt she looked like a mad-ass raccoon, sitting here in her car on a darkened city street outside Cal's apartment block with mascara smearing her face.

She started her car and pulled away from the curb. A curious calm settled over her as she drove. She felt both lighter and heavier. At last she'd acknowledged the truth of her and Cal: it was never going to happen between them.

No more pretending she was just having a fling with him for old times' sake or proving something to herself or him. It was over between them, for good this time.

It wasn't until she was pulling into the driveway of her small Victorian terrace house in Woollahara that she wondered what she was going to do when Cal called her again. She'd just spelled out the rules of their involvement in no uncertain terms—sex, no strings, no commitment. How was she supposed to back out of their deal when she'd gone to so much trouble to assure him she wasn't even remotely emotionally invested in their relationship? She couldn't very well tell him the truth— that she'd finally admitted to herself that she still loved him, which made having sex with him a really bad idea since he didn't feel even remotely the same way.

Switching off her car, she rolled her eyes at her own pride. That was what had gotten her into this stupid mess in the first place, after all. Pride had made her accept that first dinner offer. And pride had made her put on that dog-and-pony show tonight in his bedroom. And now pride was squirming in her belly at the thought of turning Cal down when he next suggested they hook up, just in case he guessed how she felt.

Okay, pride *and* lust. It would be hard to say no to more of his beautiful body and clever hands. To know that she would never again hear him sigh her name against her skin as he made love to her. That she would never again be filled with the sweaty, needy, greedy desire for him that gripped her every time they saw each other.

Tough cookies.

Her jaw hardened as she let herself into her house. She could go cold turkey on the sex. And she could definitely suck up a bit of damaged pride since the only alternative was to keep sleeping with Cal in order to maintain her facade of not caring. There was no way she was doing that to herself—making love with a man she loved but who only *liked* her was not something she was signing on for, thanks. She'd never been into sadomasochism. Self-delusion, yes. But not willful self-hurt.

She'd avoid him for a week or two, then tell him that she had a big work project coming up and she wanted to concentrate on it. Or better yet, that she'd met someone. He was in no position to challenge her. They'd made no commitments to each other. And if he suspected something deeper was going on…well, she could live with that. Whatever it took to get him out of her life once and for all.

And next time there was a Hannigan's reunion, she'd ask if he was going to be there before she blithely walked in the door and was blindsided by him all over again.

Later that morning she woke to churning nausea and just made it to the bathroom in time to lose what was left of last night's dinner. She put it down to the situation with Cal, and possibly the shrimp cocktail she'd grabbed after work with Gareth before joining Cal at his place.

When she threw up Sunday morning, and then Monday morning, an impossible suspicion began to form in the back of her mind. Tuesday morning, she rinsed her mouth out after what was becoming her traditional pre-breakfast barf and reached for her packet of contraceptive pills. No stray pills remained in the blister pack, which meant she hadn't forgotten to take one. Not this month, anyway. She pulled open the cabinet behind her mirror, scrabbling around to see if she'd left last month's blister pack lying around, so she could check that, too. She hadn't. She sighed. The odds of her being pregnant were incredibly slim. She'd been on the pill for over five years. Even if she *had* slipped up, her body would have to have been poised on the starting block, ready to explode into fertility at the first hint of an opportunity. What were the odds of that happening?

Then her gaze fell on the bottle of antibiotics she'd been prescribed last month for a nagging ear infection. She'd wanted to take care of it before she had to fly to Melbourne for Carolyn and Phil's wedding, she remembered.

She'd glanced at the bottle dozens of times over the last few weeks as she brushed her teeth and did her makeup and her hair, and not once had the familiar warning printed along the bottom of the label registered. But today it did. Big-time.

Warning—Antibiotics may decrease the effectiveness of birth control pills.

Her mind went blank. A rushing sound filled her head. She sat down on the closed toilet lid and stared at the towel rack.

She'd thrown up four mornings in a row. She'd also taken antibiotics, then had wild monkey sex with Cal in the linen closet at her friend's wedding.

She pressed her hands to her breasts and squeezed them gingerly. Were her boobs bigger? Unusually tender? Different in any way?

She didn't think so. She stared down at her belly. It

looked the same as it always had—as though she needed to really commit to doing two-hundred sit-ups a day if she wanted killer abs like Cameron Diaz.

Was it possible that right now there was a tiny new life growing behind her belly button?

She stood. She hadn't showered or had breakfast, but she didn't care. There was a convenience store on the corner, and she knew for a fact that it had pregnancy tests because she'd often noted them when she picked up milk and pitied the poor woman who was so desperate to find out whether she was pregnant that she bought her test from the quickie mart.

Hah.

She dragged on a skirt and T-shirt, not bothering with a bra, and slid her feet into flip-flops. She slung her purse over her shoulder and slammed out her front door. Once she was in the street, she became acutely aware of the fact that at thirty-one, her breasts were not as up to going out in the world sans support as they used to be. She kept her arms crossed over her chest the whole way to the convenience store.

She couldn't be pregnant. She'd have to be the unluckiest woman in the world. She'd been taking antibiotics for five days, and she'd had sex with Cal once in that time frame. Unless he possessed some kind of supersperm, there had to be another explanation for her nausea.

There was one test left on the shelf, and she lunged at it as though a horde of other desperate women might appear at any moment. She handed over cash and was out the door again in the space of a few seconds.

She tore the pack open as she walked back home, uncaring now that her breasts bounced with every step. She rapidly scanned the instructions. All she had to do was pee on a stick. She eyed the plastic indicator window. It

had better say what she wanted it to say. Otherwise…
she wasn't quite sure what she would do.

Ten minutes later, she sat on the edge of her bathtub
and stared at the blue cross in the indicator window.

She was pregnant.

Her head spun. She didn't want to be a single parent. She wasn't really sure if she wanted to have children at all. It was something she'd discussed on and off
with Jack before they'd split up, but they'd never gotten
beyond the talking stage. When they'd gone their separate ways, she'd been profoundly grateful that the only
people they'd had to consider were themselves.

But now the decision to have children had been taken
out of her hands. She was going to have Cal MacKenzie's baby.

She gasped as the top threatened to float off her head.
She bent over, gripping her knees as she shoved her
head between them. Slowly the world stopped rocking
and rolling.

A thought slid into her mind. She could take care of
it. She didn't even have to tell him. She didn't have to
tell anyone. One trip to the clinic, and this moment, this
feeling would be history.

She stood and crossed to the telephone. Punching in a
number, she counted one ring, then two, then three rings
before her sister answered at the other end.

"I need to talk to you. Do you have work today?"

Amy worked part-time, but Becky could never remember which days.

"No. I was actually going to come into the city and
raid your shoe department. Can't beat that staff discount."

"Amy, I think I'm pregnant." Becky closed her eyes.

God, she couldn't even say it properly. "I mean, I know I am. I just did a test."

There was a moment of profound silence.

"Oh my God. This is fantastic. You know I've always wanted the kids to have cousins."

Despite how desperate she felt, Becky smiled. Amy had been hassling Becky to hurry up and pop out kids for years now. Her sister was such a natural mother, she probably couldn't comprehend that news like this might be unwelcome, not to mention downright scary to Becky.

"Well, I'm glad someone's pleased," Becky said.

There was a short pause. "I'm sorry. I'm such a doo-fus. I just assumed you and Jack must have gotten back together...." Her sister trailed off, waiting for Becky to fill in the gaps.

"No. I've been, um, seeing Cal MacKenzie. You know, from back in college."

"Cal MacKenzie who broke your heart? That Cal MacKenzie?"

"That's the one."

"Isn't he married?" her sister asked.

"Not anymore."

"Thank God. Sorry, but I know how you always had such a thing for him and I thought for a moment there that maybe you'd let yourself get sucked into something ugly because you couldn't say no to him."

Becky rested her forehead on her hand and closed her eyes.

"Does that mean I can come over?" she asked. She didn't like how small and sad her voice sounded, but there was precious little she could do about it.

"Of course you can! Don't be an idiot. You could come over even if you'd humped a football team's worth of married men. You know that. What time should I expect you?"

"I need to phone in sick to work. Maybe an hour?"

She didn't feel even a moment's compunction about taking a sick day. She figured finding out she was unexpectedly pregnant by her teen crush gave her the world's biggest get-out-of-jail-free card.

"How many weeks are you?" her sister asked when she opened her front door an hour later.

"Four weeks. I think. I guess I'll need to have a scan or whatever to confirm that. Is that what happens next?" Becky asked.

Her sister pulled her into a bone-crushing hug.

"You're going to keep it," Amy said. "I'm so pleased. When you said it was Cal's and you sounded so miserable about it, I wondered."

"Of course I'm keeping it. Maybe when I was a kid I wouldn't have. But there's no reason why I can't look after a baby and be a good mum now. I've got my own place, a good job. You and Mum will help out. I'll get by."

Becky hadn't realized how much had fallen together in her mind during her shower and the drive over. The first rush of panic had subsided. She was pregnant, and it was unplanned, but she could handle it. She *would* handle it.

Amy frowned. "What about Cal? Where does he fit into all of this?"

"He doesn't," Becky said firmly.

"Why not? He made half a baby, same as you. Why shouldn't he handle half the consequences?" Her sister had her hands on her hips and a martial light in her eye.

Suddenly Becky remembered that her sister had never been Cal's biggest fan.

"Because I love him desperately, and he thinks I'm just a great lay," Becky said bluntly.

Her sister opened her mouth then shut it again without saying anything.

"Exactly," Becky said. "I am not going to spend my life eating my heart out over a man who will never feel the same way toward me that I feel toward him. Been there, done that, didn't keep the T-shirt. Having this baby tie us together forever is bad enough."

Instantly she realized what she'd said. She pressed a hand to her stomach and ducked her head to address her navel. "Sorry, little guy. I didn't mean that the way it sounded."

Her sister's eyes filled with tears as she noted the small gesture. Becky shook her head adamantly.

"No. We are not going to cry, Amy. I can't afford to. I have to sort this out. I need to come up with a way to tell Cal. And I need to set everything up so that he can see that I don't need anything from him."

"You could just not tell him, if you're so worried about it," her sister said. "Thousands of women don't."

Becky instantly shook her head. It was an easy way out, but she couldn't take it.

"No. I want my baby to know who his father is. What I don't want is Cal feeling obligated or trying to take control. He can be a part of the baby's life, but not mine."

She still wasn't sure how she was going to keep the two things separate, but she would find a way. She had to.

"Good luck with that one," Amy muttered.

"What's that supposed to mean?"

"Men come over all me-Tarzan, you-Jane when they find out they've planted a seed. Trust me on this. Craig was practically pounding his chest when I found out I was pregnant with Kyle."

"That's because he loves you and you guys had been trying for ages. This is different. Cal is different. He's a newly single guy, fresh from a divorce. He's got a new company, he's making money. He just wants to have a good time. He doesn't want the commitment of a baby. He definitely doesn't want it with me."

Her sister blinked rapidly again and Becky pointed at her.

"If you make me cry, you're going to have to go inflate a dinghy or something because it's going to be a while before I stop."

Her sister hugged her close.

"I'm so sorry. I've always wanted you to have kids so you could experience how amazing it is. I just never imagined it would be like this."

Becky closed her eyes and hugged her sister back.

"I know. Me either."

CAL SLID two champagne flutes onto his kitchen counter, then stole a black olive from the bowl he'd placed nearby. Sultry music played on the stereo, and a tray of antipasto sat alongside the bowl of olives and the champagne bucket. The lighting was low, he was fresh from the shower, and the harbor was putting on its usual spectacular nightly show.

For the fifth time in the last fifteen minutes, he checked his watch. Becky was late. He'd called her earlier in the week to tee up a time to see her, but he'd had to wait until Friday for her to be free. A whole week since he'd had her naked in his arms. Was it any wonder he was feeling distinctly edgy?

He ran an eye over his arrangements again, sliding the olive bowl a little more to the left to stop it crowding out the antipasto platter. He was just about to replace the plain glass champagne flutes with the cut-crystal ones he'd brought back from London when he realized what he was doing.

Fussing. Primping like an old lady expecting the vicar for tea. Or like a nervous man determined to woo a woman into bed.

Except he didn't need to do that, did he? Becky had made that more than clear last Friday. This thing they had together was about sex and nothing else. Whenever he felt the need to get off, he didn't have to come up with the pretext of dinner or a movie or a theater show before he could get her naked. He just had to pick up the phone and she'd arrive, ready to head straight into the bedroom and get busy.

He frowned. He wasn't sure why their deal left him feeling uneasy. On the surface, it was every man's wet dream. He craved Becky's body. Several times a day he was visited with memories from their sessions together. The clench of her hands on his butt as she urged him to go harder, faster. The taste of her on his lips. The way her body shuddered and then turned soft and languid after she came. Today, he'd been sitting in a quarterly update meeting with his business partner when he'd had a flash of Becky's face as she savored him riding high inside her.

It was crazy to question the gift he'd been given—great sex with no obligations. After the way things had ended with Natalie, it was just what he needed. She'd become so clingy toward the end, so jealous and possessive. He'd lost count of the number of times she'd accused him of having an affair. He'd been working like a dog to pay for the lifestyle they'd become accustomed to—there was no way he'd had time to squeeze in a little extra on the side, even if he'd been so inclined. Perhaps if she hadn't had trouble finding a job she enjoyed in the U.K., things might have turned out differently. But she'd been restless, dissatisfied, and she'd funneled all her anxiety into their relationship. Ironically, she was the one who'd wound up having the affair. Out of boredom, she'd said. And because she'd wanted to make Cal jealous and test his love for her.

He guessed that the fact that he'd been able to walk away from his marriage with relatively few scars was evidence that perhaps he hadn't loved her as much as he'd thought he had. He'd misjudged her. He could admit that to himself now. He'd assumed Natalie's confidence was a part of her and not just a mask that she put on like the makeup she insisted on wearing every day, no matter what.

His thoughts shifted to Becky. She was the polar opposite of Natalie. Dark to Natalie's blond, and genuinely confident, a woman with a career and life of her own. She'd always had backbone. Always known what she wanted and gone for it. It was one of the things he admired about her the most.

The doorbell chimed. On his way to answer it, he adjusted the dimmer switch, brightening the room to normal levels. He picked up the remote for the stereo and killed the smoochy music, too. For some reason, he felt stupid for trying to turn their evening into anything other than what it was.

"Hey. I was getting ready to call out the search choppers," he said as he let her in.

She gave him a tight smile and slipped past him into the apartment.

He frowned. Something was wrong.

She hadn't changed out of her work clothes, for starters. She always went home to change before meeting him. She hadn't quite met his eye when he'd opened the door, either.

"Are you okay?" he asked as he joined her in the living room.

"I'm fine," she said, but he caught a flash of distress in her big brown eyes. He stepped closer and placed a hand between her shoulder blades, rubbing her back soothingly.

"You're as stiff as a board."

She shrugged a shoulder, almost as though she was trying to shake his touch off. Then she stepped forward, out of his reach. She turned to face him, her hands clenched together in front of her.

"There's no easy way to do this. I had this big speech planned, but I'm just going to say it. I was taking some antibiotics before Carolyn and Phil's wedding, and I didn't think about what that might mean. And then I started throwing up this week."

He stared at her, confused. What was she saying? That she was sick? That something was wrong with her? A wave of protectiveness and fear raced through him. He didn't want Becky to be sick. Not when he'd just found her again.

"Cal, I'm pregnant," she said.

Two very simple words, but they changed his world forever.

CHAPTER FOUR

"Pregnant." Cal stared at her, his brain not quite putting two and two together and getting parenthood.

"As in having a baby. Our baby, to be specific."

Stupidly his first thought was for the champagne. "You won't be able to drink, then," he said.

She stared at him, and he shook his head.

"God. Sorry. I'm just…I don't know."

"It's a lot to take in." Her voice was flat, distant.

"You're on the pill, right?" he said, confused.

In the back of his mind, he was aware that there were other things he probably should be saying. Reassuring, supportive things. But he'd just been hit with the biggest surprise of his life and he didn't have a manual of political correctness on hand to guide his every move.

"Like I said, I was on antibiotics for an ear infection before Carolyn and Phil's wedding, and apparently they can affect the body's absorption of the pill in some people."

"Right."

Becky dropped her handbag onto the kitchen counter.

"I want to keep the baby, Cal," she said in a rush. "I know having a termination is maybe the smarter thing, but I think I could be a decent mother and saying no to this baby because it's not convenient doesn't sit well with me."

Cal scrubbed his face with his hands. He felt as though his brain was filled with marshmallow. Why couldn't he think straight? He was painfully aware of Becky watching him, waiting for him to say something.

"I know this is a big shock," she said after a short silence. "The last thing you want in your life."

Cal found himself staring at Becky's stomach. In a few months time, she was going to get big and round. She'd start walking with one hand on the small of her back and the other on her belly. People would want to touch her in the street.

She was having his baby. Their baby. A baby that was half him, half her.

"When are you due?" he asked.

"Carolyn and Phil's wedding was early January, so I guess that means it will be sometime in September."

"Right." Plenty of time to get things organized. To get his head around this.

"I want you to know that I've got things covered," she said. "I've spoken to my sister and my boss at work and my mum, and I can take six months maternity leave and my sister and my mum have offered to look after the baby between them when I go back to work so he won't have to go into childcare. I own my own home, I earn a good salary, I'm looking into getting a nice safe hatchback instead of my Audi."

He frowned. "Why do I feel like we're in a job interview?"

"I'm trying to explain that you don't need to worry about anything. I'd like for the baby to know who you are, to spend time with you when he or she is older, I guess, but until then there's really no reason why this should mess with your life too much."

Cal stared at her. "You're having a baby, Becky. My baby."

"Our baby. And I know this is the last thing you

need or want in your life. There's no need for you to feel trapped or anything like that."

"That's the second time you've said that," he said, his frown deepening.

"What?"

"That this is the last thing I want in my life."

"It's true, isn't it? You just got divorced three months ago. You're still finding your feet, remembering what it's like to be single again."

Why did he feel as though he'd heard those words somewhere before?

"That doesn't mean I'm not going to step up and meet my obligations. I'm thirty-one, Becky, not some kid who's going to bail at the first sign of trouble."

"I told you, you don't need to feel obligated. The baby and I are all taken care of—there's nothing for you to do."

"What if I *want* to do something? You'll need help financially, for starters."

Her full lips pressed together and her chin came up.

"I don't need your money. I told you that."

"There is no way I'm standing by and letting you shoulder the burden of bringing up our child on your own," he said.

Her lips got even thinner.

"Fine. I'll keep a record of what I spend on the baby and you can pay half. Anything else?"

"What about doctor's visits, that kind of thing? That's going to be expensive."

"I have insurance, it's covered."

"You'll need a specialist. I'll ask my brother for a recommendation." Andrew's speciality was orthopedics, but he'd know who was the best.

"I've already booked an appointment with my sister's doctor."

"Maybe we should hold off on that. My brother might know someone better."

"My sister has had four children with Dr. Martin. She trusts him, and so do I."

Her jaw was set, and her hands were crossed over her breasts. She looked the very picture of stubbornness.

"Would you like me to come to the doctor's appointment?" he asked.

"Why?"

"Why the hell do you think? To support you."

She threw her hands in the air.

"I don't need your support, Cal, and I don't want it. We're two people who happen to have good sex together, but that's it. Under any other circumstances, we'd sleep with each other until one or both of us got bored, then we'd go our separate ways. Just because this has happened shouldn't change that."

"We're a little more than two people who sleep with each other," he said. "We've known each other for more than ten years, Becky."

"No. We haven't spoken to each other for ten years. We knew each other a little when we were at university. That's it. I wouldn't even call us friends."

He'd never thought her big brown eyes could look so cold.

"Well, I consider you a friend," he said stiffly. "We worked together. We've slept with each other, I enjoy your company."

"Yeah, and when I left Hannigan's we never said another word to each other until the reunion. That's not how friends behave, Cal. Friends call each other up and drop each other e-mails every now and then. Friends are there in good times and bad. We only ever did the good times."

He shifted his feet, shoved a hand into the front pocket of his jeans.

"I thought about you. But it would have felt wrong to make contact. I was married."

She stared at him, color rising in her pale cheeks.

"Doesn't that just prove my point? It's like I said the other night. We were only ever about the sex. And just because this has happened doesn't change anything."

She slid her handbag up onto her shoulder. "I'll call you once a month to keep you up to speed on everything during the pregnancy, and I'll send you copies of the scans or anything else that comes along. We can work out child support things closer to when the baby is due, if that's what you want to do."

She headed for the door, leaving him staring at the space where she'd been standing.

"Wait a minute," he said.

She turned on the threshold of his apartment, her face perfectly calm and composed. How could she be so together when he was reeling, trying to come to terms with the fact that his whole life had changed?

"Be honest with yourself, Cal. You're a party guy— always have been. You've got this place and a sporty car and a business that's making lots of money. I know you probably feel like you have to say and do the right thing, but I don't need anything that you have to offer. I certainly don't need you coming along for the ride out of guilt. Let's just take it as read that you're off the hook and move on, okay?"

She walked away, her stride long and sure. He stared at her back until she stepped into the elevator car.

At about the same time, he started to get angry. Phrases from their conversation circled his mind. *This is the last thing you need or want in your life. You're a party guy—always have been.*

And his personal favorite: *Let's just take it as read that you're off the hook and move on, okay?*

Becky had walked in the door, broadsided him with the news of her pregnancy, then bulldozed him into a corner with about a million assumptions about who he was and what he wanted. She'd subdivided her pregnancy into neatly apportioned lots, and generously agreed to allow him access to one or two of them. He could see scans. She'd give him updates. She'd like the baby to know he was its father, and for him to have contact with the child once it was old enough.

She didn't want his money or his friendship, and she certainly didn't want him holding her hand through any of it. All she'd ever wanted from him, it seemed, was what was between his legs.

We were always only about the sex.

I wouldn't even call us friends.

Out of all the things she'd said, those two last comments burned him up the most. Yeah, it pissed him off that she thought he was some feckless playboy asshole tooling around in his Porsche, more than happy to turn a blind eye to the fact that he'd gotten someone pregnant because it might cramp his style. What the hell did that say about her opinion of him, for freak's sake?

But the thing that really got his blood boiling was the way she kept rewriting history. They *had* been friends, no matter what she said. Before they'd slept with each other, they'd spent hundreds of lunch breaks and tea breaks talking in the staff room. Every staff function, they'd wound up in a corner somewhere, making each other laugh. Yes, there had been plenty of suppressed flirtation in all of those encounters, but they'd liked each other, as well as lusted after each other.

He ran his hand through his hair, then glanced around his apartment. The champagne, the food, the stereo and lighting he'd set up and then chickened out on at the last minute—it all seemed to mock him.

He'd always wanted kids someday. He and Natalie had tried for a short while when they'd first arrived in London, but his work had become so hectic that they'd both agreed the timing wasn't right. Then their relationship had started to dissolve and the idea of kids had been well and truly off the agenda.

Now he was going to be a father. And he was damned if he was going to let Becky draw a neat little box on the ground and tell him he couldn't step outside its bounds. He had rights. He wanted to be a part of his son or daughter's life.

And despite the cool look in Becky's eyes, despite the fact that she was clearly, utterly unthrilled to find herself linked with him for life, he wanted to help her. She might not be prepared to acknowledge it, but there had always been more to them than sexual attraction. There was a reason why he'd backed off all those years ago. The same reason that she'd been the first person he'd thought of when he was single again.

Grabbing his car keys, he headed for the door.

BECKY WAS still shaking by the time she let herself in her front door. Telling Cal she was pregnant had been one of the hardest things she'd ever done.

She dressed in her favorite pair of threadbare flannel pyjamas despite the heat. She needed the comfort of the familiar. If she was the kind of woman who went in for soft toys, she'd be clutching one to her chest right about now, too. Instead, she sat on the couch with her knees pulled tight to her chest.

If she could go back in time to the night of the reunion and change things, she would. She'd turn around the moment she saw Cal, and simply walk out the door. So what if her old friends and work colleagues guessed that she still had feelings for him? A bit of self-exposure was better than this.

She rested her chin on her knees and tried not to remember the things he'd said when she'd given him the news. He'd talked about meeting his obligations. He'd used the word *burden.* She scrunched her eyes tightly shut and grit her teeth.

A burden. The last thing she wanted was to be considered a burden in Cal MacKenzie's life. Not when she loved him. Not when she craved his touch and longed for the sound of his voice.

Tears burned at the back of her eyes. She swallowed them down. She hadn't cried since that night outside Cal's apartment, and she wasn't going to now. She was going to have a baby, and that child needed her to be strong and sure. From now on, every decision she made affected both of them. The days of thinking and behaving selfishly and impulsively were over.

She uncurled from her position on the couch. She felt vaguely nauseous, and she groaned. Her sister had explained that just because it was called morning sickness didn't mean it only happened in the mornings. She'd added that she'd thrown up day and night for twelve weeks with her first child, and had warned Becky that the same might happen to her. It seemed her prediction was spot-on.

"Great. All I need," Becky muttered.

The sound of someone pounding loudly on her front door made her jump on the spot. She stared down the hallway at the glossy black door, knowing who was on the other side and dreading yet another conversation with Cal.

"Becky, I know you're in there and I'm not going anywhere so you might as well let me in," he yelled.

It was past ten, and she was sure that her neighbors wouldn't appreciate her having a yelling match through her front door.

Cal glared at her as the door swung open between them.

"I didn't even have your address," he said tightly.

His hair stood up in unruly spikes as though he'd been running his fingers through it, and his cheekbones were dark with emotion. He brushed past her, inviting himself into her home.

"I had to ring Carolyn up and ask her for your address, because I don't know where the woman who is pregnant with my child lives," Cal repeated as he swung around to face her in her living room.

Becky stood in the doorway, feeling at an acute disadvantage in her baggy pyjamas when he was fully dressed.

"It's never come up before," she said.

"Because you didn't want it to come up," he said. He stabbed a finger at the air between them. "Ever since we hooked up again you've been calling the shots. You decide when we'll meet, where we'll meet, if you'll stay the night or not."

"I didn't hear you complaining." She crossed her arms over her chest. She could feel her heart hammering against her ribs, and nausea swirled in her belly.

"I have over twenty employees," he said. "People who

rely on me to pay their mortgages and keep food in their kids' mouths. I ring my parents once a week and try to see them at least once a month, and I donate to a bunch of charities."

Becky shook her head. What the hell was he going on about?

"Cal—"

"I'm not an asshole, Becky. I don't spend my spare time partying with morons and driving around in my car showing the world how great I am. I was married for five years, and I was faithful for every one of them."

She stared at him. "I wasn't aware that I said you were an asshole who did any of those things."

"Yeah, you did. You said I was a party guy. That I always have been. That's not me. Maybe for a few years when I was in my early twenties, but not anymore."

"Okay. Well, I'm sorry if I offended you. I was simply trying to make a point. This is unexpected news, not something you planned for or even remotely want. And I'm prepared to take care of everything. So it doesn't need to make too much difference in your life."

Despite her reassurances, Cal's frown only deepened.

"You're doing it again, making assumptions about who I am and what I want and how I feel."

Becky opened her mouth, then closed it without saying a word. She didn't know how to respond to him.

"What do you want, Cal?" she finally asked.

"I want to help you. I want to do this with you. I want us to start acting as if we actually like each other."

She stared at him. He had no idea what he was asking for.

She'd worked for a year with him after their breakup, and it had been hell. Every time she'd had to go to work she'd felt half-hopeful that something may have miraculously changed since she last saw him and he'd have realized what he'd thrown away. And every time she'd had to listen to him laughing and joking about what he'd done on the weekend with his buddies, the other girls he'd met, the good times he'd had. Every work shift she'd had to face the fact that having fun with his friends was more important, more valuable to Cal than what they'd shared together.

She wasn't going through all that again.

"I've told you what I want to do. I've told you I'll take care of everything. You don't have to feel that this is a burden you have to take up or a responsibility or an obligation."

"Jesus, Becky." Cal looked to the ceiling as though seeking patience. His blue eyes burned with intensity when he returned his gaze to her. "This is not a burden to me, and if you say it one more time I'm going to get really pissed. I'm thirty-one years old, and I've always wanted to have children. I want to be a part of this."

Becky shook her head, instinctively rejecting what he was saying. She couldn't handle knowing these things about Cal. She didn't want to know that he was responsible and mature, that he'd been faithful to his wife. She definitely didn't want to know that he wanted a family.

She wanted him to be a playboy, an attractive, sexy guy she'd stupidly fallen in love with, but who would never make her happy, even if he did love her in the same way that she loved him. She wanted him to be unsuitable, impossible, out of the question. Because if he wasn't, it made the fact that he didn't love her too hard to deal with. He went from being a guy who would never settle down to a guy who wanted to settle down. A guy who wanted a family. A guy who wanted all the things she wanted—but who simply didn't want them with her.

"I don't think I can do this right now," she said.

"Tough. I'm not letting you push me into a corner and tell me what's what again," Cal said. "I'm sick of hearing you tell me what you think I am, how this is the last thing I want and how I'm thrilled to be single again. You don't know me at all, Becky."

He was standing too close, and he was too big and tall for her little living room. She felt cornered, over-whelmed. He had no idea what he was doing to her, what this meant to her.

"Don't put all this on me," she said. Suddenly she felt incredibly, incandescently angry. Not just at Cal, but at life, at the unfairness of loving a man who would never love her back. And angry at herself for putting herself in this situation in the first place.

"You said those things, Cal. *You* said you'd only been divorced three months, that you were just getting used to being single again. *You* called the baby a burden, not me. So don't you dare tell me I'm putting words in your mouth."

He frowned. "You're taking it out of context."

"Really? I asked you if you wanted a relationship with me, and you told me you'd only been single for three months. What was I supposed to take from that, Cal?"

He stared at her. "Are you saying that you want to have a relationship with me?" He sounded incredulous, mys-tified.

Becky stared at him, at his gorgeous face and strong, lean body. Why did she have to fall in love with him all those years ago? And why couldn't she get over him now?

Suddenly she felt bone weary, utterly exhausted. There was no way she could protect herself from Cal now that she was pregnant with his baby. There was no way she could allow him access to their child and hope to quarantine him from the rest of her life. He was going to be a part of her life forever. Unattainable, but always there.

"Don't worry. I'm not going to make this any more awkward than it already is," she said. She blinked furiously and turned away. "Do you want a coffee?"

Maybe they could both calm down, sit down and hammer out some kind of arrangement.

Cal caught her arm before she'd taken two steps.

"What do you mean by awkward? What's awkward about you wanting a relationship with me?"

She tried to shrug him off. "It doesn't matter."

"Yes, it does, Becky. There's been enough unsaid bullshit between us. Say what you mean for once."

She glared at him. "Why should I? Why should I lay everything at your feet so you can pick it over and see if any of it interests you? I'm done with being rejected by you, in case you hadn't noticed."

He dropped her arm at last. "If you're talking about when we were kids, we both know the timing was wrong," he said.

Years of anger and hurt swelled inside Becky.

"You have no idea, do you? You think that just because you walked away from what we had easily, it was the same for me. I loved you, Cal MacKenzie. I worshipped the ground you walked on. I used to look forward to going to work just so I could see you. I thought you were the funniest, the smartest, the sexiest guy I'd ever met. I was so jealous of your girlfriend. And then you broke up with her, and suddenly you were mine. For four whole weeks."

She took a deep breath, distantly aware that Cal was staring at her, his face pale.

"And once you'd screwed me every which way, you dumped me like yesterday's garbage. And I realized exactly what I meant to you."

"That's not how it was," Cal said tightly. "You meant something to me."

He took a step forward, but she held up a hand, warding him off.

"I know exactly what I meant to you—hanging out with your buddies and chugging beers and having sex with nameless girls was more important to you than what we had together."

"That's not true," he said, frowning. "I thought you were fantastic, Becky. God, I was obsessed with you. I used to feel so guilty when I was with Virginia because you were all I could think about. You were the reason we broke up. When we first got together, it was so good, so intense, you blew my mind."

Nausea rolled up the back of her throat. She didn't want to hear this. Didn't want to hear Cal try to justify or explain. She shouldn't have said anything. Laying out her hurts before him was worse than pathetic. She didn't want his sympathy. She definitely didn't want his guilt.

"Stop," she said. "Don't say another word. Let's just agree that I was an idiot and you had a nice time and that history has just repeated itself."

Cal stepped forward and grabbed her shoulders. She could feel the heat from his body, smell his aftershave. Helpless tears filled her eyes. Why did he have so much power over her?

"Will you let me finish? You were never just a good time to me, Becky. Being with you was the most intense, amazing time of my life. The way I used to feel when you were lying in my arms… Like my chest wasn't big enough for my heart. When we were together, all I wanted to do was get as close to you as possible. And when we weren't together, I couldn't stop thinking about you. I picked up the phone ten times for every one time I called you."

He stared down at her, his blue eyes compelling, his face tight with intensity.

"I didn't break up with you because I didn't care, Becky. I broke up with you because I cared too much, and it scared the shit out of me. When I was with you, I thought about houses and babies and being together forever. I was twenty years old. I had no idea what to do with any of that. It freaked me out. I loved you with everything I had. That's why we broke up."

Becky blinked. Cal had loved her? All those years ago, he'd broken up with her because he'd loved her too much and he couldn't handle it?

It was such a huge twist on what she'd accepted as the truth, she could barely comprehend what he was saying.

Even as her emotions overwhelmed her, bile rose in her throat and the nausea that had been threatening all evening took control of her body.

Becky clapped a hand to her mouth, spun on her heel and raced for the bathroom. The door hit the wall with a bang as she shoved it open. Then she was on her knees, her body convulsing as she lost her dinner to the toilet bowl.

Her hair hung around her face as she retched. She was vaguely aware of Cal entering the bathroom behind her. She desperately wanted to tell him to leave her alone, but was in no state to do so. Then she felt him gently gathering her hair, holding it at the nape of her neck as her stomach rebelled yet again.

The warm weight of his hand landed in the middle of her back as the nausea retreated.

"Are you okay?" he asked quietly.

"Water would be good," she said, keeping her back to him.

Her hair fell free again as he stood and moved to the vanity. She heard the rush of water filling a glass as she reached up and pressed the flush button.

"Here."

He passed her the water and a wet towel. She rinsed out her mouth until the acid taste was gone, then wiped her face.

Finally she turned around to look at him, shifting on the cool tile until her back was to the wall. He was crouched down beside her, a concerned look on his face. They stared at each other for a long silent moment.

"I'm guessing that was morning sickness?" he finally asked.

"Yep. According to my sister, I've got another eight weeks of it to look forward to."

She drew her knees into her chest. Cal sat down, leaning his back against the bathtub so that they were facing one another. Cal's gaze searched her face for a few long beats before he started talking.

"That night when we went out to dinner, I told you that I'd thought about you over the years. Not just about the sex, Becky. I thought about that great dirty laugh you have. And the way you always get so fired up for the underdog. And the fact that you're so strong and independent that sometimes it would drive me crazy when you wouldn't let me buy you dinner."

She smiled faintly as she remembered the running argument they'd had over her paying her own way.

"You were the only reason I went to the reunion, you know. I wanted to see you again. I wanted to know if I still felt the same kick in my gut every time I looked at you."

She eyed him across the space that separated them. "Do you?"

"Oh, yeah. Might even be worse now. Maybe I understand what I threw away all those years ago when I chickened out."

Becky held her breath. What was Cal actually saying? She'd been uncertain of him for too long to take anything he said at face value.

"When I told you I was just getting over my divorce, I wasn't saying that I wasn't interested in a relationship with you," he said. "I don't want to be one of those tragic guys who gets divorced and then marries again in a few months time because he can't stand being on his own. And you told me you weren't interested in a relationship. You told me your career was important to you. That we were about sex and nothing else."

Becky squirmed a little as she considered their conversation from his point of view. She'd been so busy protecting herself that she hadn't considered what signals she'd been sending Cal. She'd been so sure she knew the score where he was concerned.

"I thought that was how you felt," she said.

"You didn't give me a chance to say anything else. You were pretty clear that being with me was just about what happened in the bedroom."

Her gaze slid over his shoulder as heat rose into her cheeks. She felt ridiculously exposed and foolish.

"I thought you knew," she said. "I thought it was obvious how I felt and I was simply trying to hold on to a little dignity."

"Like I said, there's been a lot of unspoken bullshit between us. Me trying to find out if I threw away the best thing in my life all those years ago, and you throwing how not interested you were in my face at every turn."

Was that what she'd done? She'd thought her reaction to him, her longing, was evident in every glance she sent his way, in every gesture, in every word out of her mouth. She'd felt as though her love was written in the sky, huge and obvious.

"I've never been not interested in you, Cal," she said quietly.

"I realize that now. And I'm sorry I hurt you so much all those years ago, Becky. I wasn't ready for us. I think I knew on some level that I'd hurt you badly, but I never really admitted it to myself. That would have made it impossible for me to try to start things up with you again. And that was something that has been in the back of my mind ever since I knew my marriage was over."

Becky felt something hot and wet splash onto her hand, and she realized she was crying.

"Don't cry," he said. His face was twisted with regret. "I can't stand seeing you upset."

The gentleness in his voice fed the hope in her heart, and the tears fell faster. She was too scared to believe in what was happening between them, what they were both admitting to each other. She'd wanted this all her adult life.

"Becky," he said, and then he was in front of her, drawing her into his lap and holding her close as he pressed kisses onto the top of her head, her forehead, her wet cheeks.

"Please don't cry. I'm sorry I hurt you. And I'm sorry I didn't push harder when you started talking about us just being bed buddies. I should have told you how I felt, what I wanted straight up."

Becky clutched at the soft fabric of his shirt, feeling the warmth and the heat and the realness of him.

Cal. After all these years. Holding her so tightly, so closely that his voice vibrated through her body when he spoke.

"Tell me now," she whispered brokenly. "Tell me now what you want."

He took a deep breath, then she felt the nudge of his finger beneath her chin as he encouraged her to lift her face up. Tears sheened her eyes as she swallowed and met his gaze.

"I love you, Becky. I want to build a life with you. When you told me you were pregnant tonight, all I could think about was that of all the women in the world, you were the one I wanted this to happen with."

Becky absorbed his words into her soul, the certainty in his voice and the sincerity shining from his face filling the empty spaces that doubt had made inside her.

"Say it again," she said, lifting her hands to cup his face.

"Which bit?" he asked, the shadow of a smile on his lips.

"All of it."

He cupped her face in turn, his thumbs brushing the tears from her cheeks.

"I love you, I love you, I love you," he said.

He opened his mouth to say more, but she closed the space between them and pressed her lips to his. She could taste the salt of her own tears, and she could taste him, and her heart ached in her chest as she understood that she finally had the dream. After all these years, Cal loved her. They were going to be together the way she'd always wanted. And they'd made a baby together. A baby they'd watch grow together. Maybe there would be other babies, too.

She felt desperate to be as close to Cal as possible, and she began tearing at his clothes as their kiss deepened. He seemed to understand and share her need, and they peeled each other's clothes off between clinging, wet, soul-searing kisses, their hands caressing bare skin as it was uncovered, fingers clutching greedily.

Then her back was flat on the cool tile of the bathroom floor, and Cal's warm weight was on her. She felt the hardness of his erection between her thighs. She tilted her hips to invite him inside, and he filled her with his body.

"I love you," she said. "I love you so much, Cal."

"I love you, Becky," he said. "And this time, I'm going to make sure I get it right."

He began to move, and they locked eyes as the magic that had always existed between them began to heat their blood. She didn't look away once as he stroked into her, one hand cradling the nape of her neck as though she was the most precious thing in the world to him. Quickly her climax built, and still she held his gaze. She could see the love in him and his own passion rising. She could feel the tension in his body, and she loved him with her hands, mapping his strength, molding him to her, wanting to get as close as it was possible for two people to get.

"Becky," he breathed.

"Cal," she answered.

They came together, offering their vulnerability to each other along with their bodies.

Afterward, Cal rolled onto his side and pulled her against him as they both gasped for breath. Becky's heartbeat was still pounding in her ears when Cal turned his head to one side to look into her eyes.

"Marry me," he said, his face suddenly very serious and determined.

She stiffened, the old caution rising inside her. She opened her mouth to speak, but Cal pressed a finger to her lips.

"Before you answer, all I want to hear is what you want. Not what you're worried about or what you think is right or what you think I want. What do *you* want? What's your heart telling you right now, Becky?" he asked, his voice vibrating with intensity.

She blinked, and the last, unacknowledged puzzle-piece of her dream slid into place. It was crazy, the two of them making so many decisions so quickly. So many things could go wrong....

"Yes. My heart's saying yes."

Cal closed his eyes, and when he opened them again she saw a world of relief and satisfaction and happiness in them.

"Like I said, this time I'm going to get it right," Cal said. Gently, he tugged her closer still and Becky rested her head on his chest, savoring the heavy thud of his heart beneath her ear.

For the first time in more than ten years, she allowed herself to experience her love for him as a blessing and not a curse. Emotion filled her, expanding her chest, her belly, warming her arms and legs. Cal loved her. He wanted to marry her. She was going to have his baby. Their baby.

Cal kissed her again, and she felt the glide of his hand as he found her belly. The palm of his hand cupped her gently, reverentially. Becky smiled against his mouth, and she felt him smile in return.

"It's going to be all right, isn't it?" she whispered.

"It's going to be more than all right," he said. "It's going to be amazing."

Looking into his eyes, Becky knew it was the truth.

EIGHT MONTHS later, Mrs. Becky MacKenzie gave birth
to a five-pound, seven-ounce baby girl. She and Cal
had argued over names the entire course of the pregnancy, but they both took one look at her and decided
she looked exactly like a Poppy Kathleen. After an overnight stay in hospital, all three went home to the three-
bedroom Californian-style bungalow that Becky and
Cal had bought together near the sun and surf of Bondi
Beach in Sydney's east. Poppy was mostly oblivious to
proceedings, but Cal and Becky were both acutely aware
of the occasion—and blissfully, achingly happy that life
had handed them a second chance to get things right.

* * * * *

Always Emily
By **Mary Sullivan**

Emily Jordan has lived a life of adventure,
constantly leaving her hometown of
Accord, Colorado. But with that adventurous life
in shambles, she needs to regroup. What better
place to do so than home? The real question,
however, is whether Salem Pearce—the one man
she's never forgotten—will welcome her back.

Read on for an exciting excerpt of the upcoming
book ALWAYS EMILY by Mary Sullivan.

Since it was Saturday and the museum was closed for the
evening, the public areas were dark. But on the third floor, a
single yellow light shone in Salem's office.

Salem is here. The hell with his order to stay away. She
needed him.

Emily gave little thought to why he was here on a Saturday
night, and instead focused only on him. So close and yet so
far away. She needed Salem, his calming energy and his quiet
efficiency. Salem could handle anything thrown at him, and
Emily was running on empty. She needed a friend.

She managed to make her way to the building and stepped out of the rain that was coming down hard now.

She had to get up there, to him, if only her shaky legs would cooperate. He might be upset with her, but could he really turn a sick person away? She climbed the stairs gingerly, but her headache still worsened with every step.

I want…

She wasn't sure what.

She knew only that she was exhausted with the struggle to keep herself in one piece.

On the third-floor landing, she stopped and stared at Salem through glass walls.

This close to him, peace enveloped her. This, *he,* was exactly who she needed. She wanted to lay her head and her troubles on his broad chest.

When she swayed, it alerted him to her presence.

His jaw fell, his expression equal parts shock and anger. She knew she'd flitted into and out of his life too many times. *Oh, Salem, I'm home. For good.*

Will Salem welcome Emily?
Will they finally get their chance together?
Find out in ALWAYS EMILY
by Mary Sullivan, available May 2014 from
Harlequin® Superromance®.

Fate has brought them back together... but for how long?

Silver Linings
by Mary Brady

Delainey Talbot's life took a detour when she became a mother. There's no better job in the world, but that doesn't mean she isn't excited about finally becoming a lawyer—a dream she's getting close to fulfilling. So when the partnership at Bailey's Cove's only law firm is given to someone else, she's devastated. The fact that it went to Hunter Morrison only makes it worse. But maybe this is their second chance.

Pick up a copy of the second book of The Legend of Bailey's Cove miniseries.

AVAILABLE MAY 2014, WHEREVER BOOKS AND EBOOKS ARE SOLD.

They could have a future, *if* they can forgive the past

Winning Over Skylar
Julianna Morris

A respected businesswoman and city-council member, Skylar Gibson has come a long way from her teenage years. Aaron Hollister, alternatively, is still the entitled kid she remembers. He's come home to take over his family's business *and* threaten the town's livelihood. Now Skylar is the only thing standing in his way. But her first priority is protecting her secret—their daughter, Karin.

When the truth comes out, Skylar is shocked by Aaron's desire to be part of Karin's life! For the first time she's seeing past Aaron's "charmed life" to the boy she fell for. But a trip down memory lane alone won't be enough to prove he's changed....

AVAILABLE APRIL 1, 2014,
WHEREVER BOOKS AND EBOOKS ARE SOLD.

Here today, gone tomorrow?

The Soldier's Promise
Patricia Potter

A cabin and a dog—former ranger Josh Manning inherited both from a late fellow soldier, and he intends to look after them. After all, he made a promise. But as soon as he finishes renovating the cabin, he's getting out of Covenant Falls, Colorado, a town where everyone wants to know his business. A town that has an undeniably pretty mayor.

But Eve Douglas, a widow, also has a rambunctious son and a band of misfit dogs. Definitely *not* his type. Eve deserves more than he can give. Unless, against his instincts, he's ready to make another promise.

AVAILABLE APRIL 1, 2014,
WHEREVER BOOKS AND EBOOKS ARE SOLD.